THE HOLLYWOOD HIGH CHRONICLES

book 3

The Surge

by **Melissa Velasco**

ISBN 978-1-960378-10-1   (paperback)
ISBN 978-1-960378-11-8   (eBook)

1st Edition

Models contracted through DMe Talent Agency:
Deidre Michelle (Agent) @dmetalentagency11

Front Cover Models: Maddie Dawn Cordero, Julian Gopal, Zane Barber, Jordyn Nicole Ortega, Stephen Burhoe, Belle Hernandez, Joe Nava, Trey Pickett, Lillian Cordero

Back Cover Models: Maddie Dawn Cordero, Julian Gopal

Makeup and Hair: Xavier Visage
Costume Concept: Melissa Velasco
Cover Concept: Melissa Velasco
Photography: Tino Duvick @brokenchainphotography
Front Cover Design: Tino Duvick and Anna Hall
Editor: Kyle Fager
Proofreader: Doris Nehrbass

Dedicated to Daen Scott. No one enjoyed wit, candor, and a plan with high stakes quite like Daen. Her pragmatic outlook, combined with her love for laughter and sarcasm, would've made this book one of her favorites. As you surge off on the next leg of your journey, Daen, I send you away with reassurance that you, my soul sister, are a light in the dark. Until we meet again—kick ass, laugh hard, and enjoy every win, my friend.

THE SURGE

CHAPTER 1

The lights flash and strobe, music pulsating as we walk to the dance floor. My short, tight white sequined dress glimmers. Trey Valdez, my boyfriend, smiles down at me, then twirls me around in the middle of the dance floor. We laugh as we watch Hiram Friedman and his girlfriend, Susan Cranz, playfully chasing each other around our table across the way. We've earned this break, and I guess we needed it more than I thought, because everyone's acting like a bunch of rowdy kids.

Our winter dance, affectionately named the "Snow Ball" by Valerie Merser, has been a raging success. The ballroom at the historic Roosevelt Hotel is packed with kids in white and neon formal wear. Black lights hang from every rafter, bringing us all to a festive glow. Susan commissioned Mandie Malone to run the glow accessories table, and it looks like she's done a great job selling them. Everyone's wearing neon necklaces and bracelets. Even Adam Stone's gotten in on the fun—crisscrossing his chest and lining his arms is a crazy robot harness he's made from the blue glowing necklaces. Tanner Devick's wearing a matching one.

Of all of us, Adam deserves this amazing night the most. His physical bruises have healed, but the emotional damage remains, and we're all a little worried. Long story short, Adam was kidnapped last month, beaten nearly to death, and locked in a terrifying makeshift dungeon by the school's bully-group-turned-homicidal-maniacs, the Drones. Sounds insane, right? Yeah, we think so too. The list of the Drones' crimes is long and tedious, half of them potentially deadly and the other half infuriating, but we've made the collective decision to move past it . . . all of us except for Adam, but not by any fault of his own. His post-traumatic stress is mounting and multiplying. He's not okay . . . at least not yet.

As Trey and I watch him, we occasionally glance at each other with twin expressions of concern.

Eventually, Trey leans down and says over the driving beat of the music, "Something's gonna give. I can feel it."

I nod. "Adam didn't come out of that dungeon at Stan's house quite right. I need to help him."

"I still can't believe that you managed to keep him alive." Trey glances down at me, anxiety marring his handsome face. He laces his fingers with mine and sends a pulse through our soulmate connection. With Trey, it's not so much that I hear his thoughts in words. It's more like a three-dimensional emotion bubble that I can study as it passes through our hands.

I close my eyes, looking over what he sent in my mind's eye. It looks like he's insecure about Adam and me, but he wants me to try to help him. I sigh and gently pull my hand away. I'm still picking up the pieces of nearly losing Adam to the Grim Reaper, the shock of finding him, and the additional trauma of him ending our romantic entanglement. It's complicated, but this all boils down to me having a soulmate connection with both Trey and Adam. The connections are vastly different. Where Trey and I are balanced in every way—my fire and chaos balanced against his reflection and contemplation—Adam and I are made of passion, heat, and rage. Or at least we used to be before Adam became so broken.

Before you start feeling sorry for Trey, let's not forget that he had a tawdry affair with a cheerleader named Tiffany while I was close to dead. I guess it's tacky of me to try to balance the scales with that tidbit, considering that we've moved past it, but a Boy Scout he's not.

I glance up at Trey's worried eyes and sigh internally. I didn't pulse back, but that's probably for the best since I don't have enough control over my emotions about Adam quite yet. This is a mess, but we've been in bigger messes before. Just another day in paradise for our trio.

At that moment, Valerie Merser, Adam's fiancée, gives a tight half smile as she makes eye contact with us from across the room. She's been watching Adam's overzealous dance party with Tanner and Marcus, and I can see from the look on her face that she agrees: something about his boisterous partying rings hollow. Tanner and Marcus are trying, and if anyone can lift Adam's spirits, it's them. Then again, I don't know that anyone *can* lift his spirits.

Marcus Vinsky is the jokester of our group. Meanwhile, Tanner is our school's resident David Bowie, with his flashy look and sassy mouth. Even their combined efforts are falling short in the rescue attempt. Adam needs something more than this. He's a shell of the person he was before. He's always brooded, always been the kind of guy to go looking for trouble, but he's also always kept a foundation of mischief under the tough-biker-guy exterior. Yeah, he was a troublemaker, but all in good fun. Now it seems there are cracks in the foundation . . .

My thoughts are interrupted when Finley Farell and Victoria Garcia bounce up to me. Without a word of explanation, they drag me off the dance floor and out the ballroom door. I glance over my shoulder and give Trey an apologetic look, but he's grinning at me even as Tanner slides to him and they start doing the Kid-N-Play. I can't help but giggle at Trey's expression. He tolerates the school dances, but they wouldn't normally be his first choice for a fun evening.

I turn to the girls and discover that Victoria's grinning at me, which causes a moment of unsettling alarm. It's been three weeks since Victoria became a part of our group, earning a spot when she helped us save Adam. I have no doubt about her loyalty now, but old habits die hard. Victoria and I haven't always gotten along. She's got a catty, gossiping, mean side. She's also Trey's ex-girlfriend. Needless to say, I'm wary about having her around.

I take a grounding breath and grin at Finley and Victoria, my expression clearly asking what we're doing out here when all the fun's inside.

Victoria catches my flash of anxiety and smiles reassuringly at me. "So . . . I need your advice."

My eyebrows rise. "All right, shoot."

Victoria and Finley side-eye each other, and Finley grins.

"How much do you know about Demitri?" Victoria asks, glancing my way.

"You mean aside from the fact that he's drop-dead, heart-stoppingly gorgeous, *and* he's one of the most mind-blowing dancers I've ever met?"

Finley elbows Victoria. "See? It's a universal fact. Demitri's a catch."

"He would totally be on my radar if I was single," I add. "Why?"

Victoria's gorgeous face morphs with a sexy expression I know all too well. She's up to no good and it makes me wary. As Marcus would say, "That's the understatement of the year." Victoria used to be one of my biggest dramatic problems at school, so it's a relief that things have improved so much. Anything that ensures she doesn't hunt Trey for amorous sport again is welcome in my book, but I'm fiercely protective of Demitri. He's one of my best friends. I shove down the nagging additional reason I'm protective of him. I'm not ready to face some of the feelings I have about Demitri.

She smiles slyly. "I'm into him. Think I've got a shot?"

I rally, shrugging. "I know he likes nice girls, and I'm positive he has high standards. You're gorgeous, witty, and smart, which are all points in your favor. He avoids drama like the plague though."

Victoria looks down, contemplating. After a pause, she says, "I can't get him out of my head. Holy crap! He's insanely hot."

Finley and I giggle.

"He's the total package," Finley gossips.

Victoria shoots a mischievous glance toward the ballroom door. "I'm going for it." She turns her back where no one but us can see, then fluffs the ample cleavage pouring out of her white strapless floor-length gown with a slit so high I swear I can see her belly button. Victoria's a loud kind of gorgeous. Not the tiniest bit subtle. Can't really blame her, though, because if I had a body like hers, I might be also. Anyway, she's hot and she's being weirdly pleasant these days. Insecurity about her and Trey's past flairs in the back of my mind, but I stuff it down with a quick shake of my head.

Finley side-eyes me, apparently riddling out what has me looking so worried. Everyone in our group knows each other so well, it's like we're a bunch of siblings. "Victoria," she blurts, "Melanie's panicking yet again that you're going to steal Trey. Would you *please* talk to her?"

Victoria gives me a haughty look as she cocks her voluptuous hip. "I guess we've needed to discuss this long before now. Melanie,

I'm not after Trey anymore. He's a great guy, and we had a good time, but I couldn't handle his whole mysteriously pensive attitude. Frankly, we didn't have nearly what you two do anyway. Cheer up, buttercup, because I'm about to snag me a fresh piece of meat."

As Finley and I watch Victoria strut across the hotel lobby on her way to the ballroom, I cringe at the reference to Demitri as meat.

"Heaven help Demitri," I say to Finley. "That girl's on a mission."

Finley giggles. We hightail it into the ballroom to watch the show, passing into the black light glow just in time to see Victoria stalking Demitri's way, hips swaying. Arch, Kelsey, Trey, and Tanner are watching her curiously. Trey glances at me from across the room, and I grin at him, tip my head to the side, and shrug. He laughs. Bear joins their table and elbows Arch. Demitri and his best friend, Javier, are dancing on the edge of the dance floor, and Victoria's almost reached her destination. Finley grabs my hand, pulling me to our group's table for a better view.

Victoria oozes up to Demitri, who looks a little shocked. How he can be so breathtakingly perfect, and yet so unaware, is beyond me. He offers Victoria a friendly smile, but we can't hear what she says. His expression cycles through surprise and a flash of suspicion before it settles firmly on "politely aloof." Looks like Victoria wasn't on his radar.

In situations like these, Victoria likes to accentuate her ample chest by squeezing her arms together, but even that fails to help her cause. Demitri gives her a good-natured nod and turns on his heel, walking with Javier to the punch fountain across the room. Bear follows them, curiosity written on his face.

Victoria pouts, then stomps her strappy stiletto-clad foot. She flounces over to us. She sighs, exasperated, and exclaims, "He *turned me down! Meeee!* Are you looking at me? Seriously? I'm wearing *McClintock!*"

Arch rubs his forehead, clearly amused, and says to his girl-friend, "Kelsey, would you like to dance?"

Kelsey is Trey's sister. She's known Victoria for several years, and wasn't generally enthralled by her back when she was dating Trey. Victoria's got a long history as a maniacal brat, and with some in our group, a past like that dies hard.

"Yes, please," Kelsey says with a polite smile at Arch.

The happy couple side-eyes each other as they walk away. Kelsey's wearing the cutest little bouncy white dress, her raven-black hair twisted into an intricate updo. Arch has ditched his usual black anarchy trench coat for the night, and he's rocking a tux with his long, curly dark hair hanging loose around his shoulders.

As they join our group, Valerie and Adam are staring at Victoria like she's lost her mind.

Susan turns to her boyfriend Hiram and suggests, "How about we take over the glow accessories sales table and give Mandie a break?"

Looking like he would like nothing more than to escape Victoria, Hiram nods gratefully and grabs Susan by the elbow, practically dragging her across the room to the table by the door.

Well, damn, that leaves just a few of us. *Sigh.* The last thing I want is to have a conversation with Trey about Victoria's hotness.

"You know, Victoria," Tanner says, his tone dripping with sarcasm, "a nice rack isn't enough to make up for a bad reputation. Looks like you're going to have to show Demitri a new side."

Victoria huffs and glares at him. "You *knooow* I've changed." She crosses her arms defensively over her chest and fumes.

"Really? Because this looks a whole lot like the egotistical brat we all used to hate." He raises his eyebrows at her. I love Tanner.

He's usually a happy jokester with little regard for the rules, but when he chooses to, he can be such a diva. His brocade red coat and over-the-top makeup make him look particularly intimidating.

Victoria wilts a bit under his scrutiny.

"You were queen bee of the Drones," Tanner continues, "and that worked well because you didn't have to be anything but hot and mean. Guess what, Sugar Plum? The easy way ended when you decided to become a part of *this* group. You're going to have to be more than a rich bitch with a nice rack. Your *Heathers* vibe isn't going to get you anywhere."

Victoria's expression darkens with disbelief. She whips her head around, landing steely eyes on my boyfriend. "Trey, go talk to Demitri for me."

Trey laughs. "And tell him what exactly? My ex-girlfriend's rude, self-centered, and she's decided she wants you? Pony up, pretty boy! Umm . . . no, Veruca. You don't get to snap your fingers and demand that Demitri be your flavor of the week."

When Finley jumps in, she's gentler. "How about you try giving it some time? Show him that you've changed?"

Victoria whimpers and stomps both feet.

Just when Valerie starts a fresh round of advice with Victoria, Adam breaks away from the group. Valerie's one of the tough girls of our crowd. She's so tough, I find myself silently wishing Victoria luck. Trey glances my way and gives a subtle nod. He knows what I'm thinking. I slip away and follow Adam out the ballroom door, fairly certain why he left. It's time to handle some things. Adam moved quickly, it seems, because I can't figure out where he went. I close my eyes and search for the energy that's distinctly his.

There . . .

I head out the double doors into the cool night air and find Adam around the corner, leaning against the building. He's just pulling his cigarette pack from his coat pocket, but he freezes as his gaze meets mine. His eyes have that lost, darting quality to them again. He slides the pack back into his pocket. I internally ground and center, sending my excess energy down and out like an internal exhale. *Adam's so broken*, I think. Before the trauma he experienced, our energies used to match, but now my energy is too much for him. I've been working on something he doesn't know about, though.

He smiles as he feels me ground out. I raise my eyebrows, asking permission to come closer. He holds his hand out my way. I rush to him and wrap my arms around him. He puts his hand on my head, pulling it against his chest while wrapping his other arm around me. His shields are cracked and failing, leaving him little cover for me to examine everything he's dealing with. His energy is jagged and unpredictable as it spikes and flares. Half of it's about trauma, and the other half is heartbreak over me. The whole thing makes me gasp.

"Sorry," he whispers, his cheek resting on the top of my head. "I'm trying."

I look up into his ocean-blue eyes. "You don't ever have to apologize. I know better than anyone what you're dealing with."

He smiles sorrowfully and sighs.

I rest my head against him again, then ground out my suddenly manic energy. *God help me. I miss him.* I push the thought away, but not in time.

He feels it down our soulmate connection and pulses back, *"I miss you too."*

Where Trey and I send emotion bubbles, Adam and I communicate through our connection in actual thoughts. Like I said, my two soulmate bonds are vastly different.

I get control of my energy, bringing it down to a soothing hum. Then, I lace my right hand with Adam's and send the calm energy into him. He relinquishes control, something he only does with me, and lets the energy wash through him. I close my eyes and watch as the energy fills in some of the empty spots and smooths out the jagged flares firing closest to the surface.

After a time, he exhales. "I didn't know you could do that," he says quietly.

I fight the lump that threatens to rise in my throat. He doesn't need to see how much I miss him. I clamp down tight on my emotions to avoid oversharing unintentionally. "I've been working on it with Bear and Darren. They think I might be the only one who can help you."

Adam sighs. "The reason I left you was because I thought your energy would make things harder. I should've known you'd develop a new ability."

"Darren and Bear think it's developing because of our connection. Apparently, because you need it, it's surfaced in me."

He growls, "It makes this harder when you're perfect for me."

I choke out, "I know."

He whispers, "Thank you."

The tears breach my control and brim in my eyes. I bury my face in his arm and will the tears to recede. Adam tips my chin up, and I close my eyes.

Don't do this now. You can have yet another meltdown in your room later.

My control finally wins, and I pull away.

Adam's expression is one of almost desperate sadness. "We both know you need to be with Trey. I'm broken from everything that's happened."

Because I don't know if he's right, I don't know how to respond at first. "How are things working with Valerie?" I finally manage.

Adam shrugs. "We're coasting. She doesn't know what to do to help me. She's intuitive, but she isn't an energy worker like you."

I offer a soft smile. "Can we make a deal?"

He looks at me curiously.

"I know how to start to fix the issues in you, but I promise not to cross any lines. It took us months to finally come to a decision about us. I don't want to screw things up with Valerie and Trey."

Adam nods and swallows hard. He's radiating that he's unsure about what he wants, but rule number one is that I don't take advantage of the broken. It's my place to think for both of us.

"I've got you," I quietly implore. "I won't let things get insane again."

His relief floods down our connection as he pulls me in and holds me like I'm a lifeline to sanity. When he drops his internal shields, I quickly get to work directing healing energy into the bruised and battered places of his psyche. Having rescued him from his own cavernous and failing mind once before, I now have an easy route in.

After what feels like hours, even though only a few minutes have passed, I extricate myself. I blink rapidly, drained and disoriented. Moving in and out of Adam's psyche is exhausting.

He tips my chin up, his emotions still open for me, and radiates appreciation. He smiles. "You're remarkable."

I grin. "Think it's working?"

He nods.

"Would you let me heal your mind in small doses? There's a lot of ground to cover, but if it's working, then it's just a matter of time."

He glances to the side, contemplating. Finally, he says, "I don't like to ask for help, but this time, I'm going to. Would you?"

I nod and pulse to him, *"Love you."*

He smiles and pulses back, *"Love you too."*

He lets go of my hand. We turn together and walk back around the corner and through the double doors.

Trey's waiting for us in the lobby. "Did it work?" he asks me. Adam looks surprised.

"Mel's been practicing on me," Trey says with a reassuring smile. "Since she and I have a soulmate connection also, we figured it might make for a good simulation. It's disorienting, I know."

Adam exhales. "It really is, but it definitely works." He studies Trey for a moment. "You're sure this is okay with you?"

Trey looks down before meeting Adam's eyes with sincerity. "She loves you. That's not going to change. This weird double-soulmate connection isn't going away. She and I have set some boundary rules that I'm sure you can guess."

Adam smirks.

"So, if she can help you," Trey continues, "then I'm all for it." He pauses and side-eyes me before ominously adding, "We need you back, man."

I meet Trey's gaze, and we both look up at Adam, whose eyes narrow.

"Why?" Adam asks, looking to me.

Exhausted from helping him, I close my eyes and shake my head.

Trey answers for me. "Her intuition started bubbling a few days ago. Something's coming, but we don't know what."

"Shit," Adam mutters as we head back into the ballroom.

2 Unlimited's "Twilight Zone" blasts through the speakers as we enter. Demitri grabs my hand and drags me to the dance floor. We quickly clear the dance floor as all the Regulars—the students who attend the school because it's in their neighborhood—watch with their jaws on the floor. Demitri lifts me into an impressive torch over his head, and from up high, I gesture for the performing arts dancers to join us. They rush in, and together, we put on a show like only we can. Mr. Isley, the head of the dance department,

high-fives me as he joins our dance party. His film and Broadway career is seriously impressive. He doesn't dance with us often, but he quickly proves that he's still got it.

After a triple-turn, I make the mistake of flexing too hard through a backbend before whipping around to face Demitri. Quickly, I turn my back to the spectators just as my spaghetti strap gives way and the right side of my top flops down, my goods plunging from the dress. I make a high-pitched "meeping" sound.

Demitri chooses that moment to look down. His eyes widen. Instead of being embarrassed, I crack up as his gaze shifts to my face.

He laughs and quips over the raging beat, "Not bad."

I grab the front of my dress and get everything covered. A blush warms my cheeks as he winks at me, takes the broken strap between two fingers, and gestures for Dante Grunier to join us. Dante is in a goth metal band, and his suit jacket hem is lined with decorative safety pins.

"Willing to spare a pin?" Demitri asks. "Melanie's strap popped."

Dante grins at me before unhooking a pin from his coat. "Sounds like I missed a view," he jokes as he hands over the pin.

Giving a look that clearly expresses his agreement with the sentiment, Demitri cocks his head to one side. Considering that Demitri is one of my best friends, he can get away with the teasing.

"Impressing Mr. Perfect is a notch on my belt," I say.

Demitri chuckles alluringly as he pins the strap at the back of my dress. He tugs it a few times to make sure it's secure. "It'll hold as long as we don't get wild."

A hand lands on my shoulder from behind, and I freeze. I don't recognize the energy of the intruder, but my intuition says it's off. I whip around and find myself face-to-face with a security guard. He narrows his eyes at me. He's radiating malice as I back rapidly into Demitri. My friend wraps an arm around my chest and presses my back into him. We study the man, who says nothing.

"What the hell, bro?" Dante barks, right when the music hits a quiet moment before a big build.

Whether Trey has picked up my scared vibe or heard Dante, he whips around and stalks our way. Our group follows him. Everyone amps up as the entire student body watches. Trey wedges himself between me and the security guard, who takes several steps back, surprise gracing his expression as he takes in Trey's barely contained anger.

The song ends, but the deejay doesn't start a new one. I glance that way to find that he's staring at the confrontation with his mouth hanging open. Movement out of the corner of my eye catches my attention, and that's when I realize that the whole dance is crawling with black-clad security guards.

"Do our dances usually have this much security?" I send to Trey and Adam.

Trey is a sophomore and Adam is a senior, so they've been to more of these events than I have. They send back their versions of a *"No!"* in unison, both of them radiating through our connections that this is really weird.

Judging from his authoritative preening, I'm guessing the head of this security mob is the one who steps up to us through the crowd. "Melanie Slate?" he inquires.

Trey has a background in security work, having grown up working for his dad's bodyguarding company. He's trained me well enough to recognize that this moment falls into the "don't answer" category. I keep my mouth shut.

"Why?" Trey asks, his eyes narrowing.

"We need to speak to Melanie Slate." Mr. In Charge turns and asks loudly of the crowd, "Where is Melanie Slate?"

I squish further against Demitri and slide a questioning gaze to Arch.

Demitri's arm tightens around me as he leans over my shoulder and murmurs to Trey, "Something four shades of fucked is happening. We need to leave."

"Stay with my girl no matter what happens," Trey murmurs back. "This may end in blows, and I'll be in the middle of it."

Demitri nods and grabs my hand with his free one. He melts back into the crowd, and our group shifts a bit to get in front of us. Finding myself several people away from Trey makes me nervous, but I don't have time to think about it long.

"Where is Melanie Slate?" the head douchebag demands again.

"Right here," comes the brash reply. It's Susan, and she raises her hand as Hiram looks at her like she's nuts.

My eyes snap wide as the security guards all start to move Susan's way.

"They plan to take me," I whisper to Demitri. "But why?"

He squeezes me harder in response.

As they approach, Susan chirps, "Gotta catch me!" She darts out a hand and pulls the fire alarm handle on the wall next to her. Alarms shrill all through the massive building. She takes off running, skirting away from the reaching hands of the security officers.

"Scatter!" Trey yells.

Students at Hollywood High have come to trust our group, and so they gleefully make quite the production of running around and causing chaos. I glance toward our table and spot Valerie snagging all the girls' purses. Hiram grabs Susan's arm as she makes it back to our group, a little winded, her eyes showing a combination of fear and elation. Susan's never been much of a daredevil, so her brazen effort to protect me makes me respect her even more. Hiram and Susan bolt through a door marked as an emergency exit.

Demitri yanks my hand and quickly guides me to follow Susan and Hiram. Arch, Dante, Bear, and Darren surround us as we run down a service hallway to another door. Hiram shoves it open, and we pour into the alley behind the Roosevelt.

As usual, Arch takes the lead. "Head to the student parking lot. Everyone will meet there."

Since that's where we've all parked our cars, I find myself wondering if this is a bad plan. The thought dies as soon as we take off running because the damn strap on my dress pops again. I hold up the top without slowing down.

We arrive at the lot, and Mr. Isley runs up moments later, Trey and the rest of our group in tow.

"What do you know about this?" Trey demands of Mr. Isley.

Mr. Isley gestures for us to step closer, and we lean in.

"A lot has been happening that we've tried to keep from the students," he explains. "You know that fire drill we had the last day of school before winter break?"

We nod, and he continues.

"It wasn't a fire drill. A bomb threat was called into the school, and since we didn't think it was credible, we didn't want to alarm the students. The police cleared the place, but some tactical unit was brought in after. That's why it took so long to get everyone back to class."

"I didn't mind at all," Tanner chirps. "We had a great time on the front lawn."

Mr. Isley hits Tanner with a blazingly serious gaze. "Once they brought in the bomb squad, I knew something was up. But I still don't know what's happening. No bomb was found. That tactical unit all gathered in the first-floor hall in the two-story building after they roamed around for a while. I was assigned to the double doors, making sure kids didn't come back inside. I listened in, and it sounded like those guys were searching for something they didn't wind up finding. They weren't looking for a bomb, though, from what I could gather."

"What were they searching for?" Trey says. When he glances at me, I can feel through our connection how seriously he's taking this, and that's a bad sign.

Mr. Isley shakes his head. "That's the thing. They weren't really talking about *searching* for anything. They were talking about the campus layout. It's like they were trying to get more familiar with it."

"What would any of this have to do with the extra security tonight?" Arch asks.

"I have no idea," Mr. Isley says. "All I know is that I've never seen this much security at a dance, and you probably noticed how those guys weren't our usual. I mean, why wouldn't we just hire the yellow jackets you kids love so much?"

We all snort at his sarcasm. The yellow jackets are the regular campus security guards, named for their ridiculous yellow uniform windbreakers. With their bumbling ways and their tendency to catch us ditching, they annoy us on the daily.

"Either way, fancy uniforms and holstered guns aren't standard issue for school security," Mr. Isley says. He tips his head as if pondering something. "Now that I think of it, the security guards inside were wearing the same uniforms as the tactical squad."

We exchange glances around the group.

"Why would they have been asking for Melanie?" Trey demands.

Mr. Isley shakes his head and raises both hands in a "search me" gesture.

I huff and lean my head on Demitri's shoulder. "Something tells me we're going to find out."

CHAPTER *2*

For most of Saturday—at least for the part of it when I wasn't arguing over the phone with Trey about how he suddenly has problems with the whole Adam thing—I sat in my bedroom, trying not to think about how a goon squad stormed into our dance and asked for me by name. My parents have been surprisingly dismissive of the whole thing. They were unfazed, chalking it up to the idea that I probably just did something unseemly during the festivities. I argued that I was on my best behavior this time, but convincing my parents proved to be a trial I lost miserably. After a lecture about not pulling fire alarms unnecessarily, even though I wasn't the one who did it, they suggested I cool out in my room for a while. So that's what I've been doing, and the question that's been impossible to shake is this: Why, if these guys know my name and seem to want to talk to me, haven't they shown up at my house to put me through questioning?

No matter how I try, no answer seems to make sense. So now I've decided that it's time for a distraction. With my spiral-cord phone pressed to my ear, I call Demitri and ask him what he's doing tonight.

"Sitting here talking with Dad," he says. "Why? What's up?"

"Need to get my mind off things. I got my learner's permit, and Mom says I can use her car as long as I promise not to pull any more fire alarms."

"That was Susan!"

"*You* know it was Susan. *I* know it was Susan. Just try telling that to my parents." I sigh. "Anyway, I'm bored. You up for me driving over so we can have a chill night?"

"Holy crap! Clear the roads."

I laugh. "You hush. I'm a good driver!"

Demitri's dad pipes up from the background. "Sure, as long as you have a stack of phone books to sit on so you can see over the steering wheel!"

My mouth drops open, and I feign offense as I gasp, "Low blow, Dad!"

Mr. Cantrell laughs.

"I'm game," Demitri says. "What do you have in mind?"

"Your house, and I bring tacos and Twinkies."

"Tacos and Twinkies?"

"Do *not* mock the Twinkie!"

Demitri chuckles. "My stomach's going to explode if I eat a damn Twinkie, but I love tacos."

"Perfect. There's no one else I'd rather eat tacos and Twinkies with."

"I'm so glad that trying to kill me with a time-honored delight amuses you. Trey might get jealous, though. Tacos and Twinkies sounds like a big night."

I groan. "The drama with security at the dance has him all spun out. He can't do anything about what's coming, so naturally he took a sharp left, headed to crazy town. He's in one of his overanalyzing modes. Plus, he's all worked up about me helping Adam.

He was good about it in front of Adam, but then he tweaked the hell out this afternoon. Save me. I need to decompress."

"Come over. I could use some best-friend time anyway."

I bounce in place. "On my way," I chirp excitedly before hanging up the phone.

I hop out of the car, bags in hand, and Demitri opens the door before I get to the porch. He grins and takes the bag of tacos from me.

"I got chicken, beef, and fish," I explain. "Wasn't sure what you and Dad would want."

As I boing through the door behind Demitri, his dad calls out, "Hey, little imp! Thanks for bringing dinner. We were staring down the barrel of a cereal night."

"You'll have to save cereal night for tomorrow," I say with a smile.

Demitri hands his dad the greasy taco sack. Mr. Cantrell returns with paper plates from the kitchen and gives me the side-eye as I take the box of Twinkies out of the grocery bag and set it on the table.

"You really weren't joking about the Twinkies?"

I raise my eyebrows. "I never joke about Twinkies." I turn with a flourish to Demitri and hold my hands up by my shoulders with a silly shrug.

"Where did you get Fraggle Rock jammie pants and a matching T-shirt?" he asks after a once-over of my outfit. Demitri nicknamed me "Red the Fraggle" based on our shared favorite show from when we were little. I love the nickname, and calling me a Fraggle has been a theme ever since.

I bounce again. "Awesome, right?" I toss a wrapped Christmas present that Demitri catches with one hand.

"Please tell me there's Fraggle swag in this," he says, sounding amused and maybe a little suspicious.

I grin like a nut as he unwraps the package. A moment later, he's pulling out jammie pants and a T-shirt that match mine.

He throws a fist in the air. "Yes! Best friend is the best!" After hugging me, he heads to his room to change.

Mr. Cantrell cracks up as Demitri, sporting a hilariously smoldering expression, struts out in his new Fraggle-wear. Gorgeous Demitri somehow manages to make even *this* nonsense outfit look good. He poses at the end of his living room like a GQ model and then runway struts back my way. He breaks into a smile before hugging me while he sways us right and left.

"Thank you. Best present ever."

"You're welcome." I bounce in a silly circle. I love time with Demitri. "Tacos and Twinkieees! I'm so happy."

"You really are the cutest thing ever," Mr. Cantrell says.

With a mischievous smile, I pull another wrapped present from my bag, handing it to Mr. Cantrell.

"You got me a Christmas present?" he asks in disbelief.

I beam and nod.

He unwraps it, then pulls out the gift: a series of crystals and a cloth printed with a flower-of-life pattern.

"It's a house harmony grid," I explain. "Your home is already harmonized, but it reminded me of you."

Mr. Cantrell gets out of his recliner and hugs me. "Thank you, kiddo. I love it."

"You're welcome. Thank you for putting up with me. I know it's always chaos when I come over."

The "dad look" crosses Mr. Cantrell's face. "It's not chaos. I love having you around. You're welcome anytime."

We all get settled and dig into the tacos.

"Fill us in on the Adam and Trey mess," Demitri says.

"This is going to sound insane," I warn Mr. Cantrell.

He shrugs. "Go for it. I can handle it."

"Adam's been cratering. He appears functional to the unsuspecting eye, but his psyche is still in rough shape from the kidnapping. So, I started testing a theory on Trey and figured out that I may be able to fix some things in Adam."

Mr. Cantrell looks confused.

I scrunch up my face. "I know you're in the loop about how upset I was when we thought Adam died."

"That was horrible," Mr. Cantrell breaks in. "You were broken. Demitri was distraught as he was trying to help you. I'm so glad Adam's okay."

I nod, lost in thought. "That was a rough situation." I look at Mr. Cantrell, alive in the knowledge that I've gotten to know him better and can reveal more of my reality now than I could then. "I have a soulmate connection with both Trey and Adam."

Demitri's dad chokes on his taco. After his coughing fit subsides, he asks, "Both of them? Is a double soulmate bond even possible?"

I huff. "Apparently. Leave it to me to be the lucky winner. It's nothing but insanity. Trey gets all jealous, which is such a delight given that he's a pensive volcano ready to explode on a normal day. Add to it Adam's emotional torment and unhappiness with Valerie, and it's been a treat."

Mr. Cantrell rubs his face. "I despise that you have to deal with these things."

"Me too. Good times! Anyhow, while Demitri was being chased all over the dance by Victoria—"

"Who?" Mr. Cantrell cuts in.

Demitri rolls his eyes. "Gorgeous, selfish, generally tries, but really is just one of *those* girls."

His dad winces. "Please don't get tied up with a pain in the ass. I don't want to deal with some pretty brat hanging around."

Demitri shrugs. "Who knows."

I roll my eyes. "D, she's a lot." I switch gears. "Back to the story of doom. I tested out my theory on Adam, and damn if I didn't figure out that I can start to heal the cracks in his psyche. He needs help, and I'm not going to leave him floundering if I can make it better."

"How is Adam handling your help?" Demitri asks.

I tip my head right and left. "It's hard because having me in his mind ups the personal stakes. Adam does better when he can lie to himself about being in love with me, and pretend his thing with Valerie's going to work."

Demitri snorts. "He and Valerie are a disaster. All they do is fight."

"Tell me about it. He's an idiot. He had me locked, and then flip-flopped right back to her. I love her, but those two are so poorly matched."

"Sounds complicated," Mr. Cantrell says.

A sigh escapes my lips. "So, I got through a test run that was effective, but now I'll need to spend time in meditation with Adam. Trey's doing his 'Of course you should help him! How dare you help him! I'm gonna lose my girl' routine." I flop my head back. "I'm already sick of it, and it's only been a day. We talked on the phone and the squabble lasted forever. The argument's going nowhere. Unless I decide to hang Adam out to dry, which I won't, then we're at an impasse."

"My vote's that you drop them both," Demitri's dad offers. "No fifteen-year-old girl needs this much drama."

I close my eyes and shake my head. "It sounds simple, but these soulmate bonds run deep and really screw with common sense."

"Are you happy with Trey?"

"Depends on the day. We have issues. Either way, I need to help Adam. So, let the games continue."

Mr. Cantrell nods. "Sounds like you're doing what you can."

"Like usual." My mood brightens. "Anyway, I'm here and need some fun. Thank you for having me over."

"So . . . ," Demitri says in a tone that suggests he's trying to change the subject. "Dad took me to Graceland."

My mouth drops open. "No! Lucky!"

Demitri and I both love Elvis, and going to Graceland has been my all-time vacation dream since I was little.

Mr. Cantrell grins as he pulls out a gift bag from beside his recliner. He hands it to me, and I squeal.

I open it and pull out a VHS tape. A quick review of the box brings a slow smile. "A tour on tape?"

Demitri beams back at me. "I felt guilty the whole time we were there because you weren't with me. We had to get you the tour for Christmas."

His dad gestures to the TV. "Pop it in, D. She's going to love this."

Demitri hops up and puts the tape in the VCR. His dad grabs the remote and starts up the video. Demitri sits on the couch next to me. I sling a leg over his knee, curling up happily. The video starts, and a tour guide walks us up the front steps. I'm enchanted. Every detail is revealed in the video. The stories are amazing.

Partway through, I tip my gaze Demitri's way and quietly say with sincerity, "Thank you."

Demitri smiles softly at me and bumps my shoulder with his. "You're welcome. I'm glad you like it."

I lay my head on his shoulder and get lost in the tour.

When the video ends almost an hour later, I can hardly contain myself. "That was perfection! I feel like I got to go there in person."

Mr. Cantrell rises and starts gathering up our trash. "Love you, kids. I'm going to turn in."

"Good night," Demitri says. "Love you, Dad."

"Good night, Dad," I say with a girlish grin. "Thank you for the tour tape."

He smiles. "That was all Demitri's idea." He gives me an appraising look, worry marring his expression. "Demitri filled me in on the security guard demanding your presence. That's beyond worrisome."

I take a breath and my chin shakes a bit. I've been a mess about that since last night.

Demitri cups my cheek. I look into his eyes, and there's worry sitting under his surface. "We'll figure it out, Meley. We always do."

I put my forehead on Demitri's chest, and he kisses the top of my head. Mr. Cantrell gives Demitri a meaningful glance. I can't see Demitri's return expression, but it must be a whopper, because Mr. Cantrell gives him a pointed look before he heads down the hall to his room.

After we hear his bedroom door close, I ask, "What's up with the look Dad gave you?"

Demitri smiles ruefully. "It's not an issue."

"Tell me."

Demitri rolls his eyes. "Dad's worried about you, of course. But he also wants you and me to end up together. It bugs him."

I raise my eyebrows. "Interesting." I ponder a moment before asking, "Demitri, are you okay?"

"I'm good, Meley. You know that being your best friend keeps me sane. I wouldn't change anything."

My smile surely lacks luster. I close my eyes, aware yet again about how perfect the time spent with Demitri always is. I've refused to acknowledge how I actually feel about him. I keep that part of me under lock and key in the back of my mind. The last thing I need is a third romantic mess.

"Meley, are *you* okay?"

I nod and swallow hard.

He gives me a no-nonsense look. "You aren't okay. If us being friends hurts you, I need to know."

I shake my head and rally. "You being my friend is my favorite. I'm legit good."

Demitri exhales hard, closes his eyes, and shakes his head. "Does it bother Trey?"

Baffled, I blink my eyes rapidly. "Nope. Not at all." I look up at gorgeous Demitri's chiseled face.

He side-eyes me. "I try not to say egotistical things, but it's weird that Trey isn't bothered by our friendship. He's the only guy I've ever met who isn't completely wigged out by me being around their girl."

I shrug. "You want the truth?"

"Yup."

"He thinks you're out of my league." *The truth is that I think the same thing.*

Demitri rolls his eyes. "Don't let Trey's view get in your head. He doesn't know what he has."

I exhale deeply. "He was with Victoria before me, and there's no competing with her bombshell bullshit. Sometimes, he looks at me, and I know he's comparing us in his head."

"Ouch." He grimaces, then shifts to face me, and I'm suddenly uncomfortable with him staring at my profile. "You do realize you're beautiful, right?"

I belt a laugh. "Under normal circumstances, I stand a shot in the looks department. Here's the problem. All I do is dance.

Trey likes the girlie extras, and Victoria's got a whole lot of girlie extra. He became accustomed to unwrapping that prize and rolling around with it. Appreciating a six-pack is lost on him." I huff. "Sorry, D. I talk to you like you're one of the girls."

Demitri chuckles. "I like that you talk to me like I'm one of the girls. I've never had a female best friend before you. Having access to the girlie gossip you don't tell anyone else is part of the deal."

He tips my chin up, and I stare into his pretty gray-blue eyes. "I've seen part of the show thanks to your dress strap debacle. You're perfect. Any male dancer will tell you there's nothing better than a muscular female dancer. You're tiny, and the strength just adds to your whole enigma façade. Every guy I know who's walked into that dance studio and seen what you can do is floored. You've got crushes running around all over Hollywood High because you're exactly who you are. Now, I'm going to level with you about what I think is up with Trey and Adam."

"Here we go," I say with a sigh. "Let's see if I can handle this."

Demitri nods. "You're going to find out one way or the other. I'd rather give you a heads-up about my suspicions." He clears his throat. "Different things make different guys tick. For Adam, it's the chase. He likes the pursuit. It means he'll never be happy in a long-term commitment. Being brutally honest, you need to avoid anything long-term with him. Trey's a different animal. He's a 'grass is always greener on the other side' guy. I truly think he wants a deeper connection, but he's always got something nagging in the back of his mind, wondering if it would be more perfect with whatever second girl he's fixated on. He's the type that'll pick away at little things, pulling apart the perfect in front of him."

"That makes him just as shallow as Adam."

Demitri shakes his head. "It makes him as selfish as Adam. The difference is that guilt will tear Trey apart. He knows it's wrong, and he cares that he's being a dick. The question I have is, will Trey throw away a soulmate bond for someone else? It's the ultimate test, because most of the planet would worship a soulmate bond and never look back. His Tiffany affair, and his lingering Victoria admiration, are red flags."

"What kind of guy are you?"

Demitri laughs. "I'm the guy who enjoys girls casually while I wait for true love. I'll admit that I like flawless."

I raise an eyebrow. "Is that any better? Using girls who you know aren't the one seems questionable."

Demitri shrugs. "I'm still a guy."

"What's your plan with Victoria?"

Demitri ponders a moment. "I'll likely date her. As much as I hate to admit it, she's gorgeous enough that I can't pass it up. What's the worst that could happen?"

I bark out a harsh laugh. "She'll talk to you. That's the absolute worst, D. I assure you."

"I can handle conversation."

I roll my eyes. "Lucky guy. You'll get to incessantly hear all about how great she is, how rich her daddy is, and how stupid and lowly everyone else is." I raise an eyebrow at him. "Orgasms aren't worth it."

He cracks up. "I'll tune her out."

"Ugh. Guys are gross. I wish I was into girls."

Demitri side-eyes me. "That's a whole different can of nightmares."

CHAPTER 3

We pass through the alley school gate just as the first bell rings. I've been a nervous wreck all morning, half about the Trey/Adam thing and half about the black-clad gestapo, but Mom and Rich insisted I go to school. I'm not sure why, but they can't seem to wrap their heads around the idea that anyone in uniform would ever have ill intent toward a student at school.

The campus-wide loudspeaker clicks on, and as jumpy as I am, it startles me. Ms. Ferry's voice wafts through, rising and falling with enthusiasm. "Good morning, Hollywood High students! We hope you enjoyed your winter break and are ready to get back to work, refreshed. Please report to the theater auditorium for an assembly."

"Sweet!" Finley bubbles. "Looks like we're getting out of first period! This helps with the plan to stick together until we know if there's a problem. It's perfect."

We exchange pensive looks and follow the crowd of students ascending the long switchback staircase that runs the full height of the four-story-tall theater building. We enter the auditorium, blinking as our eyes adjust to the indoor light. Mr. Bentley, the

Magnet school English teacher, and Mr. Isley are just inside the door. They motion us over, and we step out of the stream of students.

"Heads up," Mr. Isley says. "Things are about to get interesting."

"How so?" Arch asks.

"You kids should stand here with us against the back wall," Mr. Bentley suggests. "We'll talk after. As student council, you'll be involved."

We exchange a look.

Hiram mutters, "Let the games begin."

We line up along the back wall, waiting for everyone else to sit down.

Ms. Ferry motions for Hiram to join her on the stage, and he squeezes through the crowded aisle with Susan in tow. They hop up the side stairs to the stage, where they confer with Ms. Ferry. Hiram nods and takes his keys out of his pocket before walking backstage.

Adam leans over and says to Trey and me, "I guarantee he's setting up a microphone. What do you think this is about?"

I shrug.

"How much could possibly happen the day school starts back?" Trey asks.

Adam scoffs. "Around here? Seriously, dude, at Hollywood High, the whole world can fall apart in five minutes flat."

"It didn't used to," Bear interjects. "This year's been bizarre. Besides, they've had two weeks with no students to get together whatever crap they've been up to."

I take a nervous breath, and Trey puts his arm around me.

Hiram crosses to center stage and sets up a microphone before heading back over to us with Susan trailing him.

Trey leans over and whispers, "Ms. Ferry seems nervous."

Hiram bypasses us, headed to the tech booth with a cassette tape in his hand. He hits us with a pensive look. A few moments later, an old song, clearly copied from a record album recording, hisses through the speaker system.

My eyes narrow as everyone in my group turns to me expectantly. I'm the history buff of the group. After a moment, I place the song. "This is an old African American chain gang song called 'Lightning.'"

My intuition suddenly blazes to life, and I gasp, my eyes widening. I reach out and grab Trey and Adam's hands at the same time. Both of their eyes widen as I send what my intuition's telling me.

Valerie looks quizzically at Adam, because somehow, she still hasn't figured out about our connection.

"It's vague, but bad," Trey says.

All further discussion is cut short as a man in a three-piece suit crosses to the microphone center stage. He leans in too close, booming, "Hello," making the speakers hiss and scream with feedback.

We all snicker, but then quickly quiet down. Something about this guy is off. I don't know what bad news he's about to deliver, but I have a feeling it's a whopper.

Darren leans my way. "Feels like this could be connected to the dance drama. Anything from your intuition?"

I snort. "Don't need intuition to know something messy is happening. But what I'm getting has a low, deep rumble. We aren't facing a quick issue here."

Three-piece-suit-man announces, "I'm Mr. Dean, an ironic name given that I'm the dean of education coordination for our public school system."

Adam hisses, "That's code for old white guy who does jack crap all day and gets paid a fortune."

We all snicker, covering our mouths and closing our eyes in an effort to control the outburst. Now's not the time to draw attention, I suspect.

"Over winter break, we made some changes that impact all of you," Mr. Dean says, "and we would like to address those changes now to avoid any rumors."

Mr. Bentley's jaw tightens, causing us all to side-eye each other. *Not good.* Our attention's brought back to the stage as Mr. Dean drops his first bombshell.

"Effective immediately, Principal Walker has been terminated. I would like to introduce his replacement. Principal Buttrum, please join me on stage."

We all lean forward, glancing up and down our line in shock.

"First, *what*?" Marcus hisses. "Principal Walker's the best! Second, this guy's last name is *Buttrum*? I can't even make fun of him because it's too easy!"

We chortle, quieting down just as Mr. Dean says, "Principal Buttrum has a seasoned military career under his belt. Upon retirement from service, he promptly became a high school principal. I can't think of anyone better to tame the abhorrent behavior at Hollywood High."

"What the hell?" Marcus fumes. "We're a little over the top, but students here aren't that bad."

"I'll show this jackass abhorrent behavior," Arch mutters.

Principal Buttrum steps up to the microphone. "Buttrum here," he says.

Well, that does it. The whole student body spontaneously howls with laughter. None of us can help it. This guy just walked right into that one.

Mr. Buttrum glares, scanning the crowd with piercing eyes until the students quiet. "Get out all your yuks now," he says, "because I'm not a fun kind of guy. From this day forward, there will be zero hijinks. No extras, no assemblies, no dances, no shows, no hall passes, and zero excuses. Let me be one hundred percent clear that you will collectively *earn* all privileges. Each week that we have zero ditchers, zero tardies, zero fights, and zero problems, you will earn back one privilege. We'll start with hall passes and work our way up. It's my understanding that this school's out of control, but lucky for the school district, I'm a *master* of control."

Valerie cusses under her breath, and just as Principal Buttrum's speech hits a lull, she says loudly to Arch, "This guy's a loser."

Buttrum glares at those of us lined up against the back wall. "Who was speaking?" he asks in a singsong voice.

"Damn," Valerie says under her breath. After a tense moment, she adds, "Screw it," and raises her hand, stepping forward.

"Name please?" the principal requests with feigned spunk.

Valerie narrows her eyes. "Valerie Merser."

"Repeat what you said so the entire school can hear it."

With a slow, deliberately clipped tone, she calls out, "I said, '*This guy's a loser!*'"

Everyone's gazes snap from Valerie to Principal Buttrum, and the students hold their breath, wondering what's going to happen.

I look down and smile. "We might be a bit more abhorrent than we thought," I say to Trey.

His lips twitch, but he doesn't reply.

"You," Principal Buttrum says. "Girl in the red dress, step forward."

Well crap. That'd be me.

I step up next to Valerie and look expectantly at our new principal. My stepfather's voice is chiming in the back of my head: *The first one who speaks loses. Wait it out, Mel.* I wait silently, my heart pounding. Even though it's happened a lot lately, I'm not generally a fan of being the center of negative attention.

Principal Buttrum huffs, waves his hands around, and stares at me without saying anything. Raising one eyebrow, I silently stare back at him.

Finally, he demands, "*Well*?"

"Well, what?"

"Well! What's so amusing?"

Damn it . . . I'm going to have to do this.

Suddenly, I feel her: my fierce side slowly rises from the dark water that has lived in my mind ever since a sedation issue earlier this school year.

"Do it," Valerie whispers. "I've got your back."

I feel Trey and Adam shift closer to Valerie and me, preparing to back us, and I decide there's no option but brutal honesty.

I take a deep breath and loudly say, "Frankly, you just strutted in here throwing your weight around for absolutely no reason. It's been five minutes, and I'm sick of it already. The students have done absolutely nothing wrong, and you're so insecure and narcissistic that you chose to flex on us to prove how powerful you are. We aren't stupid." I give him a pointed look. "We also don't need a military general around here. I wish you luck with that approach."

Judging from the confused look on many of the students' faces, it occurs to me that many of them actually are just as naïve as Buttrum seems to have thought. Glad I could enlighten them.

"I was an admiral," Principal Buttrum replies with clipped ferocity, "not a general."

"Phenomenal," Tanner snarks loudly. "Welcome to the *Titanic*! There's icebergs dead ahead, Admiral!"

Everyone chuckles as a few "You got that right" exclamations punctuate the air.

Considering that I'm likely already on the new principal's permanent shit list, I decide to go for big air. "Aren't there any administrators Mr. Dean can hire who aren't ego-driven, pathetic little boys hiding behind a cheap suit and a fancy title?"

Mr. Buttrum's eyebrows rise closer to his receding hairline. He whistles sarcastically. "Well, don't we have some bold little ladies around here?" He scans the statue-still student body. "How many of you agree with those two?"

Surprisingly, nearly every hand goes up, including most of the teachers.

Mr. Buttrum glares at our group. "Why don't all of you wallflowers come up here?"

After a laugh, Arch loudly announces, "Of all the students at this school, I promise that we're the least wallflowery you're gonna find." He pushes away from the wall and leads our pack down the center aisle and up the side steps onto the stage. Every eye follows our trek. Trey grabs my hand and Demitri shifts to my other side. I can sense that they're flanking me just in case the principal is also searching for the apparently sought-after Melanie Slate. Arch stops next to Mr. Buttrum, close enough to invade his personal space, and throws up devil horns with his right hand. The students explode, roaring and clapping. After a moment, Arch waves his hands in the air like a conductor ending a symphony, and the crowd goes silent. He turns a pointed look Mr. Buttrum's way and waits.

The principal hits us all with an evil stink eye as he takes a deep breath. "Let me guess . . . This is the infamous new student council that I've been warned about?"

Arch bends at the waist and gallantly circles his hand in front of him. "At your service, *Master*."

The crowd snickers, but then quickly goes quiet. The silence stretches uncomfortably long.

Finally, Mr. Buttrum turns to survey the crowd. "Effective immediately, the student council is disbanded." He turns to us and adds, "We won't need your services anymore because it's more than apparent that this school won't be capable of earning events."

We all glance at each other in disbelief.

"You heard the man," Arch calls out to the student body. "Student council members will *definitely* follow this latest edict by Master over here."

The students boo. Arch puts his outstretched hands at hip level, then slowly raises them. The booing gets steadily louder as his hands rise. Then, all at once, Arch signals for silence and every voice cuts off. He turns an appraising glare at Principal Buttrum.

"You think you've got control of these students, huh?" Buttrum says.

A voice cries out, "Shut up, you old bag!" It's Drew, the quarterback of the football team.

The whole student body roars and laughs at the principal, the sound deafening. My group and I exchange a look, our eyes wide. This has gone downhill fast.

Principal Buttrum demands over and over, "ORDER! ORDER!" into the microphone, but he's hardly audible over the angry students. He turns red and starts to sweat, a throbbing vein pulsating at his temple. I fight not to laugh. This guy's done a crap job handling his new students, and it looks like he's going to have to learn the hard way.

Meanwhile, Mr. Dean looks harried. He's racing and pacing along the side of the stage, panicking, hopefully seeing the grave error he made when he put Mr. Buttrum in charge of Hollywood High. The noise continues without so much as a waver, until finally Mr. Dean rushes up to Arch and whispers something to him.

Arch raises his hand, devil horns up, before performing another of his cut-the-noise hand gestures. The crowd silences instantly.

Mr. Buttrum looks like he's going to have a stroke. "How *dare* you!" he screams at Arch. "What are you trying to *prove*?"

Arch leans into the microphone so aggressively, it forces Mr. Buttrum to take two steps back. "I'm not *trying* to prove anything. I *did* prove that this school's run by respect and mutual cooperation—something you need to learn if you're going to make it around here."

Mr. Buttrum shoves his way back to the microphone and sputters at Arch, "You are *expelled*!"

The student body collectively explodes, storming toward the exits. Apparently, they've seen enough. Our group rushes to make it into the middle of the surging crowd. It's better to take our leave now. Nothing we say or do is going to help with this situation, and we need to regroup. Arch pushes his way through the crowd, and our classmates part to allow the student council to get to the front of the mob. Our school has just over fifteen hundred students, and it looks like a lot of them plan to follow us.

"Arch, what's the plan?" I yell over the noise.

He points at the gate as we round the bottom of the long, four-story staircase, riding a wave of powerful energy that apparently translates even to the yellow-jacket security guards, whose eyes widen. They throw open the front gate and back out of the way of the fast-moving crowd.

Arch puts up devil horns, and the entire crowd behind us throws up their right hands, copying the gesture. Our leader rounds the corner and heads up the side street past the parked buses, into the expansive student parking lot. He stops in the large, open driveway area, where students crowd in around us. Hiram jogs up with a bullhorn he must have grabbed from the sound storage closet before he left the theater. He hands it to Arch.

"Everyone, please sit!" Arch belts through the bullhorn.

The crowd sits down in the open space, and Arch surveys them.

"I don't know what kind of insanity we're up against," he says into the bullhorn, "but it's us against them."

"But you're expelled!" Dante hollers. "What do we do?"

Before Arch can answer, Ms. G rounds the corner and flows into the parking lot with most of the teachers behind her. "Arch isn't expelled," she calls out in her authoritative voice, "because I'm not filing the paperwork."

The crowd cheers, but then quiet down quickly as Ms. G, our Magnet school performing arts counselor, steps up next to Arch. Ms. G's an ample woman who's viewed by the students as a mother figure as well as a counselor.

She takes the bullhorn from Arch. "We've got your back," she announces. "Buttrum called us into a meeting before the assembly and treated us just as poorly as he addressed all of you. Let Little Man Buttrum think he's in charge. The teachers are with you. We'll get through this because that's what we do."

Jayla, a pretty dance student with curly hair and big brown eyes, yells out, "Maybe we should all just find new schools. This place sucks now."

Everyone murmurs in agreement, and many heads nod. The students look dejected, and who could blame them? It really has been a rough school year. We can't catch a break.

Arch shakes his head as he takes back the bullhorn. "Absolutely and unequivocally *no*! We don't back down from a challenge! We're Hollywood High!"

"What was that crap about with the security guards at the dance?" Drew calls out. "Why did they want Melanie?"

Everyone leans forward curiously.

"What happened?" Ms. G asks.

Mr. Isley snags her arm and pulls her to the edge of the parking lot to fill her in.

Arch says into the bullhorn, "We don't know, but we're looking into it. We'll stick together and figure out what's going on. I'm thinking it's all connected."

Many in the crowd are shaking their heads, looking down. Not even Arch can get through to them at this point.

Mr. Isley crosses back to us and takes the bullhorn. "Arch is right. We've been through worse than Principal Buttrum. Where's your sense of spirit?"

Everyone stares at him with dejected eyes, but they don't say anything.

Adam stands, crossing to the teachers and Arch. He takes the bullhorn from Mr. Isley. "As the resident guy who was tortured and came back from the dead, I've got a few things to say."

A ripple of appreciative laughter passes among the crowd.

"I haven't always loved this place. In fact, I spent several years ditching as often as possible, but I'm telling you right now that this is our home. I'll be damned if I let that blowhard make me his bitch."

Heads start nodding.

"So, here's the plan," Adam continues. "We don't know why administration and security have a hard-on for Melanie, but I'm asking that everyone keep an eye out. If you hear anything helpful, come to student council and we'll gladly take the info from you. We need help piecing this together, and even the most random tidbit may be key."

All eyes are on me as heads nod all around the massive student body. Several guys crack their knuckles.

"In the meantime," Adam continues, "we leave today because they can't make their attendance money if we aren't here. Hit 'em where it hurts—in their budget. Then, we show up tomorrow and it's business as usual. Be respectful, be here, do your best, but we don't fold to nonsense and rules set by a dictator. The old rules stand. He only has power if we allow it."

Kendra, Jayla's best friend and another dancer at the school, yells out, "What about student council? Do you guys still exist?"

I grin, standing up and taking the bullhorn from Adam. "We exist if you say we exist. We're your council, not the administration's council. Everyone in favor of student council remaining in place, please raise your hands."

A sea of hands rises.

"Anyone opposed?"

All hands drop. It's unanimous.

Arch takes the bullhorn. "Then it's settled. Student council remains, at least in the eyes of the students. We stay the course. Here's the key, though: everyone must be on their best behavior. Don't fill them in that we're trying to figure out what's behind this nonsense. Also, don't blindly follow them. If there's one thing my group has learned, it's that authority is often corrupt. Don't give them an excuse to clamp down, but be aware. Got it?"

Heads nod all around the parking lot.

"You need help with a plan, Arch?" Drew yells.

Arch nods. "The student council will be holding an emergency meeting. We'll have a plan by tomorrow morning. We'll involve other people as needed."

Our group exchanges looks.

"Marcus?" I say. "Can I use your cell phone to call and warn my mom? I think it's time for a student council meeting at my house."

Marcus hands me his phone.

Ms. G gets on the bullhorn. "Anyone who takes the bus, head to the buses. We've already called the bus office, and the drivers are headed to their assigned vehicles. Everyone else, you're now off campus and we see nothing. Disperse before Principal Buttrum thinks to call the police."

CHAPTER 4

My stepfather, Rich, looks confused, his face mashed up in a comical scowl. "His name's Buttrum?"

We all laugh.

"Right?" Marcus says. "He chose to be a *principal*? With that last name?"

Rich and Mom double over laughing. The full student council arrived at my house half an hour ago, and we're at the tail end of filling my parents in. Of course, Marcus and Tanner made our recount of the morning hilarious. At least we can laugh about the situation, even though we all suspect we've got a fight on our hands. Mom had a meal ready for us by the time we arrived, and we're all happily eating kid food. Mom's lunches are usually more refined, but with the short notice, all she could manage was boxed mac-n-cheese and frozen chicken strips. No one seems to mind, though.

"Well, it's never dull around there," Rich says. "What's your plan?"

"We're going back to school tomorrow with the plan to go about business as usual," Arch explains. "We're not going to cause trouble, but we're not taking any crap either. Adam asked the student body to keep an eye on Melanie in case the security guards' search for her is somehow connected."

Rich scans my group with a hard gaze. "I didn't think anything of it at first, but this certainly puts a new spin on things. Do you think it could really be connected?"

Arch shrugs, but Adam and Trey both bark, "Yes," at the same time.

"Melanie," Bear says, "what's your intuition telling you about all this?"

"It's still vague, but it has an evil undercurrent. If my intuition's accurate this time, we're in for it."

Darren grimaces. "Melanie's intuition is *always* accurate." He looks at me and adds, "You're like a weather barometer. If you say we're in for it, then we really need to pay attention."

Everyone nods in agreement.

"On a different note," Mom says, "other than the dramatic conclusion, how was the dance, everyone?"

Finley claps her hands, grinning, and her pretty blue eyes sparkle. "The dance was magic! At least until the secret police showed up. We needed a fun night so bad."

"It might be our last dance for a while if Principal Buttrum gets his way," Valerie says. "So I'm glad it was a good one." She rolls her eyes. She's been blazingly irritated that the festivities were cut short by the fire alarm fiasco. She glares in my direction, silently blaming me yet again, and I roll my eyes in response. These days, Valerie and I don't get along as well as we used to.

Rich looks to Adam. "I can't tell you how relieved we are that you're okay."

Adam looks down at his hands. "Any chance you and I can go into the den and talk?"

Concern graces Rich's expression as he stands and motions behind him. "Of course. Head that way. I'll grab us a couple of fresh sodas and meet you in there."

They exit, and we're all left in the living room staring at each other.

After a long silence, Valerie whispers, "Adam's losing it. It's worse than you all know."

We all lean forward in our seats.

"What can we do for him?" Arch asks quietly.

Bear, Darren, Trey, and I exchange a look, knowing that I'm doing what I can to fix things. No one else knows, though, and we're keeping it that way intentionally.

"Be patient," Valerie answers. "Help him when he asks for it. His shoulders and arms have a lot of nerve damage and scar tissue. It's going to take time and physical therapy to get full range of motion back, but his doctor seems to think he'll fully recover. Mentally and emotionally, he's hiding a lot from everyone. He's jumpy and reactive. Adam's always been so in control, and I think the post-traumatic stress makes him mad. He and I went to Balboa Park yesterday and took a long walk. He told me he doesn't know where to turn. His dad gets so upset when the kidnapping is mentioned that Adam ends up helping his dad, instead of the other way around. He doesn't even bother trying to talk to him anymore. I suggested that he talk with Rich, and Adam looked hopeful for the first time in weeks. I'm praying Rich can help. Adam really looks up to him."

We all nod.

"I think you made the best possible suggestion," Mom says to Valerie. "Rich will do anything to help Adam. Sometimes trauma takes time." She shifts her gaze to everyone, surveying the group. "Be there for Adam, but don't push. He needs to know that he's safe, and you'll all wait this out."

"He'll make it through," Trey says. "He doesn't know any other way."

Bear nods. "I agree. I've been talking a lot with him, and we're working on it. With Rich's help, we'll get him there."

"On a different subject," Darren says, "what's the plan with the Buttrum nightmare?"

Arch looks contemplative as he clears his throat. "Student council needs to work behind the scenes to remain one step ahead of this new problem. I stayed a few minutes after you all left earlier, and I talked to Ms. G, Mr. Bentley, and Mr. Isley. They said that the teachers are *all* furious. Everyone liked Principal Walker, and Ms. G thinks something's up with his firing. He certainly wasn't fired based on performance. Our school's student test scores are at an all-time high, our college-bound percentage is up, all the sports teams are making it at least to regionals, the Magnet performing arts programs are winning conference titles and awards right and left. Literally, there's zero logical reason for Principal Walker to have been fired for his work ethic."

We all exchange glances and Hiram says, "Marcus, why don't you see if your dad will call Principal Walker and find out what he knows?"

Marcus nods. "I'll talk to Dad as soon as he gets home from work tonight."

"Let me know what you find out," Arch says. "In the meantime, we need to stay on top of this. Principal Buttrum lunges, we dodge. He sets some insane rule, we counter. Ms. G's going to keep the teachers informed, and she assured me they'll all be allies. She seems certain that Buttrum's a loose cannon who'll end up canned soon."

We all agree.

"You're going to have to be the creative pack of mischief-makers that I know and love," Mom says. "I highly recommend that you find ways to get under his skin while you work behind the scenes to unravel this mystery. Ways that counter whatever he sets in place, but that he can't rationally get mad about. Honestly, it sounds like you're all faced with a fun game. If you play your cards right, he'll come across as a lunatic to the school board."

Everyone grins.

"You know I love a good Scooby and the gang mystery," Tanner says. "I'm looking forward to that part."

His enthusiasm isn't shared by Trey. "If someone hurts Melanie . . ." Trey's foreboding statement drifts off.

Adam cracks his knuckles while Demitri huffs and rubs his face.

"Let's not borrow trouble yet," Arch says. "We might be worried about nothing. I'm excited to see where this goes." He looks earnestly at Mom. "Thank you for having us over today. I know you didn't expect us to roll in, and I appreciate you hosting our chaos."

Mom grins. "Rich had the day off, and we needed something to do. It's too cold to swim, but Rich has a football and some Frisbees in the hall closet. Y'all are welcome to play in the front yard and have some fun."

"To the yard!" Tanner exclaims.

All smiles, we hop up and head outside to enjoy the rest of our unexpected day off.

CHAPTER 5

The next morning was met with another school assembly. I've tuned out the blathering list of rules that Principal Buttrum is going on and on about. We're broken up by grade levels, and I'm a nervous wreck sitting in the back left seating quadrant with the rest of the freshmen. Trey's across the auditorium, in the tenth-grade seating area, staring at me. His attention snaps around to Mr. Buttrum on the stage, bringing me back to reality.

"Melanie Slate?"

Enough heads turn to look my way that there's no hiding from Principal Buttrum. I wince as my heart races. Many of the students, apparently realizing they didn't handle that right, wince along with me.

My eyes narrow as I stand and meet Principal Buttrum's beady-eyed gaze. I glance to my right, up ahead, and meet Adam's blue eyes from the senior seating area. A quick glance to the left, and I find Demitri next to Arch and Hiram in the junior seating section. His eyes are narrowed as he stares at me.

Now that I know where my guys are, I look back at Principal Buttrum.

"To my office," he says. "Now."

I make an innocent face. "May I ask why?"

Principal Buttrum smiles, seemingly elated. "I have a few questions for you."

The security yellow jackets make their way to my row, where Drake, two chairs down from me, stands and blocks their way. Marcus and Tanner stand in the row behind me, hemming me in.

"The three guys that just stood," Buttrum hollers, "*sit! Now!*"

Suddenly, every guy in the auditorium stands, and a distinct sense of danger wafts through the cavernous building. My heart rate climbs. I feel Trey and Adam amp up through our connections. Unfortunately, this only serves to distract me long enough for a pair of hands to clamp down on my shoulders. I'm pulled backward across the two girls next to me, dragged into the aisle.

Tanner, Marcus, and Drake start trying to push their way through the crowd to get to me. Three yellow jackets head to them as another three escort me up the aisle. Principal Buttrum sets to squawking and carrying on at the distraction that my friends are presenting. I glance over my shoulder to spot Trey, Adam, and Demitri sliding out of their aisles and subtly heading to the exit doors closest to each of them. The principal's view of their sneaky exits is blocked by all the standing boys throughout the auditorium. The air is heavy with the knowledge that something's not right.

I'm marched out through the lobby doors and down the outside steps, then pivoted to the right. We're headed through the faculty parking lot.

Trey sends a bubble indicating that they're following.

I send to Adam, *"This isn't good, right?"*

Adam sends, *"No."*

My yellow-jacket security escort is all female, I suddenly realize, so I try the camaraderie route. They don't bite. When we get to the two-story building, I can't help but smile the slightest bit. Up ahead, casually leaning by the door to the main office, is Demitri. He's wearing a sexy smolder, his blue-gray eyes hooded flirtatiously. There's a sense that my all-female security detail is instantly enamored. Demitri casually flirts with them. They take the bait, and it's all the distraction we need. Trey and Adam grab me, and we haul ass across the hall to the conference room.

Trey closes the door, but Demitri opens it just before we can push the lock button.

"Nice job, D," Trey says, locking the door behind him.

Demitri rolls his eyes. "Out of shape, middle-aged women love me. What can I say?"

I laugh. "It's hilarious when you turn all smoldering."

Demitri juts his chin my way. "Melanie's literally the only girl on the planet my hot-guy act doesn't work on."

Trey and Adam both glare at him, and then glare at each other.

"What the hell does Buttrum want with Mel?" Trey asks, putting his arm around me.

Adam shakes his head. "We still have no clue. Whatever he wants with her is going to be a pain in our asses."

"She's clearly on his radar," Demitri says, "and that's bad. But at least now we know that the search for her at the dance can't be a coincidence."

Baffled, I look at Trey. "There's no way this whole principal switcheroo involves me." I tap my temple, muttering, "Think. What have I done . . ."

Adam laughs. "You look like Winnie the Pooh trying to think through the fluff in his head."

I smirk.

Adam pulls up a chair, sits, and puts his feet up on the conference table. "We can't leave for a while. Might as well take a load off."

Demitri takes the chair across the table next to Adam.

I sit and drape my leg over Trey's knee, then close my eyes with a huff. "This is the last damn thing I need."

Trey's rubbing his face. "Keeping you safe is a full-time nightmare, Mel. I don't know if I can handle another round."

I roll my eyes. "I don't look for trouble."

"At least it's not the Drones this time," Adam offers. "Joel and the guys who attacked Mel and me are in jail. But what the hell could it be?"

Nonchalantly, I suggest that maybe Buttrum's an old pervert who likes to use tiny teenage girls as his personal carnival ride.

Demitri winces. "Ugh." He looks at Trey. "I don't know how you do it. Every time I turn around, Melanie has some new admirer. Perverts, rapists, hot basketball players, and now we can add lumpy Napoleonic principals to the list."

"Don't forget about me!" Adam says with a grin.

Demitri laughs. "So sorry." His eyes twinkle amusedly at Trey. "Also, bad boy, blue-eyed, biker heartthrobs."

Trey gives Demitri a deadpan glare. "Thank you for that succinct summary of my personal hell."

We have time to kill, so Adam takes a set of playing cards out of his backpack and shuffles them. He deals a hand to each of us, and the guys teach me how to play poker.

Just as Trey wins a hand, we hear the maniacal squawking of Principal Buttrum in the hall. "What do you mean she disappeared? Now she's a magician? Gee *whiz*, aren't the students around here talented!"

We listen as the yellow jackets assure that they truly can't imagine what happened. I grin at Demitri. They've conveniently left out the gorgeous distraction he provided. He rolls his eyes.

Ms. G's voice cuts through their pleas. "I'll find her and deliver her to you. You can all head back to your work."

"The moment she's found," Buttrum says, "I need to speak with her."

We hear the sound die down, and then there's a soft tap on the conference room door. Trey opens it, and Ms. G skirts in, closing the door after her.

"How did you know we were in here?"

Ms. G grins. "Mr. Isley and Arch followed you. They saw Demitri's little production." Her eyes twinkle as she spots the cards on the table. "Let's play a few hands, and then I'll sneak Melanie out into the crowd when the second-period bell rings."

We return to our seats.

"What does Buttrum want with Mel?" Trey asks.

Ms. G collects the cards Adam dealt and shakes her head pensively. "No clue, but I'm not pleased about it." She looks at me. "You're a beacon for trouble."

"Any chance he's got a weird thing for me?"

Ms. G snorts. "*Really*? You're fifteen and he's a principal."

"No, seriously," Adam says. "Mel looks like a fitness model."

Trey snarls in Adam's direction. Adam nods enthusiastically, just to irritate him.

"She looks *fifteen*," Ms. G says, giving Adam a disbelieving look.

Demitri cracks up. "Like hell she does. No one from our group looks like a teenager." He gestures to Adam. "That one looks like a twenty-five-year-old biker."

Adam grins. "Bear, Darren, Arch, and I have been buying beer since we were thirteen." He gestures to Trey. "That one had a job as security at the Midsummer Night's Dream party at the Playboy mansion this summer."

Trey rubs his face hard. "Lord. That was a night."

"I didn't know that," Demitri says. "Couldn't have been all bad."

Trey grimaces. "I told my dad I'd quit if he took on another of those contracts. He shut the business down after that mess. Nothing but horny drunk celebrities who thought they had a right to do whatever they pleased. Pensive girls everywhere, half-naked and trying to stay in security's line of sight while they smiled and flirted out of obligation. It wasn't the fantasy you're thinking."

Adam shrugs. "Half-naked models sounds all right to me."

Trey gives him a look. "Ever had four scared models try to hide behind you while being pawed at by old golf pros? It's a trip."

I huff. "Seriously, Trey? The more I find out about your past, the grosser it is."

Ms. G looks flabbergasted. "The more I find out about all you kids, the more disturbed I am."

Demitri gestures to me. "I assure you that Principal Buttrum has some desire for our little solar flare here. The question is, what is it?"

"Think he's an energy worker?" Trey asks.

"Not a shot." Ms. G chuckles. "He's an energetic corpse."

— —

Ms. G managed to sneak me into the second-period passing crowd. I made it through class unscathed, but my luck has apparently run out. I'm walking from second to third period, and I've got yellow jackets subtly closing ranks from all sides. They aren't as stealthy as they think. All through my trek, I've been watching them ring me from a distance. Suddenly, I'm pissed.

I stop and whip around, barking at the one behind me, "What?"

The closest yellow jacket attempts to grab my arm, but then Drake, a hot basketball player who's had a thing for me all year, steps up. The yellow jacket cowers under the look that the tall, hazel-eyed stud gives him.

I scoot closer to Drake, who puts an arm around my shoulders. "Back off," he orders, and the yellow jackets who have us trapped take a hesitant step back.

Other students move in closer.

Dante is among them, and he steps up to my other side. "What do you want with Melanie?" he demands. Dante is a sweetheart, but he looks intimidating in the death metal gear he wears every day. He's clearly mad and does nothing to hide it.

"The principal needs Ms. Slate," one of the guards informs.

"Too damn bad," Dante says loudly enough to be heard at the back of the crowd. "So sad for him. He'll just have to rub one out by himself."

The yellow jackets exchange unsure glances as other students step up behind us, forming a bodyguard detail.

Frustration roils through me. "Leave me *alone*," I bellow at the security guards.

When they seem to stand down, we turn and continue our trek to third period. I stop at the door to my classroom, where the sound of pounding feet makes me cower. Drake wraps his arms around me as Dante steps in front of us, ready for another confrontation.

Turns out the feet belong to Trey. He gets to us, panting and out of breath as he surveys my current state. "What happened?"

Drake fills him in, and Trey gnashes his teeth.

"Damn it," Trey says. "I'm sorry, Melanie. I should have been there."

I shake my head, unsure of what to say.

Demitri rushes up and informs that word has traveled all over the school about what just occurred. "Melanie needs to leave. Can you take her, Trey?"

My boyfriend shakes his head in frustration. "If I get caught ditching again, they're going to kick me off the baseball team."

"I can leave," Demitri offers. "I'll take Melanie home and fill in her parents."

Trey nods. "Thank you."

"I'm walking them out," Drake informs. "We can't take a chance."

Trey pulls me in for a hug. "I trust Demitri, but be careful, babe. Get off campus and make a run for it. We'll figure this out."

Drake puts an arm around my shoulders again, and we make a beeline for the stairs. When we arrive outside, Drake guides me to a place in the fence I've never used to ditch. Apparently, the Regulars at the school have their own secrets. Drake leans subtly, blocking the view while he peels back the chain-link that hooks at a support pipe. I take off my clunky backpack before slipping through. Demitri slides his pack off and slips through after me. Drake tosses our backpacks over the top of the fence, and Demitri catches them effortlessly. He slings both backpacks over his shoulders and takes my hand. Together, we jog down the sidewalk.

We make it almost around to the student parking lot before we're spotted. A yellow jacket yells for us, but we ignore him and bolt for Demitri's Jeep. He unlocks my door, and I scoot in as he runs around the front of the car and gets into the driver's seat. We speed away just as Principal Buttrum and the yellow jacket arrive, winded, at the edge of the parking lot.

CHAPTER 6

My mouth is hanging open as I stare at my parents. Demitri and I didn't even manage to sit down before a talking-to started. Apparently, the principal called my parents to inform them that I ditched school, so they were seething mad when Demitri and I arrived. The talk started with a discussion about how they've pondered what my group filled them in on and they think we're jumping to unfounded conclusions. Things have escalated to a full-scale screaming match that I suspect I'm about to lose.

"What the *hell* has gotten into you? You *ran* when an authority figure demanded you stop?" Rich's tone is one I've rarely heard, and it brings instant tears to my eyes. We never fight. We're so much alike that it startles people to discover he's my stepfather. Our running family joke is that, somehow, I'm his biological child.

"They tried to pull me from an assembly," I try to explain. "*Then* they followed me during the passing period and demanded I go to the principal's office! Hell yes, I ran!"

Rich's lips turn white as he tenses. "Whatever you've done must require a discussion. We've raised you right and expect you to own up to your mistakes instead of running from them."

In an effort to calm the squabble, Demitri holds up his hands in a gesture of peace. "I can promise you that Melanie hasn't done anything wrong. There's something deeper—"

"What's your deal, Demitri?" Rich interrupts. "Why are you always around? Melanie has a boyfriend!"

Demitri appears stunned. He rattles his head before attempting to answer. "I'm her best—"

Rich waves his hand flippantly, unwilling to hear him out. "Leave, Demitri. Melanie's grounded until she meets with the principal and has the guts to face the punishment for whatever she did."

Demitri's eyes widen.

My mouth drops open, and I shake my head while tears stream down my cheeks. "I'm telling you now that I haven't done anything wrong, Rich. Something serious is happening. My intuition is—"

"Enough!" Rich snarls. "You can't use your intuition as an excuse. I don't know what the hell is wrong with you lately, but ever since you got involved with this group of yours, you've been in nothing but trouble. This ends now. No more of your friends. No more issues!"

My dark-water rage revs, and I lose control of my temper. Before I can stop myself, I turn and punch the wall. My hand goes straight through the Sheetrock.

"*Out!*" Rich bellows. "*Leave*, and don't come back until you can apologize!"

I'm stunned by the damage I've just caused, and more stunned by the realization that I've been kicked out of the house. Since I've only been grounded a handful of times in fifteen years, it never occurred to me that being kicked out was even an option. I bend at the waist and sob. I'm so desperate to be heard that I try again, but it does no good.

Rich grabs my arm, and Demitri's shoulder, and hauls us to the door. He shoves us onto the front porch and slams the door in our faces just as my mom yells, "*Richard!*"

My best friend and I stand on the porch in stunned silence as my parents bicker from the other side of the door. I keep waiting for it to open again, but the voices fade and we're left outside. Beside myself, I turn to Demitri, who's staring at the door with huge eyes.

He closes his gaping mouth and decides on a route. "We're going to my house. My dad will know what to do."

"We're going to figure this out," Mr. Cantrell promises as he wraps his arms around me.

We're standing in Demitri's living room, and it seems we've managed to find a parent who's willing to listen and be on our side.

"I'm going to help you with your parents," he offers. "You can stay with us until this boils over."

"Um, Dad?"

Mr. Cantrell and I look to Demitri, who shakes his head slightly.

"We should discuss that," Demitri says.

"What is there to discuss?" Mr. Cantrell looks stunned. "Melanie needs help."

Demitri clears his throat. "I don't think it's a good idea. It'll cause issues with Trey."

The considerate father wobbles his head right and left. "I hadn't thought about that. Do you think Trey's parents will let you stay there?" he asks me.

I shake my head, and the heat of a blush creeps up my neck. "They don't exactly like me. They think Trey and I are too serious, and that I'm trouble because there's been so much drama."

A sigh escapes Mr. Cantrell's lips.

"What about Adam's house?" Demitri asks.

I tip my head back and close my eyes. "Bad plan. I'd never hear the end of it from Valerie."

Demitri crosses to the phone by the couch. He dials a number and waits for an answer.

"Hey, Adam. We've got a problem."

My mouth drops open. "Don't do this!" I plead.

Demitri ignores me. "Melanie got thrown out by Rich."

"*What*?" Adam bellows loudly enough that I can hear him through the phone.

With a wince, Demitri holds the phone receiver away from his ear. "We're at my house," he says after Adam seems to have calmed down. "We're trying to figure out what to do with her."

Another blush rises again. I don't need a mirror to know I'm tomato red, and I hate it. I also hate being treated like a problem to be dealt with.

I'm so consumed with humiliation that I miss the last part of Demitri and Adam's chat before he hangs up.

"Demitri," Mr. Cantrell says harshly, "that was uncalled for. We aren't shuttling your best friend out the door. She's staying here."

"She's not," Demitri says venomously. "Period!"

My heart skips a beat to hear them talking to each other like this. *There's something bigger going on here.*

"Get over it, son. We don't turn our backs on the people we love."

Suddenly, Demitri is seething mad. "*I* decide what I'm comfortable with, not you!"

A pained lump forms in my throat, and I swallow hard as the realization that Demitri doesn't want me here becomes clear. I don't know why he feels that way, but since I'm empathic, there's zero doubt in my mind that I have it right. "Why don't you want me here, Demitri?" I ask, my voice tiny.

My friend squeezes his eyes closed and doesn't answer for a long moment. When he finally does, he's much calmer. "I've started dating Victoria. She's got an issue with you and me being friends. I haven't told anyone we're dating because I'm not ready to deal with the drama. No one from our crowd really likes her, and I'll catch crap from everyone. Anyway, Victoria won't be okay with this arrangement."

A million conflicting emotions rattle up. "Unbelievable. I didn't see that reason coming." Needing a new plan, I switch gears. "May I use your phone, Mr. Cantrell?"

"Of course."

I take a deep breath before picking up the receiver and dialing a number I memorized in case of an emergency. When Mr. Isley answers, I instantly tear up again. "It's Melanie," I warble out. "Melanie Slate. Sir, you know how you've always said you'd be there if any of us need anything?"

"Yes. Melanie, what's wrong?"

I barely manage to sob out, "I need a dad right now."

"Where are you?" Mr. Isley demands, sounding alarmed.

"Demitri's house." I give him the address. "Can you come get me?"

"Stay where you are. I'll be there in a few minutes." Mr. Isley hangs up, and I'm left with the buzzing receiver in my hand.

"You don't need another dad right now," Mr. Cantrell insists. "I'm here, and I promise you can trust me to help you."

I shake my head sadly.

"Melanie," Demitri says in a voice just above a whisper.

He tries to touch my arm, but I shy away and cross the room to my backpack. I take out my soft-sided CD case and flip through the CDs, finding the one I'm after. "May I?" I gesture to the CD player.

When Mr. Cantrell nods, I slip the CD in and skip several tracks before pushing *play*.

Ozzy Osbourne's "Crazy Train" blisters through the speakers.

"Shit," Demitri murmurs.

"What?"

I start dancing through the intro as Demitri informs his dad, "This is her song when everything collapses."

Several years ago, I performed to this song with a dance team I was on. The piece is incredibly complicated, with its lifts, leaps, and turn sequences. It's insanely fast, and in that way, it always helps clear my head. Demitri knows the choreography and has worked me through the piece before, back during the last time my life fell apart. He attempts to cross to me as the first lift sequence comes up, but I shoo him away, altering the choreography to dance on my own. Demitri looks abashed, but I ignore him and hit a wicked split leap.

The door opens, and I'm both unsurprised and a little annoyed when Adam invites himself in. He watches as Demitri attempts to do the next lift section in the piece.

"Leave me alone, D," I bark, pushing him away.

Adam steps to me and I stop.

"You don't know this choreo, Adam."

He smirks. "I don't need to know it. I know you."

"What about your damaged shoulders?"

Adam smiles as the song beats aggressively around us. "I'll chance it."

He takes my lead and perfectly mimics my movement. I open my connection with him and send him the choreography just before each section. He's an incredible dancer and has this in spades. Demitri is clearly stunned that I accepted Adam into my mix instead of him.

A half minute later, Mr. Isley comes through the door Adam left open just in time to watch us hit a flawless quad turn, side by side. "Yesss!" he belts. "Dance your asses off, kids."

I prep and leap. Adam launches me into the air before catching me with precise timing. I fling myself back, and Adam perfectly executes the trust fall before hooking me under the arms and spinning me round and round. He launches me up and catches me. I wrap my legs around his waist and drop back. He grips my throat and pulls me up. As we're eye to eye, my seductive dark-water side blazes. It doesn't help that my legs are wrapped around him, and we have a tanker's load of unresolved tension between us. With nothing between our connection, the seductive fire roars into Adam. His eyes blaze to match mine, and he crushes me to his chest, kissing me hard.

Lost on a wave of the best part of my dark-water side, my grasp on reality melts. All sense of right and wrong disappears, and Valerie and Trey are instantly forgotten. Fire blisters up my spine like it only does with Adam. Apparently, I'm not the only one who's been dropped into an inferno, because Adam's knees buckle. We end up on the floor, but it doesn't stop there.

Suddenly, I come back to my senses and wrench my head to the side. Adam's panting as his head drops to my shoulder.

"Okaaay," Mr. Cantrell says.

I blink rapidly, trying to get my rattling mind to slow.

Adam helps me to my feet. "I'm sorry," he says, as much to the other men in the room as to me. "I didn't expect that. Her dark-water side took over." He looks to Mr. Isley. "Why are you here?"

Our dance teacher looks scandalized but mildly amused. "I have no idea. Melanie called me to get her."

Adam looks to Demitri. "Then why am *I* here? I thought you wanted me to come get Melanie."

"I called you before she called Mr. Isley," Demitri admits. "Melanie wasn't pleased about my reaching out to you."

Adam gives me an askance look.

"We both know I can't stay with you," I say with a huff.

"Why?"

I stare at Adam like he's nuts. "Because I'll be ass up in your bed in five minutes flat."

Adam shrugs, clearly fine with the idea. "If it means you move in with me and we can try again, I'll call and dump Valerie mid-hump."

My head rolls around on my neck. "You think you'll be able to dial a phone mid-hump, let alone speak?"

Adam grins at me with such zeal that I can't help but laugh.

Mr. Isley chuckles. "Judging from what we just witnessed, it might be a great idea."

I turn a haughty look Mr. Isley's way. "Ever seen Valerie in a fistfight?"

He shakes his head.

"Just trust me. It's not on my list of yeehaw good times."

"Why aren't you staying with Demitri?" Adam asks.

I roll my eyes. "He doesn't want me here." I turn to Mr. Isley. "May I please stay on your couch tonight and get your help dealing with my latest nightmare?"

Before Mr. Isley can answer, Demitri's hand settles on my cheek. He turns my gaze his way, and there's something new in his eyes that brings my dark-water seduction to the surface again. He starts to lean toward me but stops himself just before his lips can touch mine.

"Do it," I whisper.

A wave of my dark-water intimacy thrums through Demitri's hand, and he stumbles back. His eyes are wide, and he's suddenly staring at me like he doesn't know me.

"He can't handle you, Melanie." Adam puts a hand on Demitri's shoulder. "Stick with simpletons, Peter Pan. Melanie's out of your league where it counts."

Demitri squares up, and Adam tips his head slowly to the side with suddenly fierce eyes, clearly challenging him to make a move. Demitri's jaw tenses, and the energy in the room amps up.

"Enough!" Mr. Isley strides into the middle of the looming fight. "Cool your jets, boys."

He takes me by the arm and shuttles me toward the door. I only stop long enough to grab my backpack.

Adam, Demitri, and Mr. Cantrell rush out the door behind us.

"You can come with me," Adam insists. "I promise I'll help you."

If I go with him, I'll make a mistake I quickly regret, so I don't look back or reply.

"Stop her!" Mr. Cantrell's order to his son does nothing to spur him. Demitri looks defeated.

I get in Mr. Isley's pickup truck and inhale deeply, trying to clear my head. Mr. Isley slides into the driver's seat and starts the truck. We pull away from the curb.

"Start from the beginning," he says.

CHAPTER 7

Mr. Isley pulls into the faculty parking lot at the high school and cuts the engine. "Let's see how today goes. If there's trouble, come to the dance studio."

I stare at my hands in my lap. "Thank you for talking to me. I apologize for ruining your evening."

Mr. Isley chuckles. "You aren't the first student to land on my couch, and you won't be the last. I teach at a school full of kids from all backgrounds. Your issues are nothing compared to the last one I hosted. His mother shot his dad in the head and landed in jail. That student lived with me for two years before he graduated. Proud to say he got a full-ride scholarship to a dance company in New York." He touches my arm in a fatherly way. "I called Finley and asked her to bring you some of her clothes. I hope that's okay."

There's a knock on the truck window, and there's Finley, smiling softly at me. Tanner is standing behind her, his expression sympathetic. I get out of the truck. Fin hugs me gently in that way of hers.

Tanner steps up next and cuffs me under the chin. "What do you say we get you changed and do a little makeup?" he asks.

My smile at Tanner lacks spunk, but since I'm still wearing my clothes from yesterday, I figure it couldn't hurt my mood to be on the receiving end of one of his famous glam jobs. "Yes, please."

"Meet me here after school," Mr. Isley instructs. "You're headed home with me again."

I thank him as Tanner and Finley shuttle me past Actors' Alley to the bathroom in the music building. Tanner saunters into the girls' bathroom without a thought. His disregard makes me giggle as he sets to gossiping exuberantly with two girls by the sinks. They chat as I take the clothes and head into a stall to change.

——

With a fresh Tanner makeup job finished, I follow my friends out of the music building. I'm still dreading the thought about having to come face-to-face with the new principal again—and truthfully, I'm still not sure whether I'll listen to my parents and submit to a meeting with him or go running again. Fortunately, I don't have to think about it long, because in the quad we're immediately accosted by our friends.

"What happened?" Arch asks.

I shrug. "Rich and my mom are convinced there's nothing to worry about except me being a problem. They wouldn't hear me out. It got heated and they kicked me out. I stayed with Mr. Isley last night." I intentionally leave out the part about kissing Adam, and I don't mention Demitri's reasons for not letting me stay with him. I don't need the heat that those revelations would cause.

A quick survey of the group reveals Demitri and Victoria standing on opposite sides. They're apparently avoiding each other in public, which should tell Demitri all he needs to know. I have no interest in another fight with him, and so I decide to keep my mouth shut about it.

Trey wraps his arms around me, and I put my head on his shoulder. "I'll talk with Rich and your mom," he assures me. "You aren't a troublemaker. Something is definitely happening around here."

"Are we sure it's not just some minor disciplinary thing with Buttrum?" I ask.

"It can't be that," Adam says adamantly. "Something's off. Every time one of these issues fires up around here, my empathy rages. There's a plan of some kind going on, and we need to uncover it."

I avoid looking Adam's away. Yesterday was another reminder of why I love him, a thought that I just can't handle right now.

Per the plan, we're all on our best behavior as we walk to fourth period. So far, during passing periods, Principal Buttrum hasn't seemed to be looking for me specifically. He's done little more than glare and yell into a bullhorn things like, "*Master* your discipline. If you can't *master* good behavior, then *I'll* teach *you* to master it."

Given how little he seems to be concerned about me specifically, I'm starting to think I'm insane and that we've fabricated an issue. Maybe he's just a jerk.

Presley scowls, her jaw set in a tight clamp. "This is miserable." She slides her cold green eyes my way. "It's just a matter of time before we kick his ass out of sheer irritation."

We turn the corner into quad two, where we're stopped by Principal Buttrum's bullhorn-bellowed words from behind us. "*You!* Boy in the *blue shirt*! Come here!"

Presley and I turn to look toward the commons. There, in the middle of a growing circle of students, is Principal Buttrum with his hand clamped around Tanner's bicep.

Marcus jogs up to us. "Oh crap. Here we go. This ought to be interesting. Stay with me, Mel."

We push our way toward the front of the circle of gawking students and find the rest of our group clumped together with a front-row spot.

"Boy, what's your name?" Buttrum asks.

"I'm Tanner Devick," comes the loud and boisterous reply. Tanner turns to the crowd and raises one eyebrow, his face set in a sexy pout.

The students chuckle, everyone seeming to know that this is about to be good. Tanner has a reputation for being fierce and fabulous. He shows up to school in amazing David-Bowie-inspired outfits and always has a face full of makeup that would put any glam band to shame. He's also witty and hilarious, so everyone's regularly amused by his antics. Tanner and Finley are an item, and she's standing next to Arch grinning.

"What, exactly, are you wearing?" the principal asks.

Tanner strikes a pose, his hip cocked to the side, a pose he holds dramatically before sashaying across the open area in the middle of the circle. He turns with a flourish and heads the other way, doing his favorite supermodel walk. Of course he looks fabulous.

He struts back to Principal Buttrum and flamboyantly answers for the crowd's benefit, "Today, I'm wearing the finest leather pants that Wilsons Leather Shop has to offer, complete with a pair of rad boots I found on Melrose, and a *fabulous* shimmery light-blue top, handmade by yours truly." He turns to the principal with an over-the-top, gossipy expression, putting one hand to his chest and scrunching his shoulders a bit. "It's a Devick original. Girl! Don't you love it?"

Trey cracks up at his best friend's antics. "He's laying it on thick today."

All the students are fighting not to laugh, most of us with our hands over our mouths. Adam puts his hands over his face and rubs his tired eyes hard, covering a smile. Our group exchanges side-eye glances. I don't know where this is headed, but I do know that Principal Buttrum's not likely to be amused. Tanner seems to know this too, because he's toying with him like a cat with a mouse. I love Tanner. Every school should have someone like him. He's the most open, nonjudgmental person, and he has zero toxic masculinity. He embraces the feminine and the masculine with fervor.

Principal Buttrum looks Tanner up and down with a disgusted expression, then says into the bullhorn, "I assume Tanner was part of the now defunct student council?" He shoots a glare our way, and my friends all grin at him like a bunch of idiots as I hide myself behind Trey as best I can.

Hiram and Marcus pump their arms up and down, jumping from foot to foot like circus monkeys, and all the students within view of the pair chuckle. Arch and Presley loudly guffaw.

Before Buttrum has a chance to scream at us, Tanner bounces twice on the balls of his feet and enthusiastically says, "Oh, now, now. Don't be jealous that you haven't had much time to get to know us. We're always up to something, and I *guarantee* there's more fun to come."

A murmur passes through the crowd as all the students nod in agreement.

The principal's face turns red, which seems to be a trademark for him. He really should get his blood pressure checked. The guy looks like he's going to keel over on the regular.

Buttrum puts the bullhorn to his mouth and screeches at the crowd, "*There will be no fun!*" Then he turns a fiery glare at Tanner and says into the bullhorn, "There will also be no wearing of the colors *red* or *blue*, like your friend over here!" He aggressively points his finger Tanner's way, and Tanner playfully bites at it.

Everyone laughs.

"Do you hear me?" Buttrum continues. "No red. And no *Tanner* Blue. They're *gang* colors and are now banned on these premises until further notice. I will not have *gangs* running around my school."

A male student at the back of the crowd yells, "I'm in a gang, and I'm wearing orange today!"

The students all crack up as Principal Buttrum's forehead vein throbs.

"Red is one of the school colors," Arch sensibly reminds. "Don't you want us to display our school spirit?"

Buttrum doesn't get an opportunity to respond. Tanner snatches the bullhorn from him and struts around the open space in the middle, doing his supermodel walk again. Buttrum follows after him, and they look ridiculous walking in a line. Tanner is sleek and all things fashionable; while short, fat Principal Buttrum waddles quickly behind him.

I'm suddenly having a hard time fearing this moron. I whisper to Trey, "Maybe I should just meet with that dumpling and see what he wants. He's ridiculous."

Trey snorts. "Who knows?" he whispers back. "Maybe Tanner's the new target after this show he's putting on."

"How exciting!" Tanner says into the bullhorn. "I would hereby like to invite you *all* to join my *fabulous* gang! *Oh, just imagine!* All of us dressing up in light-blue sequin outfits and heels, our makeup on point. We would rain down nothing but *terrible* fun and dance parties, like glitter, everywhere we go!"

Many of the students double over laughing, thoroughly enjoying the frustration on Buttrum's face. The principal makes a play for the bullhorn, but Tanner, in four-inch heels, towers over the short lump. Tanner reaches his arm up, dangling the bullhorn just out of his reach, and the principal hops twice, flailing.

Students are laughing so hard they're wiping tears from their cheeks. I see Mr. Isley, Ms. Ferry, Mr. Bentley, and Ms. G all clumped together, snickering at the far side of the circle. They make eye contact with our group, and Mr. Isley grins at us. Looks like even the teachers are enjoying the show.

Buttrum makes a lunge for the bullhorn, but Tanner's faster.

He jazz-slides away with a flourish. "Gotta catch me," he bellows into the bullhorn.

He performs a funny cartoon run toward our group and tosses the bullhorn at Arch, who catches it and discreetly passes it to the person behind him. I watch as the bullhorn passes back through the crowd until it's out of sight.

Somewhere at the back of the crowd, the bullhorn crackles to life with a "Buttrum is a bitch!"

It's bedlam.

"Looks like Buttrum just lost his favorite toy," I murmur to Marcus.

Marcus grins at me. This is more fun than it should be, and I have a feeling we're going to pay for Tanner's little production, but it's worth it.

His fists balled up, his pudgy leg stomping, Buttrum cries out at no one in particular, "I am not a bitch!"

The bullhorn fires off again. "Spoken like a true bitch!"

I can't help it. I double over. *This is a circus!*

Principal Buttrum rages at Tanner, "This is all your fault! *Out!* You're Ms. G's problem now!"

Ms. G rolls her eyes, and Tanner claps his hands, jumping up and down, squealing, "Yippee!"

"I want him punished!" Principal Buttrum squawks at Ms. G. The bullhorn sounds off with a sarcastic, "I bet you do!"

We all crack up again as Tanner takes a moment for a quick, deep curtsy. The students all enthusiastically clap for him before Ms. G takes him by the elbow and escorts him away.

CHAPTER 8

Mr. Bentley subtly gestures to us as the crowd disperses, heading to class. We follow him and Mr. Isley down the concrete ramp to the dance building entrance. We stop in the hall by the locker rooms and all turn to face each other. The whole student council's there, and Mr. Isley raises his eyebrows, surveying the group of twenty-one kids.

"I see the group's grown since our last meeting," he says with a laugh.

Arch fills him in. "We've added Deb, Victoria, Demitri, Javier, and Susan."

"I'm glad to see it," Mr. Isley says, "because I think you're going to need a big group. We're up against a serious problem. The teachers are worried about Principal Buttrum, and they're all secretly speculating about how your group's going to solve this issue for us. You've earned a reputation for effectively and creatively dealing with this school's nonsense."

Mr. Isley gestures toward the door leading to the quad. "Tanner just demonstrated what you little demons are capable of."

Mr. Bentley grins. "I think the students are also anxiously waiting to see how this group handles things. I passed by the cheerleaders, huddled in their little bunny hutch corner in quad two before school. They were giggling and gossiping about how the student council's going to show the principal who's boss."

When I let loose a snarl in my mind, it accidentally reaches Trey through our connection. He sighs as he recognizes my lingering hurt. He had an affair with Tiffany, the head cheerleader. While we've mostly moved past it, I have a habit of holding a grudge.

"Don't worry," Bear says to the teachers. "We've got a general plan. Looks like Tanner kicked it off with a bang."

Mr. Isley starts laughing again. "That boy's a hoot."

"As student council faculty representative," Mr. Bentley says, "I'm excusing you from fourth period. I need you all to head down to the theater department office. Please check on Tanner and help Ms. G and Ms. Austin."

"Help them with what?" Marcus asks suspiciously.

Mr. Bentley and Mr. Isley exchange a look.

"Principal Buttrum's moving the Magnet program office from the two-story building basement into the empty offices next to the conference room," Mr. Bentley explains. "He called a faculty meeting this morning and announced that the Magnet program office needs to be moved so he can 'keep an eye on them.'"

"The principal wants to keep an eye on Ms. Austin and Ms. G?" I ask skeptically.

Mr. Isley nods. "Principal Buttrum said they're on thin ice because they aren't in keeping with the standards of his master plan, whatever that means. The teachers think he's preparing to fire both of them. Ms. G has nothing to worry about because she's two years past the twenty-five years with the school district she needs to retire. She can leave with benefits and a full pension anytime.

She only stays because she loves the students so much. Ms. Austin, on the other hand, is close to tears about it. Her husband died three years ago, and she needs this job."

Arch cracks his knuckles. "Buttrum's wearing on my nerves. Ms. Austin's one of the sweetest people who work here."

"I'll talk to Ms. Austin," Marcus says. "If she gets fired, my dad will hire her at the firm. He's always looking for good assistants, and she would be perfect."

Mr. Bentley drapes his arm around Marcus's shoulders. "You kids have the biggest hearts. Doesn't matter what problem we're presented; you always find a solution."

"Let's head to the office and figure this mess out," Bear suggests.

Mr. Isley laughs as he hands us a hall pass. Confused by the laughter, we all look at it. It reads, *Master Hall Pass* across the top.

Trey snorts. "Principal Buttrum's obsession with the word *master* is bizarre." He pauses, thinking, and then adds, "I believe I'll recommend to the baseball team and the football players that we start calling him the Master-bator."

Arch beams at Trey. "Oh yeah! Buttrum's gonna *love* that!"

We all crack up as we head through the double doors toward the soon-to-be-abandoned Magnet office. Down the dingy stairs from the quad, we make our way in pairs. The school is divided into two major groups: the Regulars, who live in the area, and the Magnet performing arts kids who have to audition to get in. The two sections of the school have separate offices, and as far as I know, the Magnet program office has been in the same place for over forty years. It's going to be a big undertaking getting them packed and moved. A part of me is relieved by the news though. I'm with my group, and the yellow jackets are unlikely to start anything while we're with Ms. G. She has a reputation.

A thought suddenly occurs to me. "You guys don't think

Principal Buttrum's got the power to totally remove the whole Magnet program, do you?"

"Definitely not," Bear answers. "The program's part of a larger Magnet framework, and that's district wide. Plus, our program's federal funding makes up a huge part of the school's budget. They can't afford to let our program go. They're barely making ends meet as it is. The whole district is in a severe budget crisis."

I nod, relieved. We round the corner into the Magnet program office, where we find Ms. Austin crying at her desk. She quickly tries to dry her tears. But then Finley, the group's resident sweetheart, rounds the corner of the desk and hugs her, and Ms. Austin can't stop herself from dissolving into a burst of sobbing.

Holding a stack of folded boxes, Ms. G comes out of her office. She gives us an exhausted half smile, her head hanging at a dejected angle. "Hi, kids. What's up?"

Arch is the first to answer. "Mr. Bentley released us from class and sent us here. You have the whole student council at your disposal for the next hour. We understand you're movin' on up to a new office."

Ms. G shakes her head. "Indeed. I'm going to miss this place. The new office is nice, though. God bless Mr. Isley for sending help. Principal Buttrum—"

She's interrupted by a very uncharacteristic outburst from Ms. Austin. "*Butthole!* From now on, he's *Principal Butthole!*"

We're all shocked for a second, and then we collapse into a fit of giggles. Of all people, Ms. Austin's the *last* one I'd expect something like that from. She's usually so prim and proper, everyone's favorite Sunday school teacher type. The changes around here are clearly more than she can handle.

Ms. G's laughing so hard that she has to lean on the desk. "It's going to be okay, Patty," she says to Ms. Austin as soon as she collects herself. "Principal Buttrum can't get away with all of this for long. I'm positive he'll get fired and Principal Walker will be back soon."

Taken off guard by her own outburst, Ms. Austin looks a little shocked. She straightens her perfectly pressed blouse. "Pardon me, students. That was out of line, and I apologize."

Darren grins at Ms. Austin. "Don't apologize. Buttrum's impossible, and he's toying with your livelihood. We've got your back. By the time student council's done, Principal Butthole will be out, and Principal Walker will be back in. Leave it to us."

Ms. Austin gives the tiniest smile, then sniffles loudly and dabs at her wet eyes with a soggy tissue.

"Well, ladies," Trey says, "you've got twenty-one helpers. Let's get you packed and moved."

Tanner pokes his head out from Ms. G's little private office and says, "I'm working on things in here, but I have a suggestion."

"Get out here, Tanner," Ms. G invites. "You're the most charming troublemaker at this school." She grins and affectionately cuffs him on the arm.

Tanner blushes a little. "Aw shucks. Thanks, Ms. G." He turns to all of us. "Here's the deal. My little scheme worked. In the chaos, it seems like Melanie was forgotten. We still don't know what's happening, but I'm thinking we may be able to drive that douche-knocker to madness with some shenanigans. It'll either make him leave or give us time to sleuth things out. Either way, I get to have fun."

Arch grins mischievously. "Whatcha thinking? I love a good Tanner plan."

"I'm wearing light blue," Tanner says, "and Principal Buttrum made it abundantly clear that the color *I'm* wearing is out, but no one said anything about other shades. There's lots of shades of blue."

Arch nods, a conspiratorial sneer spreading across his face. "Driving him insane, it is." He turns to Ms. G. "Do you think you could pass on to the teachers to quietly spread the word to their students that tomorrow is 'Wear Any Blue but Tanner Blue Day? The student council hasn't hosted a spirit day in a while, after all."

I side-eye Trey, who shrugs. This plan is childish, but it'll likely irritate Principal Buttrum far more than something this minor ever should.

Ms. G, always up for shenanigans, grins at Arch. "I sure can."

CHAPTER 9

Half of our group is lined up at the end of Actors' Alley, drinking our morning coffee and surveying the school from our expansive view of the grounds. As far as the eye can see, there are students in every kind of blue outfit imaginable. I'm still out of my house, and my friends have all been supplying clothes for me, so I'm stuck in a borrowed blue shirt of Trey's.

"So far, I've seen a blue flapper," Tanner says, "three blue prom dresses, and the burner group's all made dark-blue shirts with *Gotta Catch Me* on them. So I guess I coined a new catch phrase."

Arch grins. "That was the handywork of Dante, and I love it."

A tall boy in an elf costume, complete with elf ears and a royal-blue cape, wanders by.

"That one right there," Tanner says. "That wins the award for the weirdest of the day."

Just as he finishes his sentence, someone passes by in a full body plush Smurfette costume like you'd see at an amusement park. Our eyebrows are in our hairlines as we watch Smurfette waddle by.

"Whoops," Tanner says. "Spoke too soon." He shrugs. "I guess if you're gonna wear Tanner Blue, do it with a bang."

We all crack up.

I love it here. There's nowhere else quite like Hollywood High.

"How much trouble are we about to be in?" I ask Arch.

He sneers at me with an evil gleam in his eyes. "A *whole* lot, I hope." He looks to Dante, who nods and heads around the back side of Actors' Alley. "Dante's on it."

"Well then, there's no time like the present," Adam says. "Let's find His Masterfulness. I don't want to miss any of this show."

We walk in a line down the wide quad corridor. The students are enjoying this little display of rebellion, and they seem to be in a great mood.

Trey groans in frustration. "Do you know how pathetic it is that we've been reduced to rebelling using the color blue? This is so beneath what we're capable of."

Marcus, usually the happy-go-lucky jokester of the group, uncharacteristically echoes the groan. "It makes me sick. Buttrum's dragged us down to his level, and I hate him for it."

Presley snuggles in closer to Marcus. "Don't worry, babe. Torturing the middle-aged nightmare might be fun."

"Remember what my mom told us," I remind. "We stay one step ahead and keep it creative. I kind of like the Blue Rebellion. At least the students are smiling again." Thinking about my mom right now makes my heart hurt, but I shake it off.

"Incoming," Tanner hisses.

Sure enough, here comes Principal Buttrum, his undersized shirt straining around his oversized belly as he aggressively strides toward us. He has Ms. G, Mr. Bentley, and Mr. Isley at his heels, and they're all giving us amused looks.

"Let me handle this," Arch whispers to us.

Students all around the quads come our way, quietly gathering to watch round two. The rest of our group flows over, joining our student council clump at the front of the growing crowd. Marcus situates himself in front of me to block the principal's view. I still can't believe how well this hide-and-distract tactic is working. It's like he's forgotten about me entirely.

Principal Buttrum stops in front of us, huffing and panting from his short-legged trot across the vast campus. He's so winded that it takes him a minute before he can catch his breath enough to croak out, "What's the meaning of this?"

Arch puts on his best innocent expression. "The meaning of what, sir?"

Buttrum turns in a circle and waves his arms around spastically. He looks like a short, fat pelican flapping its wings. I close my eyes tight, trying not to laugh. Only when I've gained control of my expression do I open my eyes again.

Presley's looking right at me, grinning. She quietly squawks out, "Bekack!" like a bird.

Losing it, I lean my head on Trey's shoulder and cover my rising laugh with a cough. I send the image of Buttrum as a fat pelican through our laced hands, and Trey's shoulders start shaking with laughter. That does it. Trey and I double over, quietly busting up. Bear steps in front of us, next to Marcus, while we get through our giggling fit. It's a good thing Bear's a mountain of a guy, or we'd have nowhere to hide.

After I compose myself, I shoot an amused sort of death glare at Presley. She grins at us, her striking, heart-shaped face and green eyes aglow with hilarity. Typical Presley—she couldn't care less about consequences most of the time. She's my best friend for a reason.

Arch clears his throat as if trying not to laugh. "All I see are students behaving like model citizens. No one's even making a peep! Looks to me like the students have dutifully learned how to—" He pauses, putting a finger to his lip and looking up for a moment like he's dramatically contemplating. "What was it you requested? Oh, yes, now I remember! *Master* your discipline! *Master* good behavior! Wasn't this what you wanted?"

"I said no blue!" Buttrum hollers.

So the growing, hushed crowd can hear, Arch responds loudly. "No. No. That's *not* what you said. You said, 'No red. And no Tanner Blue.' Tanner Blue is a light blue. I've only seen one rouge Smurfette running around here in Tanner Blue. The rest of us are in shades of blue that are perfectly acceptable within the parameters that you *masterfully* set for us."

The crowd of students, along with Ms. G., Mr. Isley, and Mr. Bentley, all snickers. Buttrum looks like he's going to have a stroke.

"Sir, do you need to sit down?" Finley asks sweetly. "You don't look so good."

Unexpectedly, Principal Buttrum turns on Finley, his fists balled up with rage, and starts aggressively backing her against the wall of one of the quad-one bungalows. He screeches, "*No back talk!*" He's lost it.

Tanner, Arch, Adam, and Trey all rush in front of Finley, who cowers behind them. Of all the girls in our group to bully, Buttrum picked the nicest one. We're fiercely protective of her, and this guy just made a grave error. Tanner steps up so close to Principal Buttrum that he's touching Buttrum's girthy middle with the edge of his dark-blue sequined jacket. He towers over the principal as he glares down at him, radiating barely controlled malice.

In a low, menacing voice, Tanner growls, "You just crossed a line. If you *ever* come near my girl again, you'll land in the hospital. This has all been fun and games while you throw your weight around and we pretend to give a shit, but let's be clear . . . You're playing with fire. We outnumber you, we're smarter than you, and we *will* win. Step off, *Buttrum!*"

The principal takes a few hesitant steps back, surprised by Tanner's ferocity, and Mr. Isley steps up to stand next to him. Buttrum looks up, seems to see Mr. Isley there, and turns back to us with puffed-up confidence. Mr. Isley's a force to be reckoned with, and he too towers over the principal.

Mr. Isley turns a slow, skeptical look down at Buttrum. His expression screams that he's baffled at the realization that this man thinks he's stepping up to serve as his personal bodyguard. The look on Mr. Isley's face as he stares down at the puffed-up frog would be hilarious if we weren't all so angry.

His bravery returned, Buttrum looks at Tanner and loudly says, "*You*? You have a *girlfriend*? All the makeup and sparkles?" He waves his hands dismissively in Tanner's direction. "I'm not scared of a dandy like you."

Inwardly, I grin. Tanner's one of the scrappiest guys at the school. We've all seen it. He fights like a demon straight out of hell.

Tanner narrows his perfectly eyeshadowed eyes. His heavy black eyeliner and mascara suddenly look menacing. "Good. I love being underestimated. Your day's coming, Buttrum. Mark my words."

Principal Buttrum squints his beady little eyes and turns in a circle. "You *all* broke the rules," he announces to the crowd. "What's your punishment, you ask? Until further notice, *no more bathrooms*! I'm locking every student bathroom in the school." He crosses his arms over his dumpy chest and grins like he just proclaimed a genius plan.

Motion flashes to my right. It's Marcus. He swings his backpack around and unzips the little pocket on the front. He pulls out his cell phone and steps forward to the front of our group. Cell phones are new, and Marcus is one of the few kids from a family that can afford one for him. The rest of us are stuck with pagers and pay phones. He flips open the phone, dials a number, and stares at Principal Buttrum as he waits.

Someone picks up on the other end of the line.

"Hey, Dad," Marcus says. "Principal Buttrum just physically attacked Finley, and now he's locking all the student bathrooms as punishment because students are wearing blue."

He pauses, listening. "Yes. I said blue."

He pauses again while his dad, Bruce, asks him something.

"Because he's bat-crap crazy," Marcus answers.

Marcus listens again and then answers, "Yes, Finley's okay. You know our group wouldn't let him hurt her. We're all here, and Tanner's peeved."

Now Marcus turns to us, grinning while he listens to his dad. "Yeah, Principal Buttrum just told Tanner that he's not scared of a dandy like him. His words."

A moment later, Marcus laughs. "You're telling me! If he comes near Finley again, Tanner's likely to kill him dead in the middle of the quad and solve this problem for all of us."

Another few seconds pass.

"Please call your friend Gregory," Marcus says as he stares daggers through Buttrum. "You know, the president of the school board of regents for the independent Los Angeles school district."

Buttrum runs red.

"Ahh, yes," Marcus continues. "I've always just called him Greg when he comes over for dinner, but now that you said it, I remember that his last name's Bains." Now he hits Buttrum with an uncharacteristically arrogant expression and says, "Thanks, Dad."

When Marcus snaps his phone closed, Buttrum's standing statue still with his mouth hanging open. He looks like a man who just learned that toying with the students is all fun and games until you find out how well-connected our parents are. He sputters, unsure what to say.

Marcus answers for him. "You think we're nothing but a bunch of stupid kids. You're wrong. My father will *bury* you. Keep pushing, Buttrum. We love a challenge. And we *hate* when things get dull." He smirks. "Gotta catch us."

Before the principal can respond, Adam steps forward. "Principal Buttrum, is your office the same one that Principal Walker had?"

"Yes," Buttrum answers, befuddled. "Why?"

Adam starts walking toward the two-story building. "I have to take a leak," he yells back over his shoulder. "Bathrooms are off-limits, apparently. I'll be using your trash can."

Trey grabs my arm, and we melt into the crowd before Buttrum can spot me.

The principal waddles away, and the students disperse.

Dante rushes up to our group.

"Well?" Arch asks him.

Dante's all a tizzy as he waves a paper about frantically. His eyes are huge, but he's so winded, he can't speak.

"Smokers' Corner," Arch orders. "Now."

- —

Adam, Trey, Darren, and I light up another round of smokes. Arch starts reading the paper again as I lie back in the grass. This is our third read of the cryptic memo, and by now, I've heard enough of it.

"By the authority of the LAUSD school board, funds are granted for the hire of the Cobra Militia, in the amount of thirty-five thousand dollars. Funding must be used during the 1992–93 calendar school year, ending June 30, 1993."

"All right, who are the Cobra Militia?" Bear has asked this after each illustrious reading of said memo.

I huff because, clearly, none of us know.

Marcus snaps open his cell phone and dials a number. "Hey, Dad."

Now that something new is happening, I sit up.

"Any clue who the Cobra Militia are?" Marcus asks into the phone.

Victoria chooses this moment to sashay around the hedges and join our group. Her eyes snap wide when she hears Marcus's question. "Please, no," she breathes out.

Marcus rushes to tell his dad that he'll call him back later. Victoria sinks to her knees and takes the paper from Arch. Her expression shows more and more dread as she reads.

"What is it, Vic?" Demitri asks.

We all look at him quizzically because everyone else calls her Tori when they're being nice to her.

"Cobra Militia is a mercenary group," Victoria says, fluttering her eyelashes dramatically. "Joel Stamp's dad, Daniel Stamp, runs it."

A cold sweat breaks out as I fold myself at the waist. This was an answer I never expected. That seems to be a theme lately.

"Tell me everything you know," Trey says as he takes a pen and notepad from his backpack.

Victoria looks Trey in the eyes and slowly shakes her head. "This is bad, Trey. Daniel Stamp was a sharpshooter in the military. He was a big-ass deal in Desert Storm. They wound up tossing him out with a dishonorable discharge, but he's proud of it. Long story short, he got word of a key enemy's location and defied orders for him and his men to wait. Stamp managed to get to where the mark was holed up in this huge building in Kuwait. He put a gun to the back of the guy's head and shot him at point-blank range. Then he ordered his platoon to take out every moving soul in the building. They didn't know at the time that the place used to be a hotel, and it was where the enemy's families were living. It was supposed to be a safe house for innocents. A bunch of them died, women and children mostly. It turned into a huge potential war-crimes debacle that was kept out of the news because the military had to save face."

"How do you know this?" Trey asks.

Victoria shrugs. "Both Joel and his dad would brag about it. Back when I was in the Drone group, Joel begged his dad to tell the story at a party. He didn't seem to have any problem with sharing the details."

Trey nods. "Continue." He's jotting down stuff on his notepad.

"Well, with a dishonorable discharge, the usual civilian career options for ex-military slipped away. Stamp couldn't find work, and so he opted to start his own goon-for-hire squad. He has a lot of his old military buddies on the company roster. They seem all kinds of professional to the casual observer, but they're into some seriously shady stuff. Heavy bank accounts hire his guys, and it's not always above board. Yeah, they run special security operations for a few of the shadier firms in the States, but they make most of their money on bodyguard work overseas."

"What kind of bodyguard work?" Trey asks, his ears seeming to perk up.

"I'm out of the loop now," Victoria explains, "but when Melanie and Joel were going through that rapist Olympics at the start of the school year, the Cobra Militia were bodyguarding for a group of wealthy Columbian drug runners."

We all sit back, stunned.

"Work like that was how the Stamps had all that money Joel

was always bragging about. At least until he was locked in the slammer."

"And our *school district* has hired these nutjobs for security?" Marcus says in disbelief.

"By the authority of the LAUSD school board," Bear starts reading again, "funds are granted for the hire of the Cobra Militia—"

"Yeah, Bear, we get it," I cut in.

Silence descends.

Internally, I'm panicking. "These same guys were asking for me at the dance. Are you telling us that I'm the target of someone hired by a dirty militia group with no ethics? A group owned by someone who wants my ass dead because he blames me for his son going to prison?"

Eyes widen all around the circle.

"Buttrum was asking for you too, Mel," Darren offers. "Could be connected."

"Buttrum could be a coincidence," Demitri suggests.

Marcus gestures to the memo in Bear's hand. "It's addressed to Principal Buttrum, who looks like he filed the request. And a school board member, Charlie Sisterno, authorized it."

"Why would Buttrum request funds from a random militia organization?" Darren asks.

Presley gives Demitri a pointed look. "Not to mention that all this craziness started at the same time. And we know Buttrum's *also* retired military. It can't be a coincidence."

Trey attempts to rationalize. "Buttrum's retired navy. From the sounds of it, Daniel Stamp was in the army."

"Sorry to blow your theory out of the water," Victoria says, "but Stamp has guys from all military branches in his company." When she hits me with a concerned gaze, I exhale hard.

Demitri stares at me in worry. I choose to look down again. D and I have yet to discuss what happened at his house, and on top of my life apparently being in danger, I'm uncomfortable about the whole thing.

Trey throws his pen and notepad down and jumps up. He walks off a few yards and pauses at the fence, holding on to the chain-link as he stares out at nothing for a long moment.

"We're going to figure something out, Trey," Arch assures. "We can do this."

Trey whips around and stalks our way. He gestures emphatically in my direction. "Again! It's fucking happening *again*. The Stamp family is after Melanie! Only this time is different." His face runs pale. "I'm good, Arch, but I'm not armed militia good. We're teenagers." He gestures around the group. "TEENAGERS!"

We hear footsteps coming around the hedges and look up to find Mr. Isley and Ms. G surveying our group. Their gaze stops on Trey.

Before they can say anything, Darren sarcastically announces, "Put out your smoky treats, kids. Mom and Dad are here."

Ms. G snorts. "I don't care about the cigarettes. If Trey is this upset, something much bigger than your impending lung cancer is afoot."

I take another drag off my cigarette and gesture to Trey. "We're teenagers, apparently."

"True." Ms. G. chuckles.

"We have a choice to make," I say with a shrug. "Either I give myself up to Daniel Stamp's plant, Principal Dickhead, or a militia is sure to follow."

Ms. G's eyes widen. As Trey fills our teachers in on the situation, they take a seat. Eventually, Ms. G gestures for me to bum her a cigarette. I slide one out of my pack and hand it over. Quickly, she lights it.

"Welcome to the Cancer Impending crew," Darren snarks. "So glad you could join us."

Ms. G takes a long drag and blows a huge plume of smoke. "You want to run that by me again?" she asks Trey.

"My future wife is apparently being hunted by Daniel Stamp, his military goons, and a short fat fuck."

Apparently, propriety has launched straight out the window, but Ms. G and Mr. Isley accept Trey's fowl mouth without even flinching.

"Aw!" Tanner crows. "You said 'future wife.'"

Trey looks at him like he's nuts. "Is that a surprise? I put a promise ring on her finger at homecoming." He looks down at me, and I give him girlie eyes before taking another drag of my smoke.

"Well, Trey," I say, "I guess we should probably get hitched before I'm gang-raped and murdered by a middle-aged military squadron."

Trey closes his eyes tight. "I can't take this anymore. I have zero clue what to do this time."

I shrug and put out my cigarette. "Fuck it. Let's have as much fun as we can while we're dodging the inevitable." I stand and gesture for my friends to follow me.

"Wait!" Mr. Isley calls after us. "Get back here."

We pause at the fence, and I look his way. "I'm headed home, Mr. Isley. If my parents still refuse to see the trouble I'm in, I'll let you know if I need a couch to crash on again. Thank you for helping me."

We all slip out through the hole in the fence that Arch made with bolt cutters last year. He doesn't handle being caged well—so much so that he's created exit holes and rigged the gates all over the school.

"Wait for us," Ms. G says. "We're going with you. We'll meet you at Melanie's house."

"We can't just leave! I've got classes to teach." Mr. Isley's responsible logic falls on deaf ears as Ms. G hightails it across the field, likely heading to the teachers' parking lot.

CHAPTER *10*

I refuse to cross onto my parents' property, preferring instead to wait on the sidewalk as Trey, Adam, Mr. Isley, and Ms. G walk up the brick pathway to the door. Demitri's standing by Victoria just up the sidewalk from me. He's said very little since we all arrived. He keeps side-eyeing me with a panicked expression, but I ignore him. I'm not about to get into it with Victoria in front of my parents' house.

Arch puts his arm around me, and I lean my head on his shoulder. Suddenly, my lungs are squeezing tight, and there's a rattle as I try to inhale. My heart skips when I realize I'm slipping into an asthma attack. I close my eyes, attempting to calm myself enough to loosen my lungs.

"Here, Meley," Demitri's soothing voice sparks me out of my solo efforts at survival. He hands me an inhaler. "You left it in my Jeep a while back. I kept it in the glove box and forgot to return it to you."

Gratefully, I take it and pull a puff. Then I cap it and close my eyes. I hold on to the puff for as long as I can before exhaling.

I cough like I always do when I use that damn thing. I hate it. It makes me jittery.

"You gotta cough to get off," Arch jokes.

Clearly sensing my anxiety, Tanner sparks a joint and hands it to me.

"Great plan, Tanner!" Demitri reprimands. "She just had an asthma attack."

Tanner gives Demitri a scathing look. "She's been swimming in shit soup for days. Let her unwind a little."

I take a hit off the joint just as Rich answers the door. He surveys me before loudly calling out, "I see you're making excellent choices!"

The joint held up between my index and middle fingers, I yell back, "Currently being hunted by Daniel Stamp's militia and I'm homeless! Thought I'd unwind with my vagrant friends I'm not allowed to homie around with anymore." I gesture at my outfit. "Today, I'm rocking Trey wear! His sweatpants fit like a dream. Yesterday, it was Finley's clothes."

Rich snorts, but he can't help but grin at my sass. I'm a smartass just like him, after all.

I waggle the joint around. "Want a hit?"

With an eye roll, Rich heads down the walkway. "Yup. Sure do." He takes the joint from me and pulls a hit before handing it to Tanner, who beams.

Rich surveys me. I'm not wearing any makeup, my clothes are too big, and I'm clearly out of sorts.

"You wanna run that whole militia news by me again?"

I nod pragmatically. "Sure do. I'm ass deep in alligators and need my dad."

Rich hugs me tight. "I'm sorry," he whispers in my ear.

I hang on tighter than usual, relief making me shake.

Rich lets go and surveys everyone. "Looks like the gang's all here."

Marcus's dad, Bruce, chooses that moment to pull up in his black Porsche, which he parks at the curb. Another car is quick on his tail, parking behind him. We all suck in a breath of surprise as our former principal, Mr. Walker, gets out of the mystery car.

"You kids ready to handle some stuff?" he asks with a smirk.

We all grin and rush his way as Bruce shakes hands with Rich. Now Mr. Cantrell's car rolls up, and he parks and hops out.

"While it's good to see you again, Kyle," Rich says, "why are you here?"

Mr. Cantrell gestures to me. "I was already worried, seeing as how my self-proclaimed goddaughter is homeless. Now I've heard she's being hunted by a militia, and I couldn't sit at home waiting for Demitri to stroll in with more news." He steps up toe-to-toe with Rich. "Let me be abundantly clear. If you throw Melanie out permanently, I'll sell my two-bedroom home, buy a three bedroom, and move her in."

Rich looks surprised. Meanwhile, Demitri winces slightly, and Victoria glares daggers my direction.

"Why would you do that?"

"Well, Richard, she's like a daughter to me, and I take care of my kids."

Rich appears properly chastised as he ponders Mr. Cantrell's words. After a long moment, he nods. "Understood and respected. Thank you for caring like you do." He turns to me. "Where have you been staying? I figured you were at one of the girls' houses."

I shake my head and gesture to Mr. Isley. "He took me in."

Rich's mouth drops open as he surveys Mr. Isley.

"My students are my kids," Mr. Isley says. "They will always have a home with me."

Rich swallows hard. "I was attempting to make a point, but it appears I'm the one who learned a lesson." He gestures toward the open front door. "Come inside and let's hash this out."

— —

Once the memo has made the rounds, Rich asks of no one in particular, "You wanna explain to me how this bullshit is even possible?"

Mr. Walker clears his throat. "The guy who approved the funds, Charlie Sisterno, has always been a shady jackass. We all hate him. I wouldn't be the least bit surprised if he's part of Daniel Stamp's small-dick brigade."

None of us has ever heard our beloved former principal use such colorful language, so we all just sit there, grinning.

"I knew I always liked you," Arch says.

Mr. Walker wobbles his head and breaks into a disgusted expression. "I love the kids at Hollywood High. Much like Mr. Isley and Mr. Cantrell demonstrated earlier, I have a similar soft spot for the students I was charged with the care of. While I'm always a professional at work, this news has me rattled, and so I'd prefer to be me if that's okay."

"Works for us." Rich grins at him.

My mom squeezes my hand. "Is Melanie safe at school?"

Mr. Walker shrugs. "At this point, I have no idea. I can tell you that the teachers adore her. She's an excellent student and has lots of friends." He gestures around the room. "This is the scariest pack of kids I've ever had come through Hollywood High. We've had gangbangers, drug dealers, but none of them hold a candle to these kids in a full-tilt rage. I'd say they've got a good shot against anything they're challenged with, but an armed militia wasn't on my radar."

Rich studies me. "I've always said our family doesn't lie down on the battlefield, but I meant it symbolically. This may actually *become* a battlefield."

"I'm aware," I say with a shrug. "And now that I'm allowed to be at home, I feel better. There's still something I can't figure out, though. The brigade was looking for me at the dance, and Buttrum was asking for me on day one. But ever since, *nothing*. The yellow jackets haven't come for me again. I have no idea why. But it does seem like the past few days, the stuff happening at school hasn't felt as dangerous. It's all generally either stupid or hilarious. So, I guess what I'm saying is, I want to stick it out."

Rich rubs his face hard. "You need to be at school. Failing out because a jackass principal likes to annoy you isn't grounds I can justify. With that said, I'm worried about this memo."

"We have no idea why they're being hired," Bruce interjects. "All we know at this point is that funds are allocated, and those funds run out by the end of the school year. For all we know, they've just been hired to install a security system."

Rich snorts. "A thirty-five-thousand-dollar security system?"

"You'd be surprised. A school that size would warrant an expensive system."

"Trey, what's your take on this?"

All eyes turn to Trey, who shrugs. "I'm in the same boat as Melanie. I can see why you and Carol didn't understand the pieces and thought it must be that Melanie was a problem. It all fires up, seems serious, and then dissipates. It's hard for me to decide if we're truly dealing with a grave problem or attempting to make connections where there are none."

Rich turns his attention to the other adults in the room. "Is Melanie a problem at school?"

Eyebrows rise, but Ms. G cracks up.

"That girl—" She points at me. "That girl is an angel. A foul-mouthed, fistfighting little angel. Yes, she's had her issues at the school, but she wasn't the one who started any of it, and I can't fault the girl for finishing it each time. She's tiny. She's been turned into a social target by every catty female. She's desired by half the school. And she has an energy that attracts trouble."

Victoria appears ashamed, and I think I can guess why. Back during the first semester, she made my life hell for quite a while. I ignore her and look at my parents, who are staring at each other.

"She's never been a problem that warrants your suspicion," Mr. Isley offers. "End of story."

Rich sighs and looks down at his hands. "I apologize for my rash behavior. You didn't deserve it, Melanie, and you have my word that I'll listen in the future instead of jumping to conclusions." He gives me a side hug. "In the meantime, stay the course. Stick together. Keep your eyes and ears open." He gives us all pointed looks. "I want to know the moment anything else happens, though. Carol and I are on board now. We'll take it seriously."

CHAPTER 11

"Thank goodness it's Friday. Today's been drama free. Maybe Principal Buttrum learned his lesson when Greg Bains showed up." Bear grins at Marcus. "Your dad made quick work."

Marcus is sitting next to Presley, across the table from me. We're in our lunch spot in Actors' Alley, but our group's become so big that we've had to haul a second massive picnic table over so we can all sit together.

"Whoo boy!" Marcus says enthusiastically. "You should've seen Dad when I got home that day. He was *on fire*! Greg came to our house, and they holed up in Dad's home office. I could hear Dad bellowing all the way from the living room."

Marcus's dad, Bruce, heads the top legal firm in Los Angeles County. He knows everyone, takes no guff, and has a great sense of humor. He's responsible for getting Joel locked up on attempted murder charges, and he's in the process of locking away all the Drones who faked Adam's death and tortured him. Whenever there's a legal matter—and we've had a shocking number of them—we can always count on Bruce.

"Man," Darren says, "when you pulled out that cell phone, I almost died. The look on Buttrum's face was priceless."

A loud, obnoxious beeping sound breaks into our peaceful lunch conversation, and we all look to see what the fuss is about. Principal Buttrum is aggressively stomping next to a giant truck that backs around the corner from the alley, coming toward us. The principal's wearing a hard hat, and he's clearly on a mission.

When the truck stops, Buttrum demonstrates one of his trademark freakouts. "Why are you stopping?" he screams at the driver. "Students are like dogs. They'll move. Gun it!"

The driver looks skeptically out the window in the direction of the crowded area, but he likely can't see the students behind his truck.

"Are you *deaf*?" Buttrum bellows. "Move it! I'll tell you when to stop."

"What in fresh hell," Presley says.

"Let the games begin," Hiram murmurs.

Adam's eyes go wide. "He wouldn't."

My intuition flares to life, and I yell to everyone in Actors' Alley, "Move! *Now!*"

We all jump up as the truck driver backs up toward our table. Students leap and scurry out of the way. The truck runs over two backpacks where a cluster of kids had been sitting in the walkway eating lunch only a moment before. Our group dodges out of the way. The truck doesn't stop in time, plowing into one of our picnic tables.

Buttrum grins and sarcastically chortles, "Stop."

We stare at him with our mouths hanging open.

He jumps up and down like an excited little troll as he yanks open the driver's door. "*Out!* Get them set up! I want the students to see."

The driver, a huge man with a grizzly beard and a no-nonsense expression, slams his door closed. "You're insane," he says flatly. "Get away from my truck."

Buttrum complies.

The driver pulls forward, away from the destroyed lunch table, before putting the truck in park. He jumps out, opens the back sliding door, and hefts himself into the cargo section of the large truck. We all look at each other with puzzlement written on our faces. The driver uses a hand crank lift and starts moving what looks like Porta-Potties to the tailgate. He gets them positioned and lowers the lift. Two light-blue industrial plastic boxes are unloaded.

Someone from the back of the growing crowd of students yells out, "I thought you said no Tanner Blue!"

Everyone snickers.

The driver turns to Buttrum and asks, "Where do you want these?"

The principal points to two spots. "Two here, and the other four in quads one and two."

Without hesitation, the driver places the cumbersome boxes where he's instructed, though he does it while shooting the occasional speculative glance at Buttrum. When he's finished, he hops back in his truck and follows a gleeful Buttrum around the corner to quad one.

The second the principal is out of sight, we all look at each other in confusion. Arch leads the way, opening the door of one of the boxes. We lean in and look. The box has a built-in bench and a few air vents, but that's it.

"They aren't Porta-Potties," Arch announces to the students crowded around us. He gives us a worried look and adds, "They look like solitary-confinement boxes."

Darren shakes his head. "There's no way. Not even Buttrum's that sadistic."

Arch sets a fast clip, practically running around the corner of the bungalow at the end of Actors' Alley, and the crowd swiftly follows. We get to quad one in time to see the last box unloaded.

Ms. G, Mr. Bentley, and Mr. Isley are standing near the truck, watching the process suspiciously.

Mr. Isley asks the driver, "What are these?"

"They're intended for people to change in at the county pools," the driver explains. "They're called privacy boxes, but I've never delivered them to a school before." Now he looks at the principal with suspicion on his face. "Why did you order these?"

Buttrum lets out a gleeful yip. "In accordance with my discipline plan, these are Hollywood High's new punishment boxes. Consider them time-out chairs, if you like."

An exasperated bellow escapes Mr. Isley's lips. "We can hardly afford toilet paper and soap around here, *but you can buy these things*?"

Buttrum throws an arm in the air dramatically. "Private donation funding," he sings. He looks to the driver. "Did the lockholes get drilled on the outside like I requested?"

The driver appears shocked, as if he's trying to wrap his mind around what the principal plans to do with the boxes. "Yes," he says with some hesitation. "Why do you need lockholes? The boxes already lock from the inside to allow the occupant privacy."

"We're going to padlock them from the outside." Buttrum shoots a malicious glare toward the student council, all huddled up together with a front-row view. "Some of these students need a time-out."

Students all over the quad stare at the principal in shock.

Bear whispers to our group, "He's lost it."

"This is so illegal," Tanner hisses, "I can't even wrap my mind around it."

"Where the *hell* did they find this guy?" Demitri mutters. "Alcatraz?"

The gathering teachers look as shocked as we do.

Before anyone can wrap their minds around all of this, Buttrum points at Adam and says, "You. Boy. Front and center."

Adam glances at us with sudden trepidation in his eyes as he slowly crosses quad one to Principal Buttrum. He turns sheet-white, and his eyes look sunken in. Our guys discreetly shift, lining up in front of the girls in our group. Adam is blasting panic through the connection we share, and I nearly double over.

I look across the quad at the teachers. Mr. Isley's tense as he waits to see what's going to happen. Ms. G's jaw is locked tight, and if looks could kill, Buttrum would be obliterated.

The principal announces to the growing crowd of horrified students, "Adam Stone urinated in my trash can on Wednesday. This is an infraction that violates the new Time-Out clause of my Master Behavior Contract that will be distributed today in sixth period. Each of you will receive a copy of my master plan, but I'd like to have a demonstration now so that you all understand what happens when you don't *master* your discipline."

He looks around the circle, clearly enjoying the nervous reaction from the students who are gaping at him slack-jawed.

Principal Buttrum snaps his fingers at the yellow-jacket security officers standing by the commons. "All six of you, come here."

The yellow jackets look at each other, unsure what to do. Eventually, they hesitantly walk to Buttrum. They likely don't want to lose their jobs, and Buttrum's made quite a show of threatening to fire people on the daily. The whole staff are either terrified or furious.

"Grab him," Principal Buttrum says to the yellow jackets.

Four of the six security officers walk to Adam and half-heartedly take him by his arms. They turn to look at Buttrum with confusion marring their expressions.

"Sir, he's not resisting," one of the yellow jackets says. "For the safety of the students, we're prohibited from using physical force unless absolutely necessary. But he poses no immediate physical threat."

Principal Buttrum rolls his eyes. "Do I have to do *everything* myself?" He walks to Adam with purpose, shooing the yellow jackets out of the way. He grabs Adam by the arm and yanks as hard as his pathetic body can manage.

Adam doesn't move, looking down at Buttrum with a blank expression, his eyes distant and filled with shock. I recognize this expression, as I've seen it before. Adam's on the edge of another panic attack.

Buttrum pulls again, but short of assistance, he's not going to be able to move the tall, muscular boy by himself. Adam stares across the quad, giving the teachers a pleading look. Mr. Bentley and Mr. Isley start to move just when all hell breaks loose.

"Put him in the box!" Buttrum screams at the yellow jackets.

Adam shrieks, "I'm *not* going in *there*!"

The yellow jackets latch onto him and the fight's on.

Valerie gasps and her knees buckle. She collapses to the ground, sobbing. She screams something I can't make out, but I know what she's feeling. Last month, Adam was held hostage in a tiny space by the Drones for five days. We thought he was dead, and Valerie was destroyed by the news of losing him. The thought of him being plunged into that kind of torture again looks like it's sent her back into that dark place with him.

Adam screams like a wounded animal as he fights back, bucking and kicking. All six yellow jackets try to restrain him. Adam writhes and pleads, but it doesn't stop them.

Bear and Darren rush the blue box. They start rocking it back and forth. Then, before anyone can do anything to stop them, they pick it up and hurl it into the air. It crashes to the ground and cracks down the side.

I close my eyes and wall off my connection to Adam. I need to be able to think, and his panic is invading all my abilities. My dark-water side rises. I'm raging mad. "Go help Valerie!" I call out to Finley. Then, I turn on a wave of rage and run to Adam.

I'm not alone. Most of the fighters in our group get to the yellow jackets a half second before me. Deb, Trey, Arch, Bear, Marcus, Tanner, and Demitri grab the yellow jackets and try to pull them off Adam. Any pulling on his arms is excruciating. Adam still has fresh scar tissue and injuries in his arms and shoulders from being tied by his wrists and strung up tight over a ceiling joist for five days. He screams himself hoarse, and it sends shivers up my spine. My mind sputters for a second. A wave of white-hot clarity washes over me, resolving a dilemma I've been struggling with since Buttrum was hired.

I spin around, fueled by fury like I've never felt before. I run like I'm shot out of a cannon across the quad, rocketing toward Principal Buttrum. I hear Trey scream my name, but it's too late. I take a running leap toward Buttrum, but Mr. Isley grabs me midair, spins me around, and puts me down. Then, he rounds on the principal himself.

Just as Mr. Isley balls up his fist to knock Buttrum out, a commanding voice bellows "ENOUGH," from behind the crowd of students.

Everyone freezes mid-movement. Our guys slowly back off, letting go of the yellow jackets, who seem to have come back to their senses. Adam collapses to the ground. He's so pale that he looks like a ghost. He shrieks in pain as tears stream down his face. His back convulses. He writhes, making a horrific keening sound. He's hurt so bad that he's crying in public. That doesn't happen . . . ever.

I look at the rest of our group standing to the side of quad one, and they're kneeling around Valerie, who's in a heap. With Valerie's head in her lap, Ms. Ferry makes eye contact with me, silently communicating that she's got Valerie covered.

The voice who cried "ENOUGH" turns out to belong to Mr. Jenson, the school's maintenance man. He and Adam are old friends who work on motorcycles together on the weekends. He strides through the gathered crowd into the middle of the melee and hollers the word again. He glares at the yellow jackets. "What's *wrong* with all of you?"

They don't answer, apart from shaking their heads. As they stare down at Adam, they look horrified and confused, like they just woke up from a nightmare.

"Didn't you monsters see what you were doing to the boy?" Mr. Jenson barks. "Are you that brainwashed?" He kneels next to Adam, speaking softly to him. "It's over, Adam. I won't let them touch you again."

Adam calms down and lies still at the sound of his trusted friend's voice.

Mr. Jenson gestures the teachers to come help him. Mr. Isley and Mr. Bentley gently get Adam into a more comfortable position and start checking him over. My blood boils. Adam's not okay. Every student in the quad is standing in silent shock, watching and waiting. The tension's so thick I can hardly breathe.

Arch turns slowly to watch the retreating yellow-jacket security officers, his face set in a menacing mask. "Boys," he growls into the looming silence.

Trey, Tanner, Marcus, Darren, and Bear line up next to Arch. They're all panting, and the energy vibrating from them rolls through the quad in animalistic waves that make the more intuitive students shudder all over the expansive space.

A violent sneer contorts my face. "Do it," I hiss.

All six boys rush together, each of them blasting one yellow jacket in the face as hard as they can. The security guards drop, out cold. Our group turns as one and stalks slowly toward Principal Buttrum.

Panic twists Buttrum's face. Feebly trying to escape us, he rushes back against the half wall above the dance building walkway.

Mr. Isley runs around the edge of our group, getting between us and Principal Buttrum.

"Move, Isley," I growl. "He's ours."

The shocked expression on Mr. Isley's face communicates that he hardly recognizes us. In all fairness, we must look like a bunch of demonic beings stalking prey. Mr. Isley's never seen us in a real fight.

"We're not doing this," he says in a tone laced with desperation. "The teachers will handle it the right way. I promise I'll handle it *personally*."

Trey prowls up next to me, his usually gorgeous features morphed evil from all the rage coursing through him. "There hasn't been a 'right way' since Buttrum was hired. To hell with your way! It's time to do this *our* way."

The crowd of students screams "Yeah!" in unison and starts crushing forward.

Mr. Isley puts his hands up, trying to de-escalate the situation. "Okay," he says calmly. "Let's talk about this. What's your way?"

"Move and find out," Arch snarls.

We're all seeing red, our breathing harsh, any sense of humanity washed away. In the back of my mind, it occurs to me that we aren't thinking rationally, and if Mr. Isley moves, Principal Buttrum might wind up dead. When he chose to make an example of Adam, who everyone in school thought we lost so recently, he crossed a line, and the student body's ready to rip him limb from limb.

Suddenly, Victoria saunters into the middle and faces Mr. Isley. Her demeanor's so out of sync with ours that the sight briefly confuses the mob. Everyone stares at Victoria like she's some kind of exotic, unrecognizable creature.

"Move," she says to Mr. Isley.

The teacher looks down at her. "I can't. They aren't thinking straight, and they'll regret what they're about to do."

"I've got this. I want to talk to the sniveling jackass." Victoria turns to our group. "Back up and trust me." She hollers at the students, "Everyone back up and take a breath! I've got this!" Then, she looks at me. "We talk first, and if you don't like the outcome, you get your way."

Everyone in the student council exchanges a suspicious, side-eyed glance, and after a moment, makes a collective decision to trust her.

"Back up!" Arch echoes. "We're going to let Victoria talk."

We take a few steps back, giving everyone in the quad breathing room. The student body collectively exhales.

Victoria's radiating catty rage as she turns on her heel and puts her hands on her hips. Mr. Isley looks oddly amused. He exhales, clearly relieved by how Victoria has managed to shift the energy among the student body.

"Only talk," he tells her. "We're done with violence."

Victoria hits him with a condescending expression. "A conversation with me *is* violence. Now move."

Mr. Isley steps to the side, revealing a petrified Buttrum. The principal's hands are shaking. He looks like a lump of dough wrapped in a sheen of sweat. Apparently, he's not as dumb as we thought. Our rage seems to have burned through enough of his arrogance for him to recognize how he took things too far.

Victoria glares at him. "Hello, Francis," she says in a clipped tone, loud enough for the whole crowd to hear.

Clearly shocked, Principal Buttrum tips his head to the side, pondering how Victoria knows his first name.

From the left side of the crowd, Dante Grunier yells out, "Wait! We're being bullied by a jackass named *Francis Buttrum*?"

The crowd snickers. Buttrum blushes bright pink.

Victoria raises one perfectly manicured eyebrow and turns, surveying the crowd. "Indeed." Now she looks back at the principal and loudly says in a singsong voice, "I know your secrets, Fran*ciiisss*." Victoria pivots with a flourish, her short black skirt and amethyst purple cardigan hugging her curves. She saunters around the open circle, her stiletto heels clacking. "You see, it took me a hot second to figure out how I knew him. It finally dawned on me that Francis dated my aunt years ago. I was little then, and he was *much* littler then." She glances at Buttrum and sarcastically quips, "You've enjoyed a few snacks since then, I see."

Everyone snickers.

"After I figured out who he was," Victoria continues, "I spoke with my mom." She sets a hand on the quivering Buttrum's shoulder. "My mother hates you . . . In fact, my whole family hates you. And Mom's *very* well connected. She made some phone calls." She surveys the students for a moment. "Francis cornered my cousin one night when she was fourteen. He and my aunt were loaded on a drug bender."

Students whip their heads back and forth, looking from Victoria to Buttrum, shocked.

Dante's voice rises again. "*And* the jackass is a druggie?"

Everyone laughs.

"So, as I was saying," Victoria continues, "my mother hates him and is well connected. She made phone calls and found out that the dean of education coordination is a plant. The position is new, and wouldn't you know it, Mr. Dean is best friends with Daniel Stamp, Joel's dad."

My mouth drops open.

Victoria continues pacing around the circle. She stops and looks at Arch. "Principal Buttrum has full authority granted by the education coordination office to do whatever he pleases. He's backed by powerful people who are dirty. Joel's dad's funding this little retaliation, and all his employees—at least a couple of whom happen to be the Drones' fathers—are in on the masterminding. Hence why Buttrum's gotten away with his insane bullying, nonsense rules, general irritation, and these little hump huts he's sprinkling all over campus."

By the time she turns back to Buttrum, he's practically quaking.

"I bet you didn't full think through that whole hut thing, did you? Brilliant plan, you sad little troll." She makes a dumb face to mock him. "What should I do to torture the students? Hmm . . . I know! I'll install little sex shacks all over campus." She rolls her eyes. "Everyone's just going to smoke pot, do drugs, and make sexy time in these ridiculous boxes."

Buttrum appears dumbfounded. Then, after a moment of thought, his expression changes. "You're right. I didn't think of that."

Victoria turns an appraising eye toward Demitri. "I thought of it," she purrs flirtatiously.

Someone at the back of the crowd yells, "Me too!"

Another person from the opposite side of the crowd yells, "So did Jason and Tiffany. They're in one of the Actors' Alley boxes right now."

Everyone laughs.

"Well, hell," Ms. G calls out as she storms around the corner into Actors' Alley and out of sight.

Jason's a degenerate who deals pot to fund his expensive snowboarding hobby. He's dating a girl on the softball team—not Tiffany—and that poor girl is now furiously stomping through the quad toward Actors' Alley.

I give Trey a deprecating glance. "Looks like your side-ride's at it again."

Trey watches the softball player storm past, then side-eyes me apologetically. "Tiffany has to stop playing defensive end every chance she gets."

"But, Trey!" I hiss back sarcastically. "Whatever do you mean? You said your affair wasn't Tiffany's fault. She's such a nice girl, after all."

Trey rubs his face hard.

"Fight about that soulless automaton later," Deb cuts in. "We have a principal to flatten."

"Principal Buttrum's not going anywhere," Victoria announces to the crowd. "We're guaranteed zero help from the outside. My mom found out last night that the school board is going to be forcibly replaced. All but Charlie Sisterno, that is." She gives Arch a pointed look. "We're on our own."

Everyone appears dismayed, but then Arch hollers, "*Good*! That's how we like it. Without a legit school board, we're on even playing ground. The usual rules that govern students no longer apply. It's us against the new *them*."

Victoria turns back to Principal Buttrum. "I know more of your dirty little secrets, *Francis*. A whole lot more. You have quite the shady past, and a few filthy whoppers that would set the entire school's ears to burning. You might not remember me, but I'm here to tell you that *I will end you*. Either you stand down and sit in your cushy little office with your yap trap closed, or there will be no more of your drug binge nights, no more prostitutes, no more of your perverted little foot fanta—"

"Enough!" Buttrum cuts in. "Enough. What do you want?"

Many of the students' eyes are the size of satellite dishes as we watch Victoria sway and saunter closer to Buttrum. She's radiating sex appeal from every muscle. She stops so close to him that they could easily kiss. He gasps perversely. Most of the students gag, disgusted.

"You're going to leave us the hell alone," Victoria purrs. "Sit in your office and stay there like a good dog." She places a perfectly manicured hand on his shoulder, pulls him closer, and knees him in the groin with all her might.

Buttrum groans, grabbing at his crotch as he slumps to the ground. As Victoria turns to walk away, he grabs her ankle and hangs on.

Everyone's standing still, shocked by more than one thing that just happened. Demitri's the only one thinking quick. He rushes over and grabs the back of what's left of Buttrum's thinning hair, dragging him away from Victoria.

He lets go, takes a step back, and kicks Buttrum in the gut. "Stay away from my girl," Demitri says to the sagging, gasping principal.

Now he turns to Victoria with a smoldering look. She walks to him with her curves swaying. She puts her arms around his neck and kisses him passionately.

I grimace. "Looks like the alley cat's out of the bag."

Presley cocks her head to the side, her face a mask of sheer confusion. "Well, I guess Victoria got her man, and Principal Buttrum likes to—"

She's interrupted by Tanner. "Please, God, don't say it. I'll never get the image out of my head."

Buttrum lies there silently, though it kind of looks like he's whimpering.

Meanwhile, the truck driver is still standing in the same spot with his mouth hanging open. "What the heck goes on around here?"

Arch walks by and pats him on the shoulder. "This is nothing. You should see what happens when we really get fired up."

The crowd is still gathered even though the bell rang ten minutes ago to go to fifth period. People aren't even wandering around. It's as if everyone feels safer together.

"Are those boxes paid for?" Arch asks the truck driver.

"Principal Buttrum paid for them in cash." The driver checks his clipboard and adds, "They run a thousand dollars each."

"I was told I have to supply my own Kleenex," Ms. G says, sounding exasperated, "but Principal Buttrum can buy six thousand dollars' worth of useless Tanner Blue prisons?"

"Hey now!" Tanner exclaims. "Leave me out of this!"

Everyone chuckles.

"Thank you," Arch says to the driver. "You're free to leave."

The grizzled man makes a hasty dash to his cab, hopping up and starting the truck with a rumble. The beeping sound kicks up as his truck slowly reverses down the wide walkway to the alley. He's clearly in a hurry to escape this madness, and I can't blame him.

Arch turns back to the crowd. "Listen up. I need volunteers to drag those boxes from Actors' Alley and quad two over here."

A handful of students separate from the group, and the giant boxes are quickly hauled over and set in a line in the middle of quad one.

Arch nudges Principal Buttrum with the toe of his Doc Marten boot. "Get up, degenerate! I want you to watch the show."

Glowering at Arch, Buttrum sits up.

"We're dismantling these things and getting rid of them," Arch informs the crowd.

"I'll go get screw guns," Mr. Jenson offers. "I'll be right back."

Arch raises a hand for pause. "No need." He turns to our group and gestures toward the blue box closest to us. "Have at it."

Bear, Kenji, Tanner, Trey, Hiram, Demitri, Darren, and Marcus get on either side of the box, grabbing on. The door is ripped off its hinges first, and then the box is ripped apart at each screwed-together junction. In less than a minute, Buttrum's expensive box is reduced to a pile of useless plastic.

Arch leans down and glares at the principal. "Listen here, you worthless pile of sludge," he says loudly enough for everyone to hear. "Stand down and learn to *master* your behavior, or we'll *master* it for you, just like we did with that box." With that, he stands up straight and looks out over the sea of students. "Tear them apart! *Now!*"

The students are happy to oblige. In a few blinks of an eye, the remaining boxes are reduced to piles of rubble.

Arch points at Buttrum, who's still slumped on the ground, and says to the students, "This madness is finished. We're done taking shit around here." Then he turns to glare down at the principal. "Oh, and one more thing . . . Watch what you say. You'll never be our master. By the way, if you'd done a little research, you might have realized that the term's offensive to some of us."

Mr. Isley stomps up, grabs Buttrum by the back of his suit jacket collar, and starts dragging him away like a misbehaving toddler. "You jackass, sorry sack of crap. I'll show you to use the word *master*. This is 1993, not 1793. Hurting students and acting like a dictator! Since you waddled in here, I can't even enjoy my lunch in peace!"

We all exchange an amused glance.

"Do you think we should go after them?" Presley asks. "I've never seen Mr. Isley that mad before."

"Let Mr. Isley get out some frustration," Tanner says. "He's earned it."

CHAPTER 12

The crowd disperses, and our group is left standing there after I beg Ms. G to let us handle Adam. She reluctantly agrees. Presley and Finley head to Valerie, while I cross to Adam, who's sitting up, but clearly not okay.

I lean down and grab his hand, sending a pulse through our connection. *"Will you let me help you?"*

Bear, Demitri, and Darren are watching over us. They exchange a glance as Adam hangs on to my hand with a viselike grip.

"Don't leave me," Adam pulses back frantically.

I look up at Bear and Darren from my kneeling position. I reach with my other hand to Trey and send the message his way. He quietly whispers to Bear, who turns and suggests to the others, "How about all of you take Valerie to Snow White's Café and get her cleaned up? We're going to deal with Adam. We'll meet you there shortly."

They get Valerie and head to the side gate that doesn't properly lock due to Arch's MacGyvering.

Once they're out of earshot, Bear asks me, "Can you fix him?"

I nod. "I tested it at the dance, and I can do it. But we need privacy. Let's go to the balcony lobby in the theater. No one ever checks for students up there."

The guys help Adam up.

"You should head to Snow White's with the others," I say softly to Trey.

He shakes his head. "I'm not leaving you. Just do what you need to. I can handle it."

With a sigh, I shift my gaze to Bear.

He seems to recognize my unspoken frustration. "Eventually, the three of you are going to have to face whatever this is going to be. You can set boundaries where amorous stuff is concerned, obviously, but you've also got a soulmate connection with Adam that isn't going anywhere. It's not like Trey's oblivious."

Trey's expression is strained as he nods in agreement.

Adam can walk, but the guys help him up the stairs anyway. He's obviously hurt, both physically and energetically. We get him through the main lobby and up to the shadowy balcony.

"Tell me how you'll be most comfortable," I say to him. "I know your arms hurt, but we connect best with me on your lap and your hands on my back."

Adam turns to Trey, silently inquiring about whether he's okay with this.

Trey shakes his head. "This isn't up to me. You two do what you need to."

I tip my head back and murmur, "This is about to get weird."

Adam sits, and I unzip his backpack, pulling out the Discman and little speaker he always has in there. I start to unzip my backpack for a CD, but Adam says, "Just play the CD I have in there. I made it. It'll get the job done."

The two men in my life both know that my connection to

music fuels my energetic center. I side-eye Adam, suspicious of what songs are on the CD.

After a moment, I decide to give it a try. "Crisscross applesauce," I say, like he's a little kid in a dance class.

He laughs. "You're quirky."

"Yeah, yeah, we all know."

The guys all chuckle. Adam shifts to sitting cross-legged. I settle on his lap, facing him and wrapping my legs around him. When I hit *play* on the CD player, Nine Inch Nails' "Something I Can Never Have" hauntingly thrums through the speaker.

My eyes meet Adam's. "Seriously?" I say to him. "We're going to drag Trey, Darren, Demitri, and Bear into the details of our rabbit hole?"

"With you gone," Adam says, "I have to have something to hold on to."

I hear Trey sigh and Demitri ask him, "You sure you want to be here for this?"

"It's weird," Trey admits. "But she's the only one who can fix him. I'll be fine."

I close my eyes and put my hands on either side of Adam's jaw, guiding his head down to rest on my shoulder. The music thrums methodically, and I slow my heart rate to the gentle rhythm of the music. I wrap my arms around his back, putting my hands flat on the energy center he and I always use. As usual, the music speaks volumes that I'm not thrilled about Trey knowing, but it's too late now.

Adam relaxes against me, chest to chest.

"You need to drop your shields," I murmur. "I need in."

He tenses for a second, and immediately, I know what the issue is. Everyone gathered with us is an energy worker, so he knows they'll be able to read everything that rolls off him. I know he still has a lot of feelings about me that he doesn't want Trey to be aware of. There's no need to complicate things that will take time to fix.

I glance to Bear, who's sitting next to us. "Could you shield around me and Adam?"

He catches my drift and nods.

With my eyes closed again, I whisper into Adam's ear so that only he can hear, "Bear's going to block us off."

Adam replies with an almost imperceptible nod against my shoulder as the heavy, earthy presence of Bear's energy wraps around us.

As soon as Bear's energetic shield settles in place, Adam drops his failing shields and I'm temporarily left reeling. He batters me with heartbreak, fear, and pain. I gasp, and my eyes meet Bear's. Bear gives me a pained look that indicates he can feel everything rolling off Adam. I glance at Darren, Demitri, and Trey, but they don't react.

They can't feel it, I think. *As long as Bear's shield holds, we have some layer of privacy.*

I turn my attention back to Adam and put my forehead on his shoulder. He exhales and wraps his arms around me, putting his hands flat in the middle of my back. I slip easily into the meditative trance I always use to enter Adam's psyche.

After a moment, I open my mind's eye. The damage in the cavernous main room of the cave system that makes up Adam's mind is unreal. He's barely been holding it together, and the trauma he suffered at lunch has only worsened the nightmare.

I sigh internally, then gather myself for what looks like a much more difficult process than I was expecting.

Adam's there in my mind, and he thinks to me, *"I'm trying. I'm sorry, Mel."*

I turn to his presence, and the *him* in his mind looks exhausted. I smile and think back, *"I've got this. Hang tight, okay?"*

He nods. I get to work.

The song shifts to Chris Isaak's "Wicked Game," and the *me* in Adam's head sighs. *"Letting Trey in on these songs is a disaster waiting to happen."*

Adam crosses to me in our minds, where he tips up my chin and kisses me. It sends fire up my spine in my physical body, causing me to gasp audibly. Apparently, Adam has decided it's okay for us to cheat on our significant others as long as we're not doing these things in real life.

He ends the kiss, gazing into the eyes of the mental *me*.

"This is skirting the line," I think to him.

He smirks at me. *"I know."*

I sigh in my mind, but I'm radiating that I'm secretly relieved to still have something with Adam. I'm going to be at war with myself later, but we need to get through this now.

As I examine the walls of his mind, I step to the center of the main room. *"Dark water incoming,"* I warn him.

He nods, having been through this with me before. Water rises as the song oozes through our combined psyche.

The water rushes in faster and faster. I don't stop the incoming tide until the entire cavernous space is full. Then, I gather my energetic resources and send out a massive burst of energy. It spreads through the water, flowing into the cracks and crevices in Adam's mind. Slowly but steadily, it knits together the broken places.

The physical Adam sighs against my chest. I press a little firmer with my hands against his back while he relaxes.

At this moment, the lyrics of the song seem to communicate a little too much. The music is either making things better or worse—I can't tell. Either way, it's the music that makes Adam and me *us*.

I wait as the dark-water energy does the work for me. Our

metaphysical selves are staring into each other's eyes, and Adam is radiating appreciation.

The song ends, and the next track starts. "You" by Candlebox breezes through us. My heart constricts all at once. This isn't a song we've played together, but it's obvious that he made this CD about me.

My physical body reacts. Tears start rolling down my cheeks.

"Hold it together, Melanie," Bear says, sounding farther away than he is in reality.

In his mind, the metaphysical Adam steps forward and wraps his arms around me. *"I don't know how to go on without you."*

Suddenly, his heartbreak surges, and I'm nearly torn apart by it as it shatters through my carefully held shields. My matching heartbreak slams through, and I feel Bear's shields around us tighten as he tries not to let the massive emotions leak past the barrier.

"You two need to get control of yourselves," Bear says. "You're putting a strain on my shields, and they may buckle. Work through this fast." His voice sounding muffled as he turns away from us, Bear says to Darren and Demitri, "I need you two to add a layer around what I've got. I'm good at this, but these two combined are a force to be reckoned with, and they're losing it."

Adam and I are standing in his mind, wrapped around each other, quaking in emotional pain.

"I don't know what to do," he thinks to me in a whisper.

The metaphysical me begins to sob. His disintegrating condition starts rolling through the cavernous room in his psyche. The cracks and fissures in the walls appear again. It snaps me back to the task at hand and sparks an idea. The water recedes, leaving both of us suddenly heavy.

I split my attention between Adam's mind and my physical self. "Bear," I manage to say, "I'm going to need a boost. There's not much left of me right now." I realize that my cheeks are coated with tears, and the front of my shirt is sopping wet from Adam crying down my shoulder.

"I've got you," Bear says. "Incoming."

As Bear's hands settle on my shoulders, I dive back into Adam's psyche. Bear's warm, earthy energy radiates into me, and I can feel him watching through my mind's eye. I send dark water climbing up the walls, leaving the center of the mental room dry. The water is laced with liquid steel. My entire body shakes from the effort, and Adam tightens his hands on my back. His shields always carry the illusion of steel, and I think this might be a way that he can hold it together until things calm enough for me to work on him a few more times. As the liquid steel dome reaches the top, I send out the last of my energy to forge together the two sides that meet in the middle.

"Hell of an idea, Mel," Bear says from far away.

I turn to Adam in his mind. *"Test it."*

He does, then turns to me, bewildered. *"How did you do that?"*

I shrug. *"I don't know. It's what you need, so somehow, I can do it."*

My resolve shatters, and I lunge into his arms, kissing him within the room inside his mind. His physical self gasps against my shoulder. All the pain, confusion, and heartbreak tornadoes again, and I hear Bear snarl as he tries to hold us together within his makeshift shields. Darren and Demitri clamp down over the top of Bear's energy. This only adds to the weight inside Adam's mind, but my steel barrier holds.

The metaphysical Adam pulls away and cups my face. We're both distraught, but he seems to be doing better now that I've reinforced everything.

"We'll talk about this," he thinks in a whisper. *"But not now. We need to come out of the trance. Bear can't hold on much longer."*

I shake my head frantically, sending a pulse filled with how I don't want to leave.

"I know," he mentally whispers.

My chest constricts. I moan out loud.

"She's not okay," Trey says to Bear. "She needs to come back."

"I know what's happening," Bear says. "She isn't in danger. Hang tight."

Inside his mind, Adam pulls me into his arms. *"I'm going to bring up my energy shields and cut off the connection. I love you."*

I gasp back, *"I love you too."*

Suddenly, I'm slowly backed out of Adam's mind by an unseen force. The cave system disappears, and I'm left inside my own shattered psyche. The CD switches to the next track. Depeche Mode's "Sweetest Perfection" thumps from the speaker. My heart nearly explodes as my tears soak the shoulder of Adam's shirt. I feel him lift his head, and he holds me for a long moment.

He's in no better emotional condition than me as he says softly, "Take her."

Trey steps up behind me, wraps his arms around my chest, and gently pulls me back and away from Adam's lap. As Trey cradles me, Adam stands and heads into the bathroom next to us.

"I'm going to go check on him," Bear says, following after Adam.

"Did it work?" Darren asks me.

I nod, but I'm too distraught to speak. There's just still so much heartbreak over Adam—more than even I realized.

Trey radiates calm energy as he laces his hand with mine. I clamp my shields shut on the half of me that belongs to Adam's soulmate connection. Trey's energy slows my racing heart, and I can breathe again.

"I didn't know you could do that," Demitri says.

My smile is laced with sadness. "Apparently, I can do that with my soulmates."

Adam and Bear come back out of the bathroom. Adam crosses to me. Trey lets go of my hand, and Adam wraps me up in a hug.

He slides his right hand into mine and pulses down our connection, *"Thank you. I'll get my Discman back later. Listen to the CD. I love you."*

He heads down the stairs with Bear in tow, the lyrics about how he sees me crooning as they leave.

CHAPTER *13*

We wheel into a spot in the student parking lot. Trey puts the car in park and cuts the engine.

"Thank you for picking me up today," I tell him. "My parents are worried that things might get crazy this week. They wanted to make sure we're together."

Trey nods. "I'm not complaining. We haven't had so much as a minute alone together in weeks. Anyway, it can't get any crazier around here than it was last week. Hopefully, Buttrum's learned his lesson."

"I doubt we're that lucky."

Trey meets my gaze. "Is everything okay with you and Adam?"

I shrug. "I didn't hear from him this weekend."

Most of last night, I spent listening to the CD Adam made and crying myself sick. On Friday night, and all day Saturday and Sunday, I couldn't bring myself to listen to it. But then it occurred to me that I had to get it out of my system so I could get back to something resembling normalcy with my boyfriend.

Trey leans over and cups my chin. When he kisses me, the flash of hormones makes us gasp. We've had zero time for romance, and apparently, we've both missed it.

He pulls away from the kiss. "You want to get out of here and find somewhere quiet, just the two of us?" he asks in a deep, gravely voice.

Before I can answer, there's a tap at the driver's side window. We glance over and see Arch standing outside the window in his trademark black trench coat with an anarchy symbol painted on the back.

Trey leans his head back against the headrest with his eyes closed and takes a deep breath. "If I don't get to spend some time alone with you soon, I'm gonna lose my mind."

"Same," I say with a grin. "But you better go see what Arch needs."

I unbuckle my seat belt while Trey gets out of the car. He closes his door but doesn't come around to my side. I look out the window confused because he always opens my door. He and Arch are standing still. Something's wrong. I hop out of the car. In front of me is the expansive field behind the school.

Yup, something's definitely wrong, all right.

My mouth hanging open, I close the door and round the back side of the car. Our group of friends walks our direction.

I turn to Trey, shocked. "Principal Buttrum's got to be kidding."

Adam stomps up to us, fuming. "It's early for this crap. Looks like Buttrum's been a busy bee this weekend."

"Have I lost my mind," Trey says to no one in particular, "or does our school look like a prison yard?"

We stare out at the field that now has steel bar fencing around it, with barbed wire curled all along the top.

"Well, this might just be where the thirty-five thousand was spent," Marcus says.

Adam snorts. "This fencing costs far more than thirty-five thousand." He looks at Arch. "How the hell did Buttrum accomplish this in a weekend?"

Victoria gestures to the fence. "Welcome to Daniel Stamp's world. I guarantee he footed the bill, paid overtime for a huge crew, and maniacally screamed at them all weekend to achieve this magnificent feat."

"Come on," Adam says. "Let's see what other *improvements* he's made." He and I have our emotional shields clamped so tight that neither of us can feel anything from the other. It's a relief. Meanwhile, Demitri and I have yet to discuss the awkwardness between us. I'm so sick of social drama.

We walk across the street toward the alley gate. The cinder block wall around the gate is now twelve feet tall instead of the previous eight feet, and the rolling chain-link gate has been replaced with a steel contraption, complete with an electronic control pad.

Arch laughs. "Some crackhead's going to destroy that keypad within a week."

Tanner whistles. "Is Buttrum keeping a T. rex in that paddock?"

We all stare at each other, dumbfounded. Ms. G and Mr. Isley, clearly angry, walk toward us from the Highland Avenue side of the school.

"He's at it again," Mr. Isley calls out to us as they approach.

"That's the understatement of the year," Ms. G says as they stop in front of us.

"Does this mess go around the entire school?" Arch asks.

Mr. Isley nods. "He's even shut off access to the teacher parking lot. He's erected one of these giant electronic gates where the rolling gate used to be. All the teachers now must park in the student parking lot because Buttrum won't give us the code to the new gate."

"Do you have any *idea* how much all this fencing, barbed wire, and steel gate nonsense must have cost?" Ms. G asks. "We could have funded every club, show, and team for ten years on the expense he dumped into this operation."

Finley says what we're all thinking. "I don't understand what the point of all of this is. The school already had gates and fences."

"Maybe he's trying to keep the students from ditching," Ms. G responds.

I shake my head and look down at my feet.

Bear seems to sense my concern. "Is your intuition at it again?" he asks me.

Trey puts his arms around me as I nod.

"My intuition's screaming," I say. "Feels like something sadistic."

"Like what?" Adam asks anxiously.

"Something tells me he wants to hold us in there and make sure we can't run."

Arch turns to Ms. G. "They're ramping up. I want to scope things out. How do we get into this prison to go to class?"

"There's all this new protocol. Everyone's being herded through the front doors all the way around on the other side."

Presley huffs. "I *hate* it here!" Then she throws her head back and screams. We all know how she hates having to waste time and energy. These new fences are going to irritate her on the daily.

Marcus puts his arm around her. "Screw it. We're not in yet. Wanna bounce and go to the beach?"

"Yes, please," Mr. Isley says. "Take me with you!"

We all grin at Mr. Isley.

"As much as I know we'd all love to blow this disaster off for the day," Arch says, "we can't leave the other students behind. Melanie's intuition is never wrong. Things might get dangerous in there. We're the only people who can control the chaos likely going on inside those walls. Well, all of us and Mr. Jenson, of course."

"Thanks for that little intuitive bomb, Mel," Tanner jokes, scrunching up his face at me.

"Yeah, thanks, Mel," everyone else says sarcastically.

"Yeah, thanks, Mel," I agree. "Damn intuition!"

Adam rubs at his face. He's still sporting dark circles under his eyes. "I'm warning you right now that I'm one sarcastic Buttrum bullhorn bellow from completely snapping."

"Are you okay?" Ms. G asks him.

"I'm sure as hell not. I'm tired, I'm hurt, I'm sick to death of this shit, and I just found out that Jason and Tiffany got to have naughty time in one of those damn blue boxes while I was being threatened with another one. *Let me tell you*, that pisses me off."

I growl like an irritable baby bear.

Trey glances my way. "Can we please not say the *T* word anymore?" he asks, sounding exasperated. "I don't have the energy for another fight with Mel."

Adam grins at Trey, clearly enjoying his dismay. "I'm busy being assaulted by a Napoleonic troll and six of his brainless followers in ugly yellow windbreakers, and meanwhile, Jason's having a blast with *Tiffany*. It's not fair!"

Trey glares at Adam but doesn't speak.

With a sigh, Adam takes a moment to pull himself together. "I agree with Presley. I hate it here." He looks at us earnestly. "I want you all to know how much it means to me that you stuck up for me. As much as I was hurting in that moment, I was aware enough to know that I didn't have to push through the pain and defend myself because you were all battling for me. For the second time in a month, I don't think I could've gotten through my terror alone."

"We've always got your back, brother," Bear says. "You're never alone. We'll kick ass for anyone in this group."

"As often as possible," Tanner croons. "And with gusto."

Adam turns a sly grin toward Victoria. "You earned my respect all over again. You were wicked vicious when you confronted Buttrum in the quad. The way you aired his dirty laundry was genius."

"Thank you," Victoria says demurely. "Francis Buttrum's a freak, and everyone needed to know. Plus, it was fun getting to unleash a little bit of the old Victoria."

Demitri wraps his arms around his new girlfriend and gives her a squeeze. "You kicked ass and took names."

Victoria raises an eyebrow at him. "That's what I'm best at."

"We might as well face this," Ms. G says. "Let's head around the school and see what dog and pony show awaits us today."

As if trying to put as much physical and emotional distance between him and me as possible, Adam slides his arm around Valerie and walks her to the front of the group.

A wave of irritation climbs up my spine. *I practically drained myself to nothing to help him, and he's acting like I'm invisible. Of all people,* Victoria *gets his kudos? It took all weekend to get my energy back to functional.*

Trey tries to take my hand. I cross my arms over my chest and walk ahead of him to join Bear. Bear and Trey exchange a glance over my head, and Bear puts an arm around me as we head around the corner.

CHAPTER 14

Over a thousand students are waiting on the front lawn of the school. The tardy bell rang five minutes ago, but we can't get in for some unexplained reason. Ms. G and Mr. Isley are pushing to the front of the crowd to see what the holdup is.

"Hopefully it takes forever," I say to the others. "I don't want to go in there anyway."

From across the lawn, Dante yells, "Hey, Arch! Do you know what's going on?"

Arch shakes his head. "No clue," he yells back. "I'm sure whatever it is will piss me off though."

Feeling froggy, I offer, "I'll go check it out."

Arch starts to argue, but I wave him off and announce over my shoulder as I walk away, "If the yellow jackets grab me, whatever. I don't care anymore."

Trey and Adam both give me worried side-eyes as I leave the group and start weaving my way through the crushing crowd.

From behind me, Arch hollers, "Let Melanie through. We're finding out what's going on."

People look my way and shift, allowing me an easier path to the front of the crowd. It occurs to me that the students at our school are different now. We used to be divided into the usual groups—the burners, the jocks, the Drones, the preppies, the performing arts kids, the mean girls—but now we're all one. We've overcome our differences and banded together to face a common enemy. As awful as it's been to deal with Buttrum, I'm thrilled by this side effect. Losing the usual catty teen drama has been a relief. It's a shame that more high school students can't experience what it's like to walk into their school each day free from judgment and hate . . . well, at least from their fellow students. We'll see how long this new student harmony lasts, but I have a feeling we won't slide back into old habits.

I make it to the double doors at the front of the crowd, peeking between students to see what's happening. Across the hall are two folding tables surrounded by students who look baffled. When I spot Drake, I wave him over.

He slides through the crowd. "What's up, girl?" He grins flirtatiously at me, and I can't help but smile back.

"Drake, you're a whole lot of trouble," I say suggestively.

Drake raises an alluring eyebrow. "You know, Trey's my friend and all, but remember that I'm always waiting in the wings if you suddenly pop up single."

"I'll keep that in mind," I say coyly. "Any chance you've figured out what's going on in here? Arch sent me in to do recon for the kids still stuck outside."

Drake rolls his eyes. "Principal Dickweed has installed punch card machines like they have in factories. He clearly didn't plan his new punch card rollout well, though, because he only assigned two of his lackeys to hand the stupid cards out. It's like a damn episode of *The Three Stooges*, watching these yellow jackets try to find everyone's cards. After they hand out a card, they're supposed to read through this insane list of new protocols and have each student sign that they understand the nonsense." Drake points toward a group of the usual Poindexter types all bunched up by the side of one of the tables. "Yo! Science nerds! Move."

Lionel turns our way. "We prefer to be called science geniuses, thank you very much," he says haughtily.

With a grin, Drake corrects himself. "Yo, science geniuses, scoot for a second."

The geniuses glance in every direction spastically.

"There's no danger," Drake assures them. "I just want Melanie to see the cardholders and machines on the wall behind you."

Just like Drake said, there are never-ending rows of metal cardholders screwed in all along the main hallway. The holders are covering up something I have loved about this school ever since I first toured here last summer: you can no longer see the red painted stars bearing the names of the celebrities who attended Hollywood High.

I sigh. "If it helps," I say to the science geniuses, "we're all pretty jumpy too."

Lionel and his friends give me a starry-eyed look.

"Really?" Lionel says. "I never thought you got nervous. You're always in the middle of the fight when the guys step up."

I smile back at him endearingly. I only know of Lionel because of a Santa incident with Bear last semester, but he's a nice guy. "Yes, Lionel. Really."

"You know my name?" he stutters out.

"Of course."

The science geniuses let out delighted chuckles before they all turn away and bunch up, presumably to talk about me as they head down the hall. I stare after them, amused by the unexpected breeze of admiration I can sense from the retreating geniuses.

Drake grins down at me. "Awww," he teases. "The nerds all have a crush on you." His expression morphs seductive, and he takes a step closer. "Looks like I have competition to snap you up if you're ever single."

My heart rate speeds up as I look into Drake's hazel eyes. He has that effect on me, so I've always tried to keep a polite distance, at least as often as possible. "You and I both know that if it came down to you and Lionel over there, you've got a healthy chance of winning."

Drake throws his head back, laughing.

"Anyway, I've gotta jet," I tell him. "Have to report the news to Arch."

He gives me a smoldering look. "I hate to see you go, but damn do I ever love to watch you leave."

I grin at him, feeling his electric gaze on my back as I walk out the door. *Gracious, that boy's trouble.*

Adam's waiting for me outside, and if looks could kill, his would liquify. "What the hell was that with Drake?" he barks.

I sigh. "What was up with you ignoring me earlier?"

"You first."

I roll my eyes. "A little harmless flirting, Adam. Would you *please* let me be a normal teenager for a minute? All I do is thought-share with two soulmates, warn everyone about trouble, and somehow manage to fix your busted ass psyche. I have zero clue what I'm doing, and if you're not careful, I'm going to snap under the pressure. Add to it that I'm completely heartbroken over you, and I'm a wreck down to my soul. Drake presented a fun little distraction, and I enjoyed it. Sue me."

He glowers. "This is hard enough watching my other half with her other-other half. I don't have any interest in watching Drake chase after you too."

"You chose to leave, Adam," I hiss. "*Not* me. I wanted us to be together."

"I screwed up," he hisses back. "Again. Do you think I don't know that? I left you because I thought your energy would be too much while I was broken. How the hell was I supposed to know that *yet again* you would be perfect?"

A wave of exasperation causes me to slump. "If you're so damn dense that you haven't figured out that we're perfect, then there's nothing I can do to help you."

He grabs my hand as I try to turn and walk away. Through our connection, he pulses, *"I needed space because I'm on the edge. I'm not trying to ignore you. I'm trying to stay sane."*

I squeeze his hand and pulse back a blue-tinged bubble of understanding. Then, I let go and make my way back, weaving and winding through the crowd. I find our group exactly where I left them. Quickly, I explain the punch card situation.

Arch gives me a baffled look. "What's the point of punch card machines? Our teachers all take roll."

I shrug. "Apparently spending money on stupid crap's Buttrum's latest way of flexing on us. Anyway, it's gonna be a while."

Arch turns to Hiram. "Any chance you have a boom box in the trunk of your car?"

Hiram grins. "Always."

"Go grab it. And get that mixtape you just made. If we're going to be stuck out here, we might as well have some fun."

Hiram nods and jogs across the front lawn and out of sight.

Meanwhile, Marcus gets on his knees, puffs up his chest, and squishes up his face. He says in a perfect imitation of Principal Buttrum, "There will *be no fun!*"

We all crack up.

CHAPTER 15

Yet another assembly was announced over the school loudspeaker system a few minutes ago. It took over an hour to get everyone through the punch card line, and we're already halfway through what should have been second period. We make our way up the winding four-story staircase to the theater auditorium. As has become our trend, the student council lines up against the back wall with Ms. G, Mr. Bentley, and Mr. Isley. The students give us probing looks as they pass, and Arch nods at them.

Mr. Jenson comes over. "I spent all weekend installing those metal cardholders. Principal Buttrum's a nut."

A hush falls over the auditorium as Principal Buttrum walks to the microphone center stage.

Hiram, our head sound technician at the school, radiates irritation. "I don't know who set that sound equipment up for him, but it wasn't me." Hiram has always been protective of the equipment.

On the stage, Principal Buttrum's surrounded by four tall guys wearing black suits and sunglasses.

"I see Mr. Buttrum found some strip club bouncers to accompany him today," Adam quips.

The smirks die on our lips as Principal Buttrum's voice booms out through the speakers. "As you all know, we've installed a new punch card system and advanced fencing around the school. There will be no more ditching."

Someone from the crowd hollers, "Apparently there'll be no more learning either!"

Everyone covers their snickering with their hands and sinks further in their chairs. It seems that everyone is straining under the effort to follow Arch's request that we all be on our best behavior. The goal is to give Principal Buttrum nothing reasonable to have a fit about. *Good luck with that*, I think. *The troll seems to find any excuse to throw a tantrum, reasonable or not.*

"Who just said that?" Buttrum demands.

All at once, everyone in the mystery student's seating section raises their hands in solidarity. I lean my head into Trey's shoulder to cover my laughter.

Arch grins. "Damn, these kids are getting good."

Buttrum turns his usual shade of close-to-a-stroke red as he flaps his arms in exasperation. "Enough!" he bellows into the micro-phone. "No more raising your hands!" He surveys the crowd with disdain. "You will punch in every morning. I expect order and discipline. The front doors will open at seven-fifty, and everyone must be to class by eight *sharp*."

"Are you kidding?" a man I recognize as the varsity football coach yells out. "You want fifteen hundred students to clock in on two punch card machines and get to class in *ten minutes*?"

The principal squints his beady eyes at the football coach. "Yes. And anyone who's tardy will face our new late-policy consequences."

"You've lost your marbles," the coach retorts. "Along with the jar they were stored in."

Buttrum stomps his feet rapidly and leans into the microphone. "Keep it up and you'll get the boot, just like your colleague with the baseball team did this morning." He turns back to address the students. "That's right! The baseball coach is fired. And I'll be bringing in a replacement of my choosing."

I can feel Trey's energy sag. He's on the baseball team, and he's clearly taking the news hard.

Curtis, the captain of the varsity baseball team, stands up a few rows ahead of us. "You've got to be kidding!" he hollers. "Coach Lopez took us to *state* last year!"

Baseball players all over the auditorium start groaning and complaining.

Trey adds his voice to the mix. "How dare you! We need Coach Lopez!"

Buttrum grins from ear to ear, clearly enjoying the outcry. His bodyguards step forward and fan out across the edge of the stage as if anticipating trouble.

Arch sighs. "I'm on it," he mutters to us. He pushes away from the wall and strides down the center aisle of the auditorium.

The students all quiet down when they spot our leader.

"Is this really your response to losing your solitary-confinement box battle on Friday?" Arch calls up to the stage as he makes his way through the auditorium. "Individual little prisons didn't work, so you decided to turn the whole school into a prison?"

"One way in and one way out," Buttrum says proudly.

Arch scrunches up his face, clearly baffled. "That's against fire code. You do realize that the fire marshal's guaranteed to shut this down?"

Principal Buttrum looks confused. It seems he hadn't thought of that. Finally, he says, "The chances of a fire are unlikely, so I'm risking it."

Dante stands up. "I never thought I'd say this, but if we don't get to do some schoolwork, I'm gonna torch this place myself. All we do lately is stand around wasting time arguing with you!"

The students all nod.

"You will punch card in and punch card out every day," Buttrum says, undeterred. "You will walk through campus in orderly lines. All PE classes will do nothing but jogging drills on the field. You will learn *discipline*."

Arch seems to size up each of the principal's new bodyguards in turn. "The four of you realize you've been cast in this little farce as this guy's bitches, right?"

The students all snicker as the four muscular bodyguards, clearly not enjoying being referred to as Principal Buttrum's bitches, exchange a doubtful glance. They turn in unison to look skeptically at Buttrum.

"I'm starting to figure that out," one of them says. "Come on, guys. We're done here. This is a ridiculous waste of time."

Buttrum looks frantically at the bodyguard leader. "Please, you can't leave!" he begs. "I need protection! These students are crazy."

The head bodyguard turns and surveys the quiet student body for a moment. "The only thing I've seen that's crazy is you."

As one, the bodyguards walk down the steps on the side of the stage and up the audience aisleway. The students all cheer, and we don't quiet down until all four bodyguards have exited the doors at the back of the auditorium.

Buttrum looks like he's going to keel over. He waves his hands about, and we all watch him, baffled. Choosing another tool from his limited arsenal, he barks into the microphone, "Where's Melanie Slate?"

Before Trey can stop me, I aggressively stalk down the center aisle of the auditorium. I've had enough of this bullshit. It's time to handle this. I hop up the stairs at the side of the stage and flour-ish my arms to either side as I get to Principal Buttrum. I grab the microphone off the stand and announce through the speaker system, "I'm right here."

Principal Buttrum tries to grab the microphone, but I duck my shoulders while adorably saying, "Huh-uh-uh! You like to bellow. Yell it out for everyone to hear."

I tip my head and give Buttrum my most innocent eyes. I see out of the corner of my vision that Trey and Adam are working their way closer to the stage on either side of the auditorium.

Buttrum sputters for a moment before collecting himself. "I need you in my office."

I shake my head. "No, you don't. You're a big, tough guy, after all." I gesture to the crowd sitting in rapt attention. "Your audience awaits. You can say anything in front of them that you could say to me in private." I smile sweetly. "I assure you I'll tell everyone who's willing to listen what you say anyway."

Buttrum narrows his eyes at me. He takes a step closer and says under his breath, "I'm telling you I need to speak with you privately."

My intuition flares, and I really study his expression. I cover the microphone. "Are you my enemy, or are you trying to help me?"

"I'm wondering the same thing lately," he mumbles. "I need clarity on something." His mood suddenly shifts to his usual ass-hole routine as he snatches the microphone from me, puts it back on the stand, and bellows at the student body, "I told all of you to *master* your discipline or I'll *master* it for you!"

Without hesitation, Arch hops up on the stage and aggressively stalks to the microphone. After one last glare back at Buttrum, he leans into the microphone. "I *told you* that you aren't our *master*, and that you need to quit using that *word*! This conversation is over." He lifts his arms to the crowd. "Go to second period. You're released."

A great cheer goes out. Arch leaps off the edge of the stage and heads up the center aisle as the students crush into the aisles all around him and pour toward the exit. I'm left alone with Principal Buttrum on the stage. When Trey and Adam rush up the stairs on each side of the stage, Buttrum drops his tough-guy façade.

Trey grabs my arm, but I hold up a hand to stop him.

"What do you need to discuss?" I ask the principal.

"What happened with you and Joel Stamp?"

The question takes me by surprise. I choose to answer honestly. "He tried to rape me several times. He also tried to murder me. When that didn't work, he resorted to kidnapping and holding Adam Stone hostage. Adam's best friend was murdered in the process."

Principal Buttrum's eyes snap wide. "That isn't the story I was told."

I decide to throw caution to the wind. "The Cobra Militia. Are you one of them?"

Principal Buttrum's mouth drops open, and he snaps it closed with an audible pop. He doesn't answer.

I start backing up, refusing to take my eyes off him. "We're smarter than we look, Buttrum. Choose your side carefully. I'm done with games. Whatever you allow to happen, I'll counter. You threaten. I threaten. You murder. I murder." There's blazing conviction in my eyes.

"You suddenly don't look like a sixteen-year-old," Principal Buttrum stammers.

"Actually, I'm fifteen. But I'm also really, really not."

Clarity comes into the principal's eyes. "Fifteen?"

I nod. "You're playing very adult games with someone who just got her learner's permit. Four years ago, I was playing with dolls. The amount of stress you've caused in my life is staggering. If there's a good person in you, that person needs to realize you're torturing a child." I break into a twisted smile. "Not your normal child, though. I hope we understand each other."

Trey throws his arm around my shoulders and rushes me out the closest exit, with Adam trailing behind us.

CHAPTER 16

We're forty minutes through fifth period when a runner comes in, crossing the dance room to hand Mr. Isley a piece of paper. The runner exits as the teacher reads over the sheet in his hand.

When he's finished, Mr. Isley looks at the class and grins. "Everyone please go to the locker rooms to change and gather up your stuff," he says as he shuts off the sound system. "Something tells me that we don't want to miss this."

The students all exchange excited glances as we make our way down the long hallway. At my locker, I pull out my black minidress and boots and quickly change out of my dance clothes.

Another girl in my dance class, Jayla, leans around the corner from her locker, one aisle over. "I don't know how you guys do it, but somehow your plans always work. I'm looking forward to whatever's about to happen."

"I have no clue what's happening," I answer.

We make haste packing up, putting on our backpacks, and rushing out of the locker room into the big hall by the double door exit.

Waiting for us is Mr. Isley, and he's rereading the paper the runner brought him. "Okay," he tells us, "this says that everyone needs to zip up their jackets and put their backpacks on properly. Arch wants the appearance of extreme order. You aren't supposed to speak. Not a sound, and no hand raising, no matter what Principal Buttrum says. Apparently, the marching band members are going to be stationed at each classroom, waiting for everyone when the passing bell rings. Arch wants you all to play follow-the-leader. This paper says to watch for Arch's hand signal for what he's calling 'Round Two.' Apparently, after the lines stop, you're all to stand completely still, listening for your sixth-period class teacher's name at the beginning of Round Two. I assume we'll figure out in the moment what Round Two is. Only after Arch raises his right arm may you silently walk to that line."

The bell rings, and Mr. Isley pushes open the door. One of the marching band drummers is leaning against the walkway wall, looking at his pager and waiting for us.

He grins and then clips his pager back on his pants pocket. "Please line up behind me," he says. "And if you don't know me, I'm Kurt. I'll guide you through Round One. Follow me everywhere I go and stay in your line. Don't cross over into another line or it'll ruin things."

Across campus, we hear Principal Buttrum bellow some nonsense into his newly acquired replacement bullhorn. He's interrupted by a loud drum.

CLACK, CLACK, CLACK, another drum answers.

Soon, drums are ringing out all over campus.

Our group's drummer blows his whistle, and all at once, they break into "The Ants Go Marching One by One." We follow him up the concrete walkway to quad one, all of us dutifully marching in a line behind him.

We get up to the quad, where whole classes of students are following their marching band members in perfectly straight lines all over the school. Lines of kids are marching out of bungalows, the two-story building, and around the corners from all over the campus. On the next phrase of the song, the band members start weaving and curving. They must have practiced this little routine in fourth period. We all play follow-the-leader, every face smiling. The whole student body is swirling and snaking around the school, making intricate patterns.

The teachers are watching with their mouths hanging open. Mr. Isley's grinning from ear to ear, clearly enjoying the show. We're having more fun than any student body should, reveling at the opportunity to play, even if it's in such an orderly, voiceless fashion.

Our group's drummer curves around again, and all the classes are led into a perfect sunray pattern, circling Principal Buttrum by the commons building. Classes line up next to each other, leaving enough room in the center for Buttrum to look in all directions and get a good view of his well-organized students.

As one, the drummers stop playing.

"What's the meaning of this?" Buttrum bellows into the bullhorn.

No one answers. We all remain silent, standing at attention, just like Arch's flyer instructed.

"Raise your hand if you know who planned this blatant display of disrespect," Buttrum shouts.

No one moves a muscle.

Buttrum spots Arch standing right behind the drum leader from his class line. He rushes up to him and bellows in his face through the bullhorn, "This is your doing, *isn't it*?"

Arch, continuing to stand at attention, doesn't say a word.

"Someone answer meee!" the principal screams as he spins in a circle.

Mr. Isley and Ms. G press into the middle of the students' sunray formation. They're surveying the perfectly behaved lines of kids with obvious amusement.

Buttrum rounds on them. "What's happening? I know you two are in on this!"

Before they can answer, Mr. Jenson strolls up and flashes an amused grin. "Principal Buttrum, at the assembly, you gave very specific orders that the students weren't allowed to raise their hands. You also told them that they must not speak during passing periods, and they have to walk in orderly lines. I believe they're following orders."

Principal Buttrum bellows into the bullhorn, "You disrespectful brats! Go to class!"

The marching band members pivot and walk to an open area in quad one, forming a line. One at a time, each drummer goes down the line, saying a teacher's name. The students stand still until all the drummers have voiced their Round Two assignments.

Arch raises his right arm, flashing devil horns, and all the students silently and efficiently make their way to the line for their sixth-period class. Most of the amused teachers seem to want in on the shenanigans, because they line up behind their class's assigned drummer, to the growing fury of Principal Buttrum. Ms. Ferry, my sixth-period theater teacher, silently steps in line behind our drummer. She flashes a grin, and we all smile back at her as we wait for our line to move.

Two lines down from us, the drummer gives a *CLACK, CLACK, CLACK*, and all the drummers start their "Ants go Marching One by One" song again. Perfectly in sync, we march away, leaving a flummoxed Buttrum standing by the commons building with his mouth hanging open.

CHAPTER 17

Mr. Isley's class and Ms. Ferry's class are all seated together in the theater auditorium. Adam is in Mr. Isley's sixth period, and he chose the seat next to me. We're a few rows back from everyone else, and we're instinctively leaning toward each other. I finally decide *to hell with it* and put my head on his shoulder. Adam exhales like he always does when we make contact. He sets his hand over my wrist, and I close my eyes.

"You kids are the most creatively devious people I've ever met," Ms. Ferry says. "That marching band production was one of the most hilarious things I've ever seen."

"It's all Arch," Presley says. "I have to say that as silly as it was, everyone had a good time. We needed a little fun around this miserable prison."

"I can't wait to see what you kids come up with next," Mr. Isley says. "Your antics are the only reason I haven't quit at this point."

Ms. Ferry agrees with Mr. Isley. Then, she turns to the students. "We've brought our two classes together because we share a collective new problem."

Tanner groans and dramatically throws his head back. "Another one?"

"I *hate* this place!" Marcus whines.

Ms. Ferry raises her hands to quiet the class. "I know you do, and Mr. Isley and I agree with you. We're sick of the nonsense too."

Mr. Isley takes up the thread. "Here's the deal. Principal Buttrum is insisting that the campus be locked up tight fifteen minutes after school ends every day. This leaves the dance department, theater department, music department, and all the sports teams with the unique problem of losing our rehearsal and practice spaces."

When I raise my hand, Ms. Ferry nods my way.

"Are the sports teams aware of this yet?" I ask. "Trey's going to lose it."

"I don't know if the players have been informed," Ms. Ferry says, "but they will be soon. All the teachers and coaches were called into yet another of Principal Buttrum's meetings, where he presented us with this latest bunch of garbage. The teachers and coaches who are affected had a secret meeting at lunch and—"

"Tsk, tsk, Ms. Ferry," Tanner cuts in. "That goes against the *No Unauthorized Meetings* clause in Buttrum's never-ending *master* list of rules and policies."

Mr. Isley sneers. "Soon, I'm gonna stuff that *master list* up his Napoleonic ass."

We all chuckle.

"I'm not worried about Principal Buttrum's list of nonsense," Ms. Ferry says. "Frankly, I don't think he's going to be around much longer. If he doesn't end up in jail for abusing the students, you kids and your mischief will land him in an insane asylum. I give him two more weeks, tops. Until then, I highly recommend that you keep up your antics. If nothing else, it's got the teachers curious enough that they're all planning to stick it out just to watch your performances."

"Everyone keeps saying Buttrum's days are numbered," I suggest, "but he doesn't seem to be going anywhere."

"I know it's frustrating, Mel," Mr. Isley says. "But he can't keep this up forever. Eventually, he won't have any students and staff left to boss around. The district has to give him the boot eventually. So, what the teachers and coaches have decided is that we're going to be holding practices and rehearsals during our usual classes. It'll require some shifting and cooperation. Several of you are in both the dance and theater shows. We're going to share time with those students."

I huff. *Phenomenal. Now I'm going to miss half of both rehearsals for the shows.*

"Melanie, we'll make it work," Mr. Isley assures. "Neither Ms. Ferry nor I are worried about you missing some of our time. We're prepared to work through scenes and pieces that you aren't in during the time each of you isn't with us."

I nod. "I need to fill you in on something, Mr. Isley."

"We'll discuss it shortly. First, I need a few minutes to work out the schedule with Ms. Ferry. In the meantime, you're free to roam about the theater."

We all nod, and everyone heads to our separate areas in the big space.

Adam and I are left alone in the back of the auditorium. He laces his hand with mine and pulses down our connection, "*Are you okay?*"

I sigh and pulse back, "*No worse than usual.*"

"*Thank you for helping me.*"

I smile the tiniest bit.

We sit in auditory and mental silence for a stretch before I finally send, "*Your CD broke me all over again.*"

"Me, too, Melanie. Me too." He looks down and closes his eyes. *"Can we do it this way? Friends?"*

I shake my head. *"I have no idea."*

He nods, quickly stands up, and heads down the aisle. I find myself alone and empty.

Mr. Isley comes over a few minutes later and sits down beside me. "What's up?"

I clear my throat. "Principal Buttrum had a humane moment with me after the assembly. He asked what really happened with Joel Stamp. I informed him about our history, and he looked stunned." I chuckle slightly. "Then I threatened him with a tit for tat. I'm telling you, the guy I talked with in that moment isn't the same guy who yells into bullhorns." I look at Mr. Isley with contemplative eyes. "I think he's trapped in this, just like we are."

Mr. Isley nods thoughtfully. "Sounds like we have another student council meeting to schedule."

CHAPTER *18*

I step out of my mom's car and stare pensively at Adam's house. Behind me, the passenger window rolls down.

"I'll wait here until you're inside," my mom chirps cheerfully.

Let's see how this goes.

Adam doesn't know I'm coming over, but a need to help him started nagging at me last night. I tried calling, but he didn't answer. My mom was headed this way to run errands anyway, so I decided to hitch a ride.

I take a deep breath and cross the lawn to the garage. Music rolls from the detached building, so I'm guessing Adam's inside working on a motorcycle. I softly tap on the door, then wait pensively.

"Go away," Adam barks from inside.

I grimace. I've never bothered Adam at home, and he's clearly not in a good mood. I send a pulse through our connection and feel surprise waft back. The door opens a moment later. Billy Idol hums through the open door as Adam smiles down at me. He's wearing one of his trademark tight gray undershirt tanks and a pair of black jeans. He's coated in motorcycle grease from head to toe, and I have to fight to meet his blue-eyed gaze instead of letting my eyes wander to places they shouldn't.

My lips twitch, and finally, a giggle slips out. I wave to my mom and watch as she drives away. When I look back up at Adam, he's amused.

"What's funny?"

I wiggle playfully and decide that a little flirtation can't hurt. "I've never seen you covered in your work before. It's hot."

Adam chuckles, glancing down with a touch of that sexy smolder every girl at Hollywood High is captivated by. "To what do I owe the pleasure?"

I tip my head to the side, suddenly unsure about the merits of this idea as Adam guides me inside and closes the door. The garage is hazy from the cigarette he must have just put out.

I take a grounding breath. "Trey's busy figuring out how to deal with all the baseball drama. I ended up with the afternoon free and thought I'd stop by and see if I could work on you while my mom runs errands. Your psyche still isn't healed all the way."

Adam sits on a stool and shifts his attention to something important looking on the worktable beside him. I have no clue what it is, but judging from the pieces scattered about, he's rebuilding a particularly intricate part of the deconstructed motorcycle standing in the middle of the room.

He chuckles. "So, Demitri wasn't available to laugh it up with?"

I bite my lip and shrug. "We aren't exactly speaking these days. No clue."

Adam flirtatiously slides his eyes my way. "Uh huh."

I laugh. "What?"

He motions me over and hands me a flashlight. "Don't move the light. I need to set this spring."

I carefully hold the flashlight while he works on a surprisingly delicate process. He gets the spring in place and attaches a greasy disc over it. When he's done, he sets the contraption down and takes the flashlight from me. It leaves my hand greasy.

He smiles softly. "Motorcycle grease looks good on you."

"You always faintly smell like it. I love that."

Adam's expression is unreadable as he swivels his rolling stool and faces me. He takes my greasy hand and presses it against his chest. With a seductive smirk, he wipes my hand off on his tank top. My lips part, and without intending to, I inhale sharply. He leans closer to me, and I experience a flash of conflicted anticipation. He surprises me when, instead of kissing me, he rubs the tip of his nose against mine.

Then he presses our foreheads together. "Put your hair up," he murmurs.

I pile my hair into a messy bun and tie it together with the scrunchie I'd been wearing around my wrist. Throughout the process, my hands shake. Adam has me spun out.

"How much do you care about what you're wearing?" he asks.

"Not at all," I breathe. "It's just a grungy Sunday outfit."

"Good," he says before pulling me in and wrapping his arms around me. Before I can protest, he rubs his cheek against mine.

At once, I relearn to breathe. "This is a bad idea."

Adam's arms tighten around me. "I'm just hugging you."

"You aren't just hugging me, Adam."

He chuckles darkly. My pulse thuds. He grips the back of my tank top and eases it up just enough to reveal my stomach. He stares in my eyes as he slides his hands around my sides and across my stomach, leaving a greasy black finger trail.

My resolve wavering, I squeeze my eyes closed. I reach over and run my fingers through the grease covering the gadget on his workbench. I rub my fingertips together before placing them on his shoulders. His eyes close as I run my fingers from his shoulders down his arms. I close my eyes and lace my hands with his. His energy hums erratic.

I rest my forehead on his shoulder and choke out, "We need to get your mind fixed."

"You do realize that you could fix me another way," he whispers.

"Explain."

"As many lifetimes as we've had, Mel, sex with you would fix me."

I chuckle softly. "Excellent ploy to get my clothes off."

He cups my jaw and looks in my eyes. "All bullshit aside. You and me . . ."

I take a shaky breath.

"Melanie, I don't know how many lifetimes we've had, but I know you. I know us. We can try to play this right-and-wrong game. We can try to be appropriate and maintain these boundaries. The real question I have, though, is *why*?"

"Umm . . . Because, you have a fiancée. Remember her? Blond. Like a big sister to me. Loves to fistfight."

Adam tips his face down. The light from his workbench catches his angular jaw just right. His expression looks pained as he squeezes his eyes closed. He unexpectedly pulls me in tight. I wrap my arms around his head, and he rubs his cheek against my bicep.

He stands, picking me up, before grabbing the grease container. I wrap my legs around his waist, which is a terrible idea, but apparently we're headed somewhere and I'm along for the ride. He crosses the garage and opens a door on the far side of the room. I look over my shoulder and realize that Adam lives in a room off the garage. I don't have time to contemplate this because he closes the door quickly. Sunlight faintly leaks around the edges of the blinds, pulled down over the one window on the other side of the room. The shadowy room smells of Adam's cologne.

He sets me down and pulls off his grease-covered tank top. My head drops as blazing discontent rips through me. This has always been the problem with Adam. Right or wrong, we're drawn to each other. These soulmate connections run deep, but there's nothing quite like my connection with Adam.

He tips up my chin and stares at me in the shadowed light. "We aren't going there, Mel. I won't do that to you because you're conflicted. Breathe."

Not realizing I had been holding my breath, I exhale sharply. He sets the grease container on his dresser and dips his fingers in it. He puts his fingertips on my forehead, and my breath catches again. He slowly runs his fingertips down my face, the same way Trey always does. An unexpected sob retches from me. Now Adam looks pained again. He pushes *play* on his CD player. "Careless Whisper" echoes through the room.

I can't help a surprised giggle. "George Michael? That's the last thing I expected out of you."

Adam laughs quietly. "I'm a dancer, remember? It's a good song."

My gaze shifts seductively, and his eyes turn a stormy blue. He dips me low before snapping me upright. He puts his hands around my hips and starts to dance with me. As usual, he's an excellent lead. He turns me out and back in. I slide my knee up the side of his leg as he grips my hip.

I look up at Adam with big eyes.

His expression strains around the edges. "Those eyes kill me," he whispers. "Every time you look at me like that, everything in me melts."

"I'm scared," I whimper.

"Scared of me?" he asks cautiously.

Frantically, I shake my head. "I'm scared *without* you."

His expression morphs sad, and suddenly, he looks ageless. I realize that I'm seeing the real him. He never shows all his cards. He always has a wall up. Not today.

I touch his cheek. "Do you only get that look with me?"

He nods slowly. "You're the only one who deserves to see who I really am."

"Valerie?"

He shakes his head, lacing his hand with mine. He holds our hands between us. "This . . . this doesn't exist with anyone else." He turns me around and slides his hands up my back, under my tank top.

"I'm not wearing anything under my top," I inform breathlessly.

Without a word, he pulls the tank top over my head and drops it to the floor. I glance over my shoulder, watching as he dips his hands in the oily black grease. He puts his fingertips featherlight on my shoulders and runs them slowly down my back. My head drops as he metaphysically clears my tension.

He wraps his arms around me, pressing his hands on my rib cage, leaving black prints. With his arms wrapped tight, he sways me right and left before turning me around to face him. He puts his hands around my neck and eases my head back with his thumbs on my jaw. I close my eyes but can feel his gaze slowly slide down my front.

He lifts me up. We're suddenly face-to-face, inches apart. I reach over and dip my hands in the grease container. I graze my hands across his neck before lightly running my fingertips from his forehead to his chin.

"I have past-life dreams of you," I whisper. "You're always covered in battle dirt and war paint."

Adam opens his eyes. "I have so many memory flashes of you. Old ones from lifetimes a long time ago."

I grip his jaw and ask with desperation, "What happened to us?"

He looks deeply into my eyes before turning his head. I follow his gaze, and we stare at our reflection in the mirrored doors of his closet. We're both covered in oily black lines and smudges. He sets me down and turns me to face the mirror. His hands slide over my shoulders, clasping in front of my bare chest. We stare into each other's eyes in the mirror. We both look older, lifetimes of what we mean to each other thrumming through us.

"*I* happened to us," he says softly. "This is my fault."

"Us standing here, with your handprints on me while I'm topless, is cheating."

"I don't give a damn," Adam growls. "You're my girl. Trey's lucky this is the worst we're doing."

"How can Trey be my soulmate? It doesn't work this way with him."

Adam shakes his head. "I don't know. All I know is that everything about you and me is primal. I don't need words. I feel you from miles away. I know you in a way that only thousands of years can shape."

When I turn, he loosens his grip just enough so that I can face him before he squeezes me against his chest. He stares over my head in the direction of the mirror. His breathing shallows, and I feel panic roll through him. He curls around, wrapping his arms around my head. He presses my face against his bicep, and I squeeze my eyes closed. Matching panic blazes through me as I hang on tighter around Adam's waist. We're trying, but we're both aware that we can't make it without each other.

My hands shake.

"You're okay," he whispers.

I look up at him. "You're not," I say softly.

He closes his eyes as I press my hands against either side of his head. He picks me up so I can put my forehead on his. I dive into this mind.

In my mind's eye, Adam is there. He rushes to me, grabbing my face. The metaphysical him kisses me hard. I gasp as something builds in my chest. Without warning, a booming, healing energy explodes from my hands that are pressed to Adam's head in the physical world.

He gasps, and his arms shake. We watch in our minds as healing energy reverberates through Adam's psyche. It settles, rock solid, with a resounding boom.

Adam looks at me in our minds. *"Well, all right. Looks like you fixed me."*

I can't help but laugh. *"Apparently. That was easier than I expected."*

He smiles softly. *"If we go back to reality, will you spend some time with me, just being us?"*

I shake my head. *"We've been through this. It does nothing but hurt the people we're with."*

"Trust me."

In our minds, we close our eyes.

I open my eyes in the real world to find Adam staring at me, our lips so close we could easily kiss.

"Trust me," he says.

I nod. He sets me down. He pulls me in and starts slowly dancing with me. We dip and sway, ease and breathe through the movement. He never crosses a physical boundary, but we both know this is far more erotic than the boundaries he's avoiding. He reaches over and coats his hand in grease again. He puts his fingertips on my stomach. I give in, backbending until my head touches my calf. He picks me up and drapes me over his arm before running his hand from my stomach to my neck. I gasp and ease myself upright, gracefully wrapping my arms around his neck. He guides my head to rest on his shoulder. We inhale and exhale together.

Without a word, he carries me across the room and opens a door. He sets me on my feet in the pitch-black room and closes the door behind us. I feel a tap on my ankle and lift my foot. He eases my shoe and sock off. I lift the other foot, and he takes my other shoe off. His hands land on my hips, and my black leggings drop to the floor.

"Bad idea, Adam," I whisper.

"I told you to trust me," he says.

I scoff. "It's me I don't trust."

He doesn't answer. Instead, the sound of shower water splashes nearby. Adam runs his hand down my arm until he finds my hand. I'm guided forward before he lifts me over a tile step-up. He turns me around in the darkness, and hot water cascades down my back. The smell of Irish Spring soap fills the steamy air. In the dark, the scents and sounds are profoundly vibrant. I'm usually afraid of the dark, but something about being in the pitch black with Adam allows me to breathe.

His hands slide down my sides before he turns me around and starts soaping my back. He tips my head back and rests it on his shoulder. "Close your eyes," he whispers.

I do as he instructs. His soapy hands slide down my face. I rinse my face and pivot, guiding him under the water. I run my hand along the wall, finding the little shelf where the soap sits. I make suds in my hands before running them from his shoulders to his wrists. I soap his chest, then turn him around and start on his back. He washes his face before I hear him shift. His hands slide around my waist and turn me so my back faces the water. He picks me up.

I drape myself over his chest and rest my head on his shoulder. The water slides down my back as he holds me.

"I love you," he says.

The words escape my lips in a whisper. "I love you too."

I get choked up as he holds me and I work through how perfect things always are with him. I've seen how this works, though.

"What are you thinking?" he asks. "You have me blocked."

I manage to get control of my heartache enough to say, "It's always perfect when it's just us. Then you're gone. You're like water vapor. You seem so real, but you always disappear."

All he can manage to say is, "I'm sorry." He leans in, our lips barely touching.

I make the sudden decision that if Adam wants me back, I'm his. "Are you seriously marrying Valerie?"

He freezes.

I wait, giving him the opportunity to process what I've asked. The silence that stretches speaks volumes. My stomach drops. I inhale sharply and turn my head to the side. "You almost had me," I whisper.

"Melanie . . .."

"Put me down, Adam. I'll be your girl, but I won't be your whore."

Adam sets me down. "You've never been my whore," he hisses sternly. "I can't believe you just said that!"

I step out of the shower, leaving him behind the curtain. I reach in the dark, and my hand lands on a towel hanging on the wall. I dry off quickly, leaving the towel on what I think is the sink. Then, I paw around for my clothes and grab the doorknob.

Just as I leave the bathroom, I gasp and double over. The usual Adam-heartbreak rips through me. I toss on my slightly greasy tank top and leggings, then pull my socks and shoes on quickly. Just as

I rush across the room to leave, Adam comes out of the bathroom with a towel wrapped around his waist. I look at him, and the tears I usually save for when I'm alone brim in my eyes.

"Melanie, Valerie and I make sense," he explains. "We both graduate this year. She plans to help me build my custom motorcycle business. You still have three more years of high school!"

"Three more years of high school?" I sputter out. "Are you shitting me?"

Adam looks bewildered.

I toss my hands in the air, anger burning through my tears. "What the hell happened to lifetimes together? You're worried about three years?!"

He stares at me, blinking rapidly. As usual, my logic seems to have stumped him.

"You're welcome, by the way," I say. "My soulmate obligation is done."

He looks like he can't keep up with my swift change of topic.

I gesture his way. "Why the fuck didn't you have Valerie fix your busted ass psyche? Huh, Adam?"

"She's not an energy worker," he manages. "You know that."

I nod. "Right. She couldn't fix you, because she's a Normal. We . . ." I gesture between him and me. "We aren't normal. What we deal with, what we need, isn't normal. My apologies for being three years too late for you." I take a gasping breath, my head spinning.

"Even when I seem like I've disappeared, I'm not gone."

"I'm lost," I whisper.

"You aren't lost, Melanie."

I open the door that leads into the garage. "Without you, I'm lost. Good thing Valerie's been found. That fixes everything, right, Adam?"

I leave without giving him a chance to reply.

I check my watch. My mom won't pick me up for an hour. I glance down the street, realizing that Demitri's house is only a short walk away. I head that direction, figuring that today is apparently when I further screw up the already screwed.

Might as well give this a shot. I miss my best friend.

The walk is surprisingly pleasant. I arrive at Demitri's house in a far better mood than I was in when leaving Adam's place. But then, one look at Demitri's Jeep in the driveway washes away my contentment. My heart hurts all over again.

I take a breath, warring between wanting to run and needing to do this. Before I can get up the nerve to walk up the pathway to his door, Demitri steps out to his front porch. "You planning to stand there forever, or would you prefer to come inside?"

The invitation helping still my discontent, I exhale. "Yes, please."

I cross the lawn, and at the door, Demitri hands me a Cactus Cooler. I smile slightly, and he offers an awkward smile in return. He follows me inside, where I pop the top on my soda and take a swig.

Mr. Cantrell breezes by on his way out the door. He stops long enough to hug me and tweak my messy bun before leaving.

Now that we're alone, Demitri clears his throat and gestures to the couch. I put my soda on a coaster on the coffee table and start to sit. I stop midmotion, realizing that my leggings are covered in grease.

"Any chance you have an old towel?"

Demitri looks at me quizzically.

"I'm covered in motorcycle grease from Adam's garage." I roll my eyes.

Demitri chuckles. "Lovely. I see you're making the rounds."

I laugh. "This stop may be different from that one, unless you intend to get me naked, coat me in motorcycle grease, coax me into the shower with you, and then inform me that I'm too young and immature to be yours."

"Wowww." Demitri's jaw drops.

"Indeed." I chuckle, but it holds no humor. "I fixed his noggin, though, so it wasn't a total waste."

"I guess that's something."

He leaves briefly, returning with a couple of old towels. He drapes a towel on the leather couch. I sit, and he drapes a towel over my chest. I scrunch my face, confused by the second towel.

He smiles softly. "I intend to hug you, and I like my new Rusty surf shirt."

With a giggle, I survey his white shirt. It really is nice.

Demitri sits next to me and purses his lips before making a clicking sound with his tongue. "Is it safe to assume that we both know things are confusing between us?"

My only reply is to nod.

He sighs. "Is it also safe to assume that you're as aware as I am that what we could go a lot of directions that would likely work?"

I nod again. He looks my way.

"Demitri, it's not a secret that there's a vibe. That said, I'm not in your life to complicate it."

He rubs his forehead pensively. "I respect that, but you *do* complicate it."

"Why and how?"

He shakes his head, unwilling to answer.

Uncomfortable and needing something to do with my hands, I let down my messy bun, flip my head, and gather my hair into an equally messy ponytail. I can feel Demitri watching me. I sit back up, and he turns my shoulder away from him. He studies my back before saying, "You have black finger trails on your shoulders."

I snort. "Lovely. My mom's going to be thrilled when she picks me up."

Demitri heads to the hallway and comes back with a wet washcloth in his hand. He pulls my tank top's spaghetti straps out of the way just enough to clean up the grease. He lifts the bottom of my shirt and runs the washcloth along my lower back. The usual attraction between us bubbles up, but we don't discuss it.

"Anywhere else?"

"Chest and stomach," I tease.

He hands me the washcloth. "You're welcome to finish cleaning up in my bathroom," he says with a politely caged tone.

"I didn't expect you to clean me up. Hence the playful tone."

He just stares back at me.

Awkwardly, I stand and make my way into his bedroom. In his room, there are pictures of Demitri and Victoria, newly framed. I study them briefly, and my heart hurts. *He's not mine, and it's ridiculous that I feel this way.*

In his bathroom, I attempt to get my head on straight. I quickly survey myself in the mirror and clean up what's left of the grease. It seems that Adam did a better job on my front than my back, but that's not surprising.

When I'm done, I leave the washcloth neatly folded in Demitri's sink and head back to the living room. He has his head in his hands with his elbows resting on his knees. I study him with my empathic ability. He's full of raging confliction about me, but I'm unsure if it involves the attraction between us or our friendship that's on the skids.

I cross to him and gently take his hands from his face. His hands in mine, I kneel to look him in the eyes. "I didn't come here to spin you out while you cleaned up Adam's finger trails. I came here because I miss my best friend. I'd like to get back to a good place with you."

Demitri nods. "I miss you also."

"Perfect." I smile. "Then you're D and I'm Meley. Giggle giggle, Fraggle Rock best friends."

He chuckles. "I love your quirky side."

"I know you do. That's why I'm always a Muppet with you. It's weird, but not, I suppose."

For a moment, he really studies me. "Do you want to be a Muppet with me?"

I shrug. "I want to be *something* with you, and a Muppet works. I'm good with this, D. Just please be my friend because it makes things better. That's all I ask."

"Forgive me?" His tone is hopeful.

"Always." I lean in and kiss him on the forehead. Then, I head for the door.

"Wait."

I turn expectantly. He crosses to me with the towel. He puts it over my greasy top and gathers me up, hugging me tight. I swallow hard, my heart protesting only for a moment before I decide to let this just be what it is.

He lets me go, and I open the front door.

"Cute pictures," I say over my shoulder as I step outside. "You two are stunning together."

He closes his eyes tight as I shut the door behind me.

The door opens again when I'm partway down the front walk. I turn to find that Demitri's crossing to me. He hands me my soda and kisses me on the forehead before going back inside. I leave, headed back to Adam's house, where my mom said she was planning to pick me up.

CHAPTER 19

I'm back to sleepless nights. When there's a tap at my bedroom window, I barely even stir. I set my book aside and brush the curtain back to find Trey outside. My heart flutters a little as I grin at him. He smiles back and gestures for me to come outside.

Happy to oblige, I quietly sneak down the hall and slip out the front door. Trey's waiting. He takes my hand as soon as the door closes behind me. He wordlessly guides me to his still-running car and opens the passenger door for me. I slip in with no clue where we're going, but it really doesn't matter. I need time with him to clear my head of the mess with Adam.

Trey slides in and closes his door. There's no music playing, which likely means he wants to talk. I gaze at his profile expectantly as he pulls away from the curb. He reaches out his hand, and I take it, anticipating one of our energy pulse conversations, but he doesn't send a message. I give him a slightly confused look.

"I thought I'd offer you a normal night," he says with a smile. "No confusion. No music that brings your intuition to life. Just us being us."

Tension I didn't know I was holding drains out of me as I

exhale. I lean my head back on the headrest and roll down my window, enjoying the cool night air. Trey squeezes my hand. The silence in the car is a welcome relief.

Without realizing it, I slip off on a light wave of much-needed sleep. The next thing I know, Trey is touching my arm and saying, "Babe, wake up."

I open my eyes, surprisingly refreshed from my unplanned catnap.

Trey smiles softly at me. "Apparently, you needed sleep."

"It's happening again," I explain. "I'm not sleeping much. When I'm with you, I can sleep, but I know that's not fun for you. I'm sorry. I didn't mean to doze off."

He shakes his head. "I'm relieved that you can sleep with me. For a while there, I was the one keeping you up at night, conflicted."

I glance down ruefully. "You're the one who keeps me safe in my mind now."

Something about the statement apparently serves as a relief to him because he exhales and closes his eyes. After a long pause, he subtly nods as if to answer something in his own head. He looks at me and smiles before getting out of his car and rounding to my side. He opens my door, and after I clear out of the way, he reaches into his backseat and takes out two blankets. I close the door as he puts one of the blankets on the hood of his car. He picks me up and sets me on the blanket before joining me. He gets settled, leaning against his windshield and holding out an arm to me. I snuggle against him, my head on the spot on his chest that he's deemed mine.

He covers us up with the other blanket. After a long pause, he quietly says, "Give me your hand."

I extract my hand from the blanket nest and lace my fingers with his.

"Close your eyes," he says. "I want to try something."

When I smirk up at him, he laughs.

"Not what you're thinking," he says.

"Damn," I murmur.

He chuckles.

I close my eyes.

"Drop your shields and let me in," he instructs. When I hesitate, he adds, "Just do it, please. I'm not going to dig around for information about you and Adam. I already know he has you all kinds of heartbroken. This is about fixing you, not making it worse."

I drop my shields, and he puts his other hand flat on my back. Suddenly, a gentle energy thrums through me that spreads and starts to smooth out the jagged, hurt places stemming from my heartbreak with Adam. My muscles relax one by one. After a long time, the last of the emotional pain is gone, and I exhale a breath I didn't realize I was holding. I'm so relieved, I nearly feel dizzy.

"How did you do that?" I ask quietly.

He squeezes my hand. "I just knew I could. I started to realize it a few days ago but didn't have time this weekend to meet up with you."

Hesitantly, I say, "So, I heal Adam, and you heal me. Who heals you?"

Trey shakes his head. "No one. I'm the stable one. You two nuts are the ones with issues."

I bust up, and he laughs with me.

"It feels good to laugh," I say. "You always make things better." I rest my chin on his chest and gaze up at him. "Thank you. I love you."

He smiles and pulls me up so that my face is level with his. "You're welcome. Now can we get to what you were smirking about earlier?"

I run my fingertip along his jaw and kiss him. The entire world disappears, just like it always does with Trey.

CHAPTER 20

I walk up to the lunch table and toss my backpack on the pile of my friends' packs. I lean down and gently pull one side of Demitri's headphones from his ear. Wreckx-N-Effect's "Rump Shaker" pounds through. Demitri nudges me with his shoulder, a silent hello, and scoots to make room for me. I sit and look with him through the issue of *MAD* magazine he's perusing.

Victoria is on the other side of Demitri, engaged in a heated debate with Finley about the validity of Betsey Johnson's clothing. It appears that Finley is a staunchly loyal fan of the designer, whereas Victoria thinks her flashy clothing is tacky.

Who gives a damn?

I make a sarcastic face at Trey, who chokes back his PB and J sandwich.

Apparently, Trey's had enough of the debate. "Can it, Victoria," he says once he's managed to swallow his bite. "No one cares about Betsey Johnson."

Finley starts to argue, but I tune out the discussion. I've always struggled with inane teenage chatter. Demitri apparently agrees. He gives the *MAD* magazine to Trey, gets up, and steps to an open spot next to us. I turn around, leaning my back against the table and stretching my sore legs before crossing them at the ankles. I smile as Demitri dances in place. He's usually poetry in motion, but he's just grooving this time to the fun party song playing in his headphones.

Principal Buttrum waddles around the corner just in time to spot Demitri enjoying his lunchtime vibe. The weaselly old man scowls and shakes his head obstinately before stomping over to us. He reaches out and presses the *stop* button on the Discman in Demitri's hand.

Demitri's a kind person, but he has an arrogance that stems from being the most gorgeous guy at the school. His gaze meets Principal Buttrum's narrowed eyes, and all that arrogance floods away any sense of kindness.

"May I help you?"

His uppity tone makes me chuckle quietly.

Met with Demitri's Greek god physicality, Principal Buttrum is rendered temporarily stupefied. "I'm canceling all dance classes," he finally manages.

Demitri scoffs and glances behind Principal Buttrum. Mr. Isley has abandoned his chat with Javier to join us, and he appears stunned by the news.

"What do you mean?" Mr. Isley demands.

"Dance is a privilege that must be earned," Buttrum blathers. "Until these students can earn it back, we're canceling classes."

Mr. Isley scrunches up his face. "The dance classes at this school are district recognized PE courses. You can't cancel core curriculum classes just because you're pissed on a Monday."

Buttrum looks flabbergasted.

I can't help what falls out of my mouth. "You have no clue what you're doing, do you?" My tone holds an edge of wonder at the realization.

The principal flashes an intense, hateful gaze my way.

I nod with sarcastic delight. "Yup. Not a damn clue." I stand and put my hands out to the sides. "Here we are. How about we go another round?"

Buttrum can't seem to remember how to form words.

A small group of Magnet performing arts students is forming around us. Once the crowd, and my thoughts, settle, I saunter up to Buttrum. "You have no clue how to run a school. You have no clue how the funding, credentialing, or legalities work. You've been given no training. You're flying by the seat of your cheap slacks."

Principal Buttrum sputters and blushes a mottled red. That forehead vein of his throbs. "Seeing as how I can't cancel the dance classes, let's alter my proclamation, shall we? Anyone caught dancing during lunch or passing periods will be suspended. There will be no unauthorized dancing on these premises."

I crack up, not at all worried about how rude and insubordinate it is to laugh in the principal's face. "You must be kidding!" I manage to say finally. "What is this, *Footloose*? You think you can order us not to dance? Dance is like breathing for us. You've gotten away with a lot of crap, but I assure you that I don't give a damn about your *no dancing* edict or your master list of nonsense."

Mouths drop open all around Actors' Alley, but my fellow students don't get a chance to be shocked for long.

Demitri has unplugged his headphones and plugged in a small speaker that he keeps in his backpack. He turns to address the Magnet students. "Shall we show Principal Buttrum what he's been put in charge of?"

Smiles blaze all around the crowd.

"Places for 'Swing the Mood,'" Demitri announces.

I grin as Demitri gallantly holds a hand out to me. He and I are dynamic together. The dance department has a rule that you must be a sophomore to join Mr. Isley's all-star dance team, but after seeing Demitri and me partner together in *The Pajama Game*, an exception was made. I step up to my partner, taking the center spot as all the all-star kids get into place. A crowd quickly forms around us.

Hiram hits *play* on the Discman, and Demitri quietly says, "Here we go, baby girl," like he always does when we dance.

The dance team loves this piece. "Swing the Mood" is a lively compilation song of all the greatest swing and '50s rock hits, masterfully created by Jive Bunny and the Mastermixers. It's a blast from the past, and we gleefully Charleston, Mashed Potato, Twist, and Bop through the piece. Mr. Isley outdid himself on the choreography.

Halfway through, Demitri whips me around before lifting me against him and spinning three times. I squeal like I always do during this section of the song. He tips his head back, laughing. We're all exuding the kind of joy that we only find when we dance. Mr. Isley trains performers with incredible stage presence, but we don't have to fake our smiles during this one.

The crowd claps and cheers. Many students start dancing on the sidelines. Trey gives me an askance look, tipping his head Victoria's way. I nod permission. He starts dancing with Victoria, who seems elated. She's made it clear that she desperately wants to make the all-star team, but she just doesn't have the chops. I'm happy Trey took the opportunity to heft her up and swing dance with her.

The song comes to an end, and we all hold our final poses. The crowd goes wild as Demitri scoops me up and swings me around jubilantly.

He sets me down and puts his forehead on mine before quietly informing, "I adore you."

I grin at him.

The crowd quiets as Principal Buttrum breathes out, "You're all incredible. I didn't know you could do that."

Demitri turns to Principal Buttrum and politely informs, loud enough for the crowd to hear, "First, thank you. While I usually try to be humble, I'll agree with you that we're incredible. I know you're trying to get your footing around here, and you need to understand that this school serves a purpose. It's not the purpose you think. This isn't a prison where we bend to dictators. This is a home where stars shine. Period. The buildings aren't the magic. We are. This school draws extraordinary talent that the students have worked tirelessly to cultivate. You can't take dance from the school simply because, while we're still breathing, we dance. It lives in us."

Principal Buttrum's expression shifts. The change in him is stunning. He's suddenly looking incredibly concerned, reminiscent of our brief encounter on the stage last week.

"Go enjoy your lunch," Mr. Isley announces to the crowd.

After everyone disperses, the student council and Mr. Isley step up to Buttrum.

"You all need to leave," the principal says quietly.

"Don't mind if I do," Tanner yips exuberantly.

Principal Buttrum gives him an exasperated look, but it holds an unexpected edge of fatherly humor. "I didn't mean now, Tanner."

"Tell us what's happening, and we'll help you," Mr. Isley encourages.

Principal Buttrum swallows hard. "You really are talented, smart kids." Then, almost under his breath, he adds, "You all need to find other schools. Do it fast." He walks away at a quick clip, and we're all left standing there dumbfounded.

CHAPTER 21

Trey side-eyes me. He's radiating insecurity as we wheel into the student parking lot and park in advance of another day at school.

"Love, what is it?" I ask.

He slides an uncertain gaze my way. "Do I need to be worried about Demitri?"

Concern bubbles up. "What do you mean? What do you know that I don't?"

With a sweet expression, Trey chuckles. "That's not what I meant, Mel. Demitri's your best friend. I assure you that you'd know if something was wrong with him before I would. I meant do I need to be worried about *you* and Demitri?"

I shake my head. "Where is this coming from?"

Trey shrugs. "The two of you dancing in Actors' Alley yesterday was eye-opening."

"Here's the deal." I smile softly at him. "On the dance floor, I fully admit that Demitri and I do have a connection, but you have nothing to worry about."

"He makes you happy in a way that seems different than I've ever seen in you."

I nod. "Very true. I'm grateful every day for him. I've found a joy when I dance with D that I've never had before. Dancing with him is special, and it means a great deal to me." I swallow hard and add, "I would normally say that I'd quit anything that makes you uncomfortable, but—"

"No, honey," Trey interrupts. "That's not what I'm asking for." He looks at his lap. "I just get insecure. He's kind of the whole package."

I laugh softly. "He isn't kind of the whole package. He *is* the whole package." I smirk at Trey. "But he isn't *my* package. Last time I checked, you're my package."

Trey grins slyly. "I'll give you a package."

"Oh, yeah?" I giggle.

He scoops me up and pulls me into his lap. He kisses me and tickles my sides.

When we get to class, Mr. Jenson's sitting at the teacher's desk. Presley and I grin at him and take our seats in the half-empty room.

"Hello, girls," Mr. Jenson says. "I take it the line's still around the block to get past the punch card machines?"

Presley takes off her sunglasses and slumps in her chair. "None of the cards are in alphabetical order, and it's the most mind-numbingly slow chaos I've ever been tortured with."

"The cards aren't even divided up by grade level," I inform.

Mr. Jenson nods. "I've got an idea about why Buttrum's doing this, but I can't prove it."

Everyone leans forward in their seats.

"Do tell," Deb says. "Arch's been trying to figure out Buttrum's motive."

Mr. Jenson clears his throat. "I overheard Principal Buttrum on the phone in his office while I was repairing a door that he kicked a hole in during one of his infamous fits. Apparently, the district has a policy that extensive truancy is grounds for removal of any student enrolled in a Magnet program." Mr. Jenson glances at Presley and me. "He's put together that most of the student council are Magnet students, and he's using the punch card machines to gather evidence to remove you all."

Presley slams her fist on the desk. "This explains why he's made sure the cards are all jumbled up."

The announcement system comes on, and Principal Buttrum's voice squawks through the room. "All students who punched in after the tardy bell are officially on a warning. Three late punch card marks will result in lunch detention with me. Five late punches will result in a week-long suspension. Eight late punch card marks will result in a hearing to determine your enrollment status. Also, from this moment on, *no more classes walking in lines during passing periods*. Discipline is key!"

The announcement system shuts off.

"Awww!" Mandie says sarcastically from her seat in the back row. "I liked marching to class with the drummers."

"Three punch card marks sounds awful," I say. "I'd sooner die than suffer lunch detention with Buttrum. But the five-punch-card suspension's starting to sound pretty good. I could use a break."

Presley stands up and crosses to the windows. "Half the students are still on the front lawn waiting to get into the school."

"Mr. Jenson," Deb says, "why are you in here today?"

He grins. "Looks like Principal Buttrum's insanity finally wore thin on the substitutes. The substitute teacher's union representative contacted the office this morning and said they will no longer be providing substitute teachers to our school. Buttrum gathered all the auxiliary staff and assigned me, a couple yellow jackets, several secretaries, and a few of the cafeteria ladies to classes that have absent teachers. I got to the meeting first and looked over the list. I volunteered for this room permanently until a teacher is hired—for two reasons. First, I want to make sure you student council kids stay informed. I hear things that no one else does. People always treat the maintenance man like he's invisible, and it comes in handy. Second, I want in on your plans."

I flash an evil grin at Mr. Jenson. "Welcome to the fold. We need as many allies as we can get."

Mr. Jenson nods. "Thank you. I'm always finding out helpful information. I'll make sure to pass along tidbits as I get them."

Once everyone is in their seats, Mr. Jenson stands and starts handing out worksheets that serve as a review of chapters twenty through twenty-two, which we've already learned.

We all get to work.

Five minutes before the bell, Mr. Jenson says, "Class. Your attention please. I've written your homework on the board. Please take it down in your day planners and pack up."

After she packs up, Susan comes over to sit beside me. "This is going to sound crazy, but I'm excited to have homework. I'm going over to Hiram's later, and I'll do my homework with him."

I grin at Susan, more than ready to take advantage of the rare opportunity to just be normal teens. "You and Hiram are so perfect together. How are things going with you two?"

She looks down, radiating happiness. "He's the one. We'll end up married. I love him."

Deb smiles. "I'm glad, Susan. You two deserve to be happy."

Susan grins back at Deb and squeezes her arm. Susan hasn't always been the most popular girl. She used to be a childish, ass-kissing nightmare, but pairing with Hiram seems to have made her more tolerable. We've all come to embrace her as a friend.

"I hate to break up this normalcy," Presley says, "but we need to find Arch and fill him in on what Mr. Jenson told us."

"Arch will be near the commons," I inform. "That's the best place he's found so far to keep an eye on the students and make sure everything's okay. Buttrum's usually hovering around there with his stupid bullhorn, and Arch doesn't like to let the troll out of his sight. Let's see if we can find him."

When the bell rings, we join the swiftly moving flow of students in the hall. Deb leads the way, and we rush down the south stairs and out the exit by what used to be the teacher parking lot before their access was barred by Buttrum's twelve-foot-high zookeeper gate. We make it quickly to the commons, where we find most of our group gathered. Looks like they had the same idea we did.

"Any trouble during first period?" Arch asks.

We all shake our heads.

"We had Mr. Jenson as our substitute teacher in algebra," Presley says. "He's going to be our permanent sub until a new teacher's hired. He filled us in on some insider information, and he plans to keep us in the loop. He wants to help with our plans."

Arch furrows his brow and nods. "That's going to come in handy. I like Mr. Jenson. He's a solid dude."

I fill in Arch on the punch card nonsense.

He cracks his knuckles. "None of us have a truancy problem, so Buttrum had to manufacture one for us. Crafty of him. Okay. I'll figure out a plan on that. In the meantime—"

"I think you may be wrong about—"

I'm interrupted by Marcus, who says, "Uh-oh," as he's pointing across the quad.

Trey and Curtis are at the front of a pack of varsity and junior varsity baseball players who are storming from the athletic department building and through the quad. Even from our vantage point across the school, it's easy to see that they're pissed. Our group heads that way, and Curtis stops in front of Arch, looking so mad he can't get a sentence out.

"What's happening?" I ask Trey.

He blows past me without answering. We turn around and see Principal Buttrum walking out of the two-story building with his trusty bullhorn in hand.

Trey gets to Buttrum. "Joel's *dad*?" he screams. "*Really?*"

The principal puts the bullhorn to his mouth and yells in Trey's face. "*Yes, really*! Coach Stamp is my new hire for the baseball coach position."

My heart seizes. Panic makes it hard for me to breathe. Coach Stamp helped Joel try to kidnap me from my house, but charges were dropped because he wore a ski mask and left no evidence. I know it was him. I panic at the thought of him being a teacher at the school.

"Crap," Arch says. "We better move fast or Trey's likely to beat Buttrum to death with that bullhorn."

Arch leads the pack as we run across the quad. Arch grabs Trey and pulls him back right before he can attack Principal Buttrum. Mr. Isley runs up just in time and takes Trey's place in front of the principal.

"What's this about?" Mr. Isley asks Buttrum.

The principal wears a satisfied smirk as he looks around the growing crowd of students. He raises his bullhorn to his lips. "I've hired the best baseball coach around. Coach Stamp took our team to state three years in a row in the eighties. He's agreed to return to lead our school to *victory*!"

The students start to half-heartedly clap, but then Trey steps into the open circle.

"Coach Stamp is a plant!" he hollers. "He's Joel's dad. You remember Joel? The bully who terrorized this place with his pack of Drones? The one who's in jail for attempting to murder Melanie? The guy who led the same kids who kidnapped and tortured Adam? He *murdered* Adam's best friend. Your applause is poorly timed."

Everyone exchanges glances. Then, all heads turn as a new voice rings out. The crowd splits, making a bizarre parting-of-the-Red-Sea aisle for a man I can only assume is Coach Stamp. I've never seen his face, but the resemblance to my old nemesis is uncanny. And he's wearing the old uniform that the Drones sported when they used to be the student council. His white dress shirt, thin black tie, and black slacks are enough to make some of the students around us shiver.

"Good *morning*, students!" Coach Stamp hollers jovially. "I'm so *honored* to be back at Hollywood High!"

"This is insanity," Arch hisses.

My jaw is dropped. Joel's dad, in a Drone uniform, is the last thing I expected to encounter today. My hands start to sweat, and I'm shaking. The Drones are all in jail now, but they apparently have a whole lot of backup that surfaces. They're like locusts, returning over and over.

Coach Stamp stops in the middle of the open circle surrounded by students and asks in a lilting, sugar-sweet voice, "Is Melanie Slate here?"

"Not this again," I mutter.

Bear and Darren are clearly thinking quickly because they subtly shift their stances, their shoulders coming together in front of me to block Stamp's view. I can see Trey's face between the crack in their shoulders. He has turned an ashen shade of gray. Adam's on the other side of our group. He tries to get to me, but Bear reaches out and stops him from drawing attention to us.

A student behind me gently takes my elbow and pulls me back, stepping in front of me. Another student does the same thing, and the students continue subtly shifting me back until I'm buried somewhere in the middle of the crowd. A set of arms snakes around my shoulders from behind. I look up into Drake's hazel eyes.

He leans down and whispers, "We've got you."

I glance from the right to the left, discovering that the entire basketball team is surrounding us. "You can't hide me forever," I whisper back.

"I will, if you'll let me," he says flirtatiously.

"Where is Melanie Slate?" Coach Stamp asks again, more aggressively this time.

By now, everyone knows the story about Joel hanging me over the edge of a balcony, trying to kill me. No one says a word, and no one's eyes flick my way. They're going to try to help me.

Principal Buttrum stands up on the metal railings that separate lines at the commons student store. "Come out, come out wherever you are," he yells into the bullhorn.

"Duck down, Mel," Drake whispers.

I bend at the knees, doing as he suggests. My heart's racing, and my hands are clammy. The fear has my blood rushing in my ears. I'm on the ground, surrounded by hundreds of legs, reduced to cowering. The thought causes a sudden anger to boil through the fear. This isn't supposed to be how I live my life anymore. The old Melanie was a ghost in junior high. She would've hid. But the new Melanie doesn't do this. My stepfather always tells me that our family doesn't lie down on the battlefield, and here I am doing exactly that.

The dark-water side of me starts to roil up from my depths. An adrenaline rush hits, and it only adds fuel to my anger. *This is* my *school. This is* my *home. I'm not hiding.*

I stand and start pushing my way back toward Stamp and Buttrum. Drake and the basketball team rush forward, surrounding me, acting as bodyguards while I make my way to the clear circle in the middle of the crowd.

"What are you doing?" Drake hisses.

"They're going to find me either way," I tell him. "They have the class schedules. I'd rather do this now, where all these students can see."

"No one touches her," Drake says to the basketball players. "Got it?"

"Man," one of the players says quietly, "you've got it bad for her."

Drake sighs. "Yeah, I know."

Heads swivel, everyone watching as I work my way through the crowd with the basketball team in tow. I push through Bear and Darren last before stepping into the open circle. Trey's looking at me with fear in his eyes as Drake and the basketball team form a half circle at my back. Trey looks over my shoulder, I assume at Drake, and gives him a slight nod as if silently asking him to keep me safe. Drake steps closer, putting his hand on the small of my back. Trey's gaze shifts to Principal Buttrum and Coach Stamp.

The latter locks eyes with me, and his expression morphs into a rage-filled mask that reminds me so much of his son.

My soul shrinks. *I see where Joel gets it from.* "You rang?" I say in a voice that sounds far braver than I feel. I raise an eyebrow and put my hands on my hips.

Coach Stamp glares at me. "She's a brave little skank, isn't she?"

All the students' eyes narrow as they glare at him. Jaws tighten all through the crowd. If this guy tries anything, something tells me *all* the students will attack.

I hit Coach Stamp with a sarcastic smirk. "How's the hand doing? Did it scar when I bit you?" I turn to survey the crowd.

"Joel Stamp broke into my house and tried to kidnap me the night he was released on bail. Coach Stamp here helped him. The apple doesn't fall far from the tree."

Stamp's mouth falls open. He's clearly shocked by my blunt statement. But just like his sociopath son, he quickly recovers. He grabs the bullhorn from Principal Buttrum, puts it to his mouth, and pushes the button. "Melanie Slate, head to the athletic department office. I need to speak with you privately. Security, please escort her."

The six yellow jackets rush toward me, and Drake and the basketball team step in front of me. Faced with fifteen of the tallest, most muscular guys on campus, the yellow jackets take a few hesitant steps back.

Buttrum's voice rings out through the bullhorn. "You heard Coach Stamp! *Grab her!*"

Drake turns and tells Demitri to get me out of there. Demitri pulls me back.

"Block them," Drake hollers.

Dozens of students lock hands, creating row after row of hinderances to the yellow jackets' progress.

People shift as Demitri pulls me backward through the crowd. Dante steps in front of us, his bandmates creating a circle around Demitri and me.

"Stay with us," Dante says.

"The guys around here are proving to be rather charming this morning," I say to Dante with a smile.

"You're one of the school sweethearts," Dante replies. "We don't negotiate with terrorists or trade our treasures for threats."

"Remember that line," his lead singer hisses. "I have a song brewing that I need to write down when this bullshit's over."

"First, we have to get Melanie out of here. If something

happens to her, Trey will burn this school down with all of us trapped inside."

Coach Stamp must have snatched back the bullhorn because it's his voice that bellows, "Find her!"

Demitri's arms are over my shoulders, and the heavy metal band starts shifting to the side with me in the middle. The students all do what they must, adjusting to get us to out of the crush.

Mr. Jenson and Ms. G appear just as we reach the edge of the crowd.

"We're running," Mr. Jenson says. "Come with us."

"I'm going with her," Demitri tells Dante. "Let Trey know I'm driving her to Jinky's Café in Studio City, and he needs to meet us there. He's back there in the middle of the arm-chain fiasco. He'll panic when he finds out she's gone."

"We'll leave the alley gate open," Mr. Jenson says. "To hell with it. We need to just let the students out. Today's gone sideways."

We jog to the alley gate, leaving the crowd behind us. Mr. Jenson pushes a series of numbers into a keypad on the gate. It slides open, and we storm out of the prison school.

CHAPTER *22*

Demitri took a roundabout route to make sure we weren't followed. The drive was exactly what I needed to clear my head. We pull up to Jinky's Café, where Demitri turns off his Jeep.

"Are you okay?" he asks.

I huff and open my eyes. "Nope. Not one bit. Joel's dad is dangerous, and now I'm going to be trapped with him every day in that prison." I shake my head. "I knew about the Cobra mercenaries, but I wasn't prepared to face Daniel Stamp face-to-face." I scoff. "I don't know why I thought I wouldn't have to." I look Demitri's way, my chin quivering. "Whatever this is, it's obviously real. We can't keep speculating at this phase."

Demitri gets out and rounds the back of the Jeep. He opens my door, and I look up at him with scared eyes.

He stares off into space while he slowly shakes his head. "You're a magnet for trouble, Meley." He wraps me up in his arms, and I rest my forehead on his chest. His calm vibe helps chill me out.

Suddenly, I find myself giggling.

He tips up my chin. "What?"

I grin at him. "I doubt Trey will want to go to baseball practice anymore. My afternoons just got better."

Demitri laughs.

Our discussion is interrupted as a series of car doors slam shut and footsteps storm our way. We turn just in time to see Trey rushing at Demitri with his fist balled up. Demitri lets me go and backs up.

I jump in front of Trey. "What the *hell* are you doing?"

"Fuck you!" Trey snarls at Demitri. "I thought you were my friend!"

My gaze snaps from Trey to Demitri, who looks down at me with an expression that says he's just as confused as I am.

"Trey, look at me!" I exclaim.

He slides a furious gaze my way.

"What is this about?" I ask.

Arch and Tanner catch up and grab Trey, pulling him back as the rest of our group joins us.

"I can't believe you, Melanie!" Trey barks. "I trusted the two of you."

I rattle my head. "The two of *who*?"

Trey gives me a condescending look. "Don't play stupid with me."

I glance at Demitri, who's staring quizzically at someone else. My gaze shifts, and there stands Victoria with her arms crossed over her chest. She's sporting a snotty look on her stunning face.

"What is this about?" Demitri asks her.

Trey answers for her as he glares at Demitri. "Your affair has come out."

"You're having an *affair*?" I say to Demitri, shocked. "I didn't see that coming."

Apparently, I'm a clueless idiot because Demitri looks down at me, radiating amusement. "Trey thinks *we're* having an affair."

My eyes snap wide. "We are? How exciting!" I grin at Demitri, who still looks a bit nervous, and with mischief in my eyes, I chirp, "How's our affair going?"

He laughs while he hits Trey with a baffled look. "Not so good because I seem to have amnesia and can't remember any of it. Hell of a shame, too, because that's an event I wouldn't want to miss."

Trey starts to relax as our candid responses burn through his rage. He turns to me and asks in disbelief, "You aren't having an affair?"

I shake my head and send a thought bubble his way that clearly expresses how Demitri and I are just friends. Trey studies the bubble, knowing it's close to impossible to lie mind to mind.

"Are you telling the truth?" Adam sends to me.

I send back amusement. *"I'm not with Demitri."*

Adam quietly laughs.

Trey finishes studying what I sent and turns to Victoria. "Why did you tell me they're having an affair?"

Victoria stomps her foot and gives me a death glare. "Because they are!" She turns to Demitri. "I saw you two in the dance studio! She had her head on your leg. It was more than obvious. You were leaning down kissing her!"

Demitri looks at me. I bounce on my toes and jokingly nod with over-the-top enthusiasm.

"When was this tawdry public display?" Demitri asks Victoria. His tone shines light on how wackadoodle this whole thing is.

"Yesterday," Victoria says. "Fifth period."

Demitri laughs. "Yes, her head was on my leg," he says to Trey. "She lies on her side like that and reads when we have downtime in class during pieces we're not in. Her textbook was open on the floor. I leaned over her to read a question on the chapter review page that she was struggling with. I wasn't kissing her, or whatever nonsense you've been told. My back was to the door, so Victoria likely didn't know what was actually happening."

Trey slides an irritable gaze Victoria's way. "I trusted you on this. You made it sound like they were all over each other. I nearly hit Demitri, and he just helped get my girl out of danger. For the record, I'm fully aware that Melanie and Demitri lounge in the studio. It doesn't bother me." He turns back to Demitri and me and says, "I apologize. I should have known better. It's not a secret that Victoria's a gossip."

"I don't care if you *were* doing homework!" Victoria snaps at me. "Keep your head off my boyfriend's leg."

I take a breath and close my eyes as my dark-water side rises. When I'm calm enough to speak, I open my eyes and purr, "Victoria and Trey, I don't like being accused of things I didn't do. You get a pass this time, but if you *ever* accuse me of having an affair with Demitri again, you have my word that I'll ride him until he pops like warm champagne. Then I'll tell you about it myself."

Everyone's eyes snap wide, and they exchange amusedly shocked looks.

"Don't even think about it," Victoria snarls.

I narrow my eyes at her. "You're playing with fire! How about this? You use your gifts—" I gesture up and down at her, indicating her ample curves. "And I'll use mine." I gather a massive load of my seductive dark-water energy and send it out on a slinking, sensual blast. Everyone gasps as the invisible energy wave reaches them, and I feel Demitri's energy quake next to me.

I smirk at Victoria. "We'll see who comes out on top. Screw with me. I dare you. I'll burn my universe down just to piss you off."

Victoria looks like she's been gut punched. She hasn't been on the receiving end of the fire that lives in me, and she's suddenly taking me a little more seriously.

I turn to Trey. "The next time you have an issue with me, you come to me. Demitri's one of my best friends, and if you try to attack him again, I'll put you through the floor myself. He's the most honest person I know, and he flat wouldn't do what you're accusing him of. I, on the other hand, am suddenly pissed enough to consider it."

Demitri chooses that moment to subtly run his hand down my back where no one can see what he's doing. I fight not to gasp. My expression remains neutral, but my suddenly spun-out vibe courses through his hand before I can stop it.

"You and I are new," Demitri says to Victoria, "so I'm giving you a pass this time. But I hate gossip and bullshit. Don't make up stuff, don't assume, and don't stir up shit. I'll leave you if it happens again."

Victoria looks like she's going to cry.

"One more thing," Demitri adds. "Melanie has never been anything but appropriate with me. She's welcome to lounge on my leg. You don't get to dictate what I do."

Having had enough of this, I smile enthusiastically and change the subject. "Who wants pancakes?"

Marcus raises his hand, and everyone laughs, breaking the tension.

CHAPTER 23

"There are so many of you here today that we decided to order pizzas," Rich says to the crowd. "Plus, Carol wants to hear the details, and this frees her up from the kitchen."

"Thank you for having us," Arch says with a nod. "We've brought some additions with us today." He scans the crowded room. "Thank you, Dante, Drake, our quarterback Drew, Ms. G, Mr. Isley, Greg Bains, Mr. Walker, and Mr. Jenson for being here."

Greg Bains is one of the members of the school board who was so unceremoniously removed, and Mr. Walker was our principal up until winter break. In addition, Mr. Bentley and the whole student council are gathered in my living room.

Marcus's dad, Bruce, is sitting in a chair next to Rich. He leans forward and requests that we fill him in.

"We've got a slew of new problems," Trey explains. "Principal Buttrum fired the baseball coach and hired Joel's dad in his place."

Rich whistles low, and Mom leans back in her chair, closing her eyes.

Trey continues. "Obviously, the baseball team was furious when we found out Coach Stamp was hired. We headed to the commons to confront Principal Buttrum during the passing period. Coach Stamp came striding through the crowd and demanded that Melanie step forward."

"He had the audacity to wear the old black-tie uniform that the Drones used to wear," Valerie says. "He's making a point."

Trey turns to me. "Melanie, what were you thinking coming out from the crowd?" He looks angry, and it makes me nervous. The last thing we need right now is a fight.

I meet his intense gaze with as much calm as I can manage. "Administration has the class rosters. They were going to find me either way. At least this way, the students were all there to see what happened."

Understanding seems to wash over him. But then, his stern resolve returns. "You aren't going to school anymore."

Adam chuckles from his spot leaning against the wall on the other side of the room. He clearly knows where this is headed.

Trey looks at Mom and Rich. "We aren't learning anything anyway. We've spent every moment since we returned from winter break squabbling and playing childish games with the principal. No actual schoolwork gets done. She won't miss anything but a never-ending headache. Coach Stamp tried to kidnap her, and I'm scared he's going to do it again if he gets her alone. At this point, we can no longer deny that something real is happening."

Mom glances at Rich, looking unsure about what to do.

Rich considers the situation for a moment. "As much as I appreciate you filling us in on that tidbit, Trey, there must be a way to deal with this other than hiding. I've said a thousand times that our family doesn't roll over and play dead on the battlefield." He looks at Trey and sighs. "Son, I know how much you love Melanie. You have good intentions, but you can't wrap her in Bubble Wrap and hide her in a cabinet every time a bull rushes in."

Trey clenches his teeth. "I can, and I will if I have to."

Rich and Trey stare at each other for a moment before I clear my throat and all eyes turn to me.

I level Trey with a weighty stare. "Not that *any* of you seem to give a damn what I think lately, but I'm not going to hide in my house." I narrow my eyes. "We've talked about this!"

Trey turns back to Rich without so much as acknowledging what I said. "I don't want her there."

"Then maybe she needs to switch schools," Rich counters. "If it's that bad, we have other options."

Trey's eyebrows rise. "Good point."

"I'm not switching schools," I say to Rich. "Period. My education, my choice. Isn't that what you've always said?"

Rich looks impressed. "Well played, Mel."

Trey smirks at both of us. "Looks like we have a conundrum."

I glare at Trey before rolling my eyes at Adam, who smirks.

"I agree with Rich's original assessment," Mr. Isley says. "Melanie hiding at home will bolster Principal Buttrum's resolve, and it'll likely make things worse. I hate to see anyone in this group change schools. Every one of them is incredibly talented."

"Besides," Arch chimes in, "Daniel Stamp knows where Melanie lives, what with the kidnapping attempt. If she quits coming to school, he may switch gears and come for her here, where she doesn't have an army of students coached on protecting her."

Trey flinches and grits his teeth. "Damn. You're right. She's likely safer at school."

Mom looks mad as she turns an appraising eye toward the teachers, who are all sitting on one of the couches across from me. "Stamp is only one part of the problem. How is this principal getting away with this nonsense? He literally caused physical harm to Adam and put kids in danger by locking all the exits but one. None of this is legal."

"I agree," Ms. G says. "But Principal Buttrum has friends in powerful positions who are backing him. None of this could happen without that support. We're dealing with a situation I've never seen before in the school system, and I've been at Hollywood High my entire career."

Bruce clears his throat. "Marcus has kept me apprised of the daily happenings. I asked Greg and Mr. Walker to join us, hoping they can give some insight."

"Unfortunately," Mr. Walker says, "I don't have much to tell that's likely to be helpful. I was in my office early on the Monday morning that we returned from winter break. In strolls this man who said he was Mr. Dean from some district office I've never heard of. He told me I had five minutes to pack my stuff and get out because I was being replaced by some Napoleonic guy who was bouncing around like a toddler needing to go to the bathroom."

We all laugh.

"I came here today, one, to let everyone know that I support them," he says. "And two, to find out the latest since our first meeting."

Greg Bains leans forward and sets his elbows on his knees as he gestures adamantly with his hands. "The district level school board became aware of what's happening when I got a call from Bruce that the kids had orchestrated their rather amusing blue-clothing day. He filled me in, and the board immediately started making arrangements to fire Principal Buttrum. Next thing we knew, someone from the mayor's office showed up to our closed session emergency board meeting, where we were drawing up termination paperwork. He told us our services were no longer needed. They replaced everyone but Charlie Sisterno that day."

Arch's mouth drops open, dumbfounded. "The *mayor*'s office?"

Mr. Bains nods. "When I say that Joel's dad is well connected, it's an understatement. Before I knew there was trouble afoot, Charlie Sisterno was singing the praises of the Cobra Militia to me, saying they needed to be hired as security at Hollywood High. They cost ten times more than the current security officers, and I thought he was nuts."

My eyes widen. "I still don't understand how this whole move is justifiable. Unless it really is all about Daniel Stamp's 'kill Melanie' agenda."

Mr. Bains informs, "You kids are dealing with an insurmountable problem."

"Don't underestimate us," Adam says to Mr. Bains. "Insurmountable is what we do best."

Mr. Bains smiles. "So I've heard. Bruce filled me in on everything about Joel and the Drones. I'm keeping everyone from the old school board updated."

"Okay," Arch says. "Let's deal with one problem at a time." He looks at me. "Melanie, you have to go to school. As much as Trey won't like this, we need you. You're going to offer a great distraction, keeping Principal Buttrum busy while we continue getting to the bottom of what's really going on. And anyway, there's enough of us to protect you."

Many of the heads in the room nod.

Arch looks around the circle. "Drake, I need you and the basketball players to make sure Melanie gets from first to second period."

"Nothing will happen to her," Drake says readily.

I can't help but notice how both Trey and Adam give Drake a suspicious side-eye.

"Second period's a problem," Arch continues. "None of us are in that class with Mel."

"My band and I have her covered," Dante offers. "We're all in the class next to her and will make sure she gets to third period."

"I'm in third with her," Marcus chimes in. "And so are Drew and several of the football players."

"I'll rally the guys," Drew says. "We'll get Melanie to fourth period. Half the football team has a crush on her. No one's getting through us."

Trey rolls his eyes and huffs.

Adam grins at Trey. "Don't worry, man. They'll help keep her safe."

Trey hits Adam with a death glare.

"She's in Mr. Bentley's room for fourth period," Arch says, running down the list. "We'll all meet there and keep Melanie safe at lunch. We'll get her to fifth period in the dance building, and then everyone who has sixth-period theater class can meet at the dance building to retrieve her on their way."

"I'll stand with Melanie by the walkway and wait with her until her escort arrives to take her to sixth period," Demitri says.

"Has anyone considered that I really don't want an escort everywhere I go?" I ask.

"Sorry, Mel," Arch says. "This is the only way."

"Now, we need to deal with the problem of those ridiculous punch cards," Mr. Jenson says. "It's going to take no time for all the Magnet kids to collect eight tardies and be eligible for disenrollment."

"Fill us in," Rich says.

Mr. Jenson explains the punch card situation, and when he's done, I inform, "I think you may have that wrong. Judging from his reaction after the 'Swing the Mood' demonstration, I'm wondering if Buttrum isn't just trying to get rid of us before something bad happens."

Everyone exchanges looks as they consider this.

Arch clears his throat. "It's possible he's trying to save us, given Melanie's few interactions with him that were so different. Think about it. He's obsessed with extreme order, but the cards are all mixed up. Students are racking up tardies quickly. What if he thought of this plan as a way to remove kids from danger?"

"That may track. What if he's trapped in something he can't get out of?" I pause to ponder. "We've seen it before with Nurse Betty. She needed money and agreed to poison me. Seemed like a good plan, until she was trapped in it. The Stamp family is scary. They get what they want at all costs."

Adam rubs his face hard. "I don't give a damn about the layers. We just need to shut all this nonsense down and get Principal Walker reinstated. If something bad's happening, we *will* be there and we *will* deal with it. We're the only ones capable of handling it if things go south. So, what do we do about the freaking punch cards?"

"I'm baffled that you lot of creative schemers haven't figured this one out," Rich says. "Of all the problems you've been faced with, this is the easiest."

Everyone looks at Rich.

"By all means, fill us in on what you're thinking," Arch says.

"There's no way Principal Buttrum's making copies of over fifteen hundred cards every day." Rich shrugs. "Just steal the cards and get rid of them."

We all exchange amazed looks.

"We really are off our game," Tanner says.

"All right," Arch says. "Let's make a plan to steal the cards."

Dante breaks into a wide smile. "Leave that to me and my band."

CHAPTER 24

The line at the front doors of the school is moving surprisingly fast. We all grin at each other knowingly.

"I don't know what Dante and his band did," Arch says, "but whatever it was must have worked."

When we cross through the doors, everyone in student council bunches up so we can get a look at the metal cardholders. All down the hall, each slot has a pretty daisy sticking out of it. The cards are all gone. On the walls above each of the punch card machines are posters that say, *Make Love, Not War*, with daisies painted on them.

We all laugh. The sound of happiness must have roused Principal Buttrum from his stupor. He comes storming out of his office with his trusty bullhorn. He stares at the card holders, and his face goes slack for a second before he snaps back into his usual asshole expression. He gestures to the metal boxes as he glares at us and screams into the bullhorn, "Who did this?"

Along with the rest of the students nearby, we all stare at him, amused.

Victoria takes a daisy out of one of the slots and crosses to him.

"Cheer up, buttercup," she says. She tries to hand the daisy to him while everyone fights not to laugh.

Buttrum doesn't share our amusement. He waddles down the hall and turns the corner at a fast clip.

Presley puts her sunglasses on top of her head. "Everything about that man's hilarious."

Dante chooses this moment to join us.

"How did you manage all of this?" Arch asks him, sounding awed. "It had to take time to gather the cards, put all those daisies in the slots, and tape up the posters on the wall."

Dante grins. "It was easier than I expected. We got here an hour before school. Mr. Jenson made sure the front door was unlocked. We scurried in, and no one was around. We heard noise from Buttrum's office and peeked in. That clod was sitting there with his feet up on the desk watching an episode of *All in the Family*." He shrugs. "The five of us had our assignments. Two pulled cards, two put daisies in the slots, and one hung posters. We were done in ten minutes and slipped out."

We all chuckle. Then, the group heads upstairs to deliver me safely to first period. We get to the algebra room door, where Trey turns to face me. He runs his hands down my arms as he tips his head back and closes his eyes.

"She's going to be okay, Trey," Arch says.

Trey opens his eyes and shakes his head. "No one can keep her as safe as I can because no one loves her like I do. I know you'll all try, but if I can't be there, then it's not good enough."

Drake steps up, putting his hand on Trey's shoulder. "All joking aside, you have my word that no one will get to her."

Trey turns, looking Drake in the eyes. "She's my world."

Drake nods. "I understand that. She'd be my world too if she were mine."

"I'm not going anywhere."

"I know." Drake shrugs. "I've come to terms with the fact that, short of hell or high water, you aren't leaving Melanie. I'm not trying to help so I can steal her. It's going to take all of us to get through whatever nonsense Buttrum has planned. Until he's gone, you're going to have to trust some of us. You can't be everywhere all the time."

Trey returns his attention to me. "Worst case, you run as fast and hard as you can. If things go sideways, don't fight unless you have no other option."

I grin at him. "I fight better than I run."

"That's what scares me. You tend to throw blows first and ask questions later. If you fight them, it'll give Buttrum and Stamp an excuse to lock you up in a room alone with them. Once that door's closed, we're going to have to tear the damn building apart to get to you."

Adam cracks his knuckles. "Sounds like fun."

Everyone grins.

"Run," Trey says seriously. "Don't give them an excuse."

"I love you," I say.

"I love you too," he whispers before leaning down to kiss me.

As usual, the whole world slides away when we kiss. Only faintly do I hear Presley say, "Give them a minute."

Trey hesitantly ends our kiss when the tardy bell rings. "Whatever happens, I need you to be okay."

I nod and step away from him, and for the first time, notice that Bear's standing on one side of us, leaning against the lockers and looking away as if trying to give us a little privacy. Darren's standing on our other side, watching for trouble. The whole thing makes me feel like I have the Secret Service watching my back.

I squeeze Bear's hand as I pass him on my way into class, silently thanking him for giving Trey and me a second. Bear smiles at me. Then, he heads with Darren and Trey down the hall to their first-period classes.

Adam pushes away from the lockers down the way and steps to me. He laces his right hand with mine and pulses, *"Screw that. You fight like hell. If it's bad enough, I'll be able to feel it from a distance. Send a scream my way, and I'll be there to back you."*

I nod and smile up at him.

He pulses, *"Love you."*

"Love you too," I pulse back.

We drop hands. I head into class.

I'm the last of the students to settle into her seat for algebra.

Mr. Jenson smiles at us. "Looks like entering the school went better today. You all made it on time."

"Does anyone know who stole the punch cards?" one of the girls in the class asks.

Everyone shakes their heads. Presley, Susan, Deb, Drake, and I stay quiet.

"I've got no clue," Mr. Jenson says as he pats the bulging bag next to him on the desk.

Before anyone can ask questions, Mr. Jenson passes out worksheets for the class to complete. We all do our algebra work accompanied by the sound of a paper shredder eating up punch cards.

CHAPTER **25**

A group has gathered at the bottom of the bungalow stairs next to Mr. Bentley's room, and they're all dutifully waiting to escort me to lunch.

I roll my eyes. "I know we usually walk together anyway, but I feel ridiculous having a circle of bodyguards dragging me around campus all day."

Trey smiles. "Come on, love. It's just another day strolling through hell."

I laugh as we head through the quad. Turning the corner to the commons reveals Curtis engaged in a heated screaming match with Coach Stamp and Principal Buttrum.

We all exchange a glance.

"Looks like there's trouble," Bear says.

Dozens of students start gathering, everyone clearly wondering what this latest ruckus is about. Some of them move closer to our group, intentionally gathering around the sides and the back of us, side-eyeing me. It's like the whole school's planning to stay between me and Coach Stamp.

Curtis loudly hollers at the coach. "*Tryouts?* You're going to make us *try out*? We went to *state* last year!"

"What?" Trey screams. He abandons his spot next to me and pushes through Bear and Arch. "You want the whole baseball team to *try out again*?"

Adam shifts to take Trey's spot beside me.

Coach Stamp grabs Principal Buttrum's bullhorn. "That's right. This is my team now, and I need to make sure we have only the best of the best. Trey, *you* aren't invited to *try out*."

Curtis sputters. "You want the best of the best, but Trey isn't invited? Trey can hit a ninety-mile-an-hour fastball drunk and in a straightjacket. He *is* the best of the best!"

"Anyone but Trey is welcome to try out," Coach Stamp says into the bullhorn.

I murmur to Adam and Arch, "He's targeting everyone in our group who gave depositions against Joel."

Both guys nod.

Trey's so furious that he doesn't need the bullhorn to be heard at the back of the crowd. "Varsity baseball players, step forward!"

All the baseball players make their way through the crowd and step into the open circle.

"Any of you interested in trying out for Coach Stamp's new and improved roster?" Curtis asks them.

The baseball players all shake their heads.

"If Trey's out, I'm out," one of them says.

Coach Stamp hollers into the bullhorn. "Everyone that was on the team has *mandatory* tryouts on the field. *Now!*"

The players laugh and exchange looks.

"What the hell are you gonna do?" one of them asks. "*Make us play baseball?*"

The guys all shake their heads and smirk before melting back into the crowd.

Curtis glares at Coach Stamp. "We all quit."

Stamp has a blank look on his face. Something tells me it never occurred to him that he couldn't force the players to play. He likely thought they'd all jump through his hoops to do what they must to be a part of the team. He underestimated how frustrated the players have become after a few weeks of dealing with Buttrum.

After some thought, Coach Stamp yells into the bullhorn, "Junior varsity baseball players, step forward."

The JV players all filter through the crowd, lining up in the middle of the open circle.

Coach Stamp proudly announces, "Welcome to varsity, boys. You just got a promotion."

One of them scoffs. "I hate to tell you this, Coach, but the varsity and junior varsity teams aren't in competition. JV still has skills training to go through, and the varsity guys stay after practice regularly to help us. If you think we're going against those guys, you're sadly mistaken. As far as we're concerned, we're all on the same team."

Curtis gives the boy a nod of gratitude, and the whole JV team nods back.

Principal Buttrum and Coach Stamp both look shocked as they glance at each other.

Coach Stamp surveys the rest of the JV players. "How about the rest of you? You boys up for being all-stars and showing the *former* team members how it's done?"

Apparently, flattery from a jackass will get you nowhere because the players glare at Coach Stamp, and heads shake all down the line.

The JV players all turn their backs on Coach Stamp and Principal Buttrum, then fade into the crowd.

"Looks like the baseball teams are both disbanded," Curtis says. "All you get paid to do is coach baseball, right, Coach Stamp?

Or should I call you Mr. Stamp now, since it appears that your coaching services are no longer required?"

Coach Stamp sputters, and Arch steps forward before he can say anything more.

"Go enjoy your lunches," Arch yells to the crowd. "We're done here."

Principal Buttrum isn't about to miss an opportunity to yell at the students. "Master your behavior!" he bellows.

"Shut up, Buttrum!" Dante shouts as we all walk away.

CHAPTER 26

I watch as Valerie yanks Adam's arm practically out of the socket. I'm in fifth-period dance class. Mr. Isley is using our usual class time to hold a clandestine rehearsal for the dance show, and the cast is silently suffering through one of Valerie and Adam's infamous meltdowns. They fight constantly, and today they're in rare form.

Adam unceremoniously plunks Valerie on her feet and turns his back on her. He squeezes his eyes closed, frustration throbbing through his clenched jaw. He got stuck partnering her because she's tall and muscled. He was the best choice logistically, but this challenge has put a strain on their already boiling relationship.

Valerie tips her head back. "Just get me on your shoulder, Adam," she says condescendingly.

"You have to help with that process," Adam says, giving her the evil eye. "Hold your weight, prep the leap. This isn't rocket science. My shoulders still aren't right, and I can't lug you around. Do your damn job!"

My eyebrows nearly shoot to my hairline. I turn to Demitri, who's standing next to me.

He snakes an arm around my shoulder. "These two aren't going to make it through this duet."

He's right. The duet is complicated. It's all partner work. The timing is intricate, and frankly, Valerie's in over her head. She does excellent solo work, and she turns like a demon. Where she falls short is partnered lift timing. She's good, but this piece isn't a style she can handle.

My thoughts are interrupted as Mr. Isley barks, "Valerie, take a break. Melanie, you're up."

I look over my shoulder, baffled. "I don't have a solo in the show. I'm up for what, sir?"

Mr. Isley gestures to Adam. "I want you to demo the duet. You've been in every rehearsal. I know that you know it by now."

I snap my gaze to Demitri and make one of my sarcastic Fraggle faces. He snorts.

Valerie boils over. "No way in hell! Melanie isn't dancing with Adam!"

My eyes are huge as I glance from Valerie to Mr. Isley.

"You aren't cutting it!" he roars back at her. "Can it and take a break!"

Clearly everyone's patience is paper-thin lately.

I cut my gaze to Adam, who appears amused. He taps on the blockage I've erected between our soulmate connection, and I open my side.

"*Please do this*," he sends. "*It'll piss her off, but it'll be worth it.*"

I slowly shake my head.

"Now, Melanie," Mr. Isley orders. He points to the spot he wants me to take in the center of the studio.

With a huff, I cross to the spot. Adam steps up behind me, and our eyes meet in the mirror. He drapes an arm across my chest, settling us into the starting pose.

I take a deep breath, my mind working through the choreography I've seen but never done.

"I'll give cues when you need them," Adam sends. *"You can do this. Just keep up. I've got you."*

There's no time to respond because Pat Benatar's "Heartbreaker" blisters through the speakers and we're off like a shot. This piece moves like a freight train, but with our soulmate connection open, we hit the timing perfectly in the first section.

We get to the second section, and Adam lunges, facing away from me. I run up his back, leaping off. He catches me and spins four times quickly to the right. Using the momentum, I grab his hands and fly to the side. He snaps me back, and I careen with perfect timing across his chest to the other side. We turn and leap, lift and work through the piece flawlessly. The dance is seductive and suggestive. We grip and pull, rub and drag, with ease. Adam grins at me while Valerie fumes.

I'm suddenly nervous. A blistering turn sequence hits, and this is where Valerie far exceeds my skill level. I hit a quadruple turn that whips into fouetté turns.

When I nail the sequence, Demitri crows from his spot across the room, "Yesss, baby girl!" He's danced with me long enough to know what I can do when I get fired up.

I end my fouetté turns and look Demitri's way. He crinkles his nose playfully, and his eyes flick mischievously toward a furious Valerie. I grin back at him evilly. Adam grabs my hand with perfect timing, pulling me to him. He shoots a death glare at Demitri before scowling seductively down at me. He whips me to the side, and we both slide on our knees in opposite directions. I land by Valerie's feet and look up at her. She snarls, so mad that I'm positive this is going to come to blows. My dark-water side is loving it.

I scorpion my leg up and over, rolling my head seductively as I get to my feet. Adam's across the room, ready.

"I've never done this shoulder stand trick," I say in panic.

Adam gestures. "Come on, babe. I've got you."

I bark a rushed request. "Demitri, spot this lift."

"You don't need him," Adam insists. "I've got you."

Demitri steps forward anyway, and I take off running at full speed. Adam catches me just right and launches me over his head. I tuck before straightening out.

He catches my hands in a handstand over his head and instructs, "Stay taut." He launches me up and over.

I rotate and get a grip on his shoulders. I manage to flex just in time as he spins to the left, steadying me at the hips. I'm not a skilled gymnast, and I shake with the effort to control my muscles.

"That's it, Mel," he assures me. He grips my hips, and I pike down, wrapping my legs around his waist. I dip back and snake my upper body through his legs, slinking to the floor.

Mr. Isley bellows, "YESSS!"

The entire cast, save for Valerie, lose their minds, cawing and screaming. That lift sequence has yet to be right with her, and Adam and I just nailed it.

We continue, leaping together across the room. We turn and swirl, grinning at each other. Our energy thrums in perfect synchrony.

The piece draws to a close as Adam slides me off his shoulders into a languishing dip, our faces so close that I feel his breath on my cheek. *"I know we were dancers together in a past life,"* he sends. *"Even with a soulmate connection, what just happened doesn't just happen. I love hell out of you, girl."*

I gaze up at him and grin as he pulls me to standing. We're both winded as he hugs me tight, swinging me right and left.

"That's how it's done!" Mr. Isley crows. "Again!"

Valerie explodes, snarling and threatening to kick my ass if I do the piece again. I look at Mr. Isley like he's insane, but he doesn't defend me against Valerie.

I've suddenly had enough. Between the craziness at school, and everything with Adam, I pop. "Bring it on!" I scream over Valerie's rage.

She plows across the room at a full-tilt run. Demitri and Javier think quick, racing to stop her.

Everything in me quakes. Some primal part of my brain takes over. *"Adam's mine. He's been mine for longer than this bitch has had a soul. I'm done toying with her."*

The thought slides down our connection, and Adam thinks back, *"Oh shit!"*

I stalk forward, ending up nose to nose with Valerie. The room is electric, and everyone holds their breath, wondering where this is headed.

Adam's arm snakes around my waist. He picks me up and shifts me behind him. He glares at Valerie. "Quit playing with fire. You're missing a lot of pieces to this puzzle, and I'm telling you that you'll lose if you keep pushing. Get your shit together, or we're through. Melanie's your friend."

Valerie's glaring at me even as she addresses Adam. "That seductive little display was unnecessary."

I rattle my head. "Are you *daft*? It's a choreographed hump fest! Just because *you* can't keep up with the piece well enough to *make* it seductive doesn't mean I have to be a dead dance lay!"

Demitri belts laughter and wraps his arms around my shoulders. His eyes sparkle as he gasps through his chuckles. "God, I love you, Meley."

Adam fumes in Demitri's direction.

"This is going to hell in a handbasket," I announce. I lace a hand with Demitri's, and he squeezes it, radiating amusement while he sends calming energy through his hand.

Mr. Isley breaks in on the argument. "Stop!" He raises his eyebrows at Valerie. "You don't want Melanie dancing with Adam? Fine. Load up, Demitri!"

I glance from Adam to Demitri. This is about to make things far worse. Demitri smirks at Adam.

"You have to be *kidding*," Adam yells. "Melanie and I just killed that piece, and you're considering replacing *me*?"

Demitri hits him with one of his devastatingly sexy smolders. He narrows his eyes in challenge. "She's my dance partner, after all."

Adam sees red. "Not anymore, she's not!" He whips his steely blue gaze Mr. Isley's way. "It's my piece. I pick my partner. I'm dancing with Melanie."

"*What*?" Valerie screeches. "You're *my* fiancé!"

Demitri grins devilishly. "It would be my pleasure to do the piece," he says to Mr. Isley. He shifts past Adam and guides me to the spot in front of him.

I watch Adam in the mirror while Demitri places a hand on my shoulder. He seductively slides his hand across my collarbone and down the center of my chest, getting into the opening position. I take a shuddering breath.

"Here we go, baby girl," Demitri whispers in my ear. He always says that before we dance, but damn, it's not usually so full of heat.

Just as the song starts, Trey's voice unexpectedly breaks in. "Enough!"

I have no idea when he showed up.

Mr. Isley hits *pause* on the stereo as Trey glares at him.

"Melanie's done here," Trey barks. He saunters to me, pulling me away from Demitri. "Down boy!"

Demitri chuckles as Trey wraps his arm around my shoulders. We turn, and he guides me to the door. Trey leaves me in the doorway and grabs my stuff that's against the wall.

"Where do you think you're going?" Mr. Isley demands. "We're in the middle of class!"

Trey turns to look back at him. "This school is bullshit." He points at Valerie. "This argument is bullshit." He flippantly gestures to Demitri. "Your flirting with Melanie is bullshit. Everyone knows your pretty boy ass couldn't step foot in her inferno." He points at Adam as he glares at Mr. Isley. "You pairing up Valerie with Adam is bullshit. You know for a fact that Valerie can't handle that piece, and you're stirring the pot!" He glances my way before snapping his gaze back to Mr. Isley. "Melanie isn't dancing with Adam. We're all on edge. It'll create chaos. I can't handle another shitstorm right now, and Melanie and Adam are a cyclone."

Normally, I'd have resisted all of this because I've told Trey again and again that he doesn't control me. But all that was just way too hot to resist. So, I let him turn me and escort me out the door.

"Where do you recommend we go?" I ask once we're in the hall. "We can't ditch out of this fortress."

Trey sighs. "What was all of that, Melanie?"

I hit him with exasperated eyes. "That was Mr. Isley frustratedly trying to make one of his favorite pieces in the show work. Adam is trying, but Valerie's a mess. I think Mr. Isley's had enough of their constant bickering. It's been affecting rehearsals for a while."

"Must you be so seductive with Adam and Demitri?"

I roll my neck irritably. "I'm a dancer, Trey. I perform. You might as well get used to it."

Trey rolls his eyes. Then, he takes two master hall passes from the front pocket of his backpack. "Got them from Kelsey."

Kelsey's his sister, and she serves as a TA in the copy room. He writes on each of them and hands me one. I glance at it, discovering that we're apparently headed to Mr. Bentley's room.

"Come on," Trey huffs. "Mr. Bentley's exhausted, and the class is playing board games. I want to make out at the back of the room."

I giggle as we leave the dance building. Instead of his tawdry plan, I pull him around the back of the dance building into an alcove next to a water-and-gas meter. There's a little door to a maintenance room that's unlocked, and I give him a flirtatious look over my shoulder as we slip inside. I take a pen from my backpack and wedge it between the handle and doorjamb to brace the door closed in case someone tries to open it.

Trey clicks on the light from his watch and surveys my quick thinking. "How did you know about this place?"

I chuckle. "Demitri and Victoria frequent it."

Trey grins. "Perfect." He clicks off the watch light, plunging us into darkness as his hands drift along my sides.

CHAPTER 27

Trey squeezes me tighter and slows his pace. He's sipping his coffee, deliberately looking like he's trying to spend a few extra minutes with just the two of us. He inhales deep, tipping his head back. When he looks down at me, I spot my tired reflection in his mirrored sunglasses.

"Cheer up, love," he says.

"Marcus and Presley's parents are working on enrolling them in other schools. They told the group at rehearsal."

Trey's eyebrows rise. "Damn. I didn't think this would drag on long enough for parents to switch gears. That's not good."

"It's definitely not good. If they leave, then what's the point? We might as well all leave."

We round the corner of the front of the school, only to discover that the entire front lawn is covered in students. We see Arch standing with our group by the side of the front walkway.

"Looks like we're the last from our group to arrive," I mutter. "What's happening?" I ask when we get to our friends.

Arch rolls his eyes. "The front doors are still closed. None of us can get in. Principal Buttrum's been losing his crap for the past ten minutes."

There's a haughty expression on Coach Stamp's face as he stares at Buttrum.

Principal Buttrum's screaming from the front steps of the two-story building into his trusty bullhorn. "No one will be permitted to enter until I get back my punch cards!" His little performance lacks gusto, and he looks exhausted.

Ms. G, Mr. Jenson, and Mr. Isley stroll over to us, coffees in hand.

"Well, what's the plan?" Mr. Jenson asks.

Presley laughs. "We can't give him back his punch cards because a certain model citizen who shall remain nameless shredded them." She grins at Mr. Jenson.

He smiles back. "Oh, we could give them to him, but I'd have to drive to Adam's house and get the trash bags out of the trash. It might be worth it just to watch Principal Butterball try to tape them all back together."

Adam laughs and shakes his head. "Trashman came this morning. Buttrum's shit out of luck."

Principal Buttrum sets to maniacally screaming again. "*Now*! Bring them to me! I know one of you has them."

Presley tips her head back and screams, "*Shut* uuuup!" Then, she looks at us apologetically while we wince at the noise. "Sorry. I can't take it anymore."

Dozens of other students take up Presley's call, and suddenly the lawn is alive with many voices screaming, "Shut up!"

I narrow my eyes contemplatively. "You know what, I can't take it anymore either." I ask Ms. G, "Are any of the students or teachers inside yet?"

She shakes her head. "No. I think the yellow jackets might be inside, but no one else has been allowed to enter."

I grin. "Well, guys, this looks like a perfect ditch day. If no one's inside, then we don't have to protect them. How about we spread the word, and all go have some fun?"

Mr. Isley's eyes light up. "Yes! Can the teachers come too? I need a break from this madness!"

"Of course. We're not in there yet, so it's not ditching. All I know is that Trey and I showed up to school and found the door locked. Apparently, the school's closed today, and we must not have received the notice."

"Hell yes," Adam says. "Mr. Isley, Ms. G, and Mr. Jenson spread the word to the teachers and let them know that we're all going to Santa Monica Beach. The rest of us will let the students know and make sure anyone without a ride gets one from a friend."

Finley giggles and bounces next to an already bouncing Tanner. "Yes!"

We all start making the rounds, quietly spreading the word of our ditch day beach idea. Students and teachers are equally excited. Per Arch, we let everyone know that we plan to depart with a flourish.

Arch gets into place in the middle of the crowd and waits for Principal Buttrum to take a breath from his blathering. Arch claps his hands four times. Principal Buttrum whips his head back and forth as if trying to locate the source of the intrusive sound. The students all put up devil horns on cue, and then to our surprise, guys all over the quad stick a hand in their armpits and make farting sounds. This wasn't part of the plan, and our group all cracks up.

Dante grins at us from across the lawn and puts up devil horns in our direction.

Arch laughs. "We aren't on our own anymore with the scheming," he tells us. "That particularly hilarious armpit production must have been the work of Dante." He raises devil horns in response.

"What are you losers waiting for?" Adam exclaims. "I've got a beer and a dip in the ocean waiting for me. Let's get the hell out of here!"

CHAPTER *28*

I'm lounging, happily soaking up the sun on one of the beach towels that we grabbed from Trey's house on our way to Santa Monica Beach. Kelsey let me borrow one of her swimsuits, and the tiny red bikini fits perfectly. It's a particularly warm day, perfect for the beach.

The girls are spread out in a circle with our guys on towels next to us. All the couples are snuggling, holding hands, and in the case of Demitri and Victoria, doing a lot more than that. Apparently, Victoria's jealousy streak wasn't enough to distract Demitri from her other assets. The single members of our group are lounging together on the other side of Valerie and Adam, occasionally throwing things at the happy couples, and generally having fun.

Presley sighs. "I needed this sooo bad." She has her head on Marcus's shoulder, and they're both basking in the sun with their sunglasses on. Marcus is nearly asleep as Presley adds, "We're going to take a nap."

Marcus reaches over, pulling a spare beach towel out of a huge tote bag he brought. He uses it to cover the two of them. "I ran home for supplies," he says, "and Mom made peanut butter and jelly sandwiches for all of us. They're in that Tanner Blue tote bag by Arch's cooler. Help yourselves."

Tanner laughs.

"Will you guys keep an eye on our stuff while we sleep?" Presley asks. "Save me and Marcus a couple sandwiches."

Arch laughs from his spot giving a back rub to Kelsey. "So many people showed up from the school that we ran everyone else off who wanted to enjoy the beach. Your stuff's not going anywhere. Enjoy your nap."

Within moments, Marcus is gently snoring, fast asleep with Presley curled up against him under their makeshift blanket. I sit up and start smearing suntan lotion on my legs. When I'm finished, I grab a wine cooler from the ice chest that Arch and Hiram brought. My hands are still slick from the sunscreen, so I hand the bottle to Trey, who pops the screw top off for me. We aren't supposed to have alcohol on the beach, and we're surrounded by teachers, but they're intentionally overlooking the indiscretion.

Mr. Jenson and Mr. Bentley wander over to us, and Mr. Jenson whispers something to Adam.

"Have at it," Adam says, gesturing to the ice chest.

They each grab a cold beer and head back to the spot they've chosen, conveniently out of the way where they can enjoy watching the students' hijinks but don't have to regulate anyone. They've put up a sunshade beach umbrella, and they're cooking hot dogs on a grill that Mr. Isley hauled with him. They look like peas in a pod, happily handing out hot dogs to any hungry students who pass by.

Drew jogs over. "Any of you guys up for tossing the ball around? Some of the football players suggested a game of flag football."

Adam makes puppy eyes at Valerie. "Babe, I know we're supposed to be hanging out . . ."

Valerie smiles at him. "You boys go play. You've earned some fun. All us girls will sit around and talk about how devastatingly handsome you are."

My heart rate jumps. Things are still tense with me and Valerie. Girlie chitchat isn't on my priority list today.

"Have no fear," Deb says, her tone dripping with sarcasm. "Marcus will protect us." She gestures to Marcus, who has drool slowly oozing from his open, snoring mouth.

We all crack up.

"Seriously, you guys go let loose for a little while. We're long overdue for some girl time."

Trey sits up. "You sure you'll be okay?"

"For the love of God, Trey!" Deb says with exasperation. "You act like Melanie's a delicate hothouse flower. The girl has thrown punches that have knocked guys out cold. She'll be fine sitting on her beach towel with her friends while you play football fifteen yards away."

Sure, as long as Valerie doesn't decide to turn our beach vacay into a WWF match.

Adam catches the stray thought. *"She feels bad about it,"* he sends. *"She isn't going to start shit with you. You're the one I worry will blow."*

I huff.

"Guess you're right," Trey says. "I'm going to join the guys." He kisses the end of my nose. "You've gotta cheer for me, okay?"

Adam rolls his eyes.

I grin at Trey. "Always."

He runs off with the guys as I make an ick face at the girls.

All the girls make gagging noises at me.

"Awww!" Susan razzes. "You two are so cute."

Victoria untangles herself from Demitri long enough to grin at me. "They're sickeningly gross."

Valerie shoots Victoria an ironic look and raises an eyebrow. "Yeah . . . *Melanie and Trey* are the gross ones."

Victoria's not at all embarrassed to be called out. "Give a girl a break, would you? Have you seen this guy?"

Demitri waggles his eyebrows at her. "Compliments like that'll get you everywhere. Come on, Vic. Let's go for a walk."

They hop up, and Demitri grabs his car keys from his backpack next to their towels. We watch as they head up the beach to the stairs leading to the parking lot.

Deb snorts. "A walk . . . Right."

I grimace. "I'm never sitting in his passenger seat again." I feign retching, and everyone laughs.

At the end of one of Finley's usual over-the-top funny stories, the basketball team walks by. Drake gives me an appraising look, his eyes widening appreciatively at my skimpy red bikini.

My friends all dissolve into a fit of giggles.

"I have an idea," Valerie says quietly to us before raising her voice at the basketball players. "Hey, boys! Come here a second."

Drake and the basketball team jog over.

"Offer them a beverage," Hiram yells from a distance.

Valerie nods. "There's beer in the ice chest," she informs the players as they sit down. "Help yourselves, but leave the wine coolers for our prissy girls over here." She gestures toward Finley, Kelsey, and me with the beer bottle in her hand.

"I'll show you prissy," I quip.

Valerie gives me a hesitant half smile, and I return the sentiment. *Looks like we're trying to make amends.*

"Melanie's a lot of things," Drake says with a smile, "but prissy isn't one of them."

I nod with appreciation. "I'll take that as a compliment."

One of the guys who's passing out beers says, "You should.

Drake would *never* insult the amazing, marvelous, brilliant, talented, funny Melanie." His statement drips sarcasm, but I take it lightly.

All the basketball players laugh and elbow Drake.

"Yeah, yeah, yeah," he says with good nature. "She's taken and I'm over it. Give it a rest, guys."

We don't know most of the basketball players well, but they all plop down like we're old friends. Everything at Hollywood High's been that way lately. At this point, we've all been through so much together that we're past the usual insider/outsider tension.

"For the record," the beer guy says, "and for the sake of my buddy Drake over here, how taken are you, Mel?"

I laugh.

Valerie answers for me. "She's practically an old, tired housewife at this point. But . . . Drake, have you formally been introduced to Deb over here?" She gestures to Deb, who hits her with a glare before the ferocity fades and she breaks into an impish smile.

"Yeah, hey, Deb. We have first-period class together. Good to see you." He gives her a barely concealed glance over.

Deb grins at him, not the least bit shy. "It's nice to see you also, Drake," she says, bowing her head slightly.

Finley, always quick to jump on board with the matchmaking, bubbles over. "Deb rides a Harley and looks devastating in a black leather jacket."

"She looks pretty good in a black bikini, also," one of the basketball players says of the stunning Deb.

She raises an eyebrow. Deb is unaccustomed to being flirted with. She has told all of us that the only guy who ever showed her attention was Adam's best friend, Michael, who passed away at the hands of Joel and his friends last month. "Well . . . all right. Thank you, I think."

All the girls laugh.

"That's right, Deb," Valerie teases. "Very good. This is called flirting. You see, we're in high school, and teenagers flirt as step one of a bizarre mating ritual that humans do here on Earth."

Deb plays along like she's clueless. "Got it. So, the cute boy flirts with me, and I get him drunk on Hiram's crappy beer . . . Then what?"

Finley surveys Drake mischievously. "Once the cute boy's tipsy on the crappy beer, you lead him away and *pounce*."

Drake cracks up. "Hey now, I'm not that easy."

Deb raises a flirtatious eyebrow his way. "Really? That's a shame."

We all grin at each other.

"Well, damn, Deb," Valerie says. "You just graduated from Flirting 101 to the advanced course."

"All right, I'm intrigued," Drake says. "Would you like to go for a walk?"

"With those hazel eyes," Deb says flirtatiously, "I'd follow you into hell."

Drake gives Deb a jokingly smoldering look. "You sweet talker, you."

With a laugh, Deb straightens up. "All right, here it is. Deb in a nutshell. I have no filter. I think like a guy. I take boxing classes for fun. I guarantee I can burp louder than you. I rarely date because boys are always intimidated by me. I'll embarrass you by knocking a guy out if he harasses you. I love to fistfight more than *anything*. I can fix your car. And I'm definitely not girlie."

I snort, amused. "Well, now that we've gotten past the get-to-know-you portion of the interview, what do you think, Drake? Did she woo you with all her sexy qualities?"

Drake's eyes twinkle as he smiles at Deb. "All joking aside, you haven't scared me away."

The girls' mouths drop open, and the basketball players grin while we watch Drake and Deb stand and walk away with his arm around her waist. Now the girls tumble into giggles, everyone high-fiving.

"You're all amazing at that," Susan says. "You got Hiram and me together the same way. You should be matchmakers."

"I don't know when they'd find the time," one of the basketball players says. "You're all working full time masterminding around Principal Buttrum's nonsense all damn day."

Everyone nods.

"Hey," he adds in a more serious tone, "I want you to know how much we appreciate what you're doing. We know it's been a lot."

"We also appreciate you getting Drake to look at *anyone* other than Melanie," another of the guys says. "You have *no* idea how tired we are of hearing about her." He looks my way and adds, "No offense."

I laugh. "None taken."

We say goodbye, and the guys wander away.

"Heck of an idea introducing those two, Val," Finley says.

Valerie nods. "I think they'd be perfect together. Deb needs a big beefcake who can handle her wit and filterless candor. Drake's got a good sense of humor, he's gorgeous, and he thinks on his feet. She'd score big if she can get that deal locked down."

Kelsey subtly points ahead, and we all turn to watch just as Drake delicately cups Deb's cheek and kisses her. They're standing knee-deep in the ocean.

"Yes!" Finley says. "Get it, Deb! Drake is *so* hot."

"You just lost your special secret admirer, Mel," Kelsey says with a grin.

I laugh. "There was *nothing* secret about his admiring. This is good. I want Drake to be happy, and I agree that those two just might be perfect for each other."

"Meanwhile," Valerie says, "our guys are getting their asses handed to them at flag football."

We look across the beach just in time to catch a play where the football players completely mop the floor with our guys. But at least they're all laughing and having fun. A few plays later, Adam finally catches a pass thrown by Trey and scores a touchdown. All the girls whoop and holler.

The guys jog over with Drew the quarterback in tow. They all plop down, and Hiram hands out beers.

"Did you boys have fun?" Finley asks.

"You have no idea," Tanner says. "We generally sucked compared to the varsity players, but we needed to run around and have a good time *so bad*." He looks to Drew. "Thank the football team for tolerating us out there. I know we didn't give you the challenge you're used to."

"Nah, you guys did great," Drew says. "Our varsity crew just spends every minute playing football. Even when we're not at practice, we're all at the park together tossing the ball around. It was nice to play an old school game of neighborhood ball."

"I don't care if we sucked or not," Adam says. "I had a blast."

"Gotta say that I wish I'd gotten to know you guys sooner," Drew says. "I never really knew what to make of you. These days, everyone talks about your group like you're some kind of mystical beings who can handle anything. But before all that, everyone was just baffled by the fact that most of you are practically married to your boyfriends and girlfriends."

Valerie leans into Adam and gazes at her engagement ring. "When you've been through as much as we have, the bonds get a little tighter than normal."

Drew looks wide-eyed at her hand. "You two are *engaged?*"

When Adam glances at me, I fight not to roll my eyes. We're having a good day, and I don't want to dust off this old argument.

"I couldn't imagine even being in a serious relationship, let alone getting married," Drew says, sounding baffled. "What about the rest of you?"

"Well, sleepy and drooly over there haven't started talking about marriage, from what I know," Tanner says, gesturing toward Marcus and Presley, still sound asleep. "But I'm not sure anyone else could tolerate either of them, so I think they're a forever deal."

We all laugh and nod.

Tanner gestures to me and Trey. "Those two will have precisely three kids, a white picket fence, one purebred pooch, and a bank full of money by the time Melanie's twenty-five."

Adam snarls down our connection.

"You don't get to have it both ways, Adam," I send back.

Next, Tanner looks to Arch and Kelsey. "Arch would be an idiot to let Kelsey go. I give them until six months after she graduates before they're living on some exotic island sipping piña coladas and running a tourist gift shop."

We're all smiles.

Now Tanner gestures to Hiram and Susan. "Those two are new to the dating game, but you wouldn't know it the way they're always snuggling together, gurgling about how they love each other."

He looks around. "I don't know where Victoria and Demitri are."

Valerie gestures over her shoulder toward the parking lot. "They're in a steam sauna of their own making in Demitri's Jeep, if I were to wager a guess."

Adam laughs. "Yeah. They're still at the new stage, but let's just say it's a shame we didn't save one of those Tanner Blue hump huts for them."

"Oh no, you don't!" Tanner quips. "You leave me out of their humping, and those huts."

Drew laughs. "And you two?"

Tanner turns and gazes at Finley. "I'm never letting Fin go. I'm already working on forever."

Finley looks at him with dreamy, sky-blue eyes as the girls all say, "Ooo-ooo," like a bunch of fifth graders.

"Really?" Finley mouths.

"Really," Tanner says. "Think you can clue a guy in on what your answer might be?"

"You already know I'll say yes. Do you really think I could ever be with another guy after you? He probably wouldn't even know how to fix my eyeliner."

Tanner throws his head back, laughing. "*That* would be a travesty."

We all laugh.

"Well, wherever we all wind up," Drew says, "I want all of you to know that the entire football team has your back with Principal Buttrum."

Arch sighs. "We haven't made this public knowledge, but something bigger is happening than that maniacal bottom-feeder annoying all of us regularly."

Drew pauses for a second, contemplating. Finally, he says, "Our coach was trained in Special Operations during Vietnam. Some of what Principal Buttrum is up to has him really on edge. He thinks a lot of the hijinks are a diversion tactic to wear you guys down and distract you while he does stuff like erect fences—stuff that's related to a bigger plan."

Arch side-eyes me. "This will likely sound bonkers to you, but Melanie's got an intuition that you can place a million-dollar bet on every time."

"I've heard about it," Drew cuts in. "Everyone whispers about how Melanie's psychic, or a witch, or something."

I shrug. "Honestly, my intuition likely *is* linked to an untrained psychic ability. For now, though, it's come in incredibly handy more than once."

Bear snorts. "That's an understatement. If it weren't for Melanie's intuition, I'd be barbecue."

Drew looks Bear's way. "So that story's true?"

"What version of the story have you heard?"

"The football team heard from the cheerleaders, who heard from the golf team, that you guys came out of the theater one night and went to your cars. Bear got in his car, and Melanie was told by a ghost to get Bear out of the car. She screamed, and the car blew up right after you got out."

Bear laughs. "Everything but the ghost part is spot-on. Her intuition fired up just in time."

"How does this intuition of yours work?" Drew asks me.

"I get a very specific feeling in my chest. The severity of the pain tells me how immediate the danger is. I somehow always know who it's about. It's pretty simple, actually."

"What happens when it's immediate danger like with Bear?"

"I almost doubled over that time, but I've learned not to get distracted when the pain's the most severe, because that's when we have the least amount of time."

He nods in thought. "Well, you and the football coach are on the same page then. He's positive that Principal Buttrum's hiding some gnarly plan. Keep that intuition of yours on point and let us know when it fires up. I have no intention of dying on that damn campus."

We exchange a look.

At that moment, Marcus and Presley yawn and sit up.

"What did we miss?" Marcus asks.

Valerie explains. "Well, Demitri and Victoria are currently ruining the seats in Demitri's car."

"Lucky!" Marcus says at the same time that Presley groans out, "*Gross*!"

"See?" Tanner says to Drew. "They're a match made in heaven!"

We all laugh.

Valerie continues. "Mr. Jenson and the teachers are making hot dogs for the students while they secretly drink Hiram and Arch's beers."

Marcus nods. "Sweet! I'm gonna snag a few dogs here in a minute."

"Tanner just dropped the bomb that he's scheming up a proposal for Finley," Valerie adds.

Marcus grins at Tanner. "A big congratulations in advance to the happy couple."

"Oh, and the girls managed to get Deb and Drake hooked up. They're currently making out in the ocean."

Trey throws his fist in the air. "Yes!" he says excitedly. "Thank you, girls."

"*And*," Valerie says, "Drew just informed us that the football coach was trained in Special Operations during Vietnam. He thinks the petty nonsense that the principal is up to is all a diversion tactic for a bigger plan, where we're all going to die at the school."

Marcus slumps. "Awww . . . We have to almost die, *again*?"

CHAPTER 29

"**Y**esterday seems like it was a lifetime ago," I say to Presley.

Here we are again in front of the school, and the line isn't moving.

Principal Buttrum has his bullhorn to his mouth, the volume turned all the way up. "If Melanie Slate doesn't walk to my office now," he's saying, "the entire student body will be punished."

I roll my head around dramatically. "Uuugh."

Someone yells out from the back of the group, "What are you going to do, lock the bathrooms again? No one cares, Buttrum."

"Why are you so obsessed with Melanie anyway?" Drew calls out. "You're such a filthy old man!"

Everyone laughs.

"Melanie's a bad seed!" Buttrum says into his bullhorn.

I side-eye Arch. "You remember what Drew told us?" I ask quietly.

Arch reaches past Bear's shoulder and taps Drew on the arm. Drew turns our way, and Arch motions for him to step back. Bear steps up in his place, blocking the view of our conversation.

"You'd think that if Principal Buttrum *really* wanted to find me," I say to Arch and Drew, "he'd just look over here at our group. But he hasn't even once. He knows full well who I hang out with."

The guys look contemplatively up at the principal.

"You remember what your coach thinks, right?" I ask Drew.

Drew rolls his eyes. "We're idiots. This is a diversion tactic."

I nod. "Precisely. But for what?"

Arch looks around with a pensive expression. "What could they be up to that couldn't be done while we're all in class?"

"Classrooms have windows," Drew says. "And bored students who are always gazing out, noticing everything."

"We need our own diversion so some of us can go investigate," Arch suggests.

"Leave that to me," I offer.

Arch nods at me and leans past Bear's shoulder to whisper something to Dante. He moves back behind Bear and pokes his head in with Tanner and Marcus. They both nod, and Bear whispers something to Deb and Drake. Deb grins and cracks her knuckles. Drake looks worried as he nods at Arch.

Arch, Tanner, and Marcus all shift back in the crowd, and Drew and I follow. Trey's so busy murmuring with Demitri and Adam that none of them have noticed how I've slipped away. It's probably best. Trey's on a one-man mission to ruin my fun lately, all in the name of keeping me safe. While I appreciate that he likes me in one piece, a girl's gotta have a good time every once in a while.

Coach Stamp, always overly aggressive and obnoxious, has started pushing through the crowd of students. He gets to the open circle in the middle of the students and grabs the bullhorn. "I have it on good authority that *Melanie Slate* has committed an egregious violation of Principal Buttrum's discipline policy. We need to see her in my office immediately."

"Do tell, Coach Stamp," Victoria says. "What *egregious* violation did Melanie commit?"

"She was seen in my office taking something *very* important. Theft will not be tolerated."

"I don't even know where that idiot's office is," I whisper to the guys. "They're definitely up to something. I'm going to drag this out as long as I can. You guys go now and see what you can figure out."

"No way, Melanie!" Arch hisses. "My whole plan was for you to come with me and help figure out what they're hiding."

I shake my head. "If I step up, it'll keep them extra distracted, and their eyes won't wander. Slip through the open door when their backs are turned. Move fast. I only have so many tools in my arsenal to keep them distracted."

"What are you planning to do?" Arch asks.

I shudder. "I'm going to start with flirtation and work from there."

Arch rubs his forehead. "Trey's going to kill me for allowing you to do this."

"Yeah, I know," I say with a grin. "I fully intend to blame you."

Arch chuckles and shakes his head. "That's evil, and you're a mean, nasty girl."

"You guys get ready to bolt. I'm going in."

Before Arch can object, I turn and start working my way through the crowd. Most of the guys I pass say some version of, "Get behind me. I'll hide you." It's really sweet, but I politely decline. I keep moving and round the circle of kids who are crushed up furthest from the entrance. I close my eyes for a moment, gathering my nervous energy and sending it down and out like an internal exhale. Grounded and centered, I'm ready.

I push through the three layers of kids in front of me and step into the open space in the middle. "Well, hello, gentlemen. I understand you'd like to chat with me."

Buttrum and Stamp spin around, their backs to the doors. I know Arch and the guys are making a run for it.

I clasp my hands in front of me and stretch luxuriously. "What bullshit are you two spewing now?"

Principal Buttrum does exactly what I expect. He spirals out of control, screaming and yelling about how I violated his master something or another. I grin at Buttrum while he goes on and on.

Well, that was easy. I might not even have to do anything else.

Coach Stamp holds a hand up for silence. Then, he turns a suspicious eye my way. "You're up to something. What is it?"

Crap. Going to have to work a little harder on this one. I decide to start with irritation before building up to flirtation, mostly because the thought of flirting with either of them makes me want to throw up.

"I'm not up to anything," I say. "That sniveling jackass demanded that I appear. I've been feeling particularly froggy lately, and thought whooping his ass might be a good time, so voila! Here I am." I put out my hands with a flourish.

My group's stationed to my left, close enough that I can see how Trey and Adam are gaping at me. I've intentionally blocked both soulmate connections so they can't get inside my head. I avoid making eye contact with either of them. Deb pushes up to the front, next to Trey, with Drake right behind her. Looks like the gang is all prepared to wage war.

An excited bolt of energy shoots up my back. I'm about the irritate Tweedledee and Tweedledumb to the point that it might come to blows. I'll welcome it. I want this over with already. *Time for flirtation.* I cringe internally. "What did I do now?" I ask, shining doe eyes up at Buttrum. "Did Dream Me not properly handle your grubby little feet while you enjoyed a sleepy-time fantasy last night?"

Even through the wall I've put up, I can sense Trey's confusion.

I snap my intense gaze to Coach Stamp. "And you . . . What did I do to you, Coach? You said earlier that I stole something out of your office, but I don't even know where your office is, so that can't be true."

I do my best Victoria impression, pulling my leg into a sexy mermaid stance and running my hands down my sides. I make a naughty pouting face and look at Buttrum and Stamp with smoldering eyes. Trey's confusion seems to shift to anger. He clearly knows I'm up to something, and being in the dark is making him mad. On the other hand, a quick glance at Adam says he's completely amused.

"*Why* do you want me alone, Coach Stamp?" I say flirtatiously. "I mean, you're cute and all, in an old-guy kinda way. But I'm not into it."

He's turning red.

"What's the matter, Coach?" I pile on. "Things with the wife not quite cracking anymore? Thinking you need to test things out with someone younger and hotter? Maybe the problem isn't your rapidly dropping testosterone, right? If everything gets chugging with a youngster, then you can blame your declining manhood on your aging wife."

Coach Stamp looks stunned.

"I get it," I say. "There's no shame in your pervert game."

Victoria's standing in my line of sight next to Demitri. She raises an eyebrow and whispers something to Demitri, who looks at me suspiciously. Then, he glances at Drake, who's looking past the show I'm putting on, gazing toward the front doors. Those two are smarter than the average bears. It seems they've figured out that I'm running a distraction. Drake's tall enough to see over the crowd, and he's supposed to signal to me when the guys are back.

Stamp stammers, unable to put together an audible sentence.

When Buttrum starts to lunge at me, our whole group bunches together, ready to pounce. Demitri quickly whispers something to Darren, who subtly whispers to Bear, and so on down the line. Our guys step in front of Trey to keep him from killing the principal and coach.

I giggle and bounce on the balls of my feet just like Tanner often does. "That's it, isn't it? Did I guess right?"

"To my office!" Buttrum screams into his bullhorn. "I need to speak with you privately, now!"

Interesting, I think. *He's suggesting his office instead of Coach Stamp's. More evidence he may be trying to stay between me and impending danger.*

I shake my head. "That's not going to work, sir."

Principal Buttrum huffs and rolls his eyes. "Why won't that work?"

"Because you've been such a bat-crap crazy, maniacal, loony tunes, ticking time bomb. Thanks to you, no one around here will let me go *anywhere* by myself. I have an escort to classes, to the bathroom, even on the ride home. These people won't let me take a piece of paper out of my notebook by myself! It's been *beyond* irritating, let me tell ya."

Principal Buttrum turns to survey the crowd.

Damn it! Not a good plan, Melanie. He needs to look this way.

"How many of you are in on this whole scheme to bodyguard Melanie?" the principal yells into his bullhorn.

Every hand in the crowd goes up.

Buttrum whips around, glaring at me. "You're the reason all this craziness has been happening! All the marching and stealing my cards!"

I scoff at Principal Buttrum and act over-the-top baffled. "You have *got* to be kidding. You think *I* did all of that? Principal Buttrum, you and I both know that I'm just a *girl*! Girls aren't smart enough to mastermind something so *genius* as the whole school marching to 'The Ants Go Marching One by One.'"

Everyone in the crowd snickers while Coach Stamp's chauvinistic brain seems to sputter, trying to wrap around what I'm sure he views as a completely logical statement. He turns to Principal Buttrum, and they both shrug at each other as if agreeing with me. I can't help but roll my eyes. Some of the men around here are ridiculous with their old-fashioned beliefs, but it's benefiting me right now, so I'll take it.

"You know who took my punch cards," Principal Buttrum says into his bullhorn. "Tell me, and we can work together."

I make my most innocent little-girl face. "I don't have any clue who took them, Principal Buttrum, but I think it was a low-down dirty trick. Those cards are obviously *very* important to you, and it looks like losing them has made you really sad."

Principal Buttrum nods. "I really do need them back," he says quietly.

I keep up my brainless-girl act as I pretend to agree with him. "I don't blame you. They were *really* cool punch cards, and I liked your idea a lot. Using the punch card machines was super fun, and I was so excited waiting in line every morning for my turn."

Principal Buttrum nods enthusiastically. "See! I wanted you kids to have a little fun."

Inside my mind, my dark-water side is rolling her eyes and fuming. Acting like a brainless idiot is so far beneath me that I have to fight the desire to shudder, but somehow, Coach Stamp is buying my nonsense. Plus, Drake hasn't given me the signal that the guys are back yet. I scramble for a new topic.

The guys need to get back fast. I'm running out of ideas. "I know you were thinking of us," I say. "You're just misunderstood."

Buttrum's expression softens. "I'm glad someone around here sees that. You know, Melanie, maybe I was wrong about you."

Coach Stamp looks from me to Buttrum. "You've got to be kidding. You aren't actually buying this crap, are you?"

Uh-oh. Think quick, Melanie. I decide to try something honest. "I think Principal Buttrum and I have a lot in common. In junior high, I was picked on constantly. It was awful. Every school bully made me their target. I didn't have any friends, and no one liked me. Was it like that for you also, Principal Buttrum?"

He nods, his face slack. "You just described my junior high and high school days perfectly." I recognize his tone as the same one he used during the few other times he dropped the façade.

Drake turns his head and nods once, hard and fast, in my direction.

That's my signal. Time to end this charade. I look Buttrum in the eyes. "We all have a choice to make, Francis. You can spend the rest of your life lashing out at everyone and ensuring that you're hated. That way, you don't have to wonder how people really feel about you. The other option is that you can heal your wounded ego and stop being a victim. You came into this school and victimized every person here out of retaliation against people who are nothing more than the ghosts of your past. You're perpetuating a cycle that no longer serves you, and it's weak and sad. Honestly, I think you're better than that. When you're alone and free to be who you really are, I ask that you consider this."

A distinct look of sadness fills Principal Buttrum's eyes. He glances at Stamp in a way that confirms the coach is behind all of this. For just a moment, Buttrum can't hide who he is.

My intuition blazes to life, telling me that I can't under any circumstances let Coach Stamp take me into the office. I melt into the crowd, backing up as the other students step in front of me.

Arch announces loudly enough to be heard at the back of the crowd, "We're here to learn, not play slap and tickle with two has-been G. I. Joes. We're headed to class."

The crowd surges to the school's entrance, and my friends surround me as we follow like salmon swimming upstream.

CHAPTER 30

We all make it into Mr. Isley's dance studio, and Ms. G closes the door behind us.

Trey spins around, furious. "Have you lost your mind, Melanie? What the hell were you doing back there?"

I put my hands up. "Arch's fault."

Trey whips around to face Arch. "Seriously? You put my girl in danger?"

Arch steps back. "Leave me out of this. Melanie's got a mind of her own. Principal Buttrum and Coach Stamp were hell-bent on finding her, and we needed a distraction. She was willing, and she had an idea that allowed Drew, Tanner, Marcus, and me to slip away. It worked, didn't it?"

Trey throws his head back and roars in frustration. Mr. Isley, Mr. Bentley, and Ms. G all look shocked by the display.

Mr. Jenson steps forward, near enough to Trey to stop him before he can lunge for Arch. "I know I'm the new guy to your group, but I've made some observations."

My boyfriend seems to soften.

"Melanie's going to be smack-dab in the middle of all the

action," Mr. Jenson says, "whether you like it or not. That's just who she is. The girl's a fighter deep down in her soul."

We all nod, even Trey.

"Frankly, I'm glad, because we need her. All the girls in this group are smart. And no offense, guys, but if I had to choose to go against the guys or the girls in this group in a late-night alley brawl, I'd pick the guys. I might have a shot against you, but the girls would tear me limb from limb."

Deb bows at the waist. "Thank you, kind sir. We appreciate the compliment."

Mr. Jenson grins at her and bows his head in return.

Trey throws up his hands. "It's not that I think Melanie's incapable. It's that she shouldn't have to do all of this! She shouldn't have to put herself at risk, or flirt with a dirty old man, or sink to any of the levels that she's had too lately. She's better than that."

Mr. Jenson nods. "I agree with you. You're all above what you've had to do lately." He looks at me. "You got through to Principal Buttrum back there. I saw the shift."

"I did too." I turn to Arch. "We need to fill everyone in on why I had to dance like a circus monkey distracting Buttrum and Stamp."

"Yes," Trey adds sarcastically. "Please tell me what was *so* important that my girlfriend had to practically throw herself at Coach Stamp."

For a moment, Arch looks like he's trying not to laugh. He fails. "I wasn't there to see the performance Melanie put on, and now I'm sad. It sounds like I missed something exciting."

"She laid it on thick," Victoria says. "All of you now owe Melanie *and* me for having to flirt with those trolls."

Presley shudders. "We're lucky we have Victoria and Melanie. I'd let Principal Buttrum and Coach Stamp kill everyone on campus before I'd sink to flirting with either of them."

Arch grins. "All right. Let me explain how this all came about. Halfway through Principal Buttrum's bullhorn bellowing, Melanie reminded me of what Drew told us yesterday about how Principal Buttrum and Coach Stamp are using their little tantrums as a distraction. I grabbed Drew out of the crowd, and we decided to go see if anything was happening elsewhere. Melanie's job was to keep Buttrum faced away from where we were headed."

"Did you discover anything worthwhile?" Adam asks.

Marcus nods. "The yellow jackets were split up at the two steel gates. They were messing around with the keypads."

"I'm the only one in this room with a code that opens those gates," Mr. Jenson says. "I'm going to go check it out. I'll be right back."

"Do you need any of us to go with you as backup in case something happens?" Arch asks.

Mr. Jenson shakes his head. "No one will notice me if I casually walk to the gates by myself. Maintenance men are never noticed." He leaves quickly.

"While we wait for Mr. Jenson to come back," I say, "I need to tell you all something."

Everyone looks my way.

"At the end of my speech, I saw a big shift when I told Principal Buttrum he has a choice to make about how he lives his life. That moment triggered my intuition. I was right. All the tantrums Buttrum has been displaying were as fake as my flirtation. I've noticed that his tirades fire back up lately whenever Coach Stamp is around. He's faking his game, convincing Stamp that he's still an ally, but I don't think he is. None of it was real, and most of it made no sense. It's like he was training the students, not actually trying to get a point across."

"Training the students to do what?" Hiram asks.

"To gather around every time he has a fit. It worked, because today, every single student was gathered to watch the latest show. Every set of eyes looked right where Coach Stamp wanted them to. He's been training us to become brainless followers all along, and there we stood, pawns in his plan." I pause and take a deep breath. "Something's coming soon. I can feel it."

Everyone exchanges pensive glances.

Mr. Jenson comes jogging back through the door, pulling it closed after him. We turn expectantly his way.

"You kids were right," he says. "Neither gate will open. The yellow jackets must have coded something that overrides any other code assigned to the system. This place is now a fortress with only one way in and one way out. We're trapped in here, and the only exit is through the main doors in the two-story building."

We all look at each other like we're doomed.

"Melanie," Arch says, "does your intuition tell you that something's going to happen today specifically?"

I shake my head. "I don't know. It's a big jumble."

CHAPTER 31

Dance class has been yet another disaster.

"Melanie, get over here," Mr. Isley bellows. "I'm replacing Valerie. I'm *done!*"

Valerie sets to screaming at the top of her lungs.

I tune it out, leaning against the barre with my head back. "Ugh." I'm so over Valerie, there aren't words.

Actually, apparently, there are words, because the tail end of Valerie's tirade blasts in: "That *bitch!*"

That's it for me. I launch at a full tilt toward Valerie. The sudden charge takes her off guard, and she doesn't have time to counter before I lay her flat with a brutal right hook. She hits the ground so hard, she bounces.

Everyone rushes our way, but Mr. Isley halts the helpers with a ferocious, "*Enough!*" He turns scathing eyes my direction. "Out! Go cool off. *Now!*"

"Screw you," I snarl. "Naturally, Princess Peach is perfection." My eyes narrow at Valerie. "She can replace me in every damn piece in this show. Good luck with that." I toss a flippant hand in Demitri's direction. "He won't partner her."

Mr. Isley's so mad, his lips are twitching. I don't give a damn.

"You've allowed Valerie to run rank for weeks," I say, pointing at Mr. Isley. "She's out of line, under-talented, and overly privileged. I'm not the least bit surprised, though. You regularly kiss the wrong asses." I gesture to Valerie. "Pucker up and have a field day. It worked for Adam. Valerie always wins, and she never deserves it."

I turn, stalking to the door. In the mirrors, from the corner of my eye, I notice Demitri starting to follow after me.

"Stay here, Demitri," Mr. Isley orders. "Let Melanie stew. It's what she does best."

Against my better judgment, I whip around and flash Mr. Isley the bird on my way out the door. It's rash, but I don't have anything left to give. This school has burned away every bit of my heart and soul.

I make my way into the locker room, where I stop at my locker, and it takes two tries to get the combination lock to open. I yank the lock off and turn, throwing it as hard as I can as a wave of emotion blasts from me on a silent boom. The lock shatters a full-length mirror, and I wince as glass crashes to the floor. The sound as it echoes in the empty room deflates me. I lean with both hands flat on the bank of lockers. My head hangs as I get lost in thought. *This place has affected my home life, friendships, dance life, and relationship with Trey. Nothing about this mess is worth it. Rich suggested maybe I need to transfer schools. Maybe it's time for Canoga Park High. There's nothing left for me here.*

Blazing regret creeps up my spine as I relive the unfortunate encounter I just had with Mr. Isley. He's the best dance teacher I've ever had. He's also an ally who took me in when I had nowhere to go. I don't agree with him all the time, but my meltdown was beyond rude. Not to mention, he gave me an all-star spot before the required sophomore status. He took so much heat for that. It nearly tore apart the dance department, but he defended both me and his decision to the end.

God, Melanie, what are you doing?

Without warning, a hand lands on my shoulder, and suddenly I'm stuck in an energetic shield. I blink, trying to make sense of my trapped state. I send a blasting wave of fear and confusion through my connections with Trey and Adam, but it's blocked somehow. The blast gets trapped in my psyche, bouncing around like a rubber ball in the hands of a small child. Each time it hits my psyche, a fresh gonging sound erupts. My mind is a cacophony of fear and noise. I try to cover my ears to no avail. It wouldn't have helped anyhow, seeing as how the sound is inside my mind, but not being able to move my arms is a realization that sends terror raging through every inch of me.

I try to scream, but no sound escapes. The only thing I can do is push from the inside. I swell the energy in my core and push as hard as I can, hoping the sentiment somehow escapes the trapping shield and finds someone intuitive. Nothing escapes, and a fresh round of panic boils.

From behind, I'm grabbed around the chest and hauled backward. My eyes are huge, seemingly the only part of me capable of moving. I can't see my attacker behind me, but I know his energy.

I'm dragged through the door into the second girls' locker room. We pass rows and rows of lockers, but the room is empty. With no chance of rescue, and no ability to move, I have zero choice but to hope for a miracle. Another door slams shut, and now I'm being dragged through a hallway I've never seen. I make eye contact with a girl I don't know, desperately trying to communicate that I need help. Her mouth is hanging open as she stares at me over her shoulder. She must have been headed down the hall the opposite direction. She's frozen in place, but I can sense that it's not because of this trap I'm under. It's fear that has her standing like a statue.

I hear a set of keys jingle before the sound of a door opening. I'm tossed inside a room, landing hard on a green-and-cream-colored tile floor. The checkerboard pattern makes me dizzy from my fuzzy angle—although it occurs to me at once that it actually may be from a concussion. My head aches from smacking the floor, but the pain is quickly forgotten as the door slams shut with ferocity. I have no idea where I've been locked up, but the room has that feel of a place deep in the basement.

"You're a tough little bitch to get hold of," comes the familiar voice. Coach Stamp leers over me. "Looks like your friends are off their game. I felt your rage and decided to follow it. Your energy is irresistible. No wonder Joel liked you so much."

His hand slams down on my head, and he presses with all his might. I squeeze my eyes closed and test my ability to move. I've got nothing. Earlier this year, I learned the hard way that Joel Stamp is an energy worker. Apparently, his dad is also. The shield he has me trapped within is like nothing I've ever experienced. Fear escalates as I study the metaphysical ability of this monster through his hand's contact with my head. Dejection fills me as I realize that even if I had all my abilities ready, Daniel Stamp would still have me beat, and by a long shot. He's a beast, and I'm thoroughly screwed.

I feel Coach Stamp's leg against my hip just before he grabs my arm and yanks me from my stomach to my back. Now I'm staring up at him, and I'm wearing only a tank top and little shorts. When he straddles me, I scream inside my mind, unable to scream aloud. As he sneers down at me with animalistic eyes, the memory of his son straddling me in the commons the night he tried to rape me boils up. I was wearing almost exactly the same outfit that night. The terror I experienced then is nothing compared to now. Back then, I knew Adam was on his way, and I just had to survive Joel's attack long enough for him to arrive. Now, though, I'm in deep shit.

Men in the Stamp family apparently age well, because the man pressing down on me is a carbon copy of his son. He has that same gorgeous exterior and evil interior, with just a touch more age.

Coach Stamp grabs the bottom of my tank top and rips it halfway up the front. A slow, evil smile builds across his face. "This is what he did, didn't he?"

My eyes can't get any bigger. I'm on the edge of passing out from terror, and I hope like hell it happens quick so I'm unconscious through this.

Stamp nods slowly as his eyes morph even crazier. "Joel told me the truth about everything. You understand, though. I had to try to save my son."

He gives my tank top one last yank, and it falls open. I'm not wearing a bra. He raises a speculative eyebrow. There's no humanity in his expression, just madness.

"What happened next?" he growls. "Please regale me." He must be aware that I can't speak because of the shield trap, but still he toys with me. "That's right!" He leans down and licks from my neck to my temple just like Joel did.

I close my eyes, refusing to watch this insanity. My heart's about to beat out of my chest as he pushes hard off me.

He rolls me on my side. "Is this the angle?" He has me on the wrong side, but it makes no difference. He kicks me as hard as he can in the stomach, knocking the air out of me.

Pain radiates so intensely that I'm throwing up an instant later. I'm unable to move through the trap shield, so I find myself lying with my cheek in a chunky puddle of my lunch. The smell is horrific, but I have no choice but to lie there. I focus on my lack of ability to breathe but must wait for my stunned lungs to reinflate on their own.

Finally, I'm able to take a gasping breath. Tears stream down my face into the vomit puddle.

Coach Stamps kneels where I can see his face. He looks disgusted. "You're filthy, lying there in your own vomit." He plunks down, sitting with his legs stretched out. His relaxed nature only adds to my terror. "As I said this morning, you took something very important from me that we need to discuss." He glances my way and smiles with that debonair charm only wealthy assholes are capable of. "What you took is my son. You just couldn't give in, could you? You two would have been very happy together if you'd just given in. It's what he wanted, after all. He took one look at you the first day of school, and he was in *love*." He's smiles at me with an eerie sweetness. "I was so happy for him when he got home that day. He practically bounced into my room and told me all about you."

He has to be kidding. He's turning Joel's obsession into a sweet teen rom-com?

My thoughts are interrupted as Stamp's face contorts with a vicious scowl. "Then you started rejecting him. He was sad. That made *me* sad. My son is a good boy who deserves to be happy." He slides a maniacal gaze my way. "I told him to get his girl. That's what men do. When we've found the one, we don't stop until we have her."

Holy shit! This is insane.

Coach Stamp hefts himself up with surprising grace before grabbing my ponytail and yanking me to my feet. He lets go, but my legs won't hold. I fall to the floor, my hip splatting in the vomit before my lifeless body slithers to the tile floor.

He glares down at me. "You're repulsive. I don't understand how you're the one, but you are." He claps his hands hard. "So, I need you to recant your story so my son can be released from prison. Then you two can give a relationship a shot."

This man is completely cracked. Joel's in prison because he murdered Michael. That was the charge that Marcus's dad, Bruce, brought against him because there was gas station surveillance of Michael's kidnapping by Joel and his Drone friends. *Even if I do recant my story, it won't do Joel any good.*

Coach Stamp's eyes widen as he tips his head. He looks like an asylum patient with a bat-crap crazy idea. "Not true!" he snaps. "Not *true!*"

"Did you just hear my thoughts?"

He nods once, hard and fast, before hefting me up around the waist. He grips my hips and swings me wildly to the left. With no ability to control my body, I can't stop myself as my shoulder slams into a filing cabinet. He throws me onto a metal faculty desk before rushing around the back side, out of my view. I take in what I can see, realizing that we're in a windowless office. I suspect it's his baseball coaching office. The room is small and gloomy.

I don't want to die in this room.

"Too fucking bad," Stamp snarls as he grips my ponytail tightly at the top. He yanks my head back and slams it into the hard metal desk. He yanks my head back again, and the realization that he plans to bash my skull in breezes through my chest.

My fear is suddenly replaced with relief so strong that it makes me exhale, and my tears stop. *"Do it, Coach. Get your revenge. I just want this to be over."*

Stamp releases me and rushes around the desk. He looks at me like I'm insane.

Before he can respond, there's a loud clang at the door, followed by two more. The door flies open, and Demitri rushes in with Mr. Isley hot on his heels. Adam flies through next. Demitri raises a fire extinguisher and smashes it into Daniel Stamp's face. Coach Stamp hits the floor, and Adam grabs his shirt, brutally pulling him to his feet before hitting him with a right hook that snaps my attacker's head so hard to the right, I'm scared Adam just killed him. The last thing we need is Adam up on murder charges.

Coach Stamp's head lolls, and the shield he's had over me dissolves right as Adam drops him.

Mr. Isley checks Coach Stamp's pulse. "He's alive."

I try to get up but can't. My head is pounding, and I'm seeing stars. As I lie on the desk, I'm so full of shock that nothing registers. I try again and get my arms under me. My head hangs, and blood oozes in sticky threads from my nose. I faintly realize that my top is hanging open but can't muster up the will to care.

Mr. Isley grabs the phone on the desk, and seconds later, he announces that there's no dial tone. He turns, ordering the girl I saw when I was dragged through the hall to run to Principal Buttrum's office. I look at him through my daze.

"How Principal Buttrum handles this will tell us if he's with us or not," Mr. Isley explains. "If he's not, I'll close the door and handle him myself."

Pain blazes through my shock, causing me to whimper.

There's movement at the door, and now Valerie's standing there with her mouth hanging open. "Oh my God, Melanie!"

I drop my head and swallow hard. Demitri's hand lands on my arm. He pulls me to sitting and starts to check me over. I grab on around his neck and wrap my legs around his waist. I bury my face in his neck as a torrential post-traumatic meltdown hits me.

He abandons his injury-seeking mission and picks me up from the desk. "You're okay," he whispers, holding me tight.

I cling like a terrified koala bear and gasp over and over through thick sobs. "Don't let go. Don't leave."

Demitri squeezes me tighter. "I'm not leaving, Meley. Breathe."

Shaking starts from the top of my head to my feet.

"I'll take her, D," Adam offers.

I feel Demitri shaking his head against the side of my face. "Not a shot, Adam. She asked me not to let her go."

I wince at the realization that I'm covered in vomit. I try to wiggle away, but Demitri holds me tighter.

"Stop writhing, Melanie."

"Vomit," I whisper.

"Valerie, please grab the towel from my dance bag in the studio. Wet it down and bring it back." Demitri rubs the back of my head. "We'll get you cleaned up."

I shift, putting my head on his shoulder. I blink sleepily just before Demitri turns to face Mr. Isley. Daniel Stamp comes into view, and I scream, terrified and completely out of my mind.

Adam's hands land flat on my back. "Calm down, Melanie. I won't let him touch you again. I'll kill the motherfucker if he wakes up."

I hit Adam with completely traumatized eyes. "Don't leave me here!"

He sends a huge wave of calm through his hands into my back, and I slump in Demitri's arms. I blink lethargically.

"Bad plan, Adam. She has a concussion. We need to keep her awake!" Demitri's scolding fades away as I slip into unconsciousness.

— —

I wake with a start to the word, "Ambulance." I have no clue who said it, but it makes no difference. The moment my eyes open, I know exactly where I am. Anger blisters up, and I lift my head, discovering that Demitri still has me in his arms.

The tiny office is packed. Apparently, Trey, Arch, Principal Buttrum, and Drew joined us while I took a concussion nap.

"Put me down, Demitri."

He sets me down but keeps his arms wrapped tightly around me. I give him a look, and he glances down at my bare shoulders.

I huff. "Anyone got a shirt?"

Trey crosses to a cabinet, opens a drawer, and pulls out a shirt from the baseball team's stash. He steps next to Demitri and spins me into his chest, blocking the view of my nudity from the occupants. He pulls the shirt over my head, and I get my arms through the holes. When he attempts to hug me, I step away because if he hugs me now, I'll lose it. I'll have my meltdown soon, but now isn't the time.

"Now that our first problem is fixed," I say, my tone harsh, "let's get to the second." I snap my gaze Principal Buttrum's way. "Let me be abundantly clear. I want answers, the truth, and I'm fucking done. Handle this carefully, or I'll kill you myself in this room full of people."

Principal Buttrum steps back in surprise. Everyone else chuckles.

"Well, Melanie's had the *pissed* knocked into her," Trey says with a smirk.

My face contorts into a sneer. "What do you know?" I bark at Buttrum.

For a moment, Principal Buttrum looks like he might resist, but then he softens. "I was hired by Charlie Sisternos from the school board. At first, it seemed like a legit position. I was excited about becoming the principal here. I'm alumni, class of sixty-five."

Mouths fall open.

"You were a *student* here?" I holler.

He nods and smiles wistfully. "I love this place. There's nowhere else like it."

I roll my eyes. "Phenomenal. Welcome home. Spill it."

"Anyhow, I signed the job offer, and then it started getting weird. I was called into another meeting, where it was explained to me that there were serious security issues and threats coming down on the school. The district rep and School Board Charlie were there. They filled me in on what they were claiming to be a series of bomb threats. They suggested that there was a dire need for a big security allocation. The only catch was that I, as the new principal, would have to *request* the allocation. When I heard the name of the company, I was stunned. I knew Daniel Stamp from a charity organization I used to volunteer for. We hit it off because we're both retired military. Anyhow, I was hired at his company for a brief stint years ago, but quickly discovered that he's a ruthless narcissist on a good day, and a psychotic maniac on a bad one. I quit the company, thinking that was the end of it." He makes a scoffing sound. "Little did I know."

We're all staring at Principal Buttrum with rapt fascination.

He looks my way. "Your name kept coming up as the ringleader of the trouble, but I didn't realize until later how bizarre everyone's focus on you was. I originally just took you as a bad seed that needed to be handled."

I groan.

"My first day—you're right—I came in here with my ego on fire. I'd been told that the students were a problem, and I was angry about it because I love this place. I was determined to get the school back to the reputation I think it needs. I didn't know at the time that there was nothing wrong with the students or the reputation. Daniel Stamp and School Board Charlie sauntered into my office the next day, handing me the memo you kids seem to be aware of. That's when it became apparent that I was Daniel Stamp's plant. I still might have resisted, but this time, they were accompanied by a member of the mayor's office. Turns out Daniel Stamp's connections go all the way to the top."

"What's so appealing about that jackoff?" I ask, trying to get to the bottom of the one thing I haven't worked out yet. "Why do these high-powered people care about him? He's nothing but a manipulative dick! He uses everyone to his advantage at the expense of everyone on his team!"

Principal Buttrum gives me a pointed look. "Blackmail. This is where Daniel Stamp's wife comes in. Mrs. Stamp and her society floozies troll their socialite soirees searching for gossip. One of the biggest culprits, incidentally, was Victoria's mother. They latch on to whoever's yapping and collect the details. You see, they only run in the most powerful circles. Politicians, actors, wealthy assholes. The thing about power is that it's often backed with greed. Indiscretions, whether it be an affair, murder, stealing . . . doesn't matter. Daniel Stamp collects them. If the violator wants the dirt held private badly enough, they'll bend to the person who has the information. That person is Daniel Stamp. That's his real business. His Cobra Militia is his hobby. His fortune is built on extortion."

I look down at Daniel Stamp, still an unconscious heap on the floor, then back at Principal Buttrum. "Sounds like it's time to call the police and finish this once and for all."

Principal Buttrum nods and exhales hard. "You have no idea how much I want this man out of my life."

"What are you being blackmailed for?" Adam's question is one we're all wondering.

The principal shakes his head and closes his eyes. "The same thing Victoria spilled. I didn't count on a sixteen-year-old blabbermouth when I started kowtowing to Stamp over here." He appears abashed. "I fell apart after my military service ended. Civilian life was hard. Military life was brutal. I was a disaster, and the time Victoria recounted in the quad was during my problem days. I'm not that man anymore, and you don't need to fear me." He wobbles his head. "Before you ask, I'm aware I've been insane since I got here. You have no idea how frustrating it was wanting to do the right thing but being trapped. Stamp threatened to kill my wife and me if I didn't do his bidding."

"Truthfully, none of us really care," I say with a wry smile. "We've got some odd kinks, and we're shockingly unstable too."

Everyone chuckles, even Principal Buttrum, who drops his head as he laughs.

He gestures to Stamp. "Beating a student nearly to death warrants an arrest. It's over now. I'm headed to my office to make the call. Mr. Isley, will you stay and make sure he doesn't wake up and bolt?"

Mr. Isley nods. "You got it. I hope he does wake up, though. I'm so mad I could eat a box of nails." He looks my way. "I apologize, Melanie. I was out of line in the dance studio. I know how much pressure you've been under. I should have given you a little more grace." He looks to Valerie. "You were out of line attacking Melanie verbally. She isn't the problem. Your strained relationship with Adam is the issue."

Valerie looks at me with a neutral expression.

I choose to ignore her. I'm flat done with her nonsense. I focus on Mr. Isley instead. "Please accept my apology. I was rude and completely out of line. I want you to know how much I respect you. Thank you for helping me when I had nowhere else to turn. It means a great deal."

"Why didn't you fight back when Coach Stamp trapped you in here?" Arch asks.

Everyone seems to be nervous in wait for the answer.

"I couldn't. He snapped a shield over me that froze me in place when he touched my shoulder. It blocked my ability to get a message to Trey and Adam. I even tried to blast energy to Demitri, but it didn't get through."

Concern shows in Arch's eyes. "*You* couldn't break free of his shield?"

"I'm not a superhero, Arch."

We all look down at Stamp on the floor.

"No," Arch says. "But if you couldn't escape him, then he's definitely a supervillain."

CHAPTER 32

I'm sitting cross-legged on my bed, deep in meditation. It's been long enough since my injuries that my body still aches, but the bruises have faded to a sickly green. I hear my bedroom door open and close. Trey and Adam's energy breezes through me. I slowly rise from my meditative state. It takes a long moment, but the guys are patient. I open my eyes, and they both smile at me.

"You two are supposed to be at school."

Trey shrugs. "We need to get you put back together and decided to come over."

Stunned, I ask, "You two are going to work together?"

Adam chuckles. "You scared us with this one. Not being able to feel what was happening to you has us both rattled."

"I can't believe what Stamp was capable of. I've never felt a shield like that before. If it weren't for the girl who went to Mr. Isley, I don't think I would have made it." I flop back on my pillows and rub my face hard before staring at the ceiling fan as it gently rotates.

Trey sits on the bed and scoots over to make room for Adam.

"Her name's Jennifer Luera," Adam informs. "She's in the science genius crowd. She ran in with her tail on fire. Mr. Isley immediately grabbed Demitri and me. He didn't waste time calling the office. He's caught some heat for not calling the police, but you know Isley. When a kid is in trouble, his old school thug comes out. He wanted us to handle it, and I'm relieved. We work better without the authorities doing stuff the proper way. Anyway, we ran as fast as we could. I'm sorry we didn't get there sooner, Mel. We couldn't get through the locked door, but D thought quick. He smashed the glass covering the fire extinguisher shelf in the wall. Damn glass door was stuck. He managed to bust the doorknob and then kicked the door open. I'll admit, I didn't think he had that in him."

All I can do is shake my head. I've tried not to think about what happened. It really was terrible. I make a note to myself that I'll need to track down Jennifer and thank her the first chance I get.

Trey sighs heavily. "I appreciate you getting to Melanie," he says to Adam. "I need to thank Demitri when I see him. He hasn't been at school."

"Anyone know how he's doing?" I ask, worried. "I haven't heard from him."

Adam shakes his head. "He hasn't called me, but I don't usually hear from him. I figured you'd heard."

I swallow hard. Demitri and I talked through things, but actions speak louder than words. Things between us have been strained, even after we supposedly squashed our issues and chose to remain best friends.

"It seems that Victoria has a problem with our friendship. Things have been weird. He's distant." I roll my eyes. "Whatever, though. It's his choice, and he's made it. If he prefers to cater to her, so be it."

Trey snorts his response.

Silence descends momentarily, the ceiling fan the only sound in the room.

"Daniel Stamp is in holding," Adam says after a time. "He's awaiting the judge's decision on bail until his trial. Things have calmed down at the school, and Principal Buttrum's actually proven to be fairly cool. He even jokes with the students now." He grimaces. "It's weird when he smiles. I think there's actually a human being in there somewhere. I'll always be wary of him, though."

I chuckle. "I'll take it. I'm looking forward to going back to school but needed a few days. Just about everything hurts, but it's better than it was." I grin. "Mom took me to the doctor. Can you believe my nose isn't broken?"

Trey really studies me. "I can't believe your face isn't bruised."

"Tanner came over last night with this green stuff," I explain. "It's some expensive professional makeup base that covers bruises. He did a trial run on me, and it works. I've got it under my makeup. He knew I wouldn't go back to school with my face a wreck."

"Think you can wash it off?" Trey asks. "I want to see the damage."

Dejectedly, I tip my head and grimace. "Today isn't a good day for natural Mel. I need to hide behind the makeup."

"You aren't okay, are you?" Trey puts a hand on my cheek.

I shake my head and purse my lips pensively.

Adam repositions himself so we can all sit in a circle. He takes my hand. "Let's dive in and see what we can do to fix some of this."

Trey takes my other hand, and we drop into meditation together. I open my eyes in my psyche, and they both get to work surveying my condition. Trey bolsters Adam's energy reserves while Adam calms fear in places I've stuffed it to avoid reality.

CHAPTER 33

We round the corner to the front lawn of the school. It's Monday, and I couldn't avoid the inevitable any longer. Everyone but me has coffee and donuts in hand. My friends all met in the student parking lot, jovial at my return. It was a solid reunion full of reassurance that things are different now, but I'm so nervous that I can't eat. Victoria left yesterday for a ski trip to Breckenridge, and Demitri's suddenly all kinds of Fraggle happy with me. It's annoying that he's a different person with me when his girlfriend's not around. His behavior feels fake whenever she's with us, and I despise that he's able to be such a chameleon with his girlfriends. I didn't think he had that in him.

We round the two-story building, heading up the lawn at the front of the school.

Presley's clearly annoyed. "I hate all this walking around," she says to me. "Why don't they just open the damn gates so we can walk straight in like we used to?"

"If the worst that happens is us having to walk around the school, I'll take it. We dodged a bullet." I giggle, suddenly feeling a little better. "I'm so excited that things are back to normal."

Demitri tries to put an arm around my shoulder as he agrees. I subtly step away, and he gives me a guarded look.

The bell rings, signaling time to head in.

"You guys go to class," Demitri says. "I need to talk to Meley."

Trey kisses me before giving my hand a squeeze. He, Tanner, and Marcus walk up the steps, all of them cracking up about something I can't hear.

Now that it's just us, I turn to Demitri. "What do you need?"

"Why are you acting weird?"

"*I'm* acting weird? Are you shitting me? Demitri, you're a different person around Victoria."

"I am not!" Demitri's looking at me like I've lost my mind.

I scrunch up my face. "*Yes*, you are! You don't act the same. You treat me like an acquaintance. You're fake and shallow around her. I don't get you lately, and I've never understood Victoria. I don't see what you see in her. She looks good, I suppose, but I thought you were deeper than that." I point at him, even though it's rude. "I'm not interested in a part-time friend. I'm not here to amuse you when it's convenient and be ignored when it's not. I have Adam for that."

Clearly pissed, Demitri turns on his heel, and without a word, trudges up the steps in front of the school. Left alone, I shake my head. *Looks like Demitri and I aren't the ride-or-die friends I thought we were.* I traverse the steps, the last student to enter the school as the tardy bell rings. *Damn it. Now I need a tardy slip.*

I make no effort to walk quickly to the performing arts office. Now that I'm in the building again, my intuition is stirring. At first, I think it's just a little post-traumatic residual fear, but my desire to run grows with each step. Still, I ignore it and turn into the office.

Ms. Austin smiles at me. "Good morning, Melanie. Need a tardy slip?"

I nod.

We're interrupted by the voice of Ms. G calling in from the other room. "Melanie, get in here, child."

With a chuckle, I head into her little office. I'm surprised to find Mr. Jenson sitting across from her. They greet me boisterously, and we catch up. How I'm doing seems to be the theme of the day. It feels good to be cared about in this way.

"I'm legit good," I say with a smile. "Still a little bruised, but it's getting better. I'm just glad to be back." I glance at Mr. Jenson. "You aren't teaching algebra today?"

He frowns slightly, looking a little disappointed. "A new teacher was hired. She seems all right."

Ms. Austin steps next to me and hands me the tardy slip before giving me a quick motherly hug. We all say our goodbyes, and I leave the office, taking my time heading to the stairs.

Deb and Presley round the corner as they hop down the last stair.

Presley hooks my arm. "Hey, lady. We're headed to the bathroom."

Before I can protest, they drag me with them. I reach for the door handle just as evil energy hits me like a nuclear blast. I double over, gasping, my intuition raging at full force.

Presley stops short behind me and puts her hand on my back. "Intuition or sick?"

"Intuition. Something's seriously freaking wrong."

Deb and Presley exchange a look, grab me by my hands, and pull me down the hall. They stop short as we see Coach Stamp come through the double doors. He turns and gestures. A line of black uniformed men marches through the door. Deb and Presley step in front of me, blocking me from view.

"They're wearing tactical vests," Deb says softly.

Presley's eyes narrow. "And all black," she whispers. "With combat boots."

"They're armed."

Deb's right. It's apparent they're armed to the teeth with rifles and handguns. Panic washes through me. I open the conference room door, gesturing for Presley and Deb to hurry inside. They exchange a look and rush in. I pull the door closed and lock the bolt. Presley races across the room and cracks open the door on the other side, that leads into the new Magnet office. She waves us over and opens the door just enough for us to look through.

Ms. G is across the room, standing beside Ms. Austin. Both women have their eyes narrowed as Ms. G gestures aggressively at the big guy with his back to us.

"You're what?" she says. "*Excuse* me?"

"We're taking over the school," the man says. "Stand down and sit in your office. Don't leave, or you'll be shot on sight."

Ms. G snorts. "Oh . . . I see. *You're* going to take me out?"

"Correct," the militia guy answers.

Ms. G hits him with an evil sneer. "You better hope you have an army backing you."

"We do."

Very slightly, Ms. G's gaze shifts to our position at the door.

Presley quietly closes the door and flips the deadbolt. Then, she turns to face us with huge green eyes. "Did you hear that?" she whispers.

"Who *are* they?" Deb whispers.

"Coach Stamp and his Cobra Militia," I say. "But how did he get out of jail?"

Presley snorts. "He has rich-guy lawyers. They couldn't get Joel off on the murder charges, but realistically, getting Mr. Stamp out on bail probably wasn't hard."

"What do we do?" Deb asks.

Gunshots ring out somewhere deep in the building. The three of us drop flat on the ground. I reach out and grab their hands. We hold on tight as I count three gunshots. Tears fill my eyes. *I thought we were done with this.*

Presley's hand is shaking in mine. "It's going to be okay, Mel," she whispers, but she doesn't sound sure of herself.

A realization comes to me, and terror shoots up my spine. "Shit. When Stamp attacked me, he could hear my thoughts. I don't know if it's because of the shield he had over me, but what if he can hear me at any time?"

Presley's eyes snap wide. She and Deb aren't energy workers, but they know enough to recognize that I'm talking about the very real possibility that Coach Stamp can read my mind.

Deb raises an eyebrow from her prone spot on the floor. "Think something so salacious that he's sure to react. It's better to know."

I close my eyes, gathering my nerve, and think, *Coach Stamp is a pathetic narcissist who couldn't even manage to kill a teenage girl.*

I tell the girls what I thought, and both snort their approval. We wait with bated breath, but nothing happens.

"Maybe his ability to hear my thoughts requires the trapping shield he put over me," I theorize.

A fresh round of gunshots rings out. We cower, squeezing together as tight as we can. The gunfire ceases, and we're left shaking on the ground.

"Trey, Adam, Marcus, and Drake are out there," I say. "We have to get them out."

"Don't get tunnel vision on us now, Melanie," Deb says. "We have to get everyone else out of here too. Our guys are smart. They're going to be okay. We have to make a plan."

We hear a door close on the other side of the wall.

"Sounds like Ms. G just went into her private office," Presley whispers.

Before I can answer, a piece of paper slides through the big air intake vent at the bottom of the wall. Ms. G's little office is on the other side. The three of us glance at each other before Presley and Deb army crawl to the vent, staying low in case there are more gunshots.

While they get the paper, I close my eyes and try to find Trey's energy across campus. I locate him and attempt to send him a pulse. It doesn't work. I switch gears, finding the energy that's distinctly Adam. I've got a better shot at getting a message to him because our soulmate connection has more range. I reach across the distance, straining with the effort. *"Adam!"* I pulse. *"Gunshots."*

I feel his panic as he faintly pulses back, *"Where are you?"*

"Conference room. Hang tight. We're trying to figure this out."

The exchange only takes seconds. I come back to reality as Presley crawls back and starts unfolding the paper. The note says:

> *Girls, it's Ms. G.*
> *How many of you are in the conference room?*

I pull a pen from the front pocket of my backpack. Deb takes it, grabs the paper from Presley, and writes:

> Three of us. Presley, Melanie, and Deb. We're locked in here.

Deb slides the paper back through the vent, and it's pulled through on the other side. I lie on the ground next to the others. We anxiously wait for a response. A moment later, the paper silently slides back to us through the vent. Presley opens it and we read.

Lock both doors. These intruders already searched that room and think it's empty. Don't make a sound.
They've cut the phone lines and cell service so we can't warn the rest of the school or call the police.
You kids were right.

We look at each other. I gesture for the pen and write:

We don't want to be right.
What do we do? We're trapped in here. Militiamen are in the hall.

I slip the paper back through the vent. My palms are sweating. I wipe them on my leggings.

The paper comes back through the vent.

Inside the third drawer from the left is a little tool kit.
Take the screwdriver out and unscrew the intake vent.
Mr. Jenson's going to help you. He was in my office when the school was taken over. They don't know he's in here with me.

Presley jumps up and opens the third drawer, quickly finding the tool kit. She slips a screwdriver out and rushes to the vent. She works on the screws attaching the big vent cover to the wall, then quietly removes the cover and hands it to me. We all look through. Ms. G's on her knees, peeking through from her side. She holds a finger to her lips, signaling for us to be quiet. Mr. Jenson's next to her. He silently hands her a screwdriver, then army crawls through the hole in the wall. It's a good thing the air intake hole is so big because Mr. Jenson is built like a linebacker. The vent cover on Ms. G's side is replaced. Mr. Jenson takes our vent cover and screws it back into the wall on our side.

Mr. Jenson motions for the three of us to come to the other side of the room. "I was beyond relieved when Ms. G told me that the three of you were the ones in here," he whispers. "I have a plan, but first, we need to get the blueprints from the cabinet. Are you up for this?"

We nod.

"What's happening out there?" Deb asks.

"The Cobra Militia have taken over the school. They were demanding the attendance sheets so they could have the names of everyone at school today. But Ms. G was thinking quickly. She switched today's sheets with ones from the day your group was marked absent for Adam's beach memorial service. Then, she marked Drake absent because we need Deb's head in the game. We're getting him out with us."

Deb smiles slightly and wipes at her teary eyes. "There's something about that hazel-eyed boy that's already turned my world upside down. You're right that I'll think clearer if I know he's safe."

Mr. Jenson unlocks a tall cabinet and pulls out a roll of blueprints. He unrolls them on the conference table.

"Are we safe to stand?" Presley whispers.

"Honestly, I'm not sure," Mr. Jenson says. "But we'll work faster if we can stand at the table. My old-guy knees are shot."

I smile and shake my head. "You're not old, Mr. Jenson."

"I'm older than you kids, and anyway, we're going to have to do a lot of the legwork for my plan to succeed."

We all carefully come to our feet.

"Ms. G's checking the computer system for the rest of your group's schedules," he says. "When she finds what we need, she's going to write it on a slip a paper and pass it through the vent. We need to get them out of their classes fast."

Deb crosses the room to the vent just as a paper slips through. She takes it and comes over, setting it on the table by the blueprints. We lean over to read it.

Arch & Hiram: Room 238
Drake & Susan: Room 218
Tanner & Marcus: Room 240
Trey: Room 137
Adam, Demitri & Valerie: Dance Room 1
Finley & Kenji: Room 128
Bear & Darren: Theater Building
Kelsey: Copy Room TA

"Okay," Mr. Jenson says. "We've got our list. Now all we need to do is sneak these kids out."

Deb mutters sarcastically, "Well, golly gee. Is that all?"

Presley looks at him skeptically. "These classes are all over school. How are we supposed to get to them? We're trapped in here. We can't leave through the hall door, and the other door leads to the new Magnet office. Its only exit is the same hall."

Mr. Jenson grins. "That's where these blueprints come in."

We all crowd closer to the table.

He flips through the blueprints and finds the one he's looking for. "This is it. We've got what we need. There's a series of underground maintenance tunnels that run under most of the school. We don't use them often, but they were put in to access the plumbing and heating systems. I've been down there to work on old equipment in the boiler room. Most people don't know they exist."

"If anyone can do whatever you have planned, it's us," I say.

Mr. Jenson looks the three of us over, and with a deadly serious voice, he says, "I hope you're right, or we're all dead."

"You're serious?" Deb asks.

He nods. "There's a trained ex-military militia out there. Ms. G overheard some of them discussing the plan. They have every intention of killing in retaliation for Joel and the Drones being thrown in jail. They already killed three of the yellow jackets and are holding the other three hostage in the security office."

We look at each other, shocked.

Stumped, I inquire, "I understand how phone lines are cut, but how did they cut cell service?"

Mr. Jenson shrugs. "All I know is Ms. G's cell phone doesn't work. Neither does mine. My guess is that Stamp has access to military-grade equipment. Maybe that includes some kind of cell phone jammer."

"What do we do?" Deb asks.

"This room is home base," Mr. Jenson informs softly. "No one unlocks either of those doors."

"Then how do we get in and out?" Presley asks.

Mr. Jenson walks over to a supply closet and unlocks the door, careful not to let his massive key ring jingle. "Come see."

We walk over and peer into the closet. Behind a huddle of brooms and mops is another door. Mr. Jenson unlocks it and pushes open the door. Then, he reaches in and flips on a switch. The lights make a curious buzzing pop as they come to life. There's a short, four-step staircase down to a long concrete walkway. It's not as tall as the hall walkways, but there's enough headspace for anyone under six feet tall to stand up straight. Some of our taller guys will have to duck.

"I need one of you to stay here at home base," Mr. Jenson says.

"Then you're going to have to change that nickname to the war room," Presley informs haughtily.

Mr. Jenson grins and shakes his head. "Fine. One of you stays at the war room."

"I'll stay," Presley offers.

Mr. Jenson gives a grateful look. "If you hear *anything* on the other side of either of those doors, you come in here and close the door. It automatically locks from the conference room side, so you should be safe in here. I'm going to head into the catacomb tunnels with Deb and Melanie. While we're gone, I need you to keep the toolbox and the rest of the blueprints hidden. If you must hide, we don't want anything left out that will clue in the militia. Our only shot is secrecy."

Presley nods. "I'll clean up right away."

"We're going to pull your friends out one classroom at a time. Deb will run them back here as we get them. Fill them in and make sure everyone stays quiet. Start working on a plan to get everyone out of here."

Presley's eyes widen. "You want me to work on a plan to evacuate the whole school past murdering goons with guns? With the phone lines down, I can't just call the cops!"

Mr. Jenson nods. "Correct."

I reach over and take Presley's hand.

She squeezes back, taking a quick deep breath. "Move fast."

CHAPTER 34

With the catacomb blueprint in his hand, Mr. Jenson gestures for us to follow. We make it halfway down the first hallway and turn left down another hall. He motions for us to stop while he surveys the plumbing pipes overhead. They're all marked with mysterious numbers and letters that don't mean anything to me.

I take the opportunity to pulse a message to Adam. *"Underground passageways. We're going to get you out. Lock all doors in the dance building. Coach Stamp's Cobra Militia are the ones holding the school hostage. My guess is, they plan to kill everyone in our group in retaliation. Pull aside Mr. Isley and explain about our soulmate connection so that he understands how you know all of this. He'll believe you."* The effort to send so much information leaves me reeling.

"Got it," Adam sends back. *"Are you safe?"*

"Not any safer than anyone else."

"Melanie, no matter what, you have to make it through this." His mental voice is choked with panic.

"I'm going to try."

"Does Trey know?"

"No. I can't get through to him at this distance."

Adam's mental voice holds a tinge of smug orange as he pulses back, *"Love you."*

"Love you too," I send back in an amused yellow. Leave it to Adam to be competitive about who has the stronger connection with me at a time like this.

Mr. Jenson spreads the blueprint out on the dusty concrete floor. "This floorplan is a map of the different plumbing pipes," he whispers. "Each pipe's marked with a code that correlates to the numbers on the blueprint. I know where the classrooms are located based on distance. Each classroom is thirty feet wide."

We nod.

"This should be room 137," he says, gesturing above us. "We're going to get Trey first."

My heart races with relief and fear. If we can get Trey out of danger, then I'll feel better, but the real question is, when does the danger end?

Mr. Jenson motions me over. "You see this vent?"

I nod.

"These are attached differently than the one in the war room. There's a filter behind the cover. I'll pull that out, and then you'll have to push a little metal hook away from you to unlock the vent cover on the other side. That vent cover will swing up and into the room on a hinge. Before you push up the vent, you must listen and see if you hear any of the militia in the room."

I crack my neck and wipe my clammy hands on my leggings. "Seems like all I do lately is face terror head-on."

Deb looks at me, her eyes serious. "You can do this, Mel."

"I *can* do it. But what do I do when I get in there?"

"Gesture for everyone to be silent," Mr. Jenson instructs. "Whisper to the teacher the pertinent information and explain that you need to get Trey. It's imperative that the students don't panic and try to follow you and Trey out. Make it abundantly clear that our only shot is for them to stay where they are. A suddenly empty classroom will tip off the militiamen, and all hell will break loose.

"Now, listen up because this is key. Most of these rooms have connecting doors. You need to tell the teacher to sneak to the room next door and fill in the next teacher very quietly. That teacher then needs to pass word to the room next to them, and so forth. That's how we're going to spread the word."

When I nod, Mr. Jenson reaches up and opens the hook holding the vent cover in place. He swings it up and pulls the filter out quietly. He boosts me up on the ledge, and I peek through the vent slats, listening carefully. The classroom's silent. There are students sitting on the floor, tears streaming down most of their faces. *Looks like they heard the gunshots.*

I don't see any of the militia, so I quietly push the little hook away from me, swinging the vent cover up on its hinge. I hear gasps as I shimmy through as fast as I can. When I put my finger to my lips, everyone stares silently at me like I'm a ghost that just floated into the room.

Trey rushes over and grabs my hand. I send him a giant pulse of everything that's happening. He studies it while the teacher rushes quietly to me.

"The school's being held hostage by a militia," I explain in a whisper.

"We know," he replies. "A man with a gun came in here a few minutes ago and gave us instructions."

"What did he tell you?"

"They're going to take everyone to the theater at lunch. We're supposed to stay here until then. No one's allowed to leave the room, and we can't lock the door. They're checking. The guy said he has attendance sheets and knows how many people are here."

I shake my head. "Ms. G's switched out the attendance records. The sheets these nutjobs have are for a day when my group wasn't here. Let's hope they don't figure that out." I gesture to the vent. "I'm here with Mr. Jenson. We're supposed to take Trey. He's one of the ones they're after, and the militia won't find his name on the attendance list Ms. G gave them. I need to take him before they discover an extra student."

The teacher nods.

"You need to quietly sneak over to the room attached to yours and fill in the teacher next door," I explain. "Have that teacher go to the room on the other side of them, and so on. Everyone needs to keep it quiet that there's a group working literally underground to get us out of here. We'll be back to fill you in when we have more information. The phone lines are cut, so we're going to have to do this the old-fashioned way. We'll slip a note through your vent when I know the next step of the plan. Make sure all the teachers know to watch for a note coming through their vents. Ask them all to pull the vent filters and hide them in a cabinet out of sight."

"I'll pass on the message," he assures. "All the teachers on this side of the hall will have the information."

The teacher motions for Trey to come with me. I gesture for him to grab his backpack.

"I need you to all be brave enough to stay here," I quietly explain to the other students. "I can't take you all because if the militia finds an empty classroom, it'll get people killed. We can't clue them in that something's up."

Heads nod, and the other students react in their own ways. I know they're terrified, but I can see from their expressions that they know they can do this.

Trey kneels by the vent and hands his backpack down to Deb in the catacomb.

Mr. Jenson whispers something I can't make out, then Trey gestures for me to go first. I drop down and shimmy backward through the hole. Deb and Mr. Jenson get me by the waist and guide me down. Trey looks through the hole, and then his feet slide through. He drops nimbly to the dusty catacomb floor, and the teacher closes the vent cover from the classroom side. Mr. Jenson intentionally leaves the filter out, and closes the vent cover on our side, locking it.

Trey hugs me. "You got a message to *Adam*?" he hisses.

I sigh. I hadn't intended to send him that part.

Mr. Jenson looks at us quizzically.

Deb rolls her eyes. "Nothing with you people surprises me anymore."

"Trey," Mr. Jenson says, snapping back to reality, "go with Deb to the war room. Deb, meet us back in the main catacomb walkway when you finish delivering him. Melanie and I are headed down this hall to room 128. Finley and Kenji are next."

Trey refuses to go. "I'm not leaving Melanie."

"This isn't optional," Mr. Jenson orders. "Go now. Trey, we need you to help come up with an escape strategy. We must get all these kids out of here without any more guns going off."

Trey's eyes widen, and his face sets in a determined sneer that I know all too well. He's on a mission to solve this problem.

"I'm going to be okay," I assure him. "I have to do my part, but I'll move faster if I know you're working on the next step."

Deb pulls Trey down the walkway with her. He glances over his shoulder at me but doesn't resist. I rush to him, grab his hand, and send a pulse of love. He pulses back, but the message is tinged with irritation over the Adam situation.

I sigh and follow Mr. Jenson as he counts plumbing pipes along the ceiling. The catacomb walkway narrows. He silently points to a vent overhead. He boosts me up, and I unlock the latch, pulling the filter out as quietly as possible. I squeeze my eyes closed as the filter makes a slight metallic squeak. Mr. Jenson holds his breath. We listen, but there's no sound of alarm on the other side of the vent. I peek through and see the same thing I did in the first classroom: crying students silently sitting against the wall across the room. I push the vent up on its hinge and slip through more easily this time. All the students stare at me with big eyes. Finley jumps up, rushing over to hug me.

The teacher crosses the room, and the sweet lady looks like she's going to have a heart attack. She's shaking from head to toe, her cheeks wet with tears. I quietly whisper the plan. She gestures for Kenji and Finley to follow me. They grab their backpacks, and Finley hands them through to Mr. Jenson. Finley plunges headfirst through the vent hole. I peek through and watch Mr. Jenson pull her down from the ledge. He looks up at me and gestures that he's ready for Kenji.

Kenji looks unsure. "There's no way I can fit through there."

I look from the vent hole to Kenji and snark, "If women can give birth, then you can get through that hole."

He's a big guy, but he gives it a try. After far longer than I would prefer, he finally wrestles his shoulders through the vent hole and drops down to his knees on the other side. He scampers up and moves, leaning at an awkward angle because he's too tall for the short catacomb ceiling.

I turn and hug the scared teacher. I don't know her, but we're all in this together. "We're going to get you out of here," I whisper. "I promise."

She nods and sniffs. "I know you will. You student council kids can do anything."

I inform the students that they must stay where they are. After a promise that we'll be back to fill them in, I shimmy back into the catacombs. The teacher locks the vent on her side. Mr. Jenson closes the vent cover on our side, and we hurry to meet Deb, who appears just as we turn right down the main walkway.

"Any trouble in the war room?" Mr. Jenson asks.

Deb shakes her head. "Presley listened at the hall door and heard two of the militia guys talking on the other side. They've decided that certain rooms are empty. They're going around putting signs on those doors so they don't have to check them again. It looks like they're arrogant enough to make the kinds of mistakes that will benefit us. We've moved our planning stuff back to the table since we think we're likely to be undisturbed. She also overheard that they only have Coach Stamp's master key. Presley wants to know what it opens."

"That's good news," Mr. Jenson says. "That key opens the main building doors and all classrooms, but it doesn't open any of the maintenance doors, office doors, or the conference room. If you're all silent, they should leave the war room alone. Make sure you keep Ms. G up-to-date. Slip notes through the vent to her."

Deb nods, and the trio hurries down the hall to the war room.

We move next to rescue Kelsey from the copy room, where she'd been hiding alone.

She's white as a sheet as she climbs down to us. "There were three gunshots in the room next door," she says.

"Do you know what that room is?" I ask.

"The security office. We call it the hive because of the yellow jackets."

"So I guess we can confirm that the shots we heard were meant for security," I say to Mr. Jenson, who nods mournfully.

Kelsey's eyes widen to the size of saucers. She grabs her

backpack. "We've got a plan, right?" When I nod, she breaks into an evil smile. "I knew it. We're going to kick their asses."

"That's what we do," I say with a shrug.

Since there's no one left in the copy room, Mr. Jenson and I decide to replace the filter and close the vents completely.

Deb ushers Kelsey back to the war room while Mr. Jenson and I move on to Tanner, Marcus, Arch, and Hiram, all of them set up in a pair of rooms that we can access from catacomb walkway B.

"We'll get them at the same time," Mr. Jenson tells me. "Those two classrooms are connected by a door, so as long as you're careful, there won't be any need to climb through two vents."

"But these are on the second floor," I point out. "How do we get up there?"

Mr. Jenson points up a metal ladder bolted to the side of the wall. There's no safety railing, and the ladder squeezes between a tight network of pipes and air ducts.

I shake my head. "I'm literally the most claustrophobic person on the planet. I can't squeeze between the walls and air ducts. I don't do small spaces or heights."

Mr. Jenson gives me a fatherly look. "Today, you do. You're small enough, and you know what to say to the teachers. We can't send anyone else. It'll take too long." He checks his watch. "There's no time to argue about your irrational fears right now. We have to make a plan before they start moving everyone to the theater building."

Before I can object any further, Mr. Jenson steers me toward the ladder.

I cut a terrified gaze at him.

"You can do this, Melanie. I'm going to head up the ladder first and get the vent cover propped open. I'll remove the filter and see if there's trouble. Wait for me here."

He's surprisingly nimble for such a big guy, and he makes shimmying up the ladder look easy. He disappears behind a bunch of air conditioner ductwork, and I hear the scraping of the filter being removed. I wait, holding my breath until Mr. Jenson comes back down the ladder.

"I didn't see any militia. Get up there and move fast."

I take a breath, wiping my sweaty hands on my now filthy leggings for the thousandth time. If this were any other situation, I'd flat refuse to do this, but I have no choice. So I grab the ladder rung and start my ascent.

"Don't look down," Mr. Jenson coaches. "One rung at a time. You've got this."

I take his advice, and soon discover that squeezing past the air ducts isn't the claustrophobic nightmare I anticipated. I stop for a second, feeling reasonably okay as I lean against the duct that's hugging my back. *Four more of my friends are just a few more rungs away. I can do this.*

I make it to the vent. Bright classroom light casts cheerful lines into the dusty gloom of the scary second-floor ladder space. I listen carefully for signs of the militia. When I hear nothing, I push in the hook and swing the vent cover up, then crawl through into room 238.

As has become the ritual, students gasp as I unexpectedly appear. Hiram and Arch rush to me. They're both fuming.

"What the hell's happening out there?" Arch whispers. "And how'd you get in here?"

I motion the teacher over, and the whole class gathers around. I quietly explain what I know. Everyone nods, and the teacher heads through the interior door to collect Tanner and Marcus from room 240.

"We've got a plan?" Arch asks.

I nod. "Trey's working on it."

Arch cracks his knuckles. "Then we need to move fast. I want in on this."

Quickly, I tell them how to get down the ladder, where Mr. Jenson will be waiting to hand them off to Deb.

Hiram goes first, sliding easily through the vent hole and disappearing into the catacomb abyss. The teacher returns from the classroom next door with Tanner and Marcus in tow. Just as they enter, the lookout at the door snaps at us twice. We have to get out of sight quickly. A bunch of students crowd around the coat closet as Marcus, Tanner, and I slide inside. A moment after I gently close the closet door, we hear a militiaman talking to the class. Through the tension, Marcus reaches into his backpack and silently pulls out three Twizzlers, handing one to each of us. The only light's coming through the air vent slats at the top of the cabinet door, but it's enough for Tanner and me to exchange a wry, amused glance. Tanner shrugs and takes a bite of the candy.

What the hell. Why not? Just another day battling some insane nightmare. I chuckle silently when I think about how most teens dread tests, but we dread dealing with homicidal maniacs. So, I take a bite. I've earned a treat.

After what feels like an eternity, the closet door opens.

It's Arch, and he raises an eyebrow at the sight of the three of us bunched up in everyone's coats, eating candy. "Seriously?" he whispers.

Marcus grins. "Dude, if we stopped eating every time there's a catastrophe, we'd starve to death."

"Time to go," I say. "I'll fill you in when we're in the catacombs."

Tanner grins and softly sings, "We're off to see the wizard," before gleefully heading through the vent.

Before I can follow, the teacher snakes out a hand and grasps my wrist. "The militia are checking on each room more frequently now," she says, "but he didn't seem suspicious. Move fast and lie low."

I nod and wait while Arch and Marcus scoot through the vent hole. After Marcus clears the opening, I peek through and make the mistake of looking down.

Ohhh no!

It's a long way to the ground. My heart nearly explodes. But then I pause, oddly amused that the ladder scares me more than my school being held captive by psychopaths with guns. I lie down on my stomach and back up to slide feetfirst through the vent. I find my footing on the ladder with my right foot, just as my left foot bangs into the air duct behind me. In the hushed silence of the quiet school, it sounds like a bomb just went off. The teacher hurries and closes the vent cover. The little latch slides into place just as the classroom door opens again.

I look through the vent slats to see a militiaman storming in demanding to know what he just heard.

Crap!

I reach over and grab the filter that Mr. Jenson left on the top of the air duct, sliding it silently into place just in time to block the view of the open vent on my side. An instant later, I hear the vent cover open on the classroom side. I hold my breath as I gently close and lock the vent cover on my side. Then, I take two silent steps down the ladder rungs and flatten myself against the wall, making myself as invisible as possible in the gloom.

I hold my breath until I hear the faint squeak of the vent cover closing on the other side. I exhale quietly, my heart racing.

Time to get off this damn ladder.

I hurry down to find everyone waiting for me.

"What happened?" Mr. Jenson asks.

I shake my head. "Close call. It was a stupid mistake. I accidentally kicked the air conditioner duct, but the teacher thought quickly and got the vent cover closed in time for me to slide the filter back in place and close the cover on our side. Coast is clear."

"Time's running out," Mr. Jenson says. "We need to meet Deb."

We silently race through the catacombs and find Deb waiting for us in the designated meeting spot. There, Mr. Jenson explains that Susan and Drake are next.

"I'm getting him out," I assure Deb. "It's going to be okay."

"Do you think Drake can fit through the vent?" she asks with concern in her eyes. "His shoulders are huge."

"We got Kenji through the vents. We'll get Drake through."

Before she leaves, Deb reminds me that we need to grab the backpacks that she and Presley left behind. "Two extra backpacks lying around unclaimed might clue in the militiamen."

———

Presley exhales when she sees us. "Thank God you guys are back safe."

Drake drops all the backpacks in a heap and rushes to Deb. She grabs him and they kiss.

He pulls back, leaving her breathless. "Can someone fill me in?" he asks.

I cross to Trey and take his hand. He's still mad. I sigh and pulse a thought bubble laced with being sorry. He lets go of my hand without a response.

Great. Just what I need.

Presley sighs. "This is the millionth time I've told this story. Okay, here goes. The baseball coach is a punk who, I'm guessing due to his wealth and connections, weaseled bail out of the judge. Wasting no time, he rallied his G. I. Joes and made a jump on all this hostage takeover insanity. So, as if Monday doesn't suck bad enough, we're faced with a whole militia of narcissistic cahooters with little rods and big rifles. Three security guards are dead, the school's being held hostage, we have to figure out how to get fifteen hundred people past an army of weapons, and I have to pee. Any questions?"

Drake grins. "Have we confirmed that they have little rods, or is that purely speculation?"

Everyone chuckles through the tension.

CHAPTER 35

Trey leans over the blueprints and compares the one outlining the school classrooms with the one outlining the catacombs. Everyone gathers around.

"Okay," Trey says. "Here's what we've got so far. We started with a list of to-dos, but I refuse to call it the master list."

Everyone chuckles quietly, shaking their heads.

"Buttrum's ruined that word for all of us," Arch says.

"I almost died when everyone started calling him Master Vader," Marcus says.

Trey's vibe shifts serious. "Okay. The plan. We've heard that the militia guys are waiting for lunch to round everyone up. Stupid to wait, in my opinion, but they're so damn arrogant that they think they've got this locked down. Anyway, we still need to rescue Adam, Demitri, Valerie, Bear, and Darren. They're going to be instrumental in all of this." He looks to Mr. Jenson. "We've got a few questions for you."

Mr. Jenson nods.

"Do these catacombs go as far as the dance building and the theater?"

"They do. The only classrooms we can't access are the eight bungalows in quad two, the four bungalows in quad one, and the four bungalows in Actors' Alley. That's a lot of classes."

Trey rubs his forehead. "Marcus, do you have your phone?"

"Yup, and it's fully charged." Marcus takes out his cell phone and checks the screen. "No signal."

"Then that confirms it. The militia used a jammer to impact the cell phones on campus." Mr. Jenson appears concerned.

Trey exhales. "This means we don't have access to the bungalows behind here." He points to the blueprint. "Or the four bungalows in quad one, or the four bungalows in Actors' Alley. We also can't count on help from the outside. My guess is that the police have no idea we're in trouble here. We need to send Mr. Jenson and Melanie to get Adam, Valerie, Bear, and Darren. Deb, go with them and bring back the first set. My plan originally involved getting all the students into the catacombs to hide while the police storm campus and take down the militia. I was counting on Marcus's cell phone. So now I've got to come up with a new plan."

Mr. Jenson swallows hard. "Principal Buttrum and I were shooting the shit last week. He's been far easier to chat with now that he isn't being a nutty dictator. He said that the Cobra Militia are experts in explosives."

"Are you fucking serious?" Trey breathes.

Mr. Jenson nods, and we all look at each other, dumbfounded.

Trey's eyes narrow. "Explosives, huh?"

CHAPTER 36

Mr. Jenson motions for us to be quiet as he listens at a door. I'm lost at this point. On our way to the dance building, we've had to wind and curve far deeper into the catacombs than before. No vents this time, though. Because the dance department's in a basement, there's an actual door we can take to the other side.

"Girls," Mr. Jenson says to Deb and me, "I can't tell what's happening over there. We might walk right into militia and not know it until it's too late."

"Where in the dance department does this door open to?" I ask.

"Mr. Isley's dance room."

My eyebrows rise. "Give me a second." I close my eyes and connect with Adam. *"We're on the other side of the door. Warn Mr. Isley that we're coming in."*

Adam pulses back that the understands.

"I told Adam."

They give me a quizzical look, but there's no time to explain.

I open the door, and we're met head-on by a crush of dancers and Mr. Isley.

"Hi, Mel," Mr. Isley says. "How did you get in here? I thought that door went to a mechanical closet. I've never even tried to open it."

Mr. Jenson motions for the dance teacher to see for himself.

"Where does that lead?" Mr. Isley asks as he stares into the catacomb.

"It leads to almost everywhere. It's how were pulling certain students from classes. We need to fill you all in."

"We need to fill you in also," Mr. Isley says. "Apparently, the gunmen's key doesn't work in this building. They tried to get in but couldn't get the door open. I've kept everyone silent, and we're keeping lights off in the main corridor. I've got the doors to the locker room locked, so that should bar travel between the dance department and the sports complex. So far, no one has attempted to unlock it from the other side. We've been going back and forth through the locker room and here, but no one's allowed by the double doors to the outside."

"So the militia don't know you're in here?" Mr. Jenson asks hopefully.

Mr. Isley shakes his head. "We had warning." He side-eyes me curiously, and I smirk at Adam.

"That should work in our favor." Mr. Jenson looks over the students. "How many of you were absent on the day of Adam's in-school memorial service?"

"All these students were marked absent that day," Mr. Isley informs. "I forgot to do roll with the chaos and didn't remember to correct it."

Mr. Jenson grins at Deb and me. "We just added all these students to our list of underground associates."

"You guys have a plan?" Mr. Isley asks.

Mr. Jenson nods. "Yes. Our number one issue right now,

though . . . We need to use the bathroom. We've all been working behind the scenes and don't have access to one. Our team will do a lot better if we can handle that problem first. I'm going to go get everyone from the war room. You two run to the restroom."

Deb and I about break our necks hauling tail into the ladies' room. A few minutes later, we come out feeling human again. The dance students gather around with Mr. Isley so we can explain everything that's happened.

Not long after, everyone from the war room rushes through the catacomb access door, and Mr. Isley directs them to the bathroom.

Everyone refreshed, we all gather up for an update from Trey.

My boyfriend checks his watch. "We've got an hour and forty-five minutes left to pull this off. I need everyone back to the war room. A warning that you must be quiet. Adding all of you puts us at close to forty people, but I'm going to send different people on errands through the catacombs. I need you all, and we have a lot of work to do."

"We still need to sneak Bear and Darren out of the theater building," Arch says.

"I can go get them," Mr. Jenson offers. "Access to that building is through a trap door into the lighting storage room. I can fit through. Trey, assign your errand runners to me now, and I'll show them the layout of the catacombs. Some of your runners need to be small enough to easily get through the vents."

"Sounds like a plan," Trey says. "Mel, what part of the cata-combs do you know?"

"I've got corridors A and B down, and I've got the second-floor ladders figured out."

Trey nods. "Okay. Let's have Tanner, Marcus, Adam, and Hiram learn the catacombs from Melanie on our way back to the war room." He looks over Mr. Isley's class. "Demitri, Javier, Kendra, and Jayla also need to learn the catacombs. Mr. Jenson, please show them the ropes while you get Bear and Darren. Everyone, meet back at the war room as quickly as you can. I'll have a plan ready by the time the rest of you get there."

Everyone from the dance class grabs their belongings. We stream through the maintenance catacomb access door, and Mr. Jenson double-checks that it's locked securely behind us. Everyone moves stealthily. We break off at the first T-junction, headed in opposite directions.

As we go, I quietly instruct everyone from my group on how the catacomb walkways are laid out, pointing out the numbers on the overhead plumbing pipes and how to calculate distance to determine classrooms.

After I'm done instructing them, Valerie walks swiftly up next to me. "How were you able to communicate with Adam?" she asks quietly.

I don't want to have this discussion now, but with a sigh, I decide to go with vague side-skirting. "Adam and I are both energy workers. Back when he was kidnapped, I had to use a communication line to get him out. The line is still open. We don't know how to close it."

Her eyes narrow as she radiates her displeasure. "I don't like that one bit."

"I get it, Val." Irritation bubbles up. "You're welcome, by the way. I delivered your dead fiancé back to you, not that you've shown a moment of appreciation about it. Go harp on Adam. I've got work to do."

"Stay out of my fiancés head!" she snarls.

Irritation gets the best of me. I stop in the hall and turn to Valerie. I'm radiating malice as I let my voice rise. "Leave me the fuck alone, Valerie."

She balls up a fist and moves closer, likely intending to back me against the wall. She's got the wrong girl. Trey and Adam step up on either side of us.

"Do it," I hiss. "Take your shot!"

Valerie starts to lunge, but Adam grabs her. "We're all going to die in this fucking school if we don't move fast. This can wait, you two."

I hit him with evil eyes. "Put this bitch in her place before I do."

Adam glares back at me. "Get it together, Mel."

"Get it *together*?" I gesture at my filthy clothes. "I've *had* it together! Last time I checked, you're all out of your classrooms because I'm so damn together." I slide my steely gaze Valerie's way. "I should have left you both in the dance room."

Valerie's eyes snap wide. It apparently hadn't occurred to her that she might live because of me.

"Thank you for coming to get us," Adam says, his tone calmer.

I lace my hand with Trey's. "Screw you, Adam." With my free hand, I point at Valerie. "Keep messing with me! I'll scream at the top of my lungs. I don't give a damn if I die in here, as long as I take you down with me."

Trey and Adam appear stunned at how unstable I've become.

"Pull it together, Mel," Trey says quietly. "For me. Forget them."

I scoot to the front of the crowd with Trey.

"Oh boy," Mr. Isley mutters.

We make it to the war room.

Trey listens at the door. He gives us a thumbs-up that it sounds all clear on the other side, then opens the door to find the room just like we left it. "Presley," Trey whispers, "please slip a note through to Ms. G telling her we're back."

She nods and writes the note before putting it through the vent slat.

"Mr. Isley," Trey says, "as a department head, do you have master keys that open as many doors as Mr. Jenson's key?"

"I've got an all-campus master," Mr. Isley says. "As far as I know, Mr. Jenson and I are probably the only two who have them. Ms. G was responsible for making Coach Stamp and Principal Buttrum's key sets, and she and I talked about it. Something told her not to give either of them full access."

"Good," Trey says. "My plan's crazy, but I think it'll work. I just need a few things."

Relief appears to wash over Mr. Isley as he sits in a chair. "Tell me your list and let's see what we can do."

At that moment, Mr. Jenson and his team of catacomb students slip silently through the door, and they're joined by Bear and Darren.

"What's up, losers?" Bear whispers with a grin. "Thanks for leaving us out of the fun for so long."

We all smile at him.

"You two were the farthest away," Trey explains. "It took us far longer to get to this point than I'd have liked. Did Mr. Jenson fill you in?"

Bear and Darren nod.

"This school is huge," Drake says. "If they can't get into a lot of the rooms, that may give us an advantage."

I shake my head. "We can't count on that. Mr. Isley told us after the dance fire alarm mess that the Cobra Militia searched the school under the guise of a bomb threat. They had a plan, no one was suspicious, and they were given full access with no rush. They know the school front to back."

"Who took them on their tour, Mr. Isley?"

Mr. Isley shrugs. "No one really. They marched in like they owned the place, and then they all split up. Took them twenty minutes or so. There were at least fifteen of them."

"Then they likely don't know about the catacombs," Trey says. "But everywhere else, we should assume they are aware of."

With narrowed eyes, Mr. Isley studies me. "I don't know about that. They were obviously already focused on Melanie, given their interest with her as early as the Snow Ball. My guess is that they took a tour of the places she was the most likely to be."

Trey shakes his head. "Daniel Stamp wouldn't stop at just Melanie. He wants revenge on all of us who helped put his son in jail. I guarantee they planned this little retaliation long before now. I'm positive they searched the whole school."

I nod.

"Does he want her dead, or does he want to take her?" Trey asks of no one in particular.

I chuckle humorously. "There's no telling. On one hand, he said I'm the love of Joel's life and he wants us to have a happy life together. On the other hand, he tried to bash my head in. The man is Cracker Jack crazy."

A massive crash happens behind us, and we whip around to the sight of Tanner looking horrified. On the floor is a broken decorative vase that had been full of fake flowers. Tanner is pale as he whispers, "I hopped up to sit on the counter and caught it with my elbow."

We stare at each other for a brief moment, trying to get a sense of whether the racket was heard. The sounds of running feet and yelling in the hall spur us into action. Mr. Jenson grabs the blueprints from the table while we all scurry to gather our stuff.

"Run!" I hiss.

Everyone rushes through the maintenance door, and Mr. Isley pulls it closed just as the conference room door is kicked open. The last of us make our way down the catacomb stairs. Mr. Isley eases the access door closed before flipping the catacomb light switch off. We're plunged into darkness.

I hear shifting before Mr. Isley instructs with a barely audible whisper, "No one move. Don't make a sound."

We hold our breath, waiting in the dark. My heart is pounding. Trey grabs my hand. It does nothing to make me feel better. I've stayed so busy during this ordeal that I really haven't had time to panic. This whole nightmare somehow just became more real. I'm blazingly unsure of the outcome. My intuition is doing little more than nagging at me unhelpfully.

After far longer than I'd like, Mr. Isley whispers, "I think the coast is clear." His breaking the silence makes me jump. I close my eyes in the dark and work to still my racing heart.

Trey clicks on the little screen light on his watch, faintly illuminating the group. "Where do we go? We can't stay here, and we've lost our war room."

"Back to the dance room?"

Mr. Isley's suggestion is met with a shake of Mr. Jenson's head. "I don't like it. The militia have to suspect kids are in that building, and Stamp knows how to access the dance department through the back hallways and girls' locker room." Mr. Jenson brightens up. "But there's a door at the end of catacomb B that goes straight into the old media room."

"Perfect," Trey says. "Is that room big enough for us?"

Mr. Jenson nods. "Not only that, but it should be safe. It hasn't been used since the campus TV station funding was cut. The abandoned dark room is between the media room and the hall the militia are trolling, so that gives us extra cover."

Trey appears lost in thought. "TV station, huh?"

When Mr. Jenson nods, we all contemplate that turn of potential luck.

CHAPTER 37

Mr. Isley unlocks the access door to the media room, and we peer in, finding it empty. When Mr. Isley finds the switch, the lights blaze to life, and we squint in the fluorescent wash. The room's a dusty mess.

"Someone find something they can use to dust this room," Trey instructs. "The rest of us need to figure out what's in here. This is going to be perfect."

Valerie pulls me aside while everyone else splits up, half of them cleaning as best they can and the other half opening drawers and cabinet doors in search of things we can use. Adam steps up next to Valerie, his expression hopeful.

"I'm sorry, Melanie," she says softly.

Still not in the mood to deal with her, I step past them without a word and cross the room to Trey.

Adam follows. "I talked to her," he whispers. "She's legitimately scared that you'll derail our escape plan just to spite her."

"She should be," Trey replies. "Melanie's been through hell. Today isn't a good day to mess with her."

Adam tips up my chin. "Please. For me."

I crank my head to the right, pulling my chin from his grasp. Adam sighs. I glance at Valerie, who's hovering nervously by Finley.

"She's threatened me three times." The rage in me swells, and I close my eyes in an effort to cool off. It's the wrong move. My dark-water side is waiting. She gathers my growing rage into a finely honed mass. I study it as she smirks inside my head.

Trey takes my hand as I send him the image of what just happened. He sends back alarm.

I open my eyes and curiously study the feeling of the energy mass. "Huh," I murmur. "Maybe my fistfighting days are over." I send the image to Adam, and his eyes snap wide.

He crosses rapidly to Valerie. "Don't mess with Melanie," I hear him say. "Just leave her alone until we get out of here."

Confused and delighted as I am about this new ability I seem to have discovered, I try to concentrate on Trey.

He spreads out the blueprints on the freshly dusted table in the middle of the room, along with his notes. "This room is perfect. We don't have to whisper anymore. Just keep your voices down."

"Ah, yes," Tanner sasses. "A perfect room in the basement of a militia fortress."

Trey glares at him. "Thank you for the wonderful opportunity to move us further into hell. Your clumsiness is appreciated."

Arch chuckles quietly. "Cut Tanner some slack. He never screws up like that. It was an accident, although poorly timed."

"I don't want to be the ass of the group," Darren interjects, "but is there a hidden spot in those catacombs where I can have a smoke? I'm a little jumpy."

"I'm not supposed to let students smoke on campus," Mr. Isley says.

Mr. Jenson quietly chuckles. "If a smoke is what keeps some of these kids going, then I'll show them into the boiler room. There's a vent system in there that takes air straight out through the roof. No one's going to notice. Honestly, I've been jonesing for a smoke since this all got started. Come on, Darren. I'll show you our new war room lounge."

Darren motions for Adam, Bear, and Tanner to follow, and they make their way to the boiler room across the catacomb hall.

Everyone else gathers around the big table.

"Did anyone find walkie-talkies in the cabinets?" Trey asks.

"Yup," Arch says. "We've got one." He holds it up.

Trey takes it and turns it on, discovering that it works. He exhales hard before murmuring, "Please be a sign that our luck is changing."

Mr. Jenson and his motley crew of smokers come back in, quietly closing the catacomb access door behind them.

Tanner takes the walkie-talkie and starts flipping through the five channels. He lands on channel three, and a voice comes through clearly. We all lean in and listen.

"Cobra Team, please report . . . One all clear . . . Two all clear . . . Three all clear . . . Four all clear."

Adam laughs. "These tools are so inventive. Cobra Militia, Cobra Team."

Trey rolls his eyes. "They're pathetic. I guarantee all those guys are busy living out some bizarre childhood fantasy of storming the castle. It sounds like they're broken down into four teams. Based on this school layout blueprint, I suspect they've got a team in the two-story building we're in, one in the athletic department, another in quad two, and the last one in Actors' Alley. It's where I'd put teams if the tables were turned. But we'll need confirmation."

The walkie-talkie flares to life, and a male voice says, "The Trinity system isn't in place yet. They need until one o'clock to get their shit together. We move all the students to the theater at twelve forty-five. There's an extra ten grand in it for the first person to retrieve the package. I've informed the helicopter unit, and they're pushing back their arrival. Until then, continue your checks as usual."

"*Helicopter* unit?" I bark.

Everyone shooshes me. I duck a little, embarrassed that I let shock overtake my common sense.

Trey slams his fist down on the table.

"Well, there you have it," Tanner snarks. "Apparently, the package," he gestures flippantly my way, "has a helicopter ride to look forward to."

Trey gnashes his teeth. "Damn it! They're searching for Melanie, and that asshole just upped the stakes."

Mr. Jenson raises a hand. "They aren't going to find Melanie. The good news is, we know their plan now, and knowledge is power."

Trey hits Mr. Jenson with a glare.

"Anyone know what Trinity is?" Mr. Isley asks.

Bear sets to proctoring. "The Trinity in the Bible—"

"No philosophical yap-yap," Trey cuts in. "I'm on edge. Whatever their Trinity is, it ain't the one you're about to pontificate about." He shakes his head. "God bless whatever it is, because it just bought us another hour." He slides his piercing gaze my way. "I have to get you out of here."

"What else do you need to make an escape plan happen?" Arch asks.

"We're going to use every resource available to us," Trey answers. "A high school this big is like a small city full of everything and everybody." He looks up at Jenson. "Do we have access to the metal shop?"

Mr. Jenson nods. "It's in the basement building of the athletic department. There's a door into the shop through catacomb C."

"I need a runner to go over there and get the metal shop teacher to put together some doorjamb holders. Here's the idea: a piece of metal with a plate welded on each side that can be screwed into the door on one end and the doorjamb on the other. We need enough of them for most of the classrooms, the Magnet office, and the auditorium door on the fourth floor that Bear says the militia were using to come and go. We need to block as many entrances and exits as possible."

"Screwing all those metal plates in is going to make a hell of a racket," Demitri points out.

Trey nods. "I've got that covered. Let's get them made, and we'll work from there."

"How long can you give them?" Mr. Jenson asks. "Mr. Franken's the shop teacher. He's good, and his class is trained at cutting and welding, but you're talking about at least fifty of these contraptions."

"Forty-five minutes," Trey says.

"I know how to weld. I'll pitch in and maybe we'll have just enough time. I'll be back as soon as possible with what we can get done."

"How loud is all the cutting and welding?" Presley asks.

Mr. Jenson shrugs. "It's loud, but the welding room is the furthest back in the shop building. The sound won't be heard from where we think the Cobra teams are. I think we can get away with it."

"I'm going with Mr. Jenson," Adam says. "I can knock out some of these doorjamb holders."

"Bring back every single screw gun and screws you can find," Trey instructs. "Don't be late. Get done what you can in forty-five minutes, and we'll make do with whatever you bring."

Adam takes the paper with Trey's quick sketch on it, and he and Mr. Jenson head through the catacomb access door.

"Up next, I need a runner to go to the old media teacher, Mr. Delgado, and get him over here."

"I know just where to find him," Deb says. "He has planning period at the start of the day." She checks the blueprint for her directions and then heads through the catacomb door.

"Next, I need someone to find a student from the golf team," Trey says. "We need Dante Grunier, the football coach, Drew the quarterback, Curtis from the baseball team, and whoever the lead nerd from the science club would be."

"The nerd you seek is Lionel," Drake says, "but a heads-up that his group prefers to be called geniuses instead of nerds."

Trey grins. "Noted." He grimaces. "That was rude of me. I apologize."

Drake shrugs. "I made the same mistake once before Lionel corrected me. They're nice guys. I think you'll like them."

"I need them here fast," Trey says. "We can't get a note to Ms. G now that we've lost our conference room access. Anyone know what class Lionel has?"

Presley raises her hand. "Lionel has first-period chem. I bet the other geniuses are in there too. They take every extra science class they can find."

"How do you know that?" Arch asks, amused.

Presley cocks a hip. "They follow me around. Duh." She heads through the catacomb door, followed by the sounds of our quiet laughter.

"We're going to need more stuff like bats, balls, and golf clubs especially," Trey continues. "I can't risk a raid on the sports complex building. Coach Stamp's office is connected to the storage room."

The request is met by general confusion, but then Mr. Isley grins. "There's some stuff in the dance department storage that might work," he says.

"Perfect. Run that way with a few helpers and bring the stuff back."

Mr. Isley nods and leads several members of his class through the catacomb access door.

"The rest of you, I need access to a copier."

"There's one in this room," Bear says. He points at a massive lump under a tarp. "I found it when I was searching the cabinets and snooping around."

"That's a hell of a stroke of luck," Trey says. "See if it's working."

Bear crosses the room and pulls the tarp off the machine, sending a cloud of dust up that makes us wince.

I huff. "Why do we always end up in nasty locations full of dirt and danger?"

Trey grins and pulls me in, kissing my forehead. He looks me in the eyes and quietly says, "I'm sorry I was upset. We can deal with it later, but I don't want to fight. We're going to get out of here with our usual flare and flourish."

I grin back at him, relieved, and snuggle in for a hug.

Bear flips a few switches, and the machine hums to life. "It's working, but it's out of paper."

"We found a ream of paper in the bottom of that cabinet." Finley points and Bear pulls out the package of paper just where she said it would be.

He nods in thanks and loads the paper in the machine.

"We need to put my plan down on paper and make enough copies for every teacher," Trey explains. "Finley, write this down exactly as I say it."

Finley grabs a black marker out of our pile of supplies on the table and sits down, ready to write.

Trey furrows his brow. "Title it 'The Surge Escape Plan.'"

CHAPTER 38

I can't help but chuckle. The smokers brought chairs into the boiler room and set it up as a lounge. Leave it to our group to find a unique way to survive an ordeal like this. I plunk down and light a cigarette with the lighter and pack of smokes that I'm guessing Darren conveniently left on a chair for anyone that needs it. I close my eyes and take a deep breath, hoping the distraction of the freshly delivered doorjamb contraptions keeps everyone busy. I need a few minutes alone.

Halfway through my smoke break, the dark water in my mind rises intensely. Dark-water Melanie radiates desperation so strongly that I gasp. I send a quick pulse to Adam that I need him, Trey, Bear, and Darren. I don't know what's happening, but whatever it is, I know the five of us can handle it together.

The guys come through the door, and Bear closes it behind him. "What's wrong?" he asks.

I take another drag from my cigarette and hand it to Darren. "Intuition," I gasp out. "Trey, come here. You're going in with me."

He crosses to me, looking wary of my intense expression. I lace my fingers through his and put my forehead against his chest. I drop all my shields, and he dives into the dark water in my mind with me.

"I don't know what's coming," I whisper, "but you're all supposed to be here."

We both sink below the surface of the dark water in my mind just as the intuition bubble bursts. Images start flashing across the surface of the water, rapidly rewinding through time. We see Trey, elderly and taking his final breath while I hold his hand. So many holidays with so many littles running around that my head spins. It keeps rewinding so rapidly that I can barely make sense of it, until it settles in "real time" on three separate moments. A brunette teenager walking across a film set in a bouncy red dress. She's stunning. Next is a curly haired beauty, around twelve, in a musical theater piece. She hits a flawless quadruple turn, and the audience roars. Her image is washed away, and I see Trey and me staring down at a baby boy with golden-brown eyes the exact shade of Trey's.

Trey gasps and his hands tighten on mine. "All three of them are perfect," he breathes.

Images start reversing again rapidly. Trey and me getting married, our graduations, him proposing at night with the city lights in the distance. Suddenly the images are carried away like blown ash on the wind. The water is black for a moment before the image of me lying on the pavement, dead in the quad, blazes through the water. My heart pounds when I realize that this is an image of today.

Trey moans and rips his hands away from mine. I open my eyes, terrified, as he backs up frantically.

"He broke the intuition stream," I gasp. "I need to know what happens."

Trey turns to me, his expression a mask of pure terror. "I'm sorry Melanie," he says frantically. "I shouldn't have broken away. I just couldn't see you like that."

Bear rushes over and grabs my cheeks. He puts his forehead on mine. "I'm going in. Hang tight, Melanie. I'm going to have to work on this. I don't have the same connection with you that Trey and Adam do."

I close my eyes and get a viselike grip on Bear's energy. I drag him into my psyche.

"Well, all right," he mutters. "We'll do it your way then." Once he's inside my mind, he has a look around. "You really do have a mind full of dark water! That's so weird. You're a fire sign."

Adam's voice drifts in from far away. "The water's full of oil. It'll burn."

"Light it up, Melanie," Bear says. "We're going to force the intuition back to the surface."

I've never tried this before, but somehow this insanity makes sense. I take a determined breath and light the oily water in my mind on fire. The inferno blazes high as the water on the surface starts boiling. With Bear's help, I force the intuition to the surface.

"Yes, Melanie!" Bear says. "From now on, you know how to force more information from your intuition on your terms."

Bear studies the images that Trey and I just watched. "The kids are beautiful. The oldest looks like Melanie."

We get to the death scene, and Bear does something that blocks my ability to see what he sees. I'm relieved.

Bear gets the information he needs and backs out of my psyche. He pulls me in and hugs me. "No fifteen-year-old girl should ever be faced with knowing all of that."

Trey crosses to me and pulls me against him. "What do we do?" he asks Bear.

Bear points to Trey. "You make the plan we're going to follow, but you can't call the shots when things roll." He turns to Adam. "You have to."

"Why?" Adam asks.

"Because I saw something that's pretty clearly important. Something Trey decides in the moment sends Melanie and a group of students into an ambush. She takes a bullet to the head."

Trey doubles over, and Adam's mouth drops open.

"We have to get Melanie out of here, now!" Trey orders in a panic.

Bear shakes his head. "There's no way to get her out except for the same way the rest of us exit." He looks at Darren. "I know what to do. You and I need to make a plan to stop this reality from happening."

"How sure are you that what you just saw is an actual possibility?" Darren asks.

"If we don't adjust things now, Melanie's going to die, and she and Trey's three future kids will never be born."

Darren follows Bear out the door, and I'm left reeling.

"Will you call the shots when this starts?" Trey asks Adam.

Adam nods. "Whatever we have to do, I'm in."

Trey looks from me to Adam. "We have to trust your instincts on this. Just keep Mel alive."

CHAPTER 39

Arch, Tanner, Adam, Mr. Jenson, and Marcus are all huddled up at the big table, looking down at the blueprint and talking quietly with Trey. I'm with the girls at the smaller table. Trey and Adam get into a heated debate, and the girls look their way. Only our chosen few know what happened in the boiler room lounge twenty minutes ago.

"No way, Adam!" Trey says. "Melanie's staying right here in this room, running sound during the escape."

"Not a shot in hell," Adam argues. "I need her on the dance building roof helping me. If you want me to call this thing, then I pick my second in command. I need easy access to Melanie's mind, and I can't chance it that fear will shorten our connection range."

Trey glares at him. "You want to put my girl on the roof, in full sight of an army with guns?"

"You're damn right. We need her up there. I'm telling you that this is the best route. I feel it."

Trey throws his hands in the air. "You'd seriously put her in that position after what we just heard?"

Everyone looks at each other curiously.

"What did the rest of us miss?" Valerie asks.

Trey and Adam shake their heads, unwilling to fill everyone in.

"I agree with Adam on this," Mr. Isley jumps in. "We have Dante on the way, and he and Hiram know the sound equipment better than anyone else in this group."

"If it helps settle this debate," I say from across the way, "I know nothing about sound equipment, and I have every intention of being in the middle of everything up there. I'm going with Adam's gut like we talked about."

"Yeah, come on Trey," Tanner says. "You can't let Melanie miss out on a chance to die dramatically with the rest of us!"

Trey glares at Tanner because his flippant comment hits a little too close to home. He'd have never said something like that if he'd been aware of my intuition pulse in the boiler room.

"I'm really getting sick of this group's habit of shoving Melanie to the front of every disaster," Trey says. "She's not cannon fodder."

Tanner snorts. "She does backflips trying to get to the front of every fight. You can't blame *us*."

Bear and Darren stride through the door.

"I need to speak to you three please," Bear says, gesturing to Trey, Adam, and me.

We exchange a glance and follow Darren and Bear into the boiler room across the hall.

The five of us form a circle after Darren closes the door.

"We've been talking," Darren says. "We think we know a way to get Melanie through this alive."

"Okay," Trey says. "What's your plan?"

"Melanie has a soulmate connection with both of you. She can communicate with Trey through emotion—but only with physical contact at this point, correct?"

I nod. "It helps. Trey and I don't have much range without contact."

"What about with Adam?" Darren asks.

"I can reach him from a distance, but not very far."

Bear nods. "What about between Adam and Trey?"

The boys look at each other quizzically.

"We haven't tried," Adam says.

"Do it," Darren orders.

Adam holds out a hand, and Trey rolls his eyes but takes it. After a moment, they drop hands, shaking their heads.

"Nothing," Trey says.

Bear nods. "All right. I think Darren and I have figured out a way to tear down the blockage in Melanie that separates the two soulmate connections. Generally, there's only one soulmate connection in any single person. But there's no reason we can't pull down the separation."

I shake my head adamantly. "Nope. Uh-uh. *Nooo*, sir! My life is complicated enough already."

Bear levels me with a deadly serious look. "Do you want to live through this?"

Meekly, I answer, "Yes."

"Then you need to let us try. The three of you need to work as one unit to get this done. What I saw involved a communication breakdown between Trey and Adam. If they can communicate mind to mind, then you have a shot, Mel."

"But I really don't need them involved in each other's thoughts. We've had a hell of a time keeping things to where they even *resemble* calm. After all this is over, can we put things back the way they were?"

"Honestly, we don't know," Darren answers. "Right now, we just need to get through this."

Trey, Adam, and I exchange a look.

Finally, Adam asks, "Trey, what do you think?"

Trey takes a breath and contemplates. After a moment, he says, "I'll do anything to keep Melanie alive. We've got a future family at stake." He gives me a reassuring look. "We can work out ground rules, or how to fix it, or whatever, later."

Adam sighs, frustrated.

Bear levels me with a serious look. "Describe Trey's mind and Adam's mind."

Surprised by the question, I have to think about it for a moment. "Both are made of rock," I say hesitantly. "Trey's is more like pumice. There's air, room to breathe, room for energy to flow. It's lighter somehow. Adam's is granite. Unbending." I slide an amused gaze Adam's way and add, "Difficult to deal with."

Adam scowls in jest. "Hush, Little Miss Chaos."

I laugh, and some of the tension lifts.

"For the record," Adam says to Bear and Darren, "Melanie's mind is like a damn carnival that's been drowned before it gets set on fire."

Trey bursts out laughing, and I glare at him. He shakes his head as if trying to curb his amusement. "That's the most accurate thing I've ever heard. Sorry, babe, but it's true."

I narrow my eyes at Trey. "Maybe you don't get to ride any of the carnival rides anymore."

His eyes go wide. "I'll hush."

The other guys chuckle, shaking their heads.

"That's what I love about you, Mel," Bear says. "Even faced with death, you're still quirky." He sucks in a breath. "Okay, based on Melanie's description, I need to take Adam's side of this energetic wall. Darren will be on Trey's side."

Darren nods.

"Adam and Trey," Bear continues, "each of you take one of Melanie's hands and drop any shields you have between you and her."

I close my eyes, nervous. I don't want to be in the middle of Trey and Adam's energy. It's too complicated.

"Melanie," Bear says, "I need you to ground and center. We have to use you as the foundation of this."

I roll my eyes. "I'm getting real damn sick of being the foundation of stuff."

Bear grins. "This is what you signed up for when you chose to come into this life with all these abilities. Now do it, please."

"Of course," I mutter as I close my eyes. Quickly, I gather the rogue energy and ground it down and out like an internal exhale.

I keep my eyes closed as Bear quietly instructs, "Take her hands."

Both guys gently take my hands, and I feel myself split down the middle. Half of me thrums with the fire and chaos that has always fueled Adam and me, while the other side feels like the grounded synergy of Trey and me. It's incredibly disorienting. I grimace.

"Hang tight, Kitten Little," Bear says. "You can do this." There's a pause before he starts counting down. "Three, two, one . . ."

Suddenly, Darren and Bear's energies loom behind Trey and Adam in my psyche. All four guys are taking up space in my mind, and I feel like I'm being energetically stretched somehow.

I start to pull away, and Bear says, "Keep it together, Melanie."

"Get this over with," I snarl. "You four are a lot."

Darren and Bear's energies move closer in my mind's eye, and there's suddenly pressure down the center of my energy. The pressure increases as they work together on either side of the energetic wall that blocks Adam and Trey within our soulmate connection.

The pressure suddenly ceases.

"Damn," Bear growls. "She's tougher than she looks."

"Agreed," Darren says. "Trey and Adam, on three, you need to physically grab her and hang on."

I don't have time to panic, because Darren says, "THREE!" and Adam and Trey grab me from either side. Bear and Darren shove inward, and the wall separating the soulmate connections explodes. My mouth drops open, and I double over, but the pain is so intense that I can't even scream. Trey and Adam hold me up while I relearn how to breathe.

I feel Bear and Darren extract themselves from my psyche, and I'm left with an odd mixture of Trey, Adam, and me.

When I can finally stand, head hanging, I gasp out, "I hate you guys. That was brutal." I open my eyes, and Bear and Darren are grinning at me.

"You did it though!" Bear says.

I roll my eyes. "Yeah, yeah. Yippee."

When I hold out a hand to Trey, he shakes his head and smiles. He sends a pulse my way that he loves me. It's in actual words instead of our usual image bubbles. My eyes widen. I turn to Adam, and he sends me a pulse that's carefully wrapped in energy that's a little more appropriate than usual, just in case Trey senses it.

"Did you feel the pulse from Adam?" I ask Trey.

He shakes his head. I glance Adam's way and gesture to Trey. Adam shakes his head. I send a pulse to Trey and glance at Adam. He shakes his head no again.

We keep testing the new dynamic and get a clear handle on the fact that we can communicate with anyone else in the trio, and we can still control where it goes. Finally, we discover that, if we choose, we can all three communicate simultaneously.

Satisfied with the results, Trey turns to Bear and Darren. "Looks like the three-way calling feature has been added to the phone plan."

The guys grin.

CHAPTER 40

We head through the catacombs into the war room, where there are a few new faces standing with Presley as she catches them up on the situation. I spot Drew, Lionel, Curtis, Tristin from the golf team, Mr. Delgado, and a man I vaguely recognize as the football coach. Everyone in the group turns expectant eyes on Trey.

"Good to see you, Mr. Delgado," Trey says. "Do you know how the broadcast equipment works in here?"

The former media teacher pushes his wire-rimmed glasses higher up on his nose. "I know this equipment like the back of my hand. The last time we used it was around a year ago, but it should still work."

"Is there a way to make it broadcast to a media outlet so we can get word out to police?"

"No. We're a closed-circuit system that only services our campus. Anything we broadcast only reaches the TVs in every classroom."

Trey scrunches his eyes. "That means we go with the surge plan instead of the rescue plan." He looks to Finley. "Get copies made of plan B."

Her eyes widen. Apparently plan B isn't the one she prefers. "That just upped our causality stakes," she says in a voice barely over a whisper.

"I'm aware, but we have to get out of here." Trey turns his attention back to Mr. Delgado. "Can you test that equipment without it going through to any of the rooms yet?"

Mr. Delgado nods. "I can test it. It doesn't broadcast until I throw the switch."

Trey turns his attention down the line. "Dante, I'm going to need you to run sound during the escape. Mr. Delgado's going to run the broadcast equipment. Hiram, I need you to oversee all of it. My plan's gotta go off without a hitch, and you know how to troubleshoot anything that could go wrong. Mr. Delgado, Dante, and Hiram, get started testing out all that equipment."

They move into position to work on the project.

Trey's attention shifts to the football coach. He indicates the walkie-talkie we found. "Drew told us you're retired military."

The coach nods.

"We overheard that all students are being moved to the theater at twelve forty-five. It's the only space big enough to house the entire student body. There was mention of a helicopter unit and something they called Trinity that was being set up. Any clue what that means?"

The coach's eyes widen. "That's very bad news." He makes eye contact around the room before informing, "Trinity is a high-end explosives system. It's run off connectors, cable, and strategically placed explosive packs. It's used by the military, but civilian companies also use it. When you see big high-rises in places like Vegas being leveled, Trinity is the system they use."

My eyes nearly bug out of my head. "Are you saying that the Cobra Militia plans to herd the entire student body, teachers, and staff into the auditorium, only to blow it up?"

The coach nods. "If they're using Trinity, that's likely their plan. They must be planning to helicopter out of here after."

I look to Trey. "Can we sneak all the students into the catacombs and wait it out down here? We can't take a chance that they'll be moved before we're ready."

Trey shakes his head. "We can't take a chance that more Trinity explosives have been wired around the school. It makes sense that they have a backup plan. *We* do." He stares at his surge plan paper and blinks rapidly.

Through our connection, I can see his mind racing a million miles an hour.

Finally, his gaze snaps to Mr. Isley. "Show me the supplies you found."

Mr. Isley heads out the door with half of his students, and they return carrying huge armloads of bats covered in red glitter and buckets of red-glittered baseballs.

Curtis takes one of the baseballs out of the bucket and laughs. "These are festive."

Mr. Isley shrugs. "These are all discarded stock from when the baseball team got that big equipment donation a few years back. We produced *Damn Yankees* that year and used these as props for the musical. Will they work?"

"A baseball's a baseball, right?" Trey chuckles, albeit nervously.

"If it gets us out of here alive," Curtis says, "I'll cover the whole baseball team in glitter. What's the plan?"

"Listen up because you all play a part. Our escape has to unfold in nine stages." He starts handing out copies of the escape plan, and we all look them over.

THE SURGE ESCAPE PLAN

——

STAGE ONE: The Mass Screw (War Ensemble)
STAGE TWO: Hack In (TVs on. Media Broadcast)
STAGE THREE: Chaos (:01)
STAGE FOUR: Air Assault (3:34)
STAGE FIVE: Slugger (4:48)
STAGE SIX: TNT (5:43)
STAGE SEVEN: Blitz (5:48)
STAGE EIGHT: The Steal (6:11)
STAGE NINE: The Surge

"We need to be ready," Trey says as we all review the list. "First, and foremost, every single one of you needs to tell all the students in your assigned classroom that there's going to be *really* loud music blasting through the escape stages. The music serves two purposes: first, to disorient the militia, and second, to help us coordinate different sections of our escape plan. Tell the students they need to think above the noise."

Everyone nods.

"Melanie," Trey continues, "you're going to be running rooftop visual cues from the dance department roof during steps four, five, and seven. From up there, you'll be able to see all the quads, around the side of the bungalows in quad one, and the field.

"Arch, Bear, Mr. Isley, Hiram, and Kenji are our broadcast stars. Mr. Delgado, you and Hiram are running the broadcast equipment. Dante's running sound through the announcement system.

"Adam, you're going to give watch from the two-story building roof, and if anything goes wrong, Melanie and I need to know. Most of you are dancers and musicians. I've timed the different moments perfectly with the song that'll be playing. You'll know the changes. It's obvious."

He sends a pulse to just Adam and me. *"You're sure about this, Adam?"*

Adam nods, and my palms get clammy.

Trey takes a deep breath, refocusing on the plan. He talks us through each phase, explaining to everyone present what their roles are and how important it is to time everything correctly. There's an air of nervous tension hanging over us all. We're going to be armed with bats and baseballs, and we have a coordinated counterattack planned out, but we're going up against an armed militia. These guys have guns, and they're clearly not afraid to use them. I know I'm not the only one at the table who's fearing for her life.

"Everyone needs to tell the students and teachers that they *must* be out of sight during stages four through six of the plan," Trey says. "The golf team, baseball team, and football players are going to take out everyone they see during those stages. I need Tanner, Darren, Demitri, Javier, and Marcus to leave now and go to every vent on the first floor of this building. Get the teachers' attention and ask them to collect every Coke bottle out of the trash cans that they can find and hand them through to you. Tell them it'll make sense soon, and that help's coming. Also, find out what they know about where these militia guys are stationed and how many of them there are. Mr. Jenson, supervise them in the catacombs please. Don't get caught."

Trey's select group heads out the catacomb access door, and the rest of us stare at each other.

Out of all of us, Lionel looks especially uncomfortable, and I'm guessing it's because he hasn't received his assignment yet. "Pardon my ignorance," he says, "but what exactly am I doing here?"

Trey turns to him and sets a hand on his shoulder. "Lionel, how are you with explosives?"

Lionel's expression is suddenly full of confidence. "I'm damn good."

Trey grins. "Are you Trinity-good?"

"Trinity is boring. My science club is Hollywood-High-good."

"That's what I like to hear." Trey chuckles.

Lionel smirks. "Time to kill some bad guys."

"Damn, Lionel," Deb says with a grin. "Look at you being all hot and daring."

Lionel raises an eyebrow her way. "Those assholes plan to kill our people. It's survival of the fittest. If they need to die, they die."

CHAPTER 41

Trey points to places on the campus blueprint. "Does everyone understand their part in step one?"

Heads nod all around the table.

"We managed to collect fifty-eight screw guns," Adam says. "We've tested all of them. We've also got Ziplocks with screws packed for each of our people involved in stage one."

Trey lays down the instructions for distributing the materials to the kids who need them. "Stage two," he continues. "Arch, Mr. Isley, Mr. Delgado, Bear, and Kenji. You all finish your broadcast, and then you'll only have a few minutes to head through the catacombs to the dance building. That building's secure, and I need you in the pool area, ready to collect weapons with the golf team. After those are secure, get ready to surge through the double door exit into quad two."

They nod.

"Mr. Delgado," Trey says, "would you be more comfortable waiting in here until the police can get in and rescue you? I guarantee this is going to get violent."

The media teacher smirks. "I might look like a soggy old man, but I have a fifth-degree karate black belt. Trust me when I say you need me."

Adam claps Mr. Delgado on the shoulder. "Man, some of these teachers kick ass."

Mr. Delgado grins at Adam, and Bear high-fives him.

Along with Mr. Jenson, Trey works out a way to get Adam onto the roof of the two-story building undetected. Mr. Jenson unclips the massive key ring from his belt, quickly finds the right key, removes it from the ring, and hands it to Adam, who puts it in his pocket.

"Does everyone understand the other steps of the plan?" Trey asks once everyone has the information they need.

Lionel looks up from his work and grins. He's gathered around a small table with five members of the science club that we boosted out of class through the catacombs. They're all hard at work creating Molotov cocktails in empty soda bottles we collected from every trash can we passed. With the beakers the science teacher handed Tanner through the vent, they've created a contraption they're calling the Kablooey.

"We have everything we need," Lionel says. "We're gonna blow the gate sky-high."

All his genius friends grin in agreement, but the smiles quickly fade when one of them accidentally knocks over a beaker full of mysterious liquid and they all tense up. Lionel lunges forward to mop it up.

"Just don't blow the place sky-high yet okay, guys?" Adam says once it's clear the crisis has been averted.

"Don't worry," Lionel says. "We won't. You're in good hands."

"I have no doubt," Adam says, clearly full of doubt.

The geniuses all look at Adam like they've never been in the presence of anyone cooler. For a moment, I get all warm inside about how, through it all, at least we've made some unlikely new friends.

Trey checks his watch. "We move into position in twenty minutes."

"We're as prepared as we're going to be," Darren says. "Let's spend a few minutes together and have what might be our last smoke."

Student council files through the catacomb door and into our makeshift lounge, leaving the remaining dancers and science club to finish up. As Darren distributes cigarettes, we all look at each other, realizing that we might not all make it out alive.

CHAPTER *42*

The sudden sound of gunfire rat-a-tat-tats aggressively from the first floor above. Our heads snap up, and fear reverberates as the ominous sound echoes. Bear and Darren rush out from the boiler room lounge, looking ready to fight. We hear a sound from above, and a locked doorknob at the top of the stairway wiggles.

"Get to the war room, now!" Trey hisses.

We rush silently down the stairway, through the catacombs, and into the war room. Trey silently closes the door and turns the lock. In a hushed whisper, Adam explains what just happened. Trey flips off the light switch, and we all crouch low, hoping we haven't been discovered before we can set everything in motion.

In the dark, everyone's energy amps up. Some are terrified. Others anxiously anticipate. In the case of the more flippant of our crew, they give in to the inevitable with humor. I fall into the terrified category. I feel a hand on my back and know immediately that it's Demitri. His calm vibe flows through me. I turn and hug him. He wraps his arms around me and whispers just for me to hear, "You're okay."

"Where's Melanie?" Trey whispers from across the pitch-black room.

"I've got her," Demitri murmurs.

"If shit goes south, please stay with her."

"I will." Demitri pulls my cheek against his chest and whispers in my ear. "I've got you. We're going to get out of here."

My moment of relief is short lived. More gunshots ring out. Now I'm clinging to Demitri, tears filling my eyes.

CHAPTER 43

After that last wave of gunfire, we've had ten minutes of eerie silence. We have no idea what's happening above ground, but we can't just sit here while people are being shot at.

"We're on our own now," Trey says. "Isley and Jenson can't come running to unlock a door that accidently closes. You must be to your positions in five minutes. Valerie and Tanner should be in their places as lookouts. Darren and Marcus will make a run for the bungalows in," he checks his watch, "thirty-five seconds."

Adam sends to Trey and me, *"I'm at the hatch ready to exit onto the roof of the two-story building."*

"We're going. *Now!*" Trey says to our group in the war room.

Trey turns and grabs me around the waist, yanking me against him so hard that he almost knocks the air out of me. He kisses me like it might be our last kiss in this lifetime, and I'm suddenly hit with a wave of panic. I grab him, my hands snaking around his neck, and kiss him back with the kind of fire and passion that we usually save for more private moments. When he pulls away from me, tears fill my eyes.

"Don't you do that," he says. "Not now. This isn't goodbye. We're going to make it, Melanie."

"What if we don't?"

Trey puts his hands on the sides of my face and looks deeply into my eyes. "We survive. That's what this group does. Adam was right about putting you on the roof because we all know you can handle this. You get out there and kick ass. Take down as many of those assholes as you can. I'm a pulse away." He pulls me in and sends a pulse out to Adam and me. *"Get her through this, Adam."* Along with the pulse, he sends the images of the three children we saw during my intuitive vision.

"She's going to make it," Adam sends back. Then, without dropping Trey from the communication, he sends, *"Love you, Melanie."*

I send back, *"Love you too."*

Trey accepts the exchange without argument. He hugs me one more time.

"We can't even get through a semester without having our lives be in danger," I say to him. "The thought of three kids joining this mess is insane."

"That's a long way down the road," he whispers. "You need to put everything we saw out of your mind. We can worry about all those details later." He tips my chin up. "My job is to see the big picture. It always has been. Right now, you need to focus on the present. If all goes right, we'll be out of here in thirty minutes. Just survive this, and the kids will happen whenever you're ready for them."

"What about when you're ready?"

Trey smiles softly. "I'll be ready whenever it happens. That wasn't the first time I've seen those kids. I saw them in my mind on our first date. Every time I look at you, I remember them."

I nod. He kisses me and laces his fingers with mine to send a love pulse down the connection in our old way. Even though I'm terrified, it makes me smile.

He lets go and heads one way down the catacombs, while I head the other way.

Holy crap. We're doing this!

I rush into the dance room through the catacombs, shutting the door behind me to prevent anyone else from heading down.

Tristin and the golf team cross to me.

"What do we do first?" Tristin asks.

I point at the TV mounted on the wall. "Turn it on. As soon as music blasts through the announcement system, I need two of you to take these screw guns and metal plates and screw them into the top, middle, and bottom of the main doors to this building."

Two of the guys accept the screw guns and other materials I've brought with me.

"As soon as those plates are screwed into place, rush back here. We're going up that two-story ladder to the roof."

Just as they turn, a thought occurs to me, and I panic. "Tristin, can you go up that ladder and make sure the roof access isn't locked? We're screwed if it is. We didn't think of that."

Tristin shimmies up the ladder bolted to the wall and pushes open the access hatch. He gives me a thumbs-up, then rushes back down. "Guys," he says to his teammates, "line up on this ladder and start passing up golf clubs and those buckets of golf balls. Let's get our stuff up there, fast."

While they make quick work passing the items up an assembly line, I send a pulse to Adam and Trey, letting them know that I made it to the dance building. They both send back that they're in their spots.

The golf team makes it down the ladder just as Adam's voice comes through our connection. *"Here we go. Time for the Mass Screw."*

My heart races and my hands break out in a sweaty slick. Suddenly, the loudest heavy metal music I've ever heard blasts through the campus-wide announcement system. Slayer's "War Ensemble" screams and growls, covering the sounds of screw guns fastening metal plates into doorjambs all over the school. That's everyone's cue.

Trey's plan is happening, ready or not. For stage one, we'll be blocking as many entrances into the two-story building classrooms and the bungalows as possible with the goal of barring the militia from further access to the students. We have to prevent them from getting students to the auditorium. The flip side is that blocking the exterior doors essentially forces a large amount of kids and teachers to funnel through the doors between classrooms and then out the couple of exits Trey's plan calls for keeping open. The exits he chose are at least nearest the stairs and main doors, so their paths out of the buildings and off campus should be quicker. As the song reaches the bridge, I think about how everyone should be moving through the inner classroom doors and getting into position in the two-story building by now. All the theater students are likely in a fistfight with any militia in the theater as they try to make it out through the lobby doors to the street. It's one of the few exits from campus that wasn't hindered by the steel gates and advanced fencing.

Stage two is next, but my mind is already jumping to stage three because it puts the most people in danger. During stage three, everyone from the two-story building is supposed to flood the quads, creating as much chaos as possible on their way to hide behind buildings, to disorient the militia and hopefully distract them for long enough to get the golf team, science club, basketball team, football team, and baseball team into place. There's going to be so many people out there potentially in the line of fire. I send up a prayer that everyone will stay safe.

The music stops abruptly.

"Here we go," I say to the golf team. "Time for the Hack In."

The TV above us suddenly changes from static to an image of Arch standing in front of a green screen in the media room broadcast booth. He's flanked by Mr. Isley, Kenji, Bear, and Hiram.

Every student and teacher in the school is watching this, and I hope Arch can do a good job of rallying everyone.

"This is student body president Arch Terani broadcasting live from the underground," Arch says in a histrionic tone. "This reign of terror ends now. Coach Stamp thinks he has us beat, but he forgot that this is Hollywood High. Buttrum's made quite the show of telling us that he's our master. I think not. As evidence, I present to you, live and in color . . . mass *chaaaosss!*"

All the guys on the TV raise their arms, throw their heads back, flex, and let loose a Viking roar. The screen goes to static. Over the announcement system, Metallica's "Master of Puppets" blasts to life. I grin. Trey wasn't kidding when he said we're doing this our way.

I send him a pulse. *"You just had to get in one more reminder of the obsession with the word* master, *didn't you? Well played, my love."*

He sends back a bubble of amusement, tinted yellow.

I check my watch, turn to the golf team, and yell over the

music, "Head up to the roof! Get into place. I'll cue you when it's time for our air assault. We've got three minutes and thirty-three seconds before stage four. Stay low until I give the signal."

The eighteen golf team members practically fly up the two-story ladder. I head up last. The fresh air is a welcome change as I look out from the roof. Students are running for cover behind buildings, just like they're supposed to. I spot Mr. Jenson directing the football and baseball players to run behind the bungalows to the teacher parking lot. Two linebackers grab and cover him, racing him out of sight. I'm relieved. If anything were to happen to Mr. Jenson, I'd never recover.

I turn toward the two-story building and flash devil horns, signaling to Adam that I'm in place.

He sends the signal back to me, along with a pulse. *"Here we go, Melanie."*

The song shifts to its more airy, wafting ballad section.

I turn to the golf team. "Air assault! Go!" They let out a war cry, jumping up and grabbing their clubs. They start firing golf balls into the quads in the direction of the militia pouring out of the athletic building.

"Steady your aim!" Tristin hollers to his teammates. "This isn't a drill!"

His team are a lot more precise than I expected. One after another, golf balls hit their marks, sending the militia ducking and covering all down the main campus throughway.

The song shifts out of the ballad section toward a driving beat.

"Cover them!" I yell to the golf team over the raging song. "Baseball players incoming! Slugger Stage is a go!"

The golf team shifts, repositioning to hit balls to the right and left to clear a path for the best hitters from the baseball team to form two lines in the middle of the quad, facing each direction.

Across Actors' Alley, I see a militiaman pull up his rifle. My heart stops when I see where he's aiming.

I drop to my knees and scream, "Treeey!" My whole future flashes by in the blink of an eye.

"There!" Tristin hollers. "Hit that one!"

The golfers start blasting golf balls directly at the militiaman before he can get a shot off. He lowers his weapon and retreats around the corner of the bungalow.

I slump, my eyes filling with tears, and lose it.

"*Damn, girl,*" Adam pulses. "*I can feel your despair all the way over here. You really do love that jackass. Pull it together, Mel. We need you.*"

I close my eyes tight, realizing that Adam's right. I have to do this. I take a deep breath, set my jaw in a tight clamp, and when I open my eyes again, I'm mentally back in the fight.

I stand and look down at the quad. The baseball players are smacking baseballs at eighty-five miles an hour, glitter raining down, through all the quads. Trey's back bunches as he hits a ball, his wooden bat cracking in half. The ball hits Coach Stamp smack in the chest, and he drops, clutching his ribs.

Adam's voice crackles through our connection. "*TNT. Go!*" I got so distracted watching Trey that I forgot to check my watch. Luckily Adam's on top of it.

I look out across the field, where the science club kids are lined up halfway across the grassy expanse. I give them a devil horn hand signal, and Lionel replies with a thumbs-up. He turns back to the fences and flips a switch on his homemade, remote-controlled Kablooey contraption. Time seems to slow. I hold my breath.

Suddenly, a massive explosion rocks the foundation of the school. Daniel Stamp's coveted steel-and barbwire prison fences explode in a flash of fire. A huge cloud of black smoke rises. When the smoke clears, the giant steel alley gate falls with a booming crash.

The science club starts lighting Molotov cocktails, throwing them at any militiamen running their way. I'm stunned that they're so willing to harm others this way. The science club has more balls than I gave them credit for. As my mind reels, I signal for Tristin and the golfers to rush to their second position. They disappear down the ladder though the roof access.

I turn my attention back to the field, where things have taken a turn. There's no time to send a message to Adam. The science club isn't going to make it if we don't move fast. According to the plan, this is the stage where I'm supposed to take over calling the shots in the event that anything goes wrong. I scream over the music "Blitz! *Go!*" While I frantically wave at the football players I can see. It's earlier than the musical cue, and I hope they understand.

Ninety-two football players, everyone from varsity and junior varsity, blast in tight lines from behind the bungalows on either side of quad one, the Actors' Alley bungalows, and quad two. They mow down militiamen from so many directions that the enemy doesn't know where to turn.

I look over the edge of the roof, and the science club members are all cowering against the fence by the bleachers. Several militiamen are on fire, rolling around in the grass trying to put out the flames, but they aren't alone. The science club is surrounded. That's when three of the biggest football players make a heroic charge. They plow the last three militiamen over and disarm them.

"The STEAL!" Adam and I scream the words over and over at the top of our lungs from the roofs.

Every athlete in the quad descends on the pile of football players and starts wrenching weapons away from the militia. The enemy has been pinned down with little chance of escape.

I send a pulse to my soulmates. *"Adam, take over. Trey, I'm heading down."* Without waiting for reply, I rush down the ladder, through the locker room, and to the door into the pool area where the golf team and half the student council are waiting. I push the door open just in time to see the baseball and basketball players filing in with the confiscated militia weapons. They make a pile of them in a corner out of the way.

We all exchange an urgent glance, then rush out the door. We close and secure it behind us so that the weapons can't be used to hurt anyone else.

The music ends.

Adam's voice yells from the roof into the silence, "Surge, surge, *surge!*"

AC/DC's "Thunderstruck" blares to life from the school announcement system. This wasn't part of the original plan, but I like it. This has Hiram written all over it. I can picture him grinning as he works the PA equipment.

"Hell yes!" Tristin yells over the blaring music. "You guys know how to party. Let's get out of here!"

We join the crush of students running across campus toward the exploded exit hole in the barricade fences. I come face-to-face with one of the militiamen, who makes a grab for me. I accidently send the image to Adam and Trey and feel panic jolt back through the connection from them. I ignore it, trying not to get distracted, and throw a mean right hook, dropping my attacker.

One problem solved; another quickly surfaces. My gaze meets with another militia gunman, and this one is still armed. He's steadying his rifle right at me.

Panic reverberates through my connection with Adam. I scream.

Even as I quiver under the threat of the gun, Mr. Delgado performs a wicked roundhouse kick on another militiaman. It distracts the aiming gunman long enough for Drake to get the drop on him. Drake rushes and plants his shoulder into the man's chest, dropping him to the ground. The gun fires a round harmlessly into the pavement.

I feel Trey's energy pulsing erratic and terrified down the line.

"She's okay, Trey," Adam sends. *"I can see her."*

Mr. Delgado waves me on. "Run!" he yells. "I'll bring up the rear."

The wave of students surges forward, fighting any leftover militiamen who come into our path. The cheerleaders in front of me are screaming and trying to cover their heads, not moving forward and generally not being helpful.

I realize with a start that most of them haven't been in quite as many battles as I have at fifteen. "Run as fast and hard as you can," I call out to them. "We'll cover you!"

The girls pick up the pace, squealing and racing across quad one toward the field.

I turn just in time to see hands coming my way. Another militiaman grabs me around the waist. I roar, bucking and fighting. It's clear these guys are searching for me in the crowd. The guy doesn't expect my ferocity, but he's got an iron grip and somehow holds on. Panic shoots through my end of the connection, and both of my soulmates radiate fear back toward me.

Demitri rushes up and grabs the militiaman around the neck. They start wrestling, with me trapped in the middle. I hop and wrap my legs around Demitri's waist to get leverage. I snap my head back, cracking the militiaman in the face as hard as I can. I see stars for a second, but the guy lets go, dropping to his knees, his nose pouring blood.

Drake runs up next to us and grins at me. "Damn, honey badger!" he yells over the music.

Demitri puts me down and kicks the militiaman in the face. Mr. Militia slumps, out cold.

I turn and see Trey surrounded by militia at the end of the dance building sidewalk.

"Basketball team!" Drake yells.

The whole team forms and runs off together. There must be fifteen of them charging at full speed down the concrete ramp, bum-rushing the militiamen. Though a couple of them are armed, they quickly see how outnumbered they are. Besides, rifles are useless in hand-to-hand combat. It's only a moment before Trey is free.

Drake and I high-five, and we start running again, with Demitri on my other side. Trey catches up with me and motions us over. He hollers a thank-you to Drake and Demitri for helping me.

Adam screams down the connection, *"Trey! Gunman!"* He must still have a view from his second-story vantage point.

I stop cold. Daniel Stamp is up ahead. He has a handgun raised, and it's sighted on me. The reminder that he was a military sharpshooter blisters through my memory.

Trey sends panic through our connection. I feel something odd, and Adam's suddenly in my mind. I realize at once that he can see through my eyes. This has never happened before, so it throws me.

"Oh my God!" he breathes through our connection. *"GET DOWN!"*

Out of nowhere, a blast goes off behind me, followed by a second one just as Trey yanks me off-balance. I hit the pavement. Trey drops over the top of me, and I whip my head to the side. There, handgun at the ready, is Principal Buttrum. My eyes widen as he stalks my way.

"No one messes with my students," he says. He raises the handgun again to take another shot.

I whip my head the other way just in time to see Daniel Stamp holding his chest that's oozing red. There's another loud crack, and in the blink of an eye, his head explodes. My mouth drops open as shock rages through every part of me and my eyes fill with tears.

Trey grabs my arm and hefts me up. "Pull it together, Melanie."

We look around and quickly realize that we're the last students in the quad. A militiaman rounds a corner at the other side.

Trey and Demitri grab me while Drake yells, "This way." We run into the cafeteria.

Adam sends a pulse through the connection. *"Do you have our girl, Trey?"*

"You mean my *girl?"* Trey sends back.

Adam sends yellow-tinged amusement. *"I need to get Val. Do you have Melanie covered?"*

"Yes." I can feel his love warming through our connection. *"Always."*

CHAPTER 45

Trey pulls me into the cafeteria with Drake and Demitri right behind us, and we race down a set of steps to a catacomb door. Apparently, Marcus didn't close it all the way, and I'm thrilled. Trey closes the door behind us. We rush down the catacomb hallway, stopping at the T-junction between the theater building and catacomb hall C. Trey pulls me in, hugging me tight. He lets go and turns me around, looking me over.

"I'm okay."

He shakes his head. "You aren't okay, Mel. There's blood all over your back."

I scrunch up my face, confused. "I feel fine." I roll my eyes as I realize the likely source. "It's probably from when I headbutted one of the militia thugs. I'm okay. Let's make sure everyone's alive, and then we can deal with it."

"You've lost a shocking amount of blood," Trey says.

"I can pass out later. Right now, we've got work to do."

Adam rushes in from the far side of the catacomb hall with Valerie on his heels. He kneels beside me with panic lining his handsome face. "I followed your energy line," he says, ashen.

"Melanie, you're sitting in a pool of blood."

"Yeah, yeah. Whatever. Let's finish this."

Valerie grins at me. "We're wasting time. Melanie's not quitting now. She'll black out on us later."

I stand and look Valerie in the eye. "Are we good?" I ask cautiously.

Valerie breaks into a conspiratorial smirk. "We're alive. Today, we're good."

When I laugh darkly, she reaches out an arm and hugs me. I'm filthy and covered in blood, but that doesn't faze Val. I squeeze her around the waist.

"Sorry about how things have gone," she whispers.

I take a step back and nod. The reality of what we've been through tries to invade, but I push it away. We aren't out of danger yet. I can descend into madness in a minute.

"Hold it together, love," Adam sends. *"We're almost done."*

Trey wraps his arm around my waist, and we head up the long stairway to the access door leading into the theater building. "Touch nothing," he reminds. "This building is a giant bomb."

"Think we're safe going through there?" I ask. "We have no idea who has the detonator switch."

Trey gives me a look. "I guarantee Coach Stamp had it. You know damn well he wouldn't allow anyone else the thrill of blowing up all the students."

He pushes through the hatch that opens into the lighting storage room. Adam and Trey cautiously look around. The coast is clear. We cross the backstage on the right side to the back door.

Trey stops, turning to us. "We kicked ass."

We all grin at each other.

"That's what we do," Adam says. "Now let's hope everyone made it."

Trey pushes open the door and sunlight pours in, causing us to blink and turn away as our eyes adjust. We step out on the second-floor landing above the loading dock. The entire student body is roaming through the street and student parking lot. Police cars rush up and screech to a halt with their sirens blaring.

"They made it!" someone yells.

Trey smiles and throws up both arms, flashing devil horns high for the crowd to see. Adam and I throw up devil horns on either side of Trey. A deafening cheer rises from the several thousand people arrayed in front of us. Devil horns go up from every student below. We break into laughter.

We rush down the stairs and over the collapsed steel gate into the waiting crowd.

Mom and Rich push through the crowd and grab me, hugging me tight. They gather up our group, hugging everyone and checking us over.

"You're here?" I say in disbelief. "How did you know?"

Rich grins as Bruce steps up with Marcus in tow. "Marcus had a dentist appointment scheduled for lunchtime. I showed up to get him and found the door locked. I tried to call Marcus's cell phone, but it I couldn't get a signal. I thought it was odd, so I took a walk around the school. That's when I saw the militiamen patrolling with rifles." He shakes his head. "I couldn't believe my eyes. When I pulled myself together, it occurred to me that the cell signal and the militia must be connected. So I drove until I was far enough out of range of the school to get a signal again. First, I called the police. Then, I called your parents and told them to meet me in the student parking lot. The police must have thought this was like the phony bomb threats or something because they took their sweet freaking time. I placed that call twenty minutes ago and they just arrived."

"You're covered in blood," Rich says.

"So I've heard," I say. "It doesn't hurt though."

"It will soon. You've still got an adrenaline rush."

Mom pulls Trey in for a hug, tears rolling down her face. "Thank you, Trey. I don't know what happened, but I'm positive you got her out alive."

Trey grins and returns the hug. "I don't get all the credit. You owe Adam, Demitri, Drake, and Mr. Delgado hugs also."

Mr. Isley, Mr. Jenson, and a police officer in a sergeant's uniform push their way through the crowd to us. The sergeant extends his hand to Trey, who shakes it.

"Hell of a job, young man," the sergeant says. "I've been informed by a teacher and Principal Buttrum that we owe the escape to you. I don't know how you did it."

Trey grins. "Let's just say that our group has unique talents in the masterminding arena."

The sergeant chuckles. "That's the understatement of the year. We've counted everyone, and we're missing sixteen. Eight students, six security guards, the baseball coach, and one teacher."

"Is the teacher Mr. Delgado?" Trey asks.

The sergeant nods gravely.

"The last time I saw him," I inform, "he was pounding a militiaman with a roundhouse kick."

The sergeant's eyebrows rise. "A roundhouse *kick*?"

"Our teachers have unique talents too," Trey says.

The sergeant shakes his head, appearing overwhelmed. "Where was he when you saw him last?"

"In the quad by the pool exit," I say. "He yelled for us to run, saying he'd bring up the rear. The security guards were apparently killed first. They're likely in the security office. That's rumor, but it came from the Magnet school counselor, so it's probably true.

The baseball coach took a shot to the head near the cafeteria. I'm unsure about the other missing people."

"I'll send in a team."

"Most of the doors are barred from the inside," Trey warns. "Your team's going to have trouble figuring out how to access most of the school."

"Would some of you be willing to go in with us and show us the ropes?"

There's no shortage of volunteers from our group. When I try to join, Trey stops me and gestures to my head.

"I know you want to charge back in there," he says. "But you need to get that checked out."

Rich steps in and assures that they'll take care of me. Then I hear the sergeant inform his team that it's time to go in and clear the grounds.

I watch as they walk away, relieved that this is over. All at once, my eyes go blurry. "Help," I gurgle meekly.

Demitri steps into view, and I start to fall. He grabs me just as my world goes black.

CHAPTER 46

I wake up slowly, my head pounding. A moan escapes my lips, a sound I don't so much hear as feel. My head feels like it's full of bumblebees. When I try to clear the confusion by shaking it, I quickly discover that this was a bad plan. Pain explodes like sharp needles from the back of my head all the way to my waist. I gasp.

"Lie still, Melanie," comes my mom's anxious voice. "You're safe."

I open my eyes to blinding light and see stars. "Too bright," I croak as my eyes squeeze shut.

"I'll turn out the light," says another voice that sounds like Valerie. There's a brief pause accompanied by the sound of footsteps before Valerie says, "Open your eyes, Mel."

I slowly open my eyes and sigh. The room is now lit only by the light coming in from the open door across the way. I'm both surprised and unsurprised to find that the room is packed with all my friends, Mom and Rich, Bruce, Ms. G, Mr. Isley, and Mr. Jenson. They all grin at me. Disoriented, I smile back.

"Where am I?"

"You're in the hospital," Rich says.

I squeeze my eyes closed for a second, trying to clear my jumbled head. "Were the missing people found?"

Ms. G's sitting in a chair next to me. She takes my hand, careful to avoid the IV tubes snaking up my arm. "They were found. Five of the students were pronounced dead at the scene, and the others are in the hospital recovering. We think they'll make it."

"What about Mr. Delgado?"

Arch's expression falls. "He was shot in the chest. He's in emergency surgery now. We're not sure yet, Mel."

Tears brim in my eyes. "I hope he makes it."

"We all do, Mel," Adam says. He's calm on the surface, but he pulses relief laced with panic down the connection.

The reminder of the connection brings Trey's presence to the surface, and his vibe is distraught.

Bear gently sets his big hand on my shoulder. "We'll have a party at Arch and Hiram's for you when this is all over, Kitten Little. And hopefully Mr. Delgado will be able to join. In the meantime, you've got some recovering to do."

"Over a cut on my head?" I say, trying to rise from the bed. "Screw that."

I pause when I notice the tears in my mom's eyes. Valerie and Adam step over and put their arms around her.

"She's going to be fine, Carol," Adam says to my mom. "She's one of the toughest people I know."

"The doctor's bandaged up your head wound," Rich explains. "They found a tooth lodged in your scalp when they cleaned out the gash."

I scrunch up my face. "Gross. I guess I caught that militiaman's tooth when I headbutted him. He had a hold on me. Demitri and Drake helped save me." I look across at Demitri and Drake, who are leaning against the wall. "Your timing was literally a lifesaver."

Drake nods my way. "After everything you did to help save the students, I couldn't leave you hanging, right?"

Demitri winks. "Couldn't just let my Fraggle die, now, could I?"

I smile at them.

"The head gash isn't all, Melanie," Rich says. "You have a gunshot wound in your shoulder. The doctors—hell, all of us—are shocked you were able to keep going."

I look around, baffled. "I'm telling you, I would've known if I'd been shot. I literally didn't even hear gunshots during most of the rescue chaos."

Arch raises his eyebrows. "You should get your ears checked because there was gunfire, and lots of it."

"You really didn't feel it?" Finley asks.

I shake my head, baffled. "I've got nothing." A thought comes to me. "Principal Buttrum shot Daniel Stamp in the chest. That's the main gunfire I heard. Now that I think about it, there was a sting in my shoulder when that first shot went off." I shrug. "Kinda felt like a beesting. I thought getting shot would be worse than that."

Rich chuckles. "Mystery solved. I'm just glad you're tougher than you look."

"Give Melanie a mission, and not even a bullet can slow her down," Tanner jokes. "This chick's like the Terminator."

We all laugh.

I scan the crowd of all my favorite people, and my eyes land on Trey sitting on the end of my bed. He has a steady stream of tears running down his cheeks. He's looking at me like the world might end.

"We made it, Trey. Everything's okay."

He shakes his head, unable to speak. He bends over and puts his head down on his knees.

Adam kneels in front of him. "I get it, man. She's okay though. You've been through a lot today and saved over fifteen hundred people. I think you need to take a breather." Adam sends a message down our shared connection. *"Trey, let's go outside for a smoke so you can process this."*

My boyfriend gasps and sits up. Then, slowly, he stands. Adam, Bear, and Darren lead him out through the door.

"We almost lost you," Ms. G informs. "When you passed out, Demitri caught you and discovered the bullet wound. We cleared a path to an ambulance. All hell broke loose, and you coded on the gurney. They had to shock you three times to get your heart started again. The ambulance raced off with you just before Trey came back out of the school. I broke the news to him, and it was terrible. He hasn't been okay since. I hate to tell you, but I don't think that boy will ever let you out of his sight again."

"No more fights for you, Melanie," Mom says in a shaky voice.

I snort. "Fat chance, Mom."

She sighs and rolls her eyes. Next to her, Rich serves a stark contrast by grinning at me and giving a wink.

Ms. G chuckles at our exchange, but then when she looks down, her expression morphs to sadness. "You've got a broken rib, and the bullet came within an inch of your heart. You've had two emergency surgeries, and they had to pump you full of two bags of blood. The doctors didn't think you'd make it. They prepared us for the worst. We'd just gathered, after taking turns saying our goodbyes to you, when you suddenly gasped and shook your head. Trey's goodbye was one of the sweetest and most heartbreaking things I've ever heard. That boy loves you more than life itself."

A tear falls down my cheek. "I know he does. Your story has so many layers to unpack that it's going to take me a minute to wrap my mind around it. I'll start by saying that the doctors don't know me really well. I mean, life and death? This was just another day at Hollywood High."

Everyone laughs and Presley steps forward, her cheeks wet with tears. "I hate you so, so, so much right now," she says. "Thank God you're okay, you rattlesnake nasty girl!" She moves closer, leaning down to hug me. "I love you. You scared the crap out of us."

I hug Presley with my good arm. "I love you too. Pres, you of all people should know that I'm not going anywhere. You think I'd leave you scrappy pack of alley cats to have all the fun without me?"

— —

So, how did it go? Well . . .

After five of the most boring days of my life, I was finally released from the hospital. After all the excitement we'd been through, just having to lie there wasn't the least bit relaxing. Trey, Mom, and Rich took turns staying at the hospital with me, just like old times. The only time I could sleep was when Trey was there. I'm sure he was sick to death of just sitting there watching me doze, but he never complained.

Everyone came over to the house as soon as word spread that I was released, and we had a pizza party reunion to celebrate another win in our never-ending Hollywood High battle.

Mr. Delgado didn't survive his injuries, but he went out in a blaze of glory. His wife came to the beginning of our pizza reunion at my house because she wanted to hear the story of her husband, the hero. Oddly enough, she thanked us for giving her husband the gift of being able to save the students he loved. I knew right then that she was going to be okay; she's got that Delgado fighting spirit.

Our latest war changed things, mostly for the better. Our group came out of it tighter than ever. Some of the guys are shocking the girls' parents with meetings to ask permission to propose to their daughters. Finley already has a gorgeous fire opal engagement ring on her hand from Tanner. Guess he wasn't kidding when he told us at the beach that he was working on forever with Fin. He proposed at my house during the pizza party.

The other guys haven't popped the question yet, but they will. All the parents said yes, oddly enough. Apparently, they recognize that the couples are the real deal, even though we're young. I don't know if Trey asked my parents, but we all know what my answer will be. It's just a matter of time. They're aware of my promise ring he gave me at homecoming, and that didn't faze them. So, there's no harm in a diamond ring in its place, right?

All the sports teams have been reinstated at the school, and the theater and dance shows are back on. Good thing we had so many secret rehearsals, or we would've had to cancel.

Daniel Stamp, douchebag mercenary and baseball coach extraordinaire, is dead. As much as I despise that sick monster, the image of his head blowing open still gives me nightmares. My only hope is that his wife is relieved to be done with him instead of pissed at my group and ready for revenge. I can't take another round with that family.

Principal Buttrum has been exonerated of all charges. His actions shooting Daniel Stamp were deemed necessary to protect the students. He came to the pizza party and nearly drove me crazy with apologies for hitting my shoulder with the first shot he took. Apparently, his shooting aim was a little rusty. I told him I appreciated that he tried to save me, but it did little to calm his fretting. Later at the party, he announced that he was quitting as the principal. The pressure of leading the crazy at Hollywood

High apparently proved too much for him.

To the relief of everyone, Mr. Walker's back in his old job, reinstated as principal. He's working with the reinstated school board to fix the damage all over the school. My group and I thought about apologizing for wrecking the place, but ultimately, we decided that we had to do what we had to do. It was all justifiable.

Principal Walker also convinced the school board that the students have been through so much trauma that a fresh round of fences and walls might cause further PTSD. Hollywood High is now officially a fence-free open campus, to the delight of Trey and Tanner, who have plans to ditch on the regular.

Adam, Trey, and I are learning to work around each other with the shared connection. Nothing is ever easy with us, so naturally, the opening of the connection couldn't be reversed. The messages are fainter at a distance, but at this point, I can reach both of them from as far away as across town. It's weird, but then again, we're used to weird. The guys generally keep their connection with each other sealed off and only send messages to me.

To my relief, school was canceled for a month for repairs. Making up missing assignments, while suffering through rehabilitation appointments to gain back full use of my arm and shoulder, wasn't on my list of exciting to-dos.

I'm healing faster than expected. The doctors are baffled, but I'm not. I guarantee the healing is due to the energy work everyone in my group is doing with me. They show up one at a time and sit with me, holding my hands and feeding energy into me. I meditate and focus on the spot we're trying to heal, sending the energy loads into it. It must be working because I can rotate the shoulder again already.

So, everything's back to normal . . . At least as normal as things at Hollywood High can be . . .

Special thanks to the incredible team of models that keep pulling through for me over and over. Thank you to Deidre Michelle for her endless ability to find the right people to depict these characters. Thank you to Anna Hall, Kyle Fager, and Stephen Knezovich for making this series magic. Thank you to Jordan, Bear, and Carol for their endless conceptual support.

MELISSA VELASCO is a true explorer of the arts. With a well-rounded background as a choreographer, professor, dance teacher, stage manager, author, and Crystal Grid teacher, she thrives in creation. At her core, she believes that the arts save lives and provide a route for passion and connection. The artistic ride makes life a whole lot brighter.

With a quick wit, often edgy mouth, and loud laugh, Melissa exuberantly embraces life. To find balance from the mental cacophony in her head, she enjoys expansive views in her mountain home. Her ideal day involves a mug of hot tea, music playing, and a whole day to write. Her greatest loves are her three children and husband. The four pillars of her ultimate happiness include her family, friends, dance, and laughter.